Backspin

BOOKS BY CHARLES CROSBY
italics, mine
Backspin

Backspin

a novel

*Hope you
don't find it too
shocking... :)*

Charles Crosby

| N₁ | O₂ | N₁ |

CANADA

*Publisher's note: This book is a work of fiction. Names, characters, places and
incidents are either the product of the author's imagination or are used
fictitiously, and any resemblance to actual persons living or dead
is entirely coincidental.*

Library and Archives Canada Cataloguing in Publication

Crosby, Charles, 1971–
Backspin : a novel / Charles Crosby.

ISBN 978–0–9739558–3–5

I. Title.

PS8605.R663B32 2008   C813'.6   C2007–905422–6

Printed and bound in Canada on 100% ancient forest-free paper.

Now Or Never Publishing Company
11268 Dawson Place
Delta, British Columbia
Canada V4C 3S7

nonpublishing.com
Fighting Words.

For Mike
Olie would not exist but for your voice ringing in my head

BACKSPIN

I hate Canada so much. I hate Ottawa even more. Why I came back at all is beyond me, except I have to be here at least part of the year to maintain my health benefits. And considering my lifestyle, I need them.

I've started keeping this journal because: 1) I stole it from a bookstore in the mall without looking, thinking I was grabbing a book I could read on my trip to Michigan next week; 2) I feel like this might be a good time to start recording some of the more memorable moments of my life as I approach the likely end of my career; and 3) I realize I'm forgetting a lot of days entirely. For instance, I can't remember anything I did yesterday, even though the serious partying doesn't even start until tonight. I figure if I write stuff down every day I can at least have some kind of reference. If nothing else, that might be useful in court some day.

I'm staying at Miranda's place until I leave for Michigan (I've still got to figure out what town I'm supposed to be going to, preferably before I go) and she's super pissed because Blanche Dowling took a giant dump on her carpet. It's not my fault; she just couldn't hold it. It's actually Miranda's fault. I told her Blanche Dowling can't stomach beef products, but she thought it was cute watching her suck it all down. Well fuck her. She didn't listen to me, and now she has to clean diarrhea off her new carpet. Serves her right. Still, she's so pissed she probably won't have sex with me tonight, and on New Year's Eve that just doesn't feel right. I haven't gone without getting laid on New Year's since I was like fourteen years old. It'll just seem so incomplete, like having your birthday come around and no one wishing you a Happy Birthday or anything. I'm almost tempted to help her clean it up, but I'm not going to. I have issues with shit, and I can't get anywhere near it. That's why I trained Blanche Dowling to do it outside. Keep it the hell away from me.

I acquired Blanche Dowling totally by accident one day and I'm still not all that thrilled about it. With the amount of travelling I have to do she's a huge pain in the ass. Even when she's not taking a monster dump on the carpet.

Sometimes I work as a sort of assistant to old people. Don't ask me why or what qualifications I have for this sort of work (none); sometimes you just wander into something. I just seem to hook up with a lot of geezers who pay me to walk their dog or help them get around or fix some food for them for a few weeks. I've actually got some pretty nice references somewhere in my bag.

Funny thing about a lot of old people, they're lonely as all hell and they'll talk to anyone who'll give them a little time and attention.

Anyhow, I was taking care of this crazy old lady in Willowdale a few years back where I was playing in a tournament (Total prize money for the winner: a hundred bucks. Grand total for me who lost in the semi-finals: nada. Fucking cheap-ass Canadians with their cheap-ass Canadian tournaments.), and after it was over I was broke and couldn't get back to Ottawa where Miranda was working in what would turn out to be her last year as a dancer at the Crimson Cat, having recently moved from Toronto when the federal capital finally legalized the lap dance, which she was totally not into, at least not after that one guy splooged all over her. Where the hell was I?

Oh, right. The old lady. Yeah, she was crazy as all hell. Lived alone in this shitty little apartment with her mean-ass cat. I never actually found out the name of the cat because the lady, Blanche Dowling, was so nuts, that was what she called everyone. The mailman was Blanche Dowling, her dead brother was Blanche Dowling, all her neighbours were Blanche Dowlings, and of course when I asked the cat's name, well, you get the point.

I ran into her at the Shoppers Drug Mart where she was looking confused trying to figure out how much money to give the cashier. Being the good guy I am I helped her out (I feel a little bad now remembering how I took a twenty out of her purse, but that's in the past), and she was so grateful that when she asked me to help her home with all her shit I did (especially since I was already feeling bad about the twenty), and before I knew it I was practically living with the old bird.

Her cat was evil. There's no other word for it. Except for maybe Calico. I know now that Calicos are notoriously fucked up creatures, but at the time what did I know? I just figured she was a little nuts from having lived with Mrs. Dowling for all those years. She was a little cross-eyed, and her fur was always matted in some places and falling out in others. The apartment stunk of her, and so one day I let her out, half thinking that maybe she'd take off and spare me having to smell her or having to avoid her crazy eyes and her tendency to attack my legs whenever I walked by. She also hissed at anything that moved, and let me tell you, that hiss came from a very dark place inside her. Especially at night, the sound of it would throw the fear of God right into you.

Of course it would happen that the old lady died after a couple of weeks. I kind of knew it was coming, and part of me wanted to help her get around in her last days and another part of me thought that maybe I could take some of her crap after she kicked it. As it turned out, after she passed away in her sleep, I did a quick tour of the house before calling the ambulance and there wasn't much to find. She had about fifty bucks on hand, and a whole lot of crap from when she was younger and her husband was still around. I took the fifty and this locket I liked and that was about it. I thought about taking her wedding ring, but that seemed like a really shitty thing to do, so I didn't. Besides, it wouldn't come off her big bloated finger.

After they took her body away, I stayed another two nights until the landlord finally kicked me out. I asked what was going to happen to the cat, and he told me he'd probably have the crazy bitch destroyed. "Good riddance," I thought, but as I was leaving I saw her watching me, and I swear to God her eyes uncrossed, just for a second, as she looked at me as if to say, "Jesus Christ, man, don't leave me to die! Take me with you and I'll change my evil ways and become your lifelong friend."

I don't know what I was thinking, but I took her and her carrying cage with me when I left. Maybe it was the coke I'd purchased with some of the fifty I'd borrowed from Mrs. Dowling when she died that made me so hyper I felt the need to do something, to act, to take this monster of a cat and save its wretched life, but there you go. I half hitched, half bussed my way to Ottawa where Miranda informed me I was insane and that she hated cats and that this one smelled funny and was looking at her as if it wanted to kill her.

Now when I go to tournaments I always have to sneak this stupid cat into the motels, and every time I let her outside to do her business I always half hope she'll take off, but she's always there when I get back from playing or when I come out to check on her. It's like she never moves; she's always exactly where I leave her. I'm sure she goes off to eat, or shit, or frolic or whatever it is cats do, but she always makes it back to exactly where I leave her. Something about that is eerie as all hell, let me tell you.

For a long time she'd scratch me every time I touch her, which at first was on purpose when I thought that maybe we could bond, and later by accident, and now hardly ever. Over time though she's learned to tolerate me, and even let me pat her when I absentmindedly touch her, usually when I'm drunk, or too high or too depressed after losing a match to remember I don't like her. Most of me would love it if she kicked the bucket, as it would certainly make my life a lot easier, but I don't have the heart to just kill her myself or leave her behind somewhere. She's got to be like fifteen years old now, so with any luck she'll kick it soon. I can't wait.

So New Year's is here and it always makes me take stock of my life. I'd have to call it penny stock to be more accurate, but I shouldn't complain. I can blame my bitch of a mother, and I can blame the doctor who failed to fix up my knee, and I can blame God and I can blame the world and every living thing I've ever come into contact with for making my life one giant oozing pulsating scab of a joke, but I can't complain, really. I get by. I eat. I occasionally get laid. I get to do my job in front of an audience (well sort of), and what more can one ask for, you know?

Oh right, in case someone is reading this long after I'm dead, I should probably mention that I'm a professional tennis player. Okay, I know what you're picturing, but I ain't that to be sure. When people think "professional tennis player" they tend to get an image of Pete Sampras or (evil stinking troll) Andre Agassi or, if they're of a certain age, Bjorn Borg or John McEnroe. Or maybe they follow the game a little and get an image of one of those mid-level journeyman players who make a really good living on the ATP tour, win a few titles, and maybe even squeeze out a Grand Slam title at some point in their career. Or else they picture the hundreds of lower ranked pros who play for ten years or so, make their money, win some matches, get some fame in their home country and retire to become coaches or go into management or business or, for those on the lowest rung of the ATP circuit, teach at a club somewhere. Now maybe if someone is really into the game, they'll broaden their sights to consider the struggling pros that mostly dwell on the Challenger circuit, the minor leagues of pro tennis, if you will. These guys play for ATP points which enable them to earn entry into the top level tournaments where the real money, glory and chicks reside.

I am none of these people.

See, there are a few rungs below even the Challenger circuit. I play mostly what is called the Futures circuit. It's super low rent: you earn crap money; you flip your own scoreboard; you fetch your own towels and balls on the court. In the Futures you play in shitty little towns mostly in the Southern US and South America and, like the name implies, it's typically stocked with a lot of young guys trying to work on their games. Guys who are like seventeen, eighteen, nineteen and trying to work their way up.

I'm thirty. Get the picture? That's like a hundred and fifty in tennis player years. Why do I do it? I'm too tired and anxious about the prospect of going out tonight and maybe not getting laid to get into it now, so maybe later. Let's just say I was once a prodigy. That's harder to let go of than a fistful of dollars, a bagful of weed and a pair of giant, silicone-enhanced beasts all at once, if that makes any sense whatsoever. You could say I'm one sad-assed old guy who can't stop chasing a dream he no longer has any legitimate right to have.

I played the US Open and Wimbledon once. Sure I did. I played all the big ones once upon a time. That feels like a thousand years ago now. Only problem is, I remember what it feels like, and part of me keeps thinking that maybe I'll get back there somehow. Most of me knows that ain't happening however.

Anyhow, I'm going out. If Miranda is going to be a bitch about everything I'll just go out on my own and try to hook up with someone else. Fuck her. Still, I wish to hell it weren't so god-damned cold out. End of December in Ottawa. Christ. I hate Canada and I think the feeling is mutual.

January 1

I don't remember a lot about last night so this journal thing is already paying off. I partied with some old friends, or rather some of Miranda's old friends, but they were good enough. I rang in the New Year from a bathroom stall in the strip club where I was screwing Miranda's former roommate, Chantal. Hey, I said I couldn't go a New Year's Eve without getting laid. My record remains intact.

I have to leave for Michigan (some town called Springdale apparently) tomorrow morning with the intention of arriving on the 4th. We'll have to drive like hell to get there on time, especially as I have no idea how to get there, only that it's in Michigan somewhere.

I'm supposed to play an indoor Futures tournament in Springdale, the first of the tennis season. I use that term lightly, since we don't really have a "season" any more than we have an "off-season." See, the real tour (that would be the ATP, or Association of Tennis Professionals tour) kicks off in Australia in January and runs until around October or November, at which point you get maybe six weeks off before you're supposed to be back in Australia or New Zealand or, if you're lucky, a Fijian whorehouse for New Year's Eve (in fact, now that I think about it, the first couple of events are already well underway, having started yesterday). But our tour starts now too. Only instead of attending warm-up tournaments for the Australian Open, to be played at the end of this month in front of tens of thousands of people in huge stadiums with laundered towels and fresh balls and spacious locker rooms and shitloads of prize money and cameras from TV stations all around the world, I'll be playing an event in Springdale, Michigan where I could win maybe a thousand bucks and three qualifying points towards the Challenger circuit. That's if I win. If I don't win, well then it's no points and a lot less than the grand.

But I'm not bitter, just hung-over and a little under the weather.

Miranda isn't talking to me. She says I screwed her former roommate last night and she's pissed, but that's ridiculous. . . . Oh shit, wait a minute. I just read what I wrote earlier and I guess I did. Shit. Well I hope it was worth it.

January 2

I think I'm starting to get the hang of this. I don't remember the last time I chronicled my life this consistently. I don't remember the last time I did *anything* this consistently. As it happens, I'm bored and tired and there's not much to do as we drive through northwest Michigan.

Had a few border "issues" today. Fuckers at the Windsor/Detroit checkpoint took one look at me and started grilling me about everything from the last time I did drugs (which felt like a trick question) to where I was born (and when I couldn't remember right off I was sure they were going to haul me off).

Since 9/11 these border guys have been real pricks, and no matter that I cross back and forth between the two countries on a fairly regular basis, they still give me shit each and every time. Why do they always pick on me? After all, it's not like they can see the deep well of sour defeat that fills my bitter soul.

When they realized I was travelling with a priest however, they backed off. Gary's very useful to have around in certain situations. I swear that if he wasn't wearing that collar they'd have searched him and found his monster stash of weed and busted us both. I don't like weed and I wasn't carrying anything, but I guarantee you they'd have taken me in too. Just the look of me seemed to bother these guys and, well, the slightest excuse is all they need these days.

Anyhow, we got through fine, but one of these days Gary is going to run into an atheist border guard who won't give a damn about what he happens to be wearing and his ass will be as busted as shit. I never can come up with a very good simile. I'll have to work on that.

And yeah, I know what a simile is. I'm actually unbelievably smart. Like scary smart. You wish you were as smart as me. And I'm not just saying that to be arrogant either. I was always smart as a whip, even as a kid. I was always bored in school, and I think it was because I was simply too smart for what they were teaching. Even though I dropped out in the eleventh grade, I still feel like I know more than most people, and sometimes I come up with these weird, smart things to say and have no idea where they come from. Anyhow, I got sidetracked again. Jesus, spilling your guts takes some practice. My brain is always going too fast for my pen. When I was back in school, they said that I had attention deficit disorder, and even though I told the school counsellor who told me that to suck my cock, he may have, in retrospect, been right. Too much shit in my head and not enough ways to get it out. If only you could get rid of some of these backed up thoughts through your pores when you sweat I'd be set. Because I sweat a lot.

Anyhow, I was talking about Gary who just looked over and asked me what I was doing, and when I told him I was "chronicling my life's journey and doing a philosophical study of my thoughts" he said, as he usually does no matter what you say first, "Cool," at which point he went back to watching the road for helpful signs that might actually point us in the general direction of Springdale.

I've known Gary since we were little kids. I actually lived with him and his weird parents for a year after my mother ran off when I was ten. When I (accidentally, regardless of what the slanted police report may have stated) set fire to their sofa, they kicked me out, and even though I ended up in the Ontario Juvenile Protection Centre, I still kept in touch with ol' Gar.

Gary was always the most philosophical kid I knew. Nothing ever seemed to faze him, even when he got busted for hacking into the school computer (let off with a warning, he gave up his huge talent for hacking right there). When he discovered weed in high school he was even more so. Still, even knowing Gary as I do, I was floored when he told me he was going to become a priest all those years ago.

Sure his parents were Catholics, and sure he seemed to like going to church, but there's a huge leap from that to donning the frock and fucking collar.

Besides, he's never gotten laid. Ever. I think I'd have to kill myself if that was me. That's the life of a priest though, and that's what he wanted. Go figure.

Gary did the whole deal. He went and studied with the Jesuits and did time at a Theological College, the whole shebang. He even did some time as a kind of "junior minister" with a parish just outside of Toronto, but when they caught him smoking up and told him he couldn't do that anymore he left. He insists there's nothing in the Bible about not smoking weed, and he'll stand by that for the rest of his life. I've never read it so I'll have to take his word for it.

In any case, he still wears his collar and he's still a priest but he doesn't make a living at it anymore. In fact I'm sort of afraid to ask him how he pays his rent and affords his truck, so I've never asked. I'd hate to piss him off because he's always glad to drive me around to tournaments, and he's the only person I know who can take off for weeks on end on a moment's notice and who never asks me to chip in for gas. It's all part of some grand adventure for him.

Anyhow, he's driving me to Springdale, bless his heart, and smoking a blunt as we go. I'm high just off of his fumes—he's in possession of some pretty potent stuff.

I never smoke. Not pot, not cigarettes, nothing. I'm a professional athlete, see, and I've got to think of my lung capacity.

And I *am* still a professional athlete, no matter what you might think when you meet me. I may have a little bit of a beer gut and my legs may have gone to shit, my eyesight may have seen better days and, yes, my shoulder may ache from time to time and my stomach may cause me gastrointestinal problems and my wrists may not be as flexible as they once were, but I can still move when I need to and I've still got my natural talent that promised to take me places once upon a time.

When I was a kid it all seemed so easy. Diet meant not asking for double meat on my pizza. Exercise meant spending a few hours out on the court, goofing off. Jesus, the stuff you bounce back from when you're a kid. Now I have to watch everything I eat and do and even then I don't always succeed. I once said everything I eat goes straight to my waist, but I realized I sounded like a fag and never said it again.

Oh I don't have anything against fags, by the way. There's a guy on the Futures tour named Lincoln Holmes who's a fag and I don't hate him at all. Well, actually I do, but not because he's a fag. Oh and I don't hate him because he's a black dude either. Because I'm not, like, one of those racist or homophobe-type people. I mean some of the nicest ass I ever had belonged to this black chick named Laquisha or something, and I'm all about letting the gays stick their dicks into whatever they want to. Free country and all. No, I hate Lincoln Holmes because he's a better tennis player than me. I hate him because he's got a future in the one thing that means the world to me.

Lincoln Holmes will be at this tourney. I always hate looking at the draw sheet, because I usually end up drawing someone like Holmes in the first round and my trip is all for nothing. The best is when you draw some new guy who's like really nervous, and when the top seeds end up falling early on somehow, you can coast right through to the final without having to play the guys who usually beat you. Problem for me is, more and more of them are starting to fit into that category.

Now I've made myself depressed, and I've got a headache from all the pot smoke in the cab of Gary's truck. I need a nap. Fuck.

Okay, so here's what happened, and I swear it's not my fault.

Ivan Devletshin's this punk-ass Russian kid everyone's saying has this bright future in front of him. Everyone's got their eye on him. He's got a really solid game: he's like a ball machine; he just runs everything down and you can't get anything past him, even when you're playing really well and eventually frustration gets the better of you and you start going for the lines more and you start making more mistakes which pisses you off even more and your game goes downhill even further. So when I see the draw, and first round I've got this wiry consistent kid with a good set of wheels on him and no end of energy, I figured I needed a different strategy.

So I start going for the body.

In tennis you're not supposed to try to nail your opponent. It's not seen as "sportsmanlike." Well, get to be my age and you start giving less of a fuck about sportsmanship and shit like that. I gots to do what I gots to do, am I right?

Now my aim isn't to hurt the kid, or even to hit him. It's kind of like in baseball when you're playing a little chin music, trying to teach the batter a few manners and force him back from the plate. Keep them from hanging around inside. Well, that's what I do when I play. I keep them honest. I keep them from getting into their comfort zone because they never know what ol' Olie might do. When he might snap and try to bean their sorry asses. Sometimes this strategy even works.

So we start the match, and this little shit starts trying to show me up. Okay, I suppose that, technically, to show me up there'd have to be an audience to show me up *to*, and since I'm being completely honest, even by Futures standards, I ain't all that much of a draw around here. The sum total audience was Gary, who I'm pretty sure was catching a snooze, and Dudley, the retarded kid who hangs out at the Futures events in the area. Sorry, Miranda always tells me he's not retarded, he's "brain damaged." Same difference to me; he's just really fucked up in the head. And I'm not convinced I had anything to do with it, by the way.

Where the hell was I? Oh yeah, so this Russian kid starts moving me around, showing me no respect whatsoever. And he's kicking my ass. Takes the first set in a walk, 6–1. So I'm dragging my sorry ass around the court, getting tired just going to the score cards to flip them over, and my grand strategy isn't even working because I'm barely getting to the balls, let alone getting into position to hit them with impunity. So I start getting frustrated. Just like everyone does when they play this little commie.

Only when I get frustrated, I tend to play a little better. My aim if nothing else seems a little truer when I'm looking through slitty, pissed off eyes.

So I drop serve to open the second set, and I'm down love–30 on his serve when I start losing it a little. I see this goofy teenager too tall to live with bad skin and a little patronizing smile plastered across his ugly face, and I want to hurt him. I start thinking about the fact that—at seventeen—he's already being touted as ready for the ATP within months. I start seeing me at his age and remembering how much lay ahead of me, and I take aim at his head and hit a bull's-eye.

He goes down clutching his face and I finally score a point. The one umpire charged with watching three different courts all at once comes trundling over, and I explain how it was an accident. That I'm not having any luck painting the lines so I'm trying to play closer to the body and—oops—I'm still hitting poorly, only this time the poor fella took one in the eye. I'm really sorry. *Really* sorry. Hey, can I give you a hand up, kid? No? Wow, didn't know I could still hit a ball with that kind of speed. Still got a little pepper left in the old swing, it seems.

So he's so rattled I score a couple of points and win the game. Back on serve. And when he starts pulling it together again I nail him in the shoulder so hard it leaves a bright red mark.

I plead ignorance again.

"Have you seen the way I've been playing?" I ask the umpire, shocked that he could actually think I'm playing with enough accuracy to pick a specific spot and hit it. He buys it, but is beginning to get sceptical. Interestingly, he stops following the other two matches he's supposed to be watching and just stands court-side watching me.

Now I'm a skilled professional. I know how to hit a target when I can get to the ball. I was able to tire out the kid by pummelling him to the point where he had no choice but to take a little pace off the ball. It gave me a chance to get back into things. And yet even if I won the second set, there was no way in hell I was going to survive a third. Not this day, and not after the workout I'd already had. I was puffing like a steam engine and I needed to end things quickly, but not so's you'd think I was doing something I shouldn't be. Not with this umpire watching me so closely.

So with the pace slowed enough that I was actually able to put a racquet on the ball, I seized my moment when Devletshin hit a high bouncing forehand. I end up taking a spill while making a mad, desperate dash to a ball that proved far more difficult to get to than it may have initially appeared it would. While I fell painfully to the court (I actually have very few pain receptors still firing after all these years of neglect and self-abuse), I somehow managed to rifle off a flailing forehand, nailing Devletshin right in the ear.

They said later that his eardrum shattered and that he'd be permanently deaf in that ear. It's unlikely he'll ever play tennis at the top levels, which is truly unfortunate. The kid really had some character.

The umpire tried to accuse me of hitting him on purpose, but clearly it was just a desperate flail, one of those bizarre once-in-a-lifetime things. I moved onto the second round where some forgettable American kid I had no business losing to beat me soundly. I guess my thoughts were with poor Devletshin. That and I didn't dare bean my opponent again, what with everyone watching.

Do I feel bad? Well sure I do. I didn't want to wound the kid, just retire him for the day. But then tennis is like war: you serve; you attack and you defend; you go out there and you try to survive knowing not everyone makes it back in one piece. It sucks that he's out of commission, and yeah, that'll probably stay with me a good long while, but that's the way it goes in battle. Still, I wish it hadn't gone down the way it did.

And for all my efforts I earned just enough money to pay for my half of the motel room and a case of beer.

So why do I put myself though all this? If it's this shitty, and this much of a headache to earn enough to scrape by and last another day, why don't I just grow the hell up and do something different? Because I tasted it once, and can't seem to let it go.

I was a funny kid. I couldn't have been less athletically inclined, but I had a talent for one thing that, initially at least, I had no real interest in other than as something to help pass the time.

Win Rogers was this old perv who used to hang around our neighbourhood trying to get little kids to let him suck them off. One day he was lingering around the broken-down old cement tennis court where some of the older kids went to drink at night. He beckoned me over, and being nine and stupid I went. He offered me a cracked old racquet and asked if I wanted to play. I shrugged and said sure and we batted an old ball back and forth a while. Odd thing was, I was really good at it. I'd never actually touched a racquet before, but it felt totally natural. Later on, when he was trying nervously to unzip my jeans, all I could think about was how cool it felt to hit a ball and watch it land where I wanted. I bit the end of Win's finger off and bolted. My life would never be the same again.

I was poor. Not "wish I had a new toy" poor, but "wish I had something for breakfast other than a lukewarm glass of tap water" poor. The neighbourhood in Toronto we lived was shit. The apartments we constantly moved around to were shit. And my mother, as a mother, was the human equivalent, the very epitome of shit. It all made for a rather shitrific childhood in other words.

I'm pretty sure she knew who my father was, but she always let on like she didn't. Just to screw with me she'd say it might have been a black guy or an Asian dude, but I've looked pretty closely in the mirror and, given what I look like, that would certainly be a stretch.

See I'm a white guy, but not just in the census-identification kind of way. I'm, like, whiter than white, and getting gradually whiter the older I get. And I don't know why. I get plenty of sun. I mean, Jesus, I work outside most of the time. So yeah, I get sun, but it doesn't seem to actually penetrate my skin. And I'm blonde. Well, a dark matted blonde, but blonde nevertheless. So if I'm part negro or oriental you'd sure as hell never guess it. No, I think that was just my mother being a bitch.

And growing my hair out, that might have been something of a mistake. I thought it would make me look younger, especially when I added the retro Bjorn Borg headband, but it just kind of grew off in all different directions and now I look a little too much like Nick Nolte's mug shot. You know the one. My skin's in terrible shape. There are more than a couple of broken blood vessels happening here. Especially on my nose, which I've broken twice. I always had a big head, but I don't seem to wear it very well anymore.

When I was a kid I was really good looking, and I'm not just saying that. People told me as much all the time. They said, "Olie, you're really good looking" and stuff like that. And I got laid even easier after I started playing tennis. Nowadays, though, I find myself settling more and more for skanks, tramps and old fat drunk women I wouldn't take outside in the daylight. Makes me wonder all the more what Miranda sees in me. She's both hot and young, but her temper tends to turn a lot of guys off a lot of the time. I just ignore her and everything works out great. And because I'm on the road so much our sex life is always exciting and fresh. I think she loves me for my charm and wit. That and my dink.

Anyhow, I was poor. My mother used to leave me for days on end to hook up with some guy or to go get high. I remember the first time Child Services took me away. I was really young, and I'd survived four days eating the crumbs I found in the toaster. I think I was three.

I liked Child Services. They were really nice to me, only they ended up giving me back to my mother after she went into some kind of parenting program. Guess how long that lasted? Technically until she tried to sell me to one of her clients.

I was a pretty bad kid, I guess. It was mostly because I was bored. It gave me a laugh to set fires. That was my primary form of entertainment for a while. When I started playing around with a racquet stolen from a store display downtown, I was distracted enough to keep out of trouble a little, but sometimes I just couldn't help myself. Honestly, I didn't know any better. You live alone at that age and it's hard to work out a guideline of appropriate behaviour. Add to that the fact that, when I did go to school, I was a pretty poor student. It's only because I'm as smart as I am that I know as many things as I do, despite my lack of formal education.

When my mother finally took off for good I lived with Gary's parents, Mr. and Mrs. Levandier. I really liked them—that is, once I got over the whole size thing.

See, they were midgets. Oh shit, sorry, what do we call them now? Vertically challenged? Height deprived? Jesus, I could never keep up with all that politically correct stuff. So let's just choose a nice, neutral term. They were, let's say, miniatures. No, half-pints. Yeah, half-pints, I like that better. It's cuter.

So they were half-pint people, only no one ever talked about it. You'd see people look at them funny when they walked around, but everyone, including the Levandiers, just pretended they weren't these freakish gnomes. But they really were. Tiny as all hell. Like circus tiny. I haven't a clue what they did for a living— I should ask Gary. But he's outside having a smoke and I don't have the energy to get up and get him.

Anyhow, these little hobbits went and had themselves a full-sized kid. Swear to God. He's like ten feet from me smoking a blunt in our motel parking lot. Can't imagine what that did to Mrs. Levandier, pushing out a kid as big as that. But I checked into it and apparently it happens all the time. Little wee dwarves having normal looking, human children. Life always has something fun to keep you amused.

When they let me live with them it certainly took some getting used to, because everything was, like, low. The light switches were low, the chairs were all made small and low to the floor, and even the beds were really close to the ground. Took a while to adjust, but once I did I came to like it there. I actually kind of liked it when they forced some rules on me. No one had ever tried that parental approach before.

Funny thing is, after a while you stop thinking of them as half-pints and start thinking of them as just nice, well-mannered people. That is, until the munchkin fucks throw you out.

It wasn't my fault. I sure didn't do it on purpose, like they suggested. I was just really into fire as a kid, as I said. Something so hypnotic about it, the look of a lit match or a lighter at full boil. Sometimes it got the better of me though. That particular day I was just hanging out alone in the living room, thinking to myself how good life suddenly seemed and that all that would make it better would be a little fire on the scene. So I lit a match just to watch it burn and, well, it somehow got away from me.

They said that because I'd had some previous troubles starting fires in the neighbourhood I clearly couldn't be trusted and whoosh, I was back in Child Services.

Later, when Gary had his own problems with hacking, his parents blamed my overwhelming influence. Those tiny little fuckers turned on me so hard, I was never allowed in their house again and officially banned from seeing Gary. But we found a way to hang out somehow.

I kept playing tennis whenever I had some time alone, and one day when I was thirteen I was playing a money game and Phil Tipsarevic caught my act.

Oh, the money game, right. When I was a kid I realized there was some money to be made in the "diminished expectations" of a little boy and his tennis racquet. I'd hang around the private courts in town, challenging the adults to a set and then betting them twenty bucks that I could beat them. You'd think they would've felt bad about taking twenty bucks from a ratty, badly dressed little kid who could obviously not afford to lose that much money, but they always took me up on it.

And I always beat them. Sometimes they pushed me hard, and other times I was forced to play best two out of three when they lost the first one to me, but I always beat them in the end. I never once had to cough up the twenty, though more than a few of these rich, middle-aged men stiffed me in the end. No matter. I had a lot of fun and earned myself a few hundred bucks a year in the process. At thirteen that's a fortune.

So one day I'm taking a poor sap for his twenty, whipping the pants off his flabby ass, and this youngish adult dude starts watching me through the fence. I beat the first jerk and start up another money game, and he keeps watching me. I assume he's some pervert, since I'm used to several hanging around my own neighbourhood, and I try to ignore him, but I can feel his eyes boring into me. Finally, I lose my concentration and rush him.

"What's your glitch, asshole?" I ask, kicking the fence hard enough to force him back.

"You're really good kid," he tells me with a smile.

"Go watch someone else, perv," I shoot back.

"Have you ever thought about doing something with your talent?"

"What, is that like some kind of perv code?" I ask.

"I used to play," he says, and now I'm really thinking he's a pervert flirting with me. I'm tired of playing games with him suddenly, and really want him to leave.

"Play what, asshole?" I find myself asking instead.

"That," he says, gesturing at the court.

"This how you pick up kids, huh? Get lost, homo."

"I used to be a tennis pro. Back a ways," he says. That interested me a little. I didn't follow the pro game much then, but I knew some of those guys made boatloads of cash.

"Yeah?"

"Yeah. You're good. Do you play the Juniors?"

"The what?"

"The Junior tour circuit. You really should. You're better than a lot of the kids who win those things."

"What do they win?" I ask, intrigued.

"Trophies. Pride. A glimpse into their future."

I was suddenly bored again. "Don't need 'em," I said and returned to my game. He left finally, and I put him well out of my mind. Only thing is, a couple of days later I was back at the same court playing this old banker, making him run so much that I was pretty sure he was going to die of a heart attack, and after he begged off for a break I noticed that same creepy guy was back.

"Come on, man, I'm working here!" I shouted over my shoulder.

"It's a free country, kid," he shouted back. "I'm just standing here watching an entertaining tennis match."

I tried to ignore him, but back then I didn't like having an audience. That wouldn't change for quite a while.

"Mind if I play the winner?" he finally asked.

"You got twenty bucks?"

He laughed. "Is that the going rate these days? Yeah, I've got twenty bucks."

So I finished toying with the banker, ending the match before I killed him, and let the creepy guy have a crack at me.

"What's your name?" he asked.

"None of your fucking business," I answered.

"Nice to meet you, none of your fucking business. I'm Phil."

He played me in street clothes, with a racquet borrowed from the banker who just wanted to lie down on the bench courtside a while. He played in black dress shoes and a tie. And he beat me. Bad. I'd never lost a money match before, and I wasn't sure what I was supposed to do once I had. It was hard as hell peeling a twenty off my roll, I'll tell you that.

"Want to earn it back?" he asked.

"Oh here we go, now the perv speaks up. I don't do that shit, so keep my money." It's not like I was afraid of him either; I'd been dealing with people who wanted to hurt me my whole life.

"You don't trust much, do you?" he said. "What if all I want is for you to come to the Regent Club for an hour?"

"Never heard of it."

"It's a tennis club on Bay Street."

"Get the fuck out of here."

"No, really, you should come down and play a little on the courts. You'll find them better than anything you play on here."

"Why would I? Why should I? Why the hell would you want me to?" The questions were coming to me faster than I could spit them out.

"Because you have real talent. And I'd like to see what you can do with it."

"Why would you give a shit? And if I'm so good, why'd you beat me so easily?"

"Because it's in my interest to see what kind of talent we have around here, and because I'm a teaching pro who's beaten a lot better than you before. But it doesn't mean you don't have real promise."

Funny thing was, he seemed sincere. I figured I had nothing to lose. I'd never been down to that part of the city before, but it was just a matter of hopping on the TTC, so I agreed to meet him there the next morning. He never asked me whether or not I should be in school on a Wednesday morning, and I never volunteered the information. To be honest, I just wanted to see what a nice indoor court would look like in that part of town.

Anyway, stuff happened after that and here I am. I'll maybe write more about it later. My hand is cramping worse than after that time I jacked off for four hours before letting myself come, and that's saying something. I couldn't pick up a racquet for days after that.

January 6

So I slept most of yesterday. Before he heads back to Canada, Gary is driving me to Kalamazoo where there's another tournament the top of the week. He doesn't say a whole lot when he's around, but I miss him when he's not. Sometimes I talk to Blanche Dowling but all she does is look at me a little cross-eyed. Sometimes I hook up with some locals but it isn't the same. Not anymore. When I was younger I was always into meeting and partying with new people, but that starts to get a little old after a while. Sometimes you just want to kick back with your good friends, and for me that's Gary Levandier.

I've never known someone so at peace with himself. This morning I asked him if his life was turning out like he always thought it would, and he thought for a second and just said, "Never really thought about it." When I told him I wasn't sure mine was, he just said, "Never too late to change it." Then when I said I thought I had maybe one more good run in me, he just said, "Cool." Gary never judges, but then he never offers much in the way of helpful advice either.

He was dinged for hacking as a kid. I think I mentioned that before. Even then, dragged in front of the principal with his half-pint parents smoking mad, he was still so even keeled about it. At sixteen no less, at age when most of us would have been pissing our pants over what was going down. And the kicker? He wasn't changing his own marks. No, he heard that Gus Pantalone was going to be kicked out of school for his failing marks, so he figured it was important he help the dumb-ass kid out. So he breaks into the office, hacks the computer, and changes Pantalone's marks from F's to B's. Now that illustrates two things about Gary: 1) He really seems to care about people, especially the stupid and unfortunate; and 2) He's not the most logical thinker on the globe. Of course everyone knew that Gus was too stupid to even dress himself properly, let alone get B's in any particular course. What might have worked was edging his grades up to D's so he'd pass, but not in such a way as to attract attention. But ol' Gar thought that if D's were a nice thing to do for Gus, then B's would be that much better. Shit, I'm surprised he didn't give him A+'s across the board. I mean if you're fucking around like that, why not go for broke?

Anyhow, word gets out that they're on the prowl for whoever changed the marks, and what does Gary do? He decides to "get rid of the evidence," and sneaks back into the office where he trips the new security system and gets busted.

He may be wise, but he sure couldn't be described as bright. No, that's what *I* bring to the relationship, by God.

It was his one obvious talent that he was always able to let shit
slide off his back, so after he was let off with a warning he figured
it was some kind of sign and never tried it again. Ever. And he
never seemed too bothered having to give it up. He spent most of
the rest of high school so stoned he never felt like he was missing
anything anyway.

"You ever miss hacking?" I asked him this morning.

"No."

"Not at all?"

"Nope."

But as lacking in the conversation department as he can be, I
still enjoy Gary's company, even if it's only because he's such a
familiar presence in my life.

"I'll miss ya when you go, Gar," I told him.

"Cool."

"After Kalamazoo I'm thinking of making my way down to
Arizona for this Challenger qualifying thing."

"Sounds good."

"I'll drop you a postcard so you'll know where I am."

"You know what?" he said thoughtfully. "I bet if your cat
smoked a little weed she'd mellow out a little."

"Yeah, maybe, Gar. Good point."

I got word before I left Springdale that the tournament officials
in Kalamazoo have been asked to keep an eye out for violent
activity on my part. Violent activity! Can you believe that shit? I
have no violent tendencies at all! Where do they get this kind of
crap?

Well, okay, I've done some things I'm not proud of, but I'd never
try the same thing twice. I may be violent from time to time, but
I sure ain't stupid.

I've got a good feeling about this tournament. A lot of the better American players are heading down south to prepare for the
big Arizona Grand Prix, so the field will be in my favour. I think
this time I'm going to kick some ass and take some names.

January 7

Dreams are what keep us going, right? Well as stupid as it may seem, I still have one big dream. I want to play in a Grand Slam Championship again one day. I played a few once upon a time, but it feels like it was a whole other person playing those events, in another lifetime. At the time I always assumed there'd be lots of chances. Now I realize how rarely they come along.

Oh, right. Tennis 101 again. The Grand Slams are the ones most people know about, even the non-tennis people. There are four of them—the Australian Open, the French Open, Wimbledon and the US Open. The first is played on a slow, sticky hard court called Ace Rebound, the second on red clay made from crushed bricks that plays really slow, the third on grass which plays really fast and low, and the fourth on a fast hard court. ·

Only the best players get to play the Slams. The top 80 or so in the world get straight in, while the lower ranked players battle it out in qualifying matches to fill the remaining spots to round out the 128. You play the rest of the year on all kinds of surfaces to earn enough points to qualify for the Slams. The whole year revolves around these events.

When I was a kid I played a few Slams, one in particular proving a memorable couple of weeks. You've probably seen the clip. I still think back to those couple of years and can't believe how long ago it was now. Thirteen years. My God. Not many people log that kind of time on the tour, especially those who've put in so many miles on the Futures circuit. Olie Wood really is one of a kind.

Anyhow, I still dream of one day playing at the highest level again. I know it gets less likely every year, but if I just get into a groove and start winning a few matches I know what I'm capable of. Just a couple of good weeks and I could start getting into a few Challengers up against the second tier guys, and then I could rack up some points and play a few ATP events and who knows what could happen from there.

Fuck it. It seems like so much work and such a long slog to get there from here. More and more I think this might be my last year

on the tour. Maybe instead of pipedreams I ought to try making
something of my time this year. Enjoy the travel, live a life of
adventure, whatever. I could really get something out of this year
if I tried. Damn it, I really should. As Canada's great hope I ought
to at least try something to live up to the hype.

Oh and that's not a joke by the way. I'm still kind of Canada's
big deal in the tennis world. I may be ranked 1123rd in the world,
but there aren't many Canadian men ranked higher. We've got a
couple of good doubles players, and a couple of guys ranked in
the 150–200 range, but I'm still the only guy to make some waves,
even if it was a few years ago. The real tennis fans in Canada will
know who I was, let me tell you.

Who I am! Shit, who I *am*.

                                                        January 9

Tomorrow I play in the Kalamazoo Futures Indoor Invitational.
I'm feeling pretty revved up. I slept most of the day, which is good
actually. It means I'll be well rested for tomorrow. I'd planned to
get out on the practice court, but it was too dark by the time I
woke up so I decided to warm up with a run. Only problem is, I
don't really run. I get to the gym when I can, and I practice my
game quite a lot, but I haven't been much of a runner in, like,
ever. Now my legs are starting to hurt. I'd better knock it off or
I'll feel it tomorrow.

Overall, though, I'm pumped. I think this is going to be a good
week. I'm playing an American named Oxner. He's in his mid-
twenties and that's really old for a Futures tournament, so I might
have a chance to get some momentum and start winning a few.

I'm sitting here in the Kalamazoo Holiday Inn, and I realize
now that after I pay for the room and get breakfast tomorrow I'm
going to be totally broke. I'd better win a few matches or I'm
going to be screwed royally. It's a nice room actually. I splurged; I
just wanted to get a good sleep in a clean room. Blanche Dowling
seems to like it. They've got a nice thick curtain on the window
that she can claw to her heart's content. Keeps her away from the
more shreddable things in the room, like my clothes. Don't laugh,

it's happened before. More than once I've had to go without underwear because Blanche Dowling suddenly got a hard-on for my Haines. If I hadn't solved the problem by going without underwear more often than not she'd still be doing it, I swear.

Anyhow, all is well. I'll ice my legs and rest some more, then get up early and hit a few balls and blow Mr. Oxner a whole new hole en route to my first title in three years. I'm feeling it, baby!

January 10

Okay so here's what happened, and I swear it's not my fault.

I ended up playing my match without socks. After a while I had so many blisters I could hardly walk. Add to that my muscles started to like, atrophy from my having run last night without proper stretching and, well, the fact I'm a little hung-over. I'm pretty sure that didn't have anything to do with it however.

Why do these things happen to me? I mean Jesus, I was doing fine, although my legs were feeling a little sore from the run admittedly. I just got antsy and bored and figured a couple of hours out and about couldn't hurt.

So I went out and impressed some ladies with some of my professional athlete stories over a few beers and then, later, a line or three of coke. I impressed them enough to convince them to buy the drinks and provide the coke but not enough to get them to go to bed with me unfortunately. So here I am, late as hell in the night, when I suddenly realize that, for all the time I've invested in these chicks, I'm not going to be getting any sex. So I stumble back to the hotel alone. Now I'm cold and horny from the blue balls these hot young girls were handing out, and I run into this prostitute shivering in the cold January Michigan night. She's totally gone on heroin by the look of her, and seems like she might be a tad bit old for a hooker, but when she offers me a blowjob I let her do her thing in back of a drugstore near the hotel. When she asks me to pay however, I realize I don't have any money (the main reason, I suppose, why most prostitutes who aren't old, freezing and strung-out on heroin think to ask for the money up front). She gets pretty pissed off at me, but then changes her tone and asks me for my socks instead, pointing out how cold it is. Thinking it's not a bad deal for head, I strip them off and hand them over, knowing I'm close to my hotel and won't get too cold in just my sneakers.

Now the problem here is, I forgot I went through two pairs of socks at last week's tournament. And so that's my last pair gone there with the hooker and, even if I skipped breakfast, I don't have enough money for new ones. So I had to improvise. I ended up stuffing some plastic shopping bags into my sneakers. But let me tell you, plastic equals friction. I wasn't four games into the first set of my first-round match before I started limping.

Ben Oxner, down at the other end of the court, sees this and starts screwing with me, making me chase down balls. So I'm running back and forth across the court, my feet are killing me and people are starting to laugh and point at the fringes of plastic spilling out the tops of my sneakers, and I'm getting pretty pissed off—at myself, at Ben Oxner, at all the laughing assholes—and in that moment I see my career flash before me. And it ain't pretty. Here I am reduced to a laughing stock in some penny-ante event in a creaky indoor club in the dead of winter miles from Miranda, and I lose it a little. That combined with the fact I was sweating pretty profusely (did I mention I was a profuse sweater?) and my grip on my racquet starts to get a little loose.

For whatever reason I can't get any accuracy on my shots these days unless I'm a little pissed off, and that's exactly what I was when my racquet flung out of my hand and nailed Oxner square in the face. Apparently it broke his jaw, and of course he had to retire from the match. Now it really was an accident—after all, it's not my fault I sweat as much as I do—but they kicked me out anyway. Moreover, the tournament director called me into his office and told me I was getting a reputation as someone violent and to be watched. He said there was a possibility I could be suspended from the tour as a result of my so-called "violent track record." Fucker also suggested I might be a little sociopathic.

I am the least violent person you'd ever be likely to meet, and if that greasy fucker of a tournament director doesn't realize that, he can fuck himself, and I can help with my racquet. Oh how I'd like to smash his face for even suggesting something like that.

Anyhow, I now find myself with no prize money and out of another tournament early, and since no one will play doubles with me these days I can't even try to pick up a few bucks in that event. And now I'm officially broke and have no idea what I'm going to do next. Life can be so cruel.

I should note for the record that Oxner will be just fine. He'll have to have his jaw wired shut for a few months, that's all. He'll be good as new before you know it.

My biggest short-term concern is cash flow. I have no money for dinner tonight, and though I can probably squeeze out another night at the hotel before they toss me out, I'll have housing concerns sooner than later and it's awfully cold out there.

January 11

Miranda said she'd wire me a hundred bucks to get me through the next couple of days, but made me promise to spend it on food and accommodations. Though I'm sure she wouldn't begrudge me a drink or two, or something else to help pass the time.

In the meantime I've been asked to leave the Holiday Inn. I'm now at the local shelter where I'll stay a couple of days while I figure out what my next move might be.

I'm depressed. I'm not having any fun and it feels like I'm on a serious downward spiral. It used to be so different. You know what I miss the most? Having a coach on the road with me. Except for maybe the most obvious prospects and prodigies, almost no one playing the Futures have coaches who travel with them. Even at the ATP level there's a real dividing line between the top 100 or so who can afford a travelling coach, and the rest of us shlubs who make due on our own.

It's a really segregated sport, actually. A top level guy travels with a coach, a hitting partner, a fitness trainer, a masseuse, a chef and anyone else he might need to ensure he heads into his next match in peak fitness and readiness, in this way holding an enormous advantage over the lower ranked player who, because of his financial situation, has to compete against an army all on his own.

I never had the whole entourage thing going on, but I did have my own coach and those were definitely better days. It made a big difference having someone to bounce ideas off, or even just to talk to. Phil Tipsarevic was my coach for a year and a half. I took it and him for granted, and I'd give my left nut to have him with me now. And given that I lost my right nut in that terrible drawer-slamming accident a few years back, that should give you some idea of just how much he meant to me.

If you're a big tennis fan you'd remember me. Not many seventeen-year-olds find themselves on the cover of *Sports Illustrated*. Not many seventeen-year-olds earn four million dollars in endorsements a year. Not many seventeen-year-olds get to fuck Madonna and I'm not officially saying I did, mind you, but it's safe to say, when we hooked up that one time, a good time was had by all, got me? You have no idea how big I was and how small and conquerable the world suddenly appeared to be.

I carry a picture with me from that time. It's of me and Phil after I won the Paris Masters Series. It was a huge event, and a huge win, and the look of joy on his face tells the story right there. He saw in me something I'd never been able to see myself, and it's weird to think how soon after that day it all fell apart, and all because of that fucking kookaburra I ran into down under.

Anyhow, different times. Phil turned out to be a good guy after I'd initially pegged him as your token pedophile. That day I showed up at the Regent Club in Toronto, I immediately felt like I had no business being there. I usually played on shitty, cracked outdoor courts in my own neighbourhood, oftentimes without a net, or, at best, at some of the nicer courts against the local business types, but I'd never seen anything like this before. I'd never played tennis on carpet, and I'd never seen such a large facility entirely devoted to the game. I'd never actually given tennis much thought, other than as something I could do well enough to take a few bucks off the occasional rich bastard. I'd sure as hell never thought of it as something for which facilities like this would be exclusively designed. When I walked in all I could say was, "Damn!"

That caught the attention of the jerk at the front desk. He looked at me like I'd eaten a shit sandwich and forgotten to wipe my face.

"Can I *help* you?" he said, and you can probably practically hear the way he said it.

While I was a brash little kid, I was too bowled over by the place to come up with the right smart-assed comeback. So I just stumbled around trying to think of something to say.

"Why don't you take a walk, kid?" he said. "The arcade's down the street."

I started to leave on the verge of tears (to this day I can't believe how easily overwhelmed I was by people with power or money back then) when I heard Phil's voice behind me.

"Olie. Wasn't sure if I'd see you. Come on in," he told me. I was still too emotionally fragile to take some kind of enjoyment out of walking by the fuck at the front desk, though I did manage to shoot him a glare as I passed.

Weeks later I saw him getting out of his car, and took a piss on it after he went inside. I was really patient back in the day, I guess.

I still had no idea why I was there. Phil and I hit a few balls back and forth a while, and then he called some old dude over to watch, which gave me the creeps all over again just like when Phil had started watching me.

"What do you think?" he asked the old guy. The old guy grunted. "I think there's something there myself," Phil replied.

"He can hit a forehand," said the old fart finally, after thinking about it for some time. "We've got better," he concluded sourly.

"Olie," Phil said to me without breaking stride, "serve for Mr. Tooks."

I did. Tooks, for that was his name, barely batted an eye. "So he can serve. So what. Still no power there."

"He's thirteen," Phil told him. "Olie, hit a serve here," he said, indicating a spot inside the service box. I did. "Now hit one here," he said, pointing to another spot. I did. "Give me a backhand

exactly to this spot," he said, gesturing to a spot in the back corner, near the baseline, and I did. He set markers at ten different
spots around the court, and then fed me a forehand. "Ten shots in
this rally, I want you to nail each one of these spots in exactly the
order I laid the markers."

I did. It was easy.

When I was done he turned triumphantly to Tooks, who now
couldn't help but look at least a little impressed. But all he said
was, "Yeah, okay." I had no idea what that meant.

As it turned out, that meant I was to be offered a scholarship to
join the Canadian Junior Tennis Federation and train at the Gene
Toomey Tennis Centre. Tooks insisted I was too old to be starting
the program, but he let Phil make the final call. As confused as I
was about whatever the hell they were actually talking about, I
heard one thing that sounded pretty appealing: a new place to live
and a boatload of special treatment to boot. These guys could've
been selling me into some kind of child slavery sex cult and I still
would've gone for it, believe me.

At thirteen I was already beginning to realize that I wasn't going
to have a lot of options in life. Barely attending school and flunk-
ing out whenever I did, living in the protective custody of the
good folks of the Province of Ontario and scraping up a living on
the streets, even if it was in my own inventive way, I knew I was
headed exactly nowhere fast. So these guys tell me I can live in
their facility outside the city with free meals, spending money
readily available, and little more than tennis to keep me busy (they
weren't clear at first about the school commitment they'd be
expecting from me) and I'm as there as there can be.

I didn't fit in well, though. The other kids had been playing
since they were old enough to hold a racquet, and they all had a
snobby "who the fuck do *you* think *you* are" attitude about them,
seeing me as this scummy, unwashed street kid with no business
being there breathing their rarefied air. They never tried anything
physical with me because, let's face it, these were tennis weenies
and I'd have simply killed them, but they did give me a really hard
time, trying to provoke me into taking a swing at them and

maybe losing my scholarship. As much as I would have loved to tear some of them a new hole, I really didn't want to let Phil down so quickly. I figured it would happen soon enough, and kind of wanted to enjoy this a while. As it was, I just ate alone and listened to the lot of them making remarks about how I ate like a slob or didn't know how to dress, and tried to block them out as best I could. Besides, I always got them back on the courts.

We worked on conditioning and strokes in the mornings, broke away for a couple of hours of class time, and then played some practice matches in the afternoons. While I got my ass kicked the first time I played Phil, I wasn't to be embarrassed the same way with these kids—I could beat most of them easily. After a while they were reduced to making fun of my "unorthodox style," which was easier to poke holes in than my results certainly.

We had a competition ladder, and I quickly worked my way up the rungs until it was only a few of the seventeen-year-olds still ahead of me. The older kids were simply too developed for me to handle at first, but even they got their dicks pounded into the sand as I grew more comfortable with the game.

I realized then that I had real talent. Phil had seen something in the way I played that day he'd just happened by, and he knew talent when he saw it.

Phil was once the highest ranked Canadian singles player in the world. Now that's not saying much in the big picture as his highest ranking was fifty-ninth and he never actually won a pro title, but he did win some matches in his day against some good players and once reached the fourth round at Wimbledon, briefly exciting a small nation of sporadic tennis fans. He was a small fish in the big pond of the ATP, but a huge player in the little Canadian scene. I think it was hard for him to live up to the expectations Canadian fans had of him when he got out against the best guys in the world on the biggest stages. He never came into his own as "the guy who'd finally put Canada on the tennis map." He later switched his focus to doubles where he did well and made a fair bit of money until he retired at thirty-one and came to work as a coach with the Junior Tennis Fed. I always thought a part of him was looking for that one kid who'd break through and take him along to the big show. Obviously he saw that potential in me at one time. He was on me like glue and it wasn't long before I started to like the attention.

See, no one had ever paid attention to me before. Now I know that sounds pathetic, but maybe if my mother had put me up for adoption things could have been different. As it was, she decided to keep me in some hallucinogenic moment of idiocy that the both of us would live to regret. See—and I'm not proud of this, okay—she was a whore. I don't mean she was a "whorish cow" or anything like that; she was an actual genuine practicing prostitute.

Now sure, lots of prostitutes are actually super nice people who really care about their kids and just want to catch a break in this hardscrabble world. But not my mother. She was mean and selfish and hateful and bitter, not to mention a drunk, a druggie and a hitter. As scary as it could be when she'd take off and leave me for days at a time, it was often better because at least then she wasn't actively mistreating me.

I was born in a little apartment on Bloor Street, where my mother plied her trade until frighteningly late in her pregnancy. My mother named me Oliver Drew Wood after a john she really liked named Oliver Drew, or at least that was the name he used whenever he visited her. For all I know he could've actually *been* my father.

My earliest memory was when I was maybe two. I was sitting in a diaper so full it raised me up a full three inches off the floor. When it finally popped open from the pressure I found myself covered in shit. And I was hungry and letting the world know it. But she never came. I just cried and snorted and pissed myself to pass the time and she never came. I think it might have been twelve hours or so I was left lying there in my own waste before she came home reeking of what I later knew to be hash oil. And she was pissed at me, boy. I'd made a mess she was going to have to clean up and she went wild, absolutely ballistic. It was the first time I remember anyone wailing on me. She beat me really bad.

I don't think anyone from Child Services found out about that one. She hadn't broken anything and didn't take me to the hospital, but she'd knocked my head bad enough that I felt sick for a really long time. She was a shitty, horrible excuse for a mother even then.

But I got better, and as I grew up I learned how to avoid her until she was gone for good.

I think she's dead now. When I was last in Toronto this old lady who used to live in our building told me she heard my mother had been knifed by a john. Who knows. It would certainly be in keeping with the lifestyle she enjoyed.

Huh, I think that's what they call stream of consciousness. Writing is cool. I haven't thought about this stuff in a long time—Phil, my mother, the Regent Club. All so long ago.

What now though? Well I have to get down south somehow. The cold is going to kill me up here and I need to play more events or I'm going to lose my eligibility. I have some ideas though. I always have some ideas.

January 12

I try not to steal, but sometimes it's necessary. I make a terrible thief, but it hasn't stopped me from doing what needs doing, believe me. I don't typically steal money—that seems sleazier somehow—but I've been known to take things out of cars that aren't locked or from stores when there's something specific I desperately need.

For instance, this morning I stole a box of Pop Tarts from a nearby convenience store. I'm already running dangerously low on the money Miranda sent me, and I was hungry, so I loaded up. And then, just to earn a few extra bucks, I shovelled snow off some old peoples' sidewalks for five bucks a pop (I just considered it part of my training and exercise routine), but I'm still scrambling to scrounge up enough for a bus ticket south. I tried walking, but it's so cold out you get frustrated walking for hours only to find out how little progress you've actually made in the Great Lake State.

I called Gary, but he can't come down. He has a new crop coming in and needs to monitor its progress closely for the next four or five days.

Hitchhiking always seems like such a good idea in theory, but it's hard for a guy like me. Girls can always catch a ride, and kids usually don't have any real problem getting someone to stop, but most people take one look at me and keep on driving, usually at an increased speed. And the ones who do stop are usually a little nuts or a lot lonely.

So here I sit on my ass on the side of the highway somewhere in Michigan south of Kalamazoo, munching a Pop Tart and hoping like hell someone stops for me before my last surviving nut freezes off.

                                                          January 19
Okay, I'll write this down once and not speak of it again. The past week has been a desperate blur of taunts, humiliation and pain.

I made a bit of progress in my bid to get down south, managing a few rides from people who seemed able to get past the way I look. I made it all the way to Warsaw, Indiana where my luck ran out along with my few remaining pennies. Desperate, I did some shit I'm not proud of. Most notably, I happened by an old lady with a purse just dangling off her arm in a manner so inviting I couldn't help myself. I snatched the purse and made off down the seemingly deserted street feeling a little bad, because I like old people by and large, and a little thrilled, because I had the feeling the old bag might have a few bucks.

Only problem was, she actually gave chase. Now I wasn't worried about her actually catching me, even if I was weighed down by the cat carrier, but I was surprised that someone who looked at least eighty was able to run at all.

"Bastard!" she screamed at my back. "I'll kill you. I'll fucking kill you!" I'd never heard someone so old speak so harshly before.

And still she gave chase. God she was spry. Now I'm a professional athlete, and knew it shouldn't take too much running before I shook her off eventually, but goddamn it if she wasn't catching up to me. I briefly thought about ditching Blanche Dowling to lighten my load.

"Fuck off, lady!" I shouted back over my shoulder. "Give it up or you're going to hurt yourself!"

"Drop the bag, cocksucker, or when I catch you I'm going to fuck you in the neck!" she said, whatever the heck that meant.

In spite of myself I liked this woman. I really did. But still she just kept on coming, chasing me clear out of town onto a dirt road. I was starting to panic, and envisioned having to actually fight this old lady, when suddenly the ground gave way beneath me. I landed on my ass, and the cat carrier landed on my head, as Blanche Dowling let out a bowel-loosening howl.

I'd fallen into a hole. The old lady appeared above me with a satisfied smile. She wasn't even out of breath.

"You run like a three-legged ferret," she grinned. "Now give me my purse, asshole."

"Why should I?"

"'Cause if you don't, you'll probably die in there," she said. I looked around. Sure enough, my hole was indeed a deep one. I couldn't see an obvious way to escape. "Throw me my purse and I'll get you out," she said. She had me, and so I did as requested, finally getting it out on the fourth attempt (cut me some slack, it was a deep hole!). She smiled again. Then she waved at me and whispered, "So long, ass-hat."

Ass-hat? Who was she calling an "ass-hat"? I screamed until my throat was raw but no one came. Evening arrived, and Blanche Dowling and I settled in for the long sleepless night ahead.

Finally the next morning a couple of kids appeared at the hole.

"Thank God!" I croaked. "Please get some help. I'm stuck down here."

They paused to consider the situation. And then they started throwing rocks at me, laughing like they were having the best time. I suppose they were. I was spared permanent injury when an adult finally showed up at my hole.

"What are you kids doing?" he asked them. Then he saw me and bent down for a closer look.

"Hey, man, can you throw me a rope or something?" I pleaded.

"You the guy who tried to steal old lady Edison's purse?"

"Oh fuck," I thought as he made loud, elaborate preparations to hork on my head.

It seems this Edison lady I'd assaulted was the town elder and much loved by the townsfolk. One by one, people began to stop by my hole to hurl taunts at me and throw things at my head. Sharp things mostly. But then eventually someone made the mistake of throwing some stale muffins at my head, so at least I had something to chew on. It wasn't that bad, really. At least I was eating, which I hadn't been doing outside the hole.

After a couple of days, people came by to gawk at me more like I was some kind of tourist attraction.

"That the guy in the hole?" one would ask.

"Looks like it," another would confirm. Then they'd leave. I couldn't believe it. A few took pity on Blanche Dowling, though, and instead of rocks or bottles they'd throw packets of cat food at my head. What I didn't eat myself I decided to share with my feline friend. Even in times of extreme adversity my inherent sense of kindness remains.

The police showed up eventually. However, my brief elation was punctured when it became clear that they, too, were here to laugh and point at me.

Large groups of children stopped by, and their teachers told them such things as, "Make sure you study hard, kids. Because if you don't, you'll end up broke and ugly, stuck in a hole."

"I'm not ugly, lady," I shot back. "You could afford to lay off the doughnuts yourself!"

She threw a large paving stone at me, missed by a fraction, and moved on.

I'd resigned myself to being a kept pet for the community of Warsaw, Indiana. They would care for me inasmuch as they would occasionally throw food down at me, but otherwise I was to be their entertainment. Or else their cautionary tale against intruders who would dare cross swords with their strangely agile and rabbit-quick seniors.

My saviour finally arrived in the form of a large man who fell upon my back as I was sleeping.

"What are you doing in my hole?" I asked him testily. "There's no room for anyone else in my hole."

"I was looking for the hole creature," he replied with welling eyes. "I was told he lived near here, and I fell in while I was looking."

"Yeah that would be me," I sighed.

He looked around and said, "Oh, right. That makes sense."

We stared at each other in silence.

"So you're in my hole," I said after a time.

"So I am."

"What are we going to do about that?"

"You're not going to eat me, are you?"

"No. No, I'm not."

"I heard the hole creature eats passers-by."

"No, I don't eat passers-by, dude. That's a lie."

"I have an idea. The two of us could almost reach the top. Why don't you give me a boost up?"

"Why don't you give *me* a boost?" I asked.

"Well I couldn't exactly let the hole creature out of his *hole*, now could I?"

"But you want me to help get you out."

"Well . . . yes."

"And you don't find that a little ironic."

He considered this briefly. "Okay," he said, "you go first."

It took some doing. We were fortunate no one else was around at the time, as they'd have likely tried to curtail such an attempt, but after he got me almost all the way there, I was able to scramble the remainder of the way to the top. After he tossed me the cat carrier he said, "Now find something to throw down here and pull me out."

"Sorry, dude. You're on your own."

'What do you mean?" he said.

"Hey, you were here to taunt me, so screw you. See how you like being the hole creature. Fuck you, hole creature!" I said, only I got too close to the edge when I said it and fell in again.

"Well this is sure embarrassing."

"I suppose it is," he said.

"One more time, this time I promise to pull you out."

"No way, me first this time."

"No way, you'll leave me down here."

"Then it appears we've reached something of a stalemate."

"Yeah," I said. "We have."

We sat in silence a while until we heard Blanche Dowling meowing pitifully.

"Come on, dude. She's up there stuck in her cage. She's scared and lonely. Please push me out so I can let her know I'm alive, and I promise to pull you out. I promise. You have my word this time. I'm sorry I was such an asshole before; I'm just stressed out and exhausted and tired of wallowing in my own waste."

He took a good look around and scrunched up his face.

"Let's get out of here," he said, and boosted me up.

This time I made sure to move way back from the edge before I started any taunting, and then I stole his truck and bid farewell to Warsaw and its hole. In the glove compartment, in a billfold, I found a few hundred dollars. Turned out to be a lucrative week after all.

January 21

Stupid truck. Stupid transmission. Stupid fat-assed hole creature who doesn't get his engine serviced on a regular basis.

I'm on foot again after making really good time for a couple of days. Not only was the vehicle effective transportation, but it gave me a nice place to sleep at night. I got as far south as an unmarked town outside Dresden, Tennessee before the truck finally gave out. I took it to a repair shop, but the greasy old guy running the place said it would take $800 and three days to fix. So I had to use some of my newly hard-earned hole-money to purchase myself a bus ticket.

Now I'm no snob but I hate the bus, especially when travel-ling in the States. There's always someone with a really bad, really vocal flu that everyone held hostage in this hurtling metal cylinder of death and disease will surely fall prey to. Although, in my favour, several years of medicinal experimentation, which seem to have made my system all but immune to various airborne diseases. My body's a pretty well-oiled machine when it comes to dulling the senses and keeping would-be infections at bay.

Anyhow, I had to pay three hundred bucks for my ticket. But on the upside it will get me all the way to Arkansas without having to hitch again.

There's some kind of irony at work here when it costs me more to get where I'm going than I'm at all likely to earn once I get there. Sometimes I think I'm a little out of whack in my priorities, if not a little nuts. In any case, I'm committed to this course of action, so onward I go.

There's also the matter of a little deal going down in Little Rock that I overheard a couple of the Futures guys talking about. I wouldn't mind getting in on that. Could be some serious money in it, which might make it possible to play all the tennis I want without having to worry about cash for a while.

Two birds; one big stone. When you're a travelling man like I am, you have to be able to multitask.

                                                    January 22
There's a small town called Conway in Arkansas where this next tournament is to take place. A part of me doesn't want to leave Little Rock at all. It's a real city, and as you travel through these shitty little American towns you really start yearning for that metropolitan experience.

So the bus ride. Jesus. I've had better times. Come to think about it, I've had stuff rammed up my ass (long story) that felt better than this little outing. I sat next to a fat chick who stared at me the whole trip without saying a word, and we're talking about full-on, out-and-out staring like she was trying to burn holes in my forehead with her laser eyes. No matter what I did—tried to read a magazine, pointedly looked off in the other direction, tried staring right back at her until I had to avert my eyes—it didn't make any kind of difference. She just kept her eyes glued to me like I'd done something really, really wrong.

Then there was the Tourette's guy in the back of the bus who seemed stuck on the one verbal tick, "Nigger." Now this is the American South, and naturally you're going to see a few black dudes on a bus in the American South. And naturally these fellas aren't going to tolerate some skinny white dude barking racial slurs at them for hours at a time. So not only do we get to hear the unnatural barking from the back, but we also get to hear the following exchange:

Tourette's guy: "Nigger."

Well-dressed black dude with a short temper: "Better knock that shit out, mister."

Bus driver: "Keep it down back there."

Well-dressed black dude with a short temper: "I apologize. But I will not tolerate racial epithets on my time."

Tourette's guy: "Nigger."

Well-dressed black guy with a short temper: "Mister, if you're not careful, I'm going to come back there and beat your head in."

Bus driver: "Hey, I'm the only one gonna be doing any beating on this bus. So shut up."

Well-dressed black guy with a short temper: "Don't oppress me, white man."

Unwise little white cracker sitting in front of the well-dressed black guy with a short temper: "This guy at the back is just telling it like it is, so shut your mouth, boy."

Well-dressed black guy with a short temper: "Clearly more than one person here is screaming out for a severe beating!"

Tourette's guy: "Nigger."

Old black lady as she whips out an umbrella and starts waving it about: "I've heard about enough. I'm takin' y'all out!"

Bus driver: "I'll pull this bus over! I mean it!"

"Nigger!"

This kind of went on for a while. Eight straight hours in fact, during which time something clearly crawled up someone's ass and died before being pushed out into the world in the one

backed-up bathroom we had access to the entire trip. Add to this
a lot of angry, screaming Americans and a crazed, staring freak
(who I now realize may have been blind, so my bad) and, needless to say, I was pretty much ready to kill by the end of it. I actually ran off the bus when we finally arrived in Little Rock.

So anyway, here I am, and I'm supposed to go to the Pittman
Hotel, a shitty little dive on the west end of the city where I overheard a couple of the tour players say there was some money to
be had. And yes, I have a feeling that what's going down may not
be totally on the up and up. The talk of free money, and the
hushed tones with which these guys talked about it, suggested
otherwise.

Now if anyone ever reads this, let me just say that money
obtained from disreputable means is still necessary for the desperate, and frankly more than a few of the Futures players fit square-
ly into that category.

January 23

You know you're unpopular when you show up at a meeting of
your peers in which they're talking about doing something really
morally wrong and they still look like you're not good enough to
be there amongst them. Well fuck you too. I received some seriously dirty looks when I arrived, but I just took my seat and said,
"So, guys, what's on the agenda?" There wasn't much they could
do. I knew what they were up to (well, to be fair, I knew they
were up to *something*, but still) and could've easily ratted them out.
So I was in, though increasingly aware of just how disliked I am
by the other players on the tour.

Mike Zahn owns and carries a gun. That's key to this next little
scene. Who's Mike Zahn, you ask? Doesn't matter. You'll never
hear of him unless he ends up killing someone someday, which he
more than likely will, now that I think about it. He's an undistin-
guished player with minimal talent. A hanger-on who plays an
average game of tennis, who uses his status as a "professional athlete" to get tennis groupie tail (and yes, there is such a thing) in
various places around the globe.

Now as a Canadian I still find it surprising when someone who isn't a cop or a secret agent carries a gun (okay, I haven't actually met a secret agent, but I feel pretty sure they'd carry guns). It just isn't done in my neck of the woods. Down here, though, it isn't that big a deal. Of course it would be if someone wore a gun strapped to their thigh on the tennis court or into the 7–11, but when kept in one's suitcase no one seems to think anything of it. The sight of a gun gives me the shits myself, but I know enough to stay quiet even when I get spooked.

"Holy cow," I said, "that's a gun!"

"Shut up!" Zahn hissed. "Get your head out of your skanky old-man ass and realize where we are."

A hotel lobby, to be exact. And for the record my ass is neither skanky nor remotely similar to an old-man's. I just want that on the record.

Anyhow, I tried to listen as Zahn told us of his great plan.

It seems he has family in Little Rock. Well, more than family, I suppose—his parents to be exact. Now Zahn hates his family like death. And to make matters worse, they've disowned him, and worse still, they've got boatloads of money. And Zahn's got none. (Except for what he makes as a Futures tennis professional, and by now I think we're all up to speed on how much, or rather how little, that amounts to.) Now he can't very well show his face around their house, but he knows where they keep their family safe (and what the fuck kind of world is it where people have "family safes"? I definitely missed out on something growing up like I did). His big plan is to feed a few of the guys the information about his parents' house, have us burgle the place and walk off with whatever cash and sellable goodies they have on site, and split the haul.

I, for the record, do not approve of any illegal activity, be it drugs, theft, or any form of assault. If I happen to have taken part in any such activities in the past, it's only because I needed to survive. And again, for the record, guns really do give me the willies, and so I refused to use it or so much as touch it during the break-in.

Okay, so I ended up being the guy with the gun. What else could I do? Zahn made me on account of no one really wanting me to be a part of this thing in the first place. So I paid my way into the arrangement by accepting the shit detail.

I'm not convincing with a gun. I just don't look the part. Some people you see with a gun and it just looks right. Just *feels* right. John Wayne looked great with a gun. Clint Eastwood pulls off the gun brilliantly. I look like a small child, tentative and awkward, holding a giant mousetrap that might snap back on me at any time. The thing looked and felt huge in my hands. Zahn assured me it wouldn't even be necessary since his parents always went out for dinner on Sunday nights, but felt we needed something "just in case." So I stuffed the thing into my sweatpants, and the five of us went off to rob the Zahns.

We were advised to go around back to the kitchen, where we could break a small pane of glass, reach in, and unlock the door. Then we were to make our way to the spare bedroom upstairs, two doors down from the master bedroom, where we'd find a closet with a secret panel, behind which was the safe. The combination was Zahn's and his older sister's birthdays, in that order. We were to grab all the cash that was there, as well as any worthwhile trinkets we found along the way, then get out and back to the hotel where we'd divvy up the take and make our way to Conway in time for the tournament the next day. No problems—quick, easy and painless. And if anyone surprised us, I was to point the gun at them until we made our getaway. Less painless, but still quick and easy. I had half a mind to remove the bullets, since I wouldn't actually be needing to fire the thing, but when I suggested as much Zahn smacked me on the head.

"I'm gonna regret letting the old guy in on this," he muttered to himself as he walked away. So I left the bullets in.

So four young guys—three Americans and a Serbian who spoke very little English—and of course me, all hustled over to a nice leafy street in a nice old neighbourhood with nice old houses for our big criminal moment in life. And as evidence that we were all pretty bad, not to mention new, at this, we took a cab.

Hey, none of us had a car! Zahn hadn't thought that part through, I guess.

Anyhow, the five us squeezed into the cab and prayed we wouldn't be at all memorable to the driver. For his part, the driver just smoked his cigarette and stared at us in the rear-view mirror. I prayed he wasn't committing our faces to memory in case of future police line-ups.

All went as it was supposed to, at first. Mario Kosavic, the Serb kid, broke the back window with a rock and we entered uncontested. The house seemed quiet, and I was relieved at not having to brandish the gun, although its weight was starting to pull my sweatpants down. Still, I preferred it there, dragging my pants down, rather than in my hand where really bad things could happen.

We crept upstairs, each of us doing his best impression of a burglar he'd seen on any number of television shows. We counted off rooms beyond what looked to be the master bedroom, and a guy named Jimmy Locke triumphantly burst open the door to the spare bedroom . . . whereupon he fell flat on his face as said door was yanked open from within. The rest of us just stood there, too stupid to move, unable to comprehend that someone else was there with us.

With Jimmy down I was next up, and found myself staring up into the face of the largest woman I've ever seen. Not as in fat, but as in big. Like BIG big. Maybe six-foot-four with arm muscles that looked like dolphins swimming under her skin. Clearly she'd heard us dorks break in, and was ready for whatever we were bringing. She hauled back and punched me square in the nose. I went down hard, and heard a couple of the guys behind me squeal and run away. Only Kosavic, poor Jimmy still on the floor and me, now down there next to him, remained.

"Fuckers!" the big girl bellowed as she grabbed Mario and threw him—literally threw him—across what looked to be her bedroom. He landed in a heap on her bed as she turned her glare back to me, now scrambling to get to my feet.

"I know who you are," she announced in a deep booming voice that literally shook the windows. "I recognize tennis players when

I see them," she added, grabbing my nut sack with her humungous hand. "Same fruity, Nancy-boy, 'look at me, I'm sort of an athlete' way about you. Gotta be friends of Michael's."

Meanwhile, I remind you, she's holding my balls (and I use the plural here only because any reference to my one remaining ball and it's plastic surrogate twin is just too hard to bear and, frankly, sounds pathetic somehow) and starts rolling them around her palm like dice. And I'm feeling a dead weight in my stomach that feels like I'm about to barf.

Mario stood beside me clutching a comically large flashlight, seemingly unable to move. "So big, the woman," he managed to mutter. "Like demon." And then it sounded like he might have started praying in Serbian, or whatever the fuck they speak where he's from.

"See this, asshole," she said to Mario, brandishing my sack. "You're next."

As inconsistent as his grasp of the English language may have been, Mario understood perfectly well what she meant, and promptly recovered from his temporary paralysis and disappeared with the others.

Jimmy tried to get up. But she nailed him so hard in the side of the head with her elbow that he went down again, cold this time. She pulled me closer by the balls until we were face-to-face, so close that I could smell that she'd recently eaten seafood of some kind.

"Michael's a pussy," she breathed. "He always sent weak little pricks like you to do his dirty work. Shit, the guy couldn't even delegate properly."

"Maybe you could take that up with him personally," I whimpered through clenched teeth.

"You violated my personal space," she said, seemingly not hearing me. "I was having a private moment!"

I shuddered to think what that might mean exactly, but it was starting to look like I might not get out of this in possession of all the body parts I'd come in with. I suddenly remembered the gun, now pulling my sweatpants two thirds of the way down my ass, and started to dig for it. But she noticed me digging and squeezed that much harder, which I didn't realize was even possible until that point. In desperation I punched her in the eye and she staggered back, only she didn't let go of my scrot and I collapsed forward onto her. I started to lose all feeling in my rod and stones as her other monster hand grabbed me by the throat and squeezed that too.

As I started to black out I heard her scream, incredulous, "You hit a *girl*? You break in and scare me and then you *hit* me?" Before she could squeeze the life out of me I managed to get my pants off; then stood up and brandished the gun through the fleece-polyester blend. The gun, still in the pocket, looked a bit like a giant fleecy turkey baster, but she seemed to understand what I had in there. So she started wailing on me. I didn't even mind the beating so much since she had to let go of my nads to start hitting me.

"Back up offa me, bitch," I wheezed, adding, "I will so waste you!" as I kicked out at her, meaning to boot her square in the stomach but actually catching her down around the shin.

"You have to be the least threatening gunman I've ever seen," she said disdainfully, giving me a good looking-over. I suppose she was right. There I stood in my raggedy drawers, holding my pants around a gunnish-shaped thing that might or might not have been a firearm, with hair dishevelled and eyes bloodshot from the working over I'd just received. But I wasn't done. I wanted the money I'd come for. I hadn't suffered for nothing.

"Don't push me, man. I am one nasty muthafucka. I've used this thing before and I ain't above using it again."

"You've never used that before," she told me, almost laughing while I scrambled to remove the gun from my pants. "That's Michael's gun. You don't even know how to hold it properly."

"Stay the fuck back, dude," I told her, tossing my sweatpants across the floor. "I'm crazy and you never know when I might go off. I killed a man once I'll have you know." And suddenly she wasn't sure. Something about me told her I might just be crazy enough to do it. Somehow I was able to convince her.

By the way, I wasn't bluffing. I did kill a man once. Though technically it wasn't, like, from hand-to-hand combat, or with a knife or a gun or anything of that nature. I suppose, technically speaking, I once killed a man with a key lime pie.

Okay, so I think I mentioned before that I often do some part-time work tending to the elderly. Again, weird shit, I know, but there you go. What sometimes happens is, I have just enough money to get to a tournament on some remote part of the globe. The idea is I'll win enough prize money to get myself back, with maybe a little left over for some fun while I'm there. Unfortunately, from time to time, I lose earlier than would allow for any real money to be made. So I do what work I'm able to find.

Well, one of the plum B-level tournaments is in Bermuda. I won the event back when I was a kid just starting out, and they still hold a spot for me, though truth be told, after the incident with the chief of police last year, I'm not expecting another invitation anytime soon. But a few years before that unfortunate day I was in Bermuda to play, and I lost early and found myself with no money to get home. Of course, if you're going to be stranded anywhere, Bermuda's not a bad place to be. But I didn't have enough to survive there for more than a few days.

So I ended up hooked up with a guy named Alfred Brenner. Met him like I do so many of these old geezers, at the grocery store. You see them struggling with their bags and you help them out, and before you know it they're so grateful for your actually taking the time to talk to them and listen to their boring stories that you're in their living rooms pulling out impressive reference letters from previous employers prior to running errands and cleaning toilets and, on particularly unfortunate occasions, wiping asses and whatnot. Brenner didn't need much help; he just liked having someone to talk to, and it was worth the odd twenty to have me move some furniture around and then sit over coffee listening to what life was like in the motherland back when he was a little boy.

Alfred was actually a pretty nice guy, and though he could bore you to tears with tales of Merry Olde England, I didn't mind sitting with him for extended periods of time. And one of my many make-work projects was to pick up his groceries, which worked out well because I could buy him his stuff but get the cheaper no-name options and keep the change for myself.

One day when I went to pick up the grocery money and his shopping list for the week, he was having himself a crying jag. Seems it was the anniversary of his wife's death, so truth be told, I felt bad for the guy. Thought I'd do something nice for old Alfred.

He always got these boring, low-fat, low-sugar arrowroot cookies as his snack—you know, the kind babies eat—so for once I splurged on something nice instead of keeping most of the money for myself. I bought him this beautiful, only-in-Bermuda, bright green key lime pie. Thought it might cheer him up.

He was asleep in his chair when I got back, so I just put his groceries away and left the pie on the table for him with a note saying, "Thought you might enjoy something special!"

But when I came by the next day to check on him, he was face down in the pie with half of it eaten. At that moment I seemed to recall something he'd said when we'd first met about being severely diabetic, but he'd gone on so long in that monotone of his that I kind of blanked it out at the time.

I felt like shit of course, but it wasn't like he had a long full life ahead of him. Besides, he should have known not to eat the goddamned thing! I beat it out of there (taking with me my friendly note of course), taught private lessons to some rich kids outside Hamilton until I earned enough money to get back home, and never heard anything about it again. But I always remember—I killed a dude. Death by pie. That's my admission of guilt right there.

And so this huge horse of a woman deserved to know what exactly she was in for if she pushed me too far.

"I'll do it again," I told her.

"You're no killer. You look like a bum who wouldn't know his ass from his elbow."

Now that pissed me off, because I most certainly knew my ass from my elbow. Who didn't? And besides, what did this cow know?

"I tell you what. I'm going to take what I came for out of that there safe, I'm going to leave the way I came in, and you're going to behave like a good girl. Understand?"

She just laughed. "You can't think I'm going to let you steal from my family."

"I think my little friend here says you will." I was starting to feel pretty cool, standing there holding my big American gun.

She shook her head in disgust. "My brother is friends with the biggest assholes—"

"Hey! I'm not your brother's friend. Now look," I told her, "I'm stepping over to that safe." I did, and without taking my eyes off of her. "And I'm putting in the combination." This was harder to do without taking my eyes off her, but after only four or five minutes I got it open. "Now I'm taking out the money." And I did that too. Only I had nowhere to put it. There wasn't as much as I thought or hoped there'd be, but it was more than I could easily carry. I would've put it in my pants, but they were on the floor across the room. "Have you got a bag or something?" I asked.

"Like I'd tell *you*." Her eyes narrowed.

I tried to rouse Jimmy. "Jimmy!" I said, that being the obvious thing to say. "Jimmy, dude, get up!" I nudged him with my foot a few times and he eventually started to come to.

"What in the hell . . ." he started, but then he saw this woman standing there and he remembered. "Holy shit, I thought it was some kind of twisted fucking nightmare!" he said, beating it out of there, leaving me alone with the gun, the money, and this big ol' bitch here.

"Gimme my pants," I told her. She just bared her teeth in answer. "I'm gonna put a bullet in you, I swear to God!" I said, getting so frustrated that I felt like I actually could have. But she still said and did nothing, so I stacked up the money and balanced it on one hand while I kept the gun trained on her with the other. I shimmied along the wall with my back flat against it. I made it to the door and started to relax a bit, realizing I was going to get out of here after all.

Then, faster than I've ever seen a human being move (except for maybe that old bird in Warsaw, Indiana), she bolted across the room and karate-chopped my wrist—actually karate-chopped it—causing me to drop the gun. She pushed me up against the doorjamb, bringing her meaty swollen lips up close to my face and whispering, "I don't think so, little man." She held both my wrists in her one big meat hook, and pinned me back with the other.

"Such a bad man, sneaking in here and scaring me," she breathed, her seafood breath still pungent. "Such a bad man, trying to steal from me. Gonna have to be punished."

And then she kissed me. On the mouth.

Now . . . No, that won't do it justice. See . . . No, I can't quite explain it. Okay, picture a cow's tongue, all thick and meaty and rough, pushing itself into your mouth, cutting off all air that might want in or out. Then picture the largest hand you ever saw aggressively grabbing your member and twisting it into some sort of appalling balloon animal and you might get some sense of the many terrible things befalling my person at that moment.

I have never known true terror before. Now I am intimate with it.

Finally she released my dong and said with a smile, "Go on, tennis player. Get your skinny ass out of here. You're done."

I tried to shuffle away, but she pulled me back.

"What now?" I asked, turning to see what new horror awaited me.

And she handed me my sweatpants. "You should probably take these," she said. "You'd look stupid as hell running around in your ginch, and I'd hate to think what my parents would do if they found them here."

"Thanks," I mumbled, reaching gingerly for them.

"And this," she said, handing me the pile of money.

"What, are you fucking with me?"

She shrugged. "Nope. What do I care. It's nothing to me. Besides," she said with a disturbing smile, "you earned it, my friend." Then she winked. She actually winked her giant cow-lid at me like we had some sort of "understanding." And then she turned her back on me, lay down on her bed, and opened a book by Jane Austen.

I wasn't sure what to do. I was convinced she was setting me up somehow, and that she'd call the cops the minute I stepped out the door. But I'd suffered for that money. I'd truly suffered. So I grabbed it and ran like hell.

When I finally made it back to base, the other guys insisted on their cut. At first I tried to protest. Tried to point out that I'd been the one who sacrificed for this bling; that I'd given up some blood, some bruises and more than a little pride, and thus deserved the bulk of it. But as I imagined trying to explain exactly what had happened, I felt reluctant to tell the story. I realized it would be easier to share the money than share all those mortifying details. But little do they know I kept an extra fifty in my shoe for myself, so ha! I goddamn well earned it and have the twisted dink and crushed ball to prove it.

"Why didn't you tell us about your sister?' I asked Michael as I was leaving.

"Didn't realize she still lived at home," he answered with a grin. In that moment I wondered if he knew more than he was saying. If he and his scary-ass sister had some sort of weird deal going on here. But then I suppose I'll never know for certain.

I felt totally wasted and I hadn't even had a drink. I returned to my shitty hotel and checked myself out in the mirror, scaring myself silly in the process. I was puffy and swollen—even more than usual—and I'd picked up a black eye at some point. My scrot hurt like hell and I was so weak I could hardly stand up. It was almost not worth the four hundred bucks I'd hauled in for the night's work. Almost, but not quite.

To top things off, Blanche Dowling went a little nuts, and as some sort of punishment for leaving her alone for so long, attacked and scratched my left shin to shit.

And just to make the night complete, I'm feeling like I might have a flu coming on, and I just realized the tournament starts up tomorrow. And me with my one remaining testicle swollen

up like a tennis ball. No idea how I'm going to play in the
morning. Jesus, and the month isn't even out yet.

January 24

Jesus Christ up in his heaven, I won a match. Well, okay, technically I got a walkover when whatever flu bug I've been carrying
but haven't contracted—due to my iron constitution—spread to
a bunch of the guys last night. But still, a win's a win. One more
and it's officially a streak. And thank God, because I could barely
walk today. I wouldn't have lasted five minutes.

January 25

Everyone is sick. You've never seen so many guys puking their
guts out on court. I got three defaults. One of them actually
ended up in hospital. What a fantastic day!

And best of all, not only am I in my first final in three years
tomorrow, but my ball is healing nicely, I feel pretty good, and my
opponent, good ol' Lincoln Holmes, has the flu as well. He probably won't be able to take the court at all, and if he does, he'll fall
apart for sure. I'll get a win without actually having to hit a ball
all week, and I'll chalk up a victory over the hottest prospect in
the Futures. That'll not only earn me a couple of precious ATP
ranking points and a few bucks for a change, but also the attention of the tennis world for having beaten—no, crushed—the big
new stud.

Why couldn't everyone be sick every day? For the first time in
a long time everything seems to be going perfectly.

January 26

Oh shut the fuck up. So I lost to a guy who could barely walk.
It happens.

I really thought I had it in the bag. To my surprise, Holmes staggered out onto the court and stood there looking like death, but
he was clearly determined to try.

I actually hadn't planned on playing. In fact I spent some of my
newly hard-earned money getting wasted. Call it a pre-emptive

celebration. I assumed ol' Lincoln wouldn't show. But he did. Goddamn it if he didn't show up and stand there like an idiot, swaying in the breeze, barely able to keep his balance.

You can't help but feel a little humbled losing to a guy in that condition, but truth be told, I suddenly wasn't in the greatest shape myself. Hung-over and out of practice from not having played all week, I was hitting my shots every which way but straight. All I had to do was get my serves and returns in and there was no way he was getting to the ball. But I hit a personal record thirty-nine double faults over two sets and couldn't seem to hit a return off even the weakest, kitteny-soft lobs he was getting over the net. I think I was trying too hard and went wailing away on the balls, much as Zahn's sister had wailed away on mine a few days ago. Bottom line, he kicked my ass. I won't even mention the score. Because really, what does the score matter as long as you're having fun?

Way I figure, he just wanted it more. I mean the kid was desperate.

On the bright side, as a finalist I earned $750 and a few computer points, and feel like I've got some wind in my sails. I see good things in the near future. Do I hear the beating hoofs of momentum? Do I? I really think I do.

January 27

I was supposed to get myself to a border town called San Felipe on the Mexican coast for the next tournament, a clay-court Challenger, and I only had a couple of days to get there, what with my playing through to the final of this last event. I'd forgotten what a squeeze it could be when you play past the first day. As least I've got a few bucks to get me there. I really want to keep this magical momentum going.

I'm doubly determined to make something happen. This could very well be my last year on the tour. Who knows what I'll be doing this time next year. I get a little scared thinking about it, to be honest. I'm so going to get into real shape and keep my recent winning ways alive.

It was so much easier when I was younger and thinner and, to be honest, more talented. I never realized just how good I was. Phil Tipsarevic knew it though.

I lived at the Gene Toomey Tennis Centre outside Toronto from the time I was thirteen until I was seventeen. Hard to believe it was a full four years, but most of what I was to become came about as a result of my time there. Phil was directly responsible for most of my on-court training, and it was he who kept my scholarship on track, always making sure I was taken care of financially. I never appreciated just how much he did for me. Not then anyway.

School was the worst part. Before I attended Toomey, school and I were little more than passing acquaintances. But they monitored class attendance really closely at the Centre. They were always worried about the province coming in and shutting them down for not providing for the education of all the minors they were responsible for.

I never felt more stupid. I couldn't talk good, like I can now, and I didn't know shit about shit. But I went because I didn't want to screw things up with my scholarship, or for Phil who'd really put a lot on the line for me. And I actually learned stuff. For instance, I learned a bunch of words to throw into conversations to make myself look and feel smarter. I enjoyed history and discovered a few things about Canada, like the fact there are ten provinces, a couple of territories and a prime minister, who's like our version of a president, only gayer. Yeah I learned a lot there. I actually became quite well educated compared to what I'd been before. I became this weird combination of wily street smarts and highly schooled athleticism. I didn't know if I was coming or going for a while there.

But I was coming on a few fronts to be sure. I lost my virginity that second year for one thing, which was huge. Suddenly I all but brimmed with newfound confidence. I was still tough, but didn't feel like I had to prove it to everyone anymore. And moreover, Phil was constantly telling me how I was going to be some kind of star, so much so that I started to believe it. So one day when the sister of another student there, Danny something or other, came to visit him, I was in a position to be über charming. She was a couple of years older than me, but she was also kind of slutty and liked the feel of this punk-assed kid mixed in with the preppy nerds like her brother, so she fucked me in the locker room. God bless her. I'll never forget her. Margaret something. No, Mary. Yes, definitely Mary. God bless you, Mary.

Molly?

Anyhow, I digress. (See? I learned a lot of useful shit at Toomey.) I started playing junior events around Toronto, and then Phil started taking me around the country. And I was winning. And winning. And winning. It all seemed so easy. Most of these kids seemed a step too slow for me. It felt like everything was happening in slow motion. I could literally do no wrong, and I quickly put together the best record in junior play at Toomey. Needless to say, the other kids hated me. It was like I didn't deserve to be there in the first place, and when I started beating them all it only made them detest me that much more.

I won the Canadian Junior National Championships at fifteen, the youngest ever to do so. Then I was sent to play the Orange Bowl in Florida, kind of the World Championships of junior tennis, and I was then, at sixteen, the first Canadian kid to win it. Tennis Canada sponsored me to travel to Paris to play the Junior French Open and I reached the finals, and then they sent me to London to play the Junior Wimbledon and I won that too.

I became a minor celebrity in Canadian tennis circles. Again, you've got to understand, tennis greatness in Canada is a rare thing outside of doubles. The first sign of a star and every tennis official in the country gets collectively wet. And ol' Olie Wood had them drenched before long.

I was the number one-ranked junior player in the world. I'd outgrown Toomey and it was time to move on.

Phil took me aside one afternoon after practice. I'll never forget that conversation.

"I think it's time, kid."

"Time for what?" I asked suspiciously. (I tended to ask everything suspiciously; old habits died hard, it seems.)

"We've produced fourteen pros out of Toomey," he said, side-stepping the question. "Did you know that?"

"I heard it somewhere." (Like every fucking day at breakfast from desperate, ambitious kids and desperate, career-minded teaching pros.)

"Did you also know that we've produced two doubles stars, as well as two young men who cracked the top one hundred in the world?"

This was getting a little tiring. "Yeah, it's common knowledge. It's, like, in the Toomey bible."

"Do you know what their highest achievements were?"

"Haven't a clue. Never followed the sport, dude."

"Greg Shellenberger won the Australian Open doubles with a German partner. It made maybe page six of the sports section in most Canadian papers. And Ashram Sellig went as high as number ninety in the world, and maybe a dozen people in this country could actually have identified him on sight."

"So?"

"So you could be the first real star, Olie."

"What about you, dude?"

"Had you ever heard of me before we met?"

"Well . . . no, not exactly. But surely you were *kinda* famous—"

"Never got recognized in my life. Even at tournaments. Even when I won the Canadian Nationals. Made a little money, sure, but I was small-time in the grand scheme of things."

"I had no idea." I really hadn't. I'd always considered Phil a big-time star.

"But you, Olie, you are unlike anything I've ever seen before. Not in Canada, not anywhere. You're a rare gem. A jewel."

I didn't know what to say, but it was clear what he was getting at. He felt it was time for me to turn pro.

I'd never really understood what turning pro meant. I had no concept of what tennis players made and didn't realize there was potential fame to be had in this racket. But Phil wanted this for me and was determined to see me succeed. All I really cared about was making him happy. He actually cared about me, which made me feel weird inside, like my guts were being squeezed and like I wanted to cry. And I never cry. Funny thing about those early years, it didn't matter that I'd found something I was good at, and it sure as hell didn't matter that I was picked on and shunned by the other kids. The only thing that mattered was this guy here who was looking out for me. You have no idea how much something like that could mean to a guy like me.

Anyway, Phil signed on as my private coach and we went to Vancouver to play a Futures, an event I won easily. It seemed so easy. These were professional tennis players and I felt like I was in total control. If I wanted to move them around the court, I could. If I wanted to pin them to the baseline, I could do that too. If I wanted to bring them in to the net and then fire lobs over their heads, the courts were mine to control. I was fast and could run down any ball; I was accurate and could put the ball exactly where I wanted. I earned the first real money of my life, took home a nice silver trophy for my efforts, and we were off.

I played a series of Futures and then some Challengers in the US and South America, winning several. When I was beaten, it was usually by a seasoned veteran who knew how to deal with a whippersnapper like me, but they too would eventually fall as I learned how to push and pull them around the court.

One of my greatest gifts was my ability to adapt. Most players, depending on their style, are strong on one surface or another, but I could adjust on the fly. I predominately played an attacking, serve-and-volley style of tennis, but I could also be patient and stay back and win from the baseline if, say, I was playing on the slower clay. Crowds didn't bother me; I was able to block them out and focus on that little yellow ball exclusively.

My first ATP event was the Canadian Open. I was seventeen. I got in thanks to a wildcard the officials gave me as the Great Canadian Hope, and I started beating top-ranked professionals regularly. I got all the way to the semi-finals where I lost to Andre Agassi, who was then in his prime. Even at that I pushed him to the wall and it took a third-set tiebreak to beat me.

"You're something else, kid," he told me as we shook hands at the net. I was starting to believe it.

I won a big Challenger in Surbiton, England, and played through to the main draw at Wimbledon where I upset two top-ten players en route to the quarterfinals. That's where people really started to take notice of me. They started writing articles about me in Canadian papers and then, the holy grail, in some American papers too. After I won ATP events on grass in Newport, on hard court in Long Island, on clay in San Paolo and indoors in Hong Kong, winning on all four major surfaces (the only player in the world to accomplish such a feat that year) and all before I turned eighteen, I ended up on the cover of *Tennis Magazine* and then the cover of *Sports Illustrated* under the headline, "The Prodigy." The money started to get nuts and then the sponsors started piling on, offering me almost pornographic amounts of cash to shill their products, especially in Japan where I developed a weird, almost cult-like following. Phil was in heaven, enjoying being right in his instincts and living vicariously through my successes. I was among the youngest players to crack the top 40, and then the top 20, in the world.

And for all that, nothing compared to the simple pure joy of standing on the service line of a hot steamy asphalt court at a pro event in, say, Florida, or on the clumpy red clay in Portugal, seeing people in the stands out of the corner of my eye yet hearing nothing but my own breathing as I tossed the ball into the air, leapt up after it, springing upward from the balls of my feet and making contact right at the sweet-spot of my racquet, then rushing to the net to put away the return with a nice crisp volley, when finally the sounds of the crowd would return to me as they applauded and smiled down on me, a stupid, rough, dirty pseudo-orphan no longer.

I became a little famous, especially after I turned eighteen, at which point I won three Masters Series events, reached the French Open final, and broke into the top 10.

One thing I never knew, and would've found valuable to have known beforehand, was the fact that movie stars and models date

tennis players. Think that's bullshit? Brooke Shields married Andre
Agassi. Mandy Moore dated Andy Roddick. Look at the player's
box anytime you see a match on TV: the wives and girlfriends are
almost always blonde, Nordic and unearthly looking, I swear to
God. And rest assured I used my newfound status to my advantage. I started dating a Russian model, and then dumped her for
an American TV actress several years older than me. Then one
night I was partying in a club in Los Angeles and ran into
Madonna, back before she got married and old and boring and,
well, as I've said before, I'm not allowed to talk details under court
order.

I thought life couldn't possibly get any better. I was pretty much
right too.

                                                        January 28
Will wonders never cease? I called Miranda (collect) to check
in, and after she finished tearing me a new one for not calling
since she wired me that money earlier this month, she mentioned
that a letter had arrived from Tennis Canada. I told her to open it.
She did, and apparently they were interested in sponsoring me to
play some qualifying events in Europe. It seems the number one-
ranked Canadian (read: #129 in the world), Sebastien Laliberté,
busted his knee playing the first round of the Australian Open
(poor baby; I'd pay good money to get to bust my knee at the
Australian Open, even though that's the very scene of my own
unfortunate demise), and at the same time the #2 Canadian, Steve
Turrell, is getting married soon and retiring from the tour, and
our #3, Omar Toumar, is feuding with Tennis Canada over their
refusal to allow him to accept sponsorship money from some gun
manufacturer. Bottom line, the European clay court circuit won't
have a single Canadian player anywhere to be seen and the TC
guys see this as embarrassing. So I'm guessing one of these dudes
said, "Hey, remember that Wood guy? Isn't he still playing?" to
which some other dude probably said something like, "Nah, I
heard he died or something." Then the first dude would have
been all, "No, I'm sure I heard about him getting banned from

some Challenger for attacking his opponent recently." And then some other dude might have asked, "But is that really the best we can do? Is that really the state of men's tennis in this country?" and someone else would have answered, "Unfortunately, yes. Is it. Things are pretty desperate. But then again, he was always good for a laugh, if nothing else. Might even get us a bit of attention." And then some fuckwad would have put in, "Maybe not the kind of attention we want!" and they all would have laughed but at the same time realized that I'm the best left of a bad lot, and so decided to send me over to Europe.

I haven't been in a long time. I used to do the European swing routinely every spring and early summer. That was back when I made money. Back when I had sponsors.

Sponsors are what make the tennis world go round. You need sponsors to supply you with equipment. A racquet company will sponsor you and supply you with racquets so that people will see you using their product. Clothing companies will provide you with clothes so that people will see you wearing their product. Lately I haven't had any sponsors. The only time Futures players have sponsors is when they're young and on the rise, when the sponsors hope to establish relationships with them that might pay off down the line. That's not me. Last time I had a sponsor was Maxx4 Razors, a Canadian razorblade company. I'd been doing ads for them for years until they wised up and realized no one knew who the hell I was anymore and they cut me loose. That was about five years ago. Since that time I've been buying my own razors, and as for racquets, well, I have two and, unlike myself, I do everything I can to keep them in decent playing shape. Once last year I was playing in a tournament and I broke a string on one, and then broke a string on the second one and almost had to default. It was admittedly a bit of a horror show playing with a racquet with a broken string, but my perfect no-default record remained intact. My opponent had a bagful of racquets that I kept an envious eye on, trying to figure out how I could steal one without anyone noticing, but that's a difficult thing to do in daylight with everybody watching. I also buy my own clothes, such as they are, and rely on prize money, such as it is, supplemented here and there by whatever I can beg, borrow or steal (or get assaulted by a giantess to earn), whatever the case may be.

While a player can earn hundreds of thousands in prize money, even millions at the very top of the game, the real money is in the sponsors. What I wouldn't give to have a sponsor again.

Then again, countries like Canada, even with their shitty player-development programs, have ways of supporting their people from time to time, and when the rest of the players are injured, or out of commission, or retiring or dead, they might even look my way. And it seems they have. Maybe it's a nice going-away present as I enter the twilight of my career. It just makes me want to capitalize on these opportunities all the more. I'm deadly serious about buckling down and working hard to get back in shape and better at this game. I have the talent; I just have to let it loose.

On an unrelated note, I've decided to set Blanche Dowling free. It feels like the right decision for a couple of reasons: 1) I'll be going to Europe after the San Felipe tournament and she won't travel well overseas; 2) Shouldn't all animals be free really, to live life as God intended? 3) She's a bitch and I'm really sick of her; and 4) I accidentally set her on fire and think I might be a hazard to her health and wellbeing.

I didn't mean to do it, even though there have been numerous times when I've thought seriously, if not graphically, about how it might be done.

The motel I'm currently holed up in has this odd stink to it. It's got that southern border town, armpit-mixed-with-sulphur kind of smell I've experienced in this part of the world before. You find it especially in the cheaper motels, such as my current abode.

Miranda's a candle nut, like most women I've known. Has them everywhere: ones that smell, ones that burn slowly, ones that come in funny weird shapes and colours, and of course the ones that are just for show. So I know my candles. She even packs a couple for me when I travel as a way to remember her. So, thinking on my feet, and knowing that when someone lets one or takes a giant dump lighting a candle often takes the smell away, I figured I'd blaze one of these babies up and maybe it'd take the stink out of the place.

Only problem is, ever try to light some of these things? The ones with the cute colours but the crappy wicks? Sometimes hard to do. So I'm flicking my lighter, trying to get the thing to light, getting frustrated, trying to dig out the wick from the base of the candle so I have more to work with but still getting nothing, when suddenly I come up with this great idea: I'll light a piece of paper and rest it on the candle. That would create so much flame and so much heat that the wick would have no choice but to eventually take the light. The only difficulty was, the flame kind of got away on me. The index page from the motel Bible (the only paper I could find) went right up and, well, bits of burning Old Testament started floating around the room. Meanwhile Blanche Dowling was napping on the bed in that creepy way of hers, the one where she keeps that one freaky eye open and trained on you, following you as you move around the room, but otherwise still snoring and clearly sound asleep. And of course one of the embers landed right on her, and she started to smoke. Something about that matted, unclean fur of hers was pretty flammable, it turns out. She really went up, and naturally went a little nuts, screaming (I honestly didn't realize a cat could scream) and tearing around the room like a little furry madman.

I desperately tried to catch her and hold her down so that I could put the flames out, but the faster she ran the more oxygen seemed to get at the flame and the bigger the fire got. Meanwhile the bed is also in flames, and I'm trying to put it out with my one foot while chasing down Blanche Dowling with the rest of me. Finally I leap out with every last ounce of my professional athlete's ability and land square on her. I singed the hair on my arms and chest (and I'm a bit of a hairy guy, so this was a risk I should've pondered a bit beforehand), but I was able to get the fire out while she lay there pinned beneath me, hissing and spitting, yet at the same time seeming almost grateful for my quick reactions.

Strangely enough, she wasn't too badly burned. Apparently that same fur that seemed so flammable was also so thickly matted that it acted like a kind of armour protection. In fact, all the fire treatment seemed to do was even out her gross coat a little. If anything it was actually a bit of an improvement.

But regardless of how well she may have come out of it, it just makes me realize that I'm not really meant to be in charge of anything. I can't be trusted to care for something other than myself, when even that is sometimes hardly manageable. So I'm setting her free, which is what I should have done ages ago. It's the best thing for her and certainly for me.

Huh. For a second there she looked like she wasn't sure whether she wanted to go, but after some light coercion and a tossed Bible (missing one index page) she trotted off to her new life. Go, I said. Be free. Go play and screw and live off the land the way you animals were meant to. It's so for the best. *So*. Believe me.

January 30

What of women's tennis, you say? What about the little lovelies in the skirts and the ankle socks with the finely honed bodies? What encounters have I had with this similar yet wholly unique creature? Well I'm glad you asked. First, let me just say that I firmly believe everyone would be much happier, not to mention more productive on court, if they did a better job of combining the men's and women's tours. As it is, it's only rarely that the men and women get to play together, and never at the Futures level once you graduate from juniors. At the top levels, say the Grand Slams and a few Masters events and a handful more, the men and women do their thing at the same time, but everywhere else it's a regular apartheid system. But the juniors, that's a different story.

There was this little thing called Nancy True (no lie), an up-and-coming junior girls player I assumed liked me as much or more as I liked her. See, back when I was on the cusp of turning pro and had all that buzz about me, the chicklets were all about ol' Olie Wood. And yeah, I took advantage. At that age the idea is to conquer as much terrain as you can possibly squeeze into your schedule, and I did my best to rack up some frequent flier miles. But Nancy True brought me back down to earth a while.

I usually liked blondes, especially from Sweden and Scandinavia and that part of the world, but Nancy was a brunette, and she kept her hair cut really short. She looked like a pixie, or like I figure a pixie would look, seeing as how I've never actually seen one in real life other than this one time when I was done up on Angel Dust and swore I saw tiny fairies dancing around my head. But then pixies and fairies, they're not really the same thing, are they?

Where the hell was I? Nancy! Right! Man do I love being able to read back over what I just wrote. It's so much better than talking, when I can't ever remember what the hell it was I just said.

Oh, right! Nancy! Sweet as all hell. That was what I remember most about her, her sweetness. I hadn't known real sweetness before.

Now it's worth noting that I was a bit of an insufferable asshole at times. I know that's hard to believe now, but back then I let my ever-accelerating success get the better of me, and I developed a little arrogance problem. But the chicks loved it. Take it from me, they like a confident dude. And need I remind you, I was getting the ladies every which way in my youth. Funny thing about Nancy, though, she wasn't all that impressed with me, and certainly not with my act. She was the only chick who routinely ignored my advances, and I confess it got to me. Made me want her even more, but to no avail. She wouldn't touch Olie's Wood. Eventually I came to the conclusion that she must have been a rug-muncher not to have been interested, even though she really didn't fit the bill. Trust me, there are plenty of dykes in women's tennis, and they're not the kind you see on TV.

Anyhow, it turned out Nancy wasn't a lesbian. She just didn't seem to dig me, and that bothered me, especially because she seemed so smart and interesting, and I didn't know too many people like that, especially women. She was willing to hang out with me a little bit, just so long as I promised not to talk. Turned out to be a pretty good thing, too, because I got to learn a little bit about her, which was odd. She was a scholarship girl, planning on attending UCLA on a full tennis scholarship, and she wasn't sure if she was ever going to turn pro. She just wanted a good education, which was totally lost on me, though at the same time kind of new and interesting, even if a little insane.

I actually fell in love with her. The better I got at listening to her and being able to actually converse with her (once she allowed me to speak again), the less of an asshole I became and the more she started to like me back.

We started dating, and it got pretty serious. I think she came to like my casual fun approach to life, if nothing else. When I started playing professionally and making money, I flew her out to tournaments when she could get away from school.

"Will you stay faithful to me?" she asked me one night before a big final.

"Of course. I love you. Why would you even ask that?"

"I worry about all this . . . this glamour."

"It ain't that glamorous," I told her. I was only lying a little.

"What happens if you start getting groupies?"

I laughed. "They still wouldn't have a thing on you."

Of course two weeks later I had sex with this model, Linda Evangelista, and Nancy turned out to be kind of right about me.

I tried to be good, but the temptations were just too huge. I was drawn into a world that wanted to turn me into something different and new. It wanted to corrupt me and twist me and I kind of allowed it to.

Nancy came to the conclusion that I was officially a shithead when one of her classmates showed her my picture in the *Examiner* sucking face with some soap opera actress who'd just won a daytime Emmy. It didn't take too much to convince her that was I pretty worthless apparently. I was actually a little taken aback by how easily she dumped me and seemed to get over me.

Last I heard she'd become a sports psychologist, and recently she had her second kid. She and her husband live in San Diego, probably in some big suburban house. Good for her, really. I like to think that some people who crossed my path could still turn out for the better.

I loved Nancy, I honestly did. I realize this now, all these years later. Thing is, at the time, I'd developed an appetite for this new life that eclipsed whatever it was I felt for her. It wasn't the last time I'd screw over someone I loved.

February 2

In some border town, no idea what it's called, but it's a shit hole. Yet shit hole or not, there is of course a *NuBodys*. I "worked out" for the first time in, well, I can't actually remember the last time I actually worked out at all. I was never the most disciplined person when it came to off-court training. But at my age I realize it's the only way I'm ever going to get more mobile.

I lope around the court where once I glided. (Glode?) It's so hard to get to any balls now unless they're hit right to me, something very few of my opponents seem willing to do. Bottom line, if I'm serious about turning my game around, I need to actually start working at it for the first time in my life.

So I went to a gym. Sorry, a "gym." I guess these places mean something different than back when I was a kid. Sometimes I'd sneak into the Y and screw around with the weights back when I thought if I was stronger I could fight my way through childhood. But the rundown weight room and running track of my youth has been replaced by a social club stocked with big shiny machines and neon-lit juice bars. I used equipment like this at Toomey, but even that was nothing in comparison to the bizarre cultural shift these places characterize now.

There are mirrors everywhere. And people use them too. I've never seen so many people trying not to be seen checking themselves out. It's like it's not enough to just work out; they've got to look good doing it too.

You'll have to excuse the slight air of bitterness. I'm a professional athlete who's feeling pretty humbled after surviving barely twenty minutes on this stair-climbing thing. For Christ's sake, there were chicks there fitter than me. I was so depressed by the whole thing that I didn't even try to pick any of them up, and that's saying something.

I need to focus on fitness. I need to get quicker and stronger and I don't have a lot of time to do it. I'm going to run more (which I can better afford to do), and when I can I'm going to bench and lift and strap myself to every bullshit workout machine I can get my hands on. And I'm going to lay off the booze and the drugs and all the late nights too. Well the drugs and the late nights at least. And let's be honest, the odd late night won't kill me. After all, I've got to take advantage of *some* of these places I may be visiting for the final time in my career. But the drugs for sure. Most of the time.

Yeah, going to get strong. Going to get healthy. Going to get qualified for the fucking US Open, just watch me.

No, it is glided.

Glade?

Tomorrow I'll use some of my precious dollars to catch a bus to the next tournament. Even travelling by bus starts to really add up though. It won't be too long before I'm out of money again. I've really got to make the most of this trip to San Felipe. I've really got to kick some ass and take some names and then (somehow) get back home, at which point I'm Europe-bound with a small per diem. Maybe two of the sweetest words in the English language you'll ever hear—"per" and "diem"—at least when used together. On their own they aren't so sweet. Anyhow, can't wait. All part of Olie Wood's new Big Picture.

I've been clean for three days now. Not even a beer. And I don't miss it or anything. I feel fine—great, actually—because I'm already healthier, even if my gym experiment was a bit of a bust. I may have gotten this little gift from Tennis Canada because I was the only player available, but I'm going to show them how worth it I really am. Also, there's this grass court event in Rossmallen, in the Netherlands, where I hear you can score some amazing hash oil. I'm going to see if I can somehow beg my way into the qualifying rounds so I can check out the scene a little.

February 3

Not sleeping well. Keep having weird dreams that I can't remember afterwards. I need a night off more than I've ever needed anything in my life. My body might actually be *too* free of toxins. I've been eating too well and working out too much and I need a little reprieve from it all. I need some fun. My eyes are still on the prize, and I'm taking the shiny new me seriously, but I need to reconnect with what keeps me sane. Maybe after San Felipe.

February 5

Jesus. Cheap busses in the South are bad, but cheap busses in Mexico, well, I'd prefer to never mention it again, except to say, why do we bother putting bathrooms on busses if they're always going to break down and be so backed up with shit that the entire bus stinks? Just asking.

Three days of hellish transit and I confess I'm really starting to miss certain things. I'm in Mexico and I have to at least try a cerveza. Just one of course; I do have the tournament tomorrow. Just enough to even me out a little. I've been good and I've been exercising, even while on the bus (hand flexing and sitting crunches, though I think some of the other passengers may have thought me a bit troubled), so I deserve a break, especially since my hands are shaking a little and I really need to straighten them out before I play. Just the one and everything'll be cool. I mean really, what damage could one beer possibly do?

February 8

I have just enough money to get me back to Michigan by bus. I'd love to fly, but I'm broke. Once I reach Michigan I'll call Gary and hope he can come down and get me. He always makes it easier to get across the boarder anyhow.

So yeah, I'm a fuckup. I know it. All I can say is, Mexicans know how to party like no one else in the world. I have no evidence of actually having played in the San Felipe Satellite Invitational, except for a letter officially banning me from the event in the future, a two-day hangover, and a deep cut running at an angle across my chin. I know I played though, because I have red clay in my shoes. I can only assume I lost. I earned $115 for playing but was fined $250, so I forfeited my prize money. My fine citation says something about some kind of bodily function on the court but my Spanish sucks. I'll have to have Miranda read it to me when I get home.

Home. Do I have a home? I guess wherever Miranda is qualifies as such. I feel a little sad to be heading back, seeing the miles pass under the bus (which will soon turn into kilometres again after I get over the boarder—sadder still). As shitty as the road can be, at least it feels like I'm living a life. In Ottawa it just feels like life's ebbing away. At least there's Gary and Miranda.

Europe will be good for me. I'll only be in Ottawa for four days before it's off to Portugal to play in a series of events neither you nor I have ever heard of. But it'll be great. I'll feel like a professional athlete again, especially if I get into some qualifying events at the smaller ATP tournaments.

Countries often have what they call reciprocal wildcard deals. A wildcard is basically a free pass into the main draw of a tournament, usually saved for lower ranked players from the host country. For example, I received wildcards to the Canadian Open for years after my star faded. If you don't get wildcards, but aren't ranked high enough to get into the main draw, they have qualifying events, usually three rounds of tennis to determine the handful of main draw spots remaining. But players like me aren't ranked high enough for even qualifying rounds of most tournaments. So they usually have some wildcards for the *qualifying* events as well. Now sometimes a country will decide it would be neat to have a couple of their up-and-comers play in, say, Italy at the Tennis Masters Event in Rome. They may offer up a couple of wildcard spots at their own event to some Italian players in exchange for the same treatment for theirs in Rome. Tennis Canada made a few such deals with some European countries with the idea that Sebastien Laliberté or Steve Turrell would get to play more. Yet another reason why they'd come to me to play in Europe—they'd worked out the reciprocal deal for some wildcard spots at the Canadian Open but had no one to take advantage of the returns. Cue me playing the top guys on European

clay. I'll take the charity. Fuck Sebastien Laliberté. Fuck Steve
Turrell. Fuck the lot of them. This sport is all about making the
most of your opportunities, and make the most of them I will.

I can feel the air growing colder the further north we go. After
I retire from the game I'd love to be a teaching pro in Florida or
some place like that. Never have to be cold again. I hate the cold.
From the time when I was a little kid shivering in any number of
cruddy apartments in Toronto with no heat till now, freezing my
ass off heading for Ottawa, it's all been horrible. Then again, if I
didn't return to Canada every once in a while, I wouldn't be in
line for goodies like my upcoming European trip, so I'm stuck
with it for now.

I've been thinking a lot about Miranda as the wheels of the bus
go round and round. I often wonder when she's going to leave me.
I used to be the one who did the leaving, but that was many moons
and many pounds ago. Back when I was good-looking, talented,
famous and rich I had women wanting to be with me in the worst
way. Famous women, beautiful women, young, hot and perfectly
proportioned women, they were all into the Oliemeister. But with
each passing year following the kookaburra incident that number
grew smaller and smaller. And the skank factor of my girlfriends
increased steadily as the classier famous chicks started to look the
other way. Miranda, though, she was different. She may take her
clothes off and dance naked in front of strange men, but she's no
skank. She's smart and funny and lovely to look at, and she's with
me. No idea why, really. She doesn't talk about it much but I think
she's had a hard life, what with the requisite abusive father who got
way too friendly with her, the neglectful mother, the lack of formal education and so on. I think I'm the first guy to stay with her
for any length of time. As if I'd ever leave. I may have a problem
being faithful to her, but I love her all the same. One of these days
I'm determined to clean up and settle down properly with her.
Maybe even marry her, though that feels a long way off right now.

In any case, I'm missing her more the closer I get to her. I hope
we can make the most of our four days together. I know she'll be
pleased to hear of Blanche Dowling's liberation.

February 10

What a change of pace. I'm riding shotgun in Gary's truck. God bless the guy, he drove right down to get me and bring me across the border, back into the land of the cold, the desolate, and the almost depressingly loyal.

I've got to clean up. I still feel hung-over from a drunk four days ago. My body can't keep up the way it once did, back when I was a kid. And boy could I put it away then.

When I first tasted success, people were always wanting to do things for me—buy me a drink, take me to clubs, suck my dick, you name it. Sweet times. At home I was the poster boy for Canadian sports. Pierre Trudeau had me out to his club in Montreal for a session, and even at nearly seventy he more than held his own. The media loved that, and they were out in full force to photograph the event. It was one of the most popular photos of the year judging by the number of times it ran in various magazines and newspapers. I was shilling for more Canadian companies than I can remember. My every win led the sports report on the news, a huge thing considering this was tennis in a hockey country. Between that and the commercials I shot you couldn't go a day without seeing my gob on your set.

I was what people wanted in a celebrity. I was young, good-looking and successful, and I had a winking, bad boy quality about me that made the girls hot. When Canadians find success at something, we're not usually known for it outside of certain circles. But with me, it was more like Wayne Gretzky and hockey. Yep, that was Olie Wood and tennis, baby.

In the States it was even crazier. Tennis doesn't matter much to the masses, but if you can hook into the world of celebrity—and happen to play tennis too—life can get pretty weird pretty damned quickly. Professional athletes are held in very high regard there, even tennis players. When I was the flavour of the month, the prodigy (and nothing beats a door to fame faster than *that* word), people really wanted me around.

So I drank to socialize. When I was hanging out in Hollywood I experimented with coke. And travelling to various A-list parties, other substances were tried and enjoyed. I became quite the connoisseur of illegal narcotics. I was always looking for some way to make sure I fit into this fabulous new life.

And yet my tennis didn't suffer at all. When I was eighteen I won six tournaments and finished the year ranked number three in the world. I beat Pete Sampras on grass and a bunch of nameless but otherwise clay-expert Spaniards on their turf. I reached the finals at Wimbledon and lost a close five-setter. I was on fire. It was only a matter of time before I was to win a Grand Slam and become number one.

I was living my life in fast-forward. Consuming as much as I could, enjoying all the extras as much as I could, cashing in as much as I possibly ever could.

The year I turned nineteen was supposed to be my breakthrough year. I went into the Australian Open in January tapped to win. This was going to be my coming-out party. But at the same time there was so much attention on me that I felt the need to take the edge off. I partied all over Melbourne. I played my opening round match totally wasted and yet still won (God, those were great times). But by the third round I had nothing left in the tank and lost badly to some no-name Swede who bowed out in the next round and has long since retired.

Phil was devastated. He had so much invested in me that he couldn't help but feel disappointed, and I resented the hell out of him for feeling that way.

"Lay off me, man!" I screamed after he chastised me for my apparent indifference to my career. "I'm the reason you're even close to this world again, so back off!"

"Kind of the other way around, isn't it?" he asked with the first real bitterness I'd ever heard in his voice.

"So I had an off day. So what. Leave me alone, I'm entitled. Here," I said, tossing him a handful of Australian dollars. "Go out and have a drink or two on me."

Now that was the wrong thing to do. Even then I knew it, how humiliating it was to show such disrespect to the only father-like figure I'd ever had. But I was so full of myself and so defensive of my place in the world that I couldn't help it.

"Fuck you, Olie," he said quietly as he left my hotel room. We didn't speak for a while after that as Phil returned to Toronto while I went on to play some hard court events in Florida and Indian Wells on my own.

My results were mixed that year. I won a couple of tournaments, sure, but my momentum had slowed noticeably. I was still winning more often than not, and I was still ranked in the top 10, but I couldn't break through to the top. I lost in the quarterfinals at the French Open and Wimbledon, and in the semi-finals at the US Open. I was still a winner, and sponsors and celebrities still wanted me in their lives, but something was different. I'd morphed from being the "prodigy" to "one of the pack." It didn't matter that I was still one of the best players in the world, I was suddenly "not hot."

And I was pissed off about it. I felt supremely entitled, and when my star faded a little I was not fun to be around. If I'd only known then what I know now I'd have learned to appreciate what I had while I had it, you know?

Phil and I got back together that summer, but there was a tension there and it never felt quite the same again. I still resented his questioning me, and he was irate at my lack of respect and gratitude. The relationship was all but doomed by that point.

Man I miss Phil. Haven't seen the guy in like nine years. He sent me a Christmas gift a couple of years back, a dry-mounted copy of the *Maclean's* magazine cover from years ago, with the two of us under the headline "Hooray for Olie Wood!" written in the style of the Hollywood sign. Shit, that joke was tired even then. And when I saw it again it just made me feel old and used up. I didn't respond to Phil's overture and he never tried again. I kind of suck.

Anyhow, I'm headed home, and it's all about the forward momentum. Fuck the past, it's best left there.

Oh and it's my birthday in two days! I'll be thirty-one!

On the downside, it's my birthday in two days. I'll be thirty-one.
I'm inching toward oblivion. I'd been hoping Miranda would
have some kind of birthday thing lined up for me, but now I'm
mostly wishing it would simply pass unnoticed. Each month I
peel off the calendar brings me that much closer to the time
when I'm going to have to actually start working for a living, and
frankly that terrifies me. On the other hand, maybe Miranda will
wear something sexy.

February 9

Gary is possessed. He hasn't slept and we're nearly in Ottawa.
He's been up for days, and yet he doesn't look particularly bad.
He just keeps on keeping on, this guy.

"I'll rest when we're home," is all he said when I asked whether
he wanted to pull over or switch places. Meanwhile, I've had several naps and one or two genuine sleeps. I love naps—they're a
recent addition to my existence, but a welcome one. Another sign
of getting old, I guess, when at about one in the afternoon my
eyes start getting really heavy. It particularly sucks when I'm in
the middle of a match, but then the one time I asked the umpire
for a nap break he looked at me like I was nuts, so now I just go
along to get along. But when I'm in the car and someone else is
doing the driving, I'm gone.

"I think you should start winning more," Gary announced after
we passed through the border without incident. I was startled, not
just because of my looming slumber, but because I'm so unused
to my buddy actually starting conversations.

"Who in the what now?"

"You should start winning more," he repeated. "It's time, I feel."

"Yeah, okay. Good idea, Gar. I'll be sure to try that out."

"Good," he said, and that was pretty much all he said for the rest
of the trip until we turned onto the street where Miranda lives. I
told him he was a good friend and a rockin' priest, and that not
many people would've come all that way to Michigan to get me.

"I had nothing better to do," he informed me.

February 10

Miranda. Lovely Miranda. Still as honey-sweet as the day I met her. I'll never forget it. I was drunk and she was giving me a lap dance. Good times.

So today I'm thirty-one. Sucks to be me. Andre Agassi won a Grand Slam title at thirty-three so anything's possible, but somehow I think that's a long shot for ol' Olie. Bottom line is, I'm coming to the end and even I know it.

I was thinking last night about what I was going to do next and I decided I'd make a good celebrity journalist. I like being around famous people and I think I'd find it easy work. Think I'll start looking into it later in the year when the season starts to taper off, ignoring as I am Gary's utterly unhelpful suggestion that I consider the priesthood at some point.

Sometimes I wonder how Blanche Dowling is doing. It's been a few days of freedom for her now and I hope she's enjoying it. I've started to wonder if I did the right thing. Not that I care what happens to her really, but I hate to think of her getting attacked by a wild animal (though she could more than hold her own, I'm sure) or having a hard time finding something to eat. Ah well, nothing I can do about it now.

For my birthday I received a genuine gold-plated man-bracelet from Miranda, who's always been keen to see me wearing more jewellery, and a book about tennis greats from Gary, who I'm sure wasn't trying to make me feel bad by rubbing the success of others in my face like that. Feels like I ought to have gotten more presents, but then I don't really have any more friends or family. Makes me feel kind of alone all of a sudden. Of all the people I've touched over the years, none of them have any place in my life now. That's like really sad. Now I understand all those people who say they get depressed around the holidays, not that my birthday qualifies as a holiday. Not saying it should either, so back off. I realize it's just another day to everyone but me.

But to me it's more than just another day; it's another bead on the abacus that's counting down my remaining days of utility. Hey,

I like the way that sounds. Maybe I'll be a writer after I retire from the tour.

Tonight Miranda totally freaked me out when she casually brought up the subject of marriage. And when I say "casually brought up," I mean she said, "Hey, y'ever think we maybe oughta get married?" with a hopeful gleam in her eye, now purple thanks to the contacts she's been wearing of late as part of her act.

"Why would I ever think that?" I asked back, a little too quickly I might add.

"Because you've got a good thing going here and wouldn't want to fuck it up. And also because you ain't getting any younger, pal, and might want to start thinking about planting your seed before long."

Now this really threw me, because I'd swear she was talking about kids, only she was being really subtle and metaphorical about it and all.

"I don't want kids. Too many kids in the world," I said as conclusively as I could manage.

"I think a kid would be cool. Someone to keep me company while you're out on the road."

"Won't be on the road forever, you know. Then it can be just the two of us."

"Still, I think a little kid would be cool. Don't rule it out, sweetie. Promise me at least that."

I wavered a while, but then figured I'd at least buy myself some time. "Yeah, okay, I won't rule it out."

"That's my baby," she said happily. "Now come here and let me give you a blowjob!"

It's not that I wouldn't want a life with Miranda. Or kids. I mean if I had them with anyone, it would definitely be her. It's just that I only recently got rid of a cat I couldn't take care of, so what the hell would I do with a kid? If I set a child on fire it wouldn't blow over so easily as with a cat, I'm guessing. Besides, what do I know about being a parent? Can't say I had really good role models in that particular department. The prudent thing to do then is put this discussion off as long as possible.

I would honestly have no idea how it is a father should act. I never met mine. And I couldn't really relate to Gary's, and not just because he was a half-pint either. I guess Phil would be the most obvious choice to emulate, but God, where did he ever get the energy to be so supportive all the time? I can't begin to imagine it, what with being busy with my career and all. No, I'm just going to slip out of here and get to Portugal and I'll put all thought of this baby-making business behind me.

Still, a little version of me might be cool, you know?

February 12

Had to meet up with the rep from Tennis Canada today to get my per diem and plane tickets. The man I met, Wesley Goodie, was a bit of a surprise though. For one, he was a much smaller guy than I'd expected. More of a toady bureaucrat than the athletic director-type I'd had in mind.

"Got your passport in order?" he asked.

"Always keep it up to date," I told him. "You never know when you might have to leave the country, if you know what I mean."

He laughed, but unsmilingly.

"So you understand how this works. We've paid for your ticket and a Eurorail pass to get you to the four events you're entered in. You'll play two Challengers, as well as receive wildcards to play in both Lisbon and Milan. As I recall, you had a good clay-court game once upon a time."

After I stopped laughing at "Lisbon" (it always made me laugh) I said yes, I had some "mad skillz on the dirt." He didn't laugh at that. In fact, he really didn't seem to like me much at all. I figured that out when he said, "I'm not your biggest fan, Olie. I should probably be upfront about that."

"Sorry to hear that," I said. Funny, people have never been shy when it comes to telling me what they think of me. As a result, criticism in whatever form stopped having any kind of impact on me years ago.

"This program was set up to aid our emerging stars."

"Yeah. Great. So about my per diem?"

"Tennis Canada wants to promote our best and brightest. That's why we've set aside funding, to help them play tournaments and gain valuable experience worldwide."

"And I appreciate that," I said. "Now about my—"

"You should know that, as a result of this little boondoggle, the entire program is to be completely re-examined. I hope you're happy."

"Oh yeah, I am, absolutely." I confess I hadn't entirely understood what it was he was saying to this point, and wasn't being in any way flippant.

"I'm just sorry this isn't going to someone who's going to make the most of it."

"Me too, man. Me too."

He shook his head in disappointment. "Anyway, I hope you'll at least enjoy the trip. I'd imagine you're thinking about retirement soon?"

"Well not if I kick some serious booty in Lisbon and Milan!"

"Right," he said. "In any case, I'll need you to run an errand while you're in Lisbon."

"Is this part of the deal?" I asked, suddenly sceptical. "I have to do you personal favours?"

"No, but it would go a long way to making me happy, and if I'm happy I could make sure you remain situated to receive further undeserved funding from Tennis Canada."

Well that seemed fair. "So what am I packing in then?"

Turns out it's just a book. A frigging huge hardcover book, mind you, but nothing I can't handle. I'm a professional athlete after all. I'm supposed to deliver it to some guy named Raphael Farnel in Lisbon. Again, nothing I can't handle. Hell, I was happy to take it just so Goodie would give me my documentation and my cheque.

So I had my teary goodbyes with Miranda at the airport. How cool to be on a plane again. No busses, no weird smells, no crazy people. Just the luxury of a coach-class ticket and eight hours alone in the air.

I love airplane food by the way. I like how it comes in miniature sizes. I like things that come in miniature, like forks and
knives and parental units. I even eat the vegetables on an airplane
I like the miniature portions they serve so much.

I love being waited on too. When I was younger I was being
waited on all the time. Now, not so much. But these babes
onboard, even the ones who are dudes, *have* to wait on me. It's like
a law or something.

However, it's been a while since I've flown, and I've somehow
allowed myself to forget the rough treatment they always seem to
give me at check-in. They always search my luggage and even
rough me up a little if they can find a way to do it without looking like they're harassing me. This time proved no exception. But
I never carry when I travel internationally. I mean why bother,
especially when anything I might bring over would no doubt pale
in comparison to the good shit I'd acquire when I get there?

So they searched my bags and gave me a pat down, but ultimately let me on the plane.

I've never had any fear of flying. In fact there's something about
being all those hundreds of miles off the ground that makes me
feel truly free somehow. No one can get at me when I'm that far
up in the air.

"Portugal, huh?" said the big guy sitting next to me, pulling me
out of my thoughts.

"Huh? Yeah. For sure." I hoped he would just leave me alone. I
like to do my own thing when travelling, and not have strangers
talk to me.

"Me too. I'm not a great flier, I have to admit." Oh great. "First
time to Europe and I don't much like the idea of flying over all
that water," he said, and I noticed he was starting to sweat a lot.
Something I could relate to of course, though not in this particular air-conditioned environment.

"My daughter is 'marrying' her same sex partner in Estoril," he
went on. "I'm pretty sure it's illegal there, Catholic country and
all, but she always had her own ways, that's for sure." He just kept

on talking, as if that would keep his nerves at bay. Considering we
were due to be in the air for five and a half hours, I wasn't relish-
ing being this dude's best friend the entire time we were sitting
here together.

"I should tell you," I said, leaning into him. "I have a serious
mental imbalance and I'm kinda hangin' on by a loose thread
here. So no offence, but it's really in your best interest that I find
a way to relax."

That had the desired effect as he quickly turned away, keeping
to himself after that. The only thing I heard out of him was the
occasional nervous whimper, at which point I stared at him until
he stopped.

Only problem then was the sheer boredom. I'm not the world's
biggest reader, but I can get lost in a book if the situation warrants
it. So I rifled through my carry-on to see what I could find to
help pass the time. The only books I had with me were this journal, the tennis heroes book Gary gave me (which was just too
depressing to read), and the big-assed tome Goodie gave me.

It was called *Medieval Portraiture: A Detailed Study.* Jesus Christ,
I'd sooner pluck my eyeballs out with a fork than subject myself
to that, but I figured there might be pictures of naked ladies in
there so I tried my best to thumb through it. Only problem was,
these pages weren't for thumbing. They seemed to be stuck
together. "What the fuck?" I thought as I opened the front cover.
Turns out it was just a hollowed-out box containing a large bag
of white powder.

My heart stopped. Christ, if the security people had found this.
And what was going to happen when we landed? The customs
folks in Lisbon would surely be more thorough than those lazy
asses back in Ottawa. What the hell was I going to do? I started
to panic.

"*Oh my God,*" whispered the guy sitting beside me. "Drugs!
Those are *drugs!*"

"Shut up!" I whispered back. "Everything is going to be okay.
Now I need to get rid of this shit, so you just sit tight, breathe
deep, and we'll get through this, all right?"

I made my way to the bathroom with the "book," locked myself in, and tried to think about what I should do. In movies, people in this situation often stick the contraband up their asses, but this was a really big bag. I couldn't imagine how I was going to make it all fit. My ass has never been all that accommodating, even at the best of times. I had no idea how I was going to get this stuff hidden, and my imagination has never been my strongest attribute. In retrospect, I suppose I could have flushed it, but at the time I didn't think of that. I just didn't. So I did what I had to do. I accommodated.

I waddled back to my seat and tried to get comfortable. "Everything's fine now," I told my seatmate with a wink and a knowing nod. He didn't seem all that reassured, and my awkward shifting in my seat didn't seem to make him feel much better.

I can honestly say it felt like I was going to explode. I've heard people use that expression in the past, but I never realized exactly what it meant. But I felt somewhat safer at least.

I somehow survived the flight. Even managed to sleep a little. But I was a little afraid of what would happen when we landed. I gradually adjusted to the feeling of pressure in my ass, but if you looked closely enough you could see that something was off all right. I wasn't sure how on the ball the Portuguese officials would be, but I was worried and expected the worst.

When I stepped off the plane everything seemed okay. It was only when the dude who'd been sitting next to me made a big production of steering clear of me that the guards started paying closer attention.

"É algo a questão aqui?" one of them asked. (For the record I always pictured the Portuguese as kind of a small attractive people, but these guards were anything but. They looked overcooked and generally unhappy, not to mention large and intimidating.)

"Sorry, no habla," I replied, trying not to look scared. Failing, it turns out.

"Eu'necessidade de ll procurar seuas sacolas e se," the security guy said as his buddies dragged me off to their office.

Well I thought for sure I was done for. Strangely enough, I'd never gotten arrested before, at least not since I was a kid committing petty crimes around Toronto. I'd always had a weird sort of luck where avoiding the law was concerned. But my luck had obviously run out here in Portugal.

"You are English, yes?" a smaller dude with a moustache asked me.

"No."

"No?"

"Canadian."

"Ah yes. You are Canada. Very good. And you are here why?"

"To play tennis."

"A long way to play the tennis, no?"

"Yes, but I'm a professional. I'm here to play the Lisbon Open."

At that he chuckled heartily, and then the two others in the room who I'm pretty sure didn't understand any English at all, they started chuckling too.

"I am thinking no."

"Oh you should be thinking yes."

"You are not athlete. I think maybe you here for some trouble, no?"

"I'm a professional athlete!" I said far too loudly, drowning out all the fake levity currently on display. "Why doesn't anyone ever believe that? Look at my documentation," I told him. "I have papers from Tennis Canada."

He looked sceptical, but had one of the others search my bags.

"Tennis Canada. They are—how you say—hard up, no?" And he chuckled again, sending the others off on another round of contrived hilarity.

"Yeah. Maybe." Damn, surely there were wittier comebacks than that, but I was a little scared what with all the police and a large bag of God-knows-what shoved up my ass. The brain simply wasn't firing on all cylinders.

"Mr. Whipple say you are drugs," he said.

I wasn't quite sure how to respond to this. "Who in the what now?"

"Mr. Whipple say you are drugs." Nope, no clearer the second time. I just shook my head in confusion. He sighed deeply. "Mr. Whipple who sit next to you. Mr. Whipple—W-E-B-B-E-R— Whipple. He says he see you drugs! We search the bags and find nothing. Now we search you."

They proceeded to strip me down, and the two unilingual ones chuckled again. I comforted myself with the idea they were an easy laugh, rather than that they saw something particularly amusing about my package. Can't recall if I've ever heard anything about the Portuguese being all that well hung, though I could be wrong.

"You will bend down," the one in charge told me. And as I did I realized that, at some point over the years, my ability to feel shame had pretty much disappeared along with my pride. I was more afraid of what they might do to me once they pulled that huge bag of whatever out of my ass than I was embarrassed at the idea they might actually be laughing at the size of my dong.

Moustache man wasn't a gentle sort. A good time was not had by all. Well, maybe by him, and judging by the constant chuckling coming from the peanut gallery, maybe by the others too.

After he rooted around in there a while, he withdrew, snapped the rubber glove off his hand and announced, "He clean."

I was thrilled. I was free to go. They had nothing on me. Only then it struck me: *Where in the hell did it go?*

They let me go, but I could have sworn they put a tail on me. (I admit I'm not entirely sure what a tail looks like, but I swear I sensed one back there behind me.) Meanwhile, here I am trying to figure out what the hell happened to the stash. The cab driver gave me a funny look when he caught me digging around in my ass, but I didn't give a damn. The bag was gone. I couldn't imagine it had fallen out anywhere—I'm sure I would have noticed that—unless it happened while I was asleep. Maybe Whipple— Webber, whatever his name was—fished it out while I was napping, though I'm more than sure I would have noticed that. The only thing I could think was, if it didn't come out, well then it must have gone in. But even that seemed hard to believe. Where exactly could it have gotten to then? It couldn't just *disappear*. It had to have ended up *some*where.

And sure enough, at that exact moment, the world appeared about ready to tip over. Everything was suddenly pitched over at an angle and I felt like I was swimming through the air. "Hotel," I managed to blurt at the cab driver. "Fast."

"You betcha, baby," he said with a smile. He got me to my hotel in impressive time, and I managed to check in without too much trouble.

Once I was safely installed in my room, I ran for the bathroom and willed myself to take a dump. It took a lot of effort (one of the side effects of taking a lot of certain types of drugs is that they sometimes leave you a bit constipated), but I managed to get a little something out with a huge grunt and push while socking myself in the gut a few times. And sure enough, there among the other usual suspects, a completely empty plastic bag. Of course I was relieved to no longer have a huge bag of drugs crammed up my ass, and I tried to calculate how much of whatever drug it was had been absorbed by my system. That was when the bathroom walls started to bleed into odd geometric patterns. I won't go into too much detail here, except to say that there was way too much nudity on my part that day. And if it hadn't been for all my quick thinking, and those seemingly soundproof bathroom walls, I might have ended up in prison anyway.

As it is, I'm in my bedroom and still fairly stoned, though if I stay right here on the floor with a wet towel on my forehead and my tennis racquet at the ready, I'm pretty sure I'm safe from all those creatures lurking outside my door. If I somehow don't make it, if they drag me back to their secret lair to sell me into some underground sex-slave trade ring, let this journal be a record of my life and hopefully an inspiration. Okay fine, a cautionary tale, for all those aspiring athletes who think they might be the next big thing.

Okay, you sick bastards, no more pussy stuff. I'm coming out to do this like a man, and I'm bringing my racquet with me.

One strange thing that came out of the subsequent drug-induced, racquet-swinging frenzy is I seem to have stolen a lawn ornament. It's a small skunk holding its nose and I think it's supposed to be cute, but it's actually kind of creepy. I scribbled down the address from where I stole it on a parking ticket, which is also weird since I don't have a car. I'm sure I'll take the time to return it while I'm still here in Lisbon.

Actually, I think I'll keep it as a souvenir of my European experience, a memento of all the good times I've had so far. Fuckers are stupid enough to have a skunk ornament on their lawn, they deserve to lose it, whoever they are.

I haven't slept for forty-eight hours straight in a really long time. Probably not since Christmas. I feel pretty refreshed though, so that's good. The downside: I arrived here with enough time to warm up and practice before tomorrow's match, but now here it is, like, almost tomorrow, and I haven't done anything but get really high.

By the way, the hotel Tennis Canada put me up in is actually kind of shitty. I didn't exactly have time to notice before. When you think of a "hotel in Europe," your mind inevitably drifts to big castle-type things with a lot of gold leaf decor. Well I'm in a Portuguese version of a HoJo, and not a very good one at that. Still I can't complain. I am in Europe after all.

One thing I hadn't considered was the fact they all seem to speak Portuguese in Portugal. Almost no one speaks English. Weird! I haven't been to Europe in a really long time, and I've never been to Lisbon (hee hee!) before, but I thought people spoke at least *some* English everywhere. Maybe when I was more well-known and had more money people simply made more of an effort with me.

I was supposed to meet up with Raphael Farnel today, but I haven't got anything to give him. Well I suppose I could give him *Medieval Portraiture: A Detailed Study*, but I have a feeling it wasn't the fake book he was interested in. Then again, I could blow him off and he'd never know how to find me. He doesn't know what I look like. Screw him, he's nothing to me.

You know, I wasn't sure I'd ever come down. Now I've experienced my share of, let's say, extra-sensory experiences in the past, but never anything quite like this. Truth be told, I'm still high as a kite, but at least I'm no longer trying to eat my headband and sneakers or rip my clothes off because they're burning me. So that's good. I swear, if it had been anyone else, they'd have died for sure. Good thing Goodie chose me. Hell, maybe that's *why* he chose me. I will say this for the little toad-man, he carries some good shit, whatever it may be. Does make you wonder though. Is he using other players to move his drugs? I mean what a *scandal* if he were. I could really have his job! Then again, he might be able to score for me, so I probably shouldn't mess with that.

No! I'm clean these days. Clean living and exercise to get myself back in shape. I'm not into that stuff anymore. Except for this major three-day high I'm still on of course, but obviously that doesn't count since I had no choice. No, Olie Wood no longer has a need for a source. He's clean. I'd go for a run but I'm still a bit too wobbly. Maybe a nap'll do me.

February 17

Qualifying time at a full-fledged ATP clay-courter. I think it's been a full three years since I last played an ATP event, and yet the nerves haven't caught up with me yet. I think most of what I'm feeling is an odd sense of returning home to where it is I'm supposed to be. Another thing I'm feeling is a bit of pressure to perform, not just for me but also for the Tennis Canada people who put me here, regardless of the reasoning behind their decision.

I haven't felt this way in a long time. For so many years now I've been playing for Olie Wood alone. On the one hand that's easier, what with no one else counting on you, no one else to disappoint when you perform badly. But on the other hand, there's always a bit of an empty feeling associated with going it solo. It's harder to get motivated, and when you do happen to win there's no one there to share it with.

When Phil was around it was so different. That summer we got back together was a good one. I was picking up my game and focusing. I was tired of glass ceilings and I wanted to finally break through. I thought I might do it at the Australian Open at the beginning of the new year. I'd recently won a major warm-up tournament in Sydney and was feeling at the top of my game. I laid off the partying for a while and worked hard to stay in shape. It was all coming together as I breezed through the first week without dropping a set. In the quarterfinals I played and beat one of the top guys in a tough five-setter—don't remember which one—Sampras most likely. I fought my way past Boris Becker in the semis to face Andre Agassi in the finals. It was going totally according to script.

Now I should mention that during this time I had what you might call an on-court temper. For all that's happened to me since, that's the one problem I seem to have moved well beyond. I've gotten mellow in my old age, and lately haven't felt the need to lose it quite so much. Maybe, when the stakes go down, so does the need to snap. But back then, watch out. The better I got and the more I won, the more difficult I became on the court. When I was winning, I was a gracious though determined leader. But when I was losing, or wasn't able to make the ball do exactly what I wanted it to, I was considerably less so. I could rant and rave with the best of them. I broke a lot of racquets back when I had enough racquets to break. I cursed out umpires. I picked fights with line judges. I once even threw a water bottle at a fan that was heckling me in Germany. It was the first time I was penalized a full game in a match.

So one cloudy day we were playing in the final of the Australian Open, hoping to beat the rain in the days before the retractable roof. (Rain delays were always a pain in the ass since they forced you off the court until it was clear; meantime you lose your concentration and any momentum you might've been building.) On that particular day, for whatever reason, I started dropping serve early and badly. Agassi's long frosted hair bounced to and fro as he skipped about the court with that big stupid smile on his face, back in the days before he thought to rein in his rapidly receding hairline with a good close shave. His hair he gets rid of, not the smile, which I would have preferred. The sight of his arrogant puss always did piss me off, and I quickly lost my concentration that day. Before I could take a breath he had the first set, and I was already up against it.

He kept the pressure on and ran me ragged around the court, while I grew angrier and angrier. At the scene of my horrible momentum killer, Australia did it to me again and I completely fell apart out there.

I kicked the umpire's chair after he refused to overrule a shot Agassi'd made that was clearly out by a mile but had been inexplicably called good. I racked up ten thousand dollars in fines for swearing, stalling before I served, threatening a linesman, and making a "lewd gesture," which is what the tennis world calls it when a player grabs his dick through his shorts and shakes it menacingly at his opponent.

The match actually became a famous one. They still run it all the time on TV, in slow motion no less, the moment I horked up a lung at Agassi. Some commentators suggested that when I later swung my racquet at a female photographer, it was the worst on-court moment in the history of the game. An overstatement if I ever heard one. And for the record I insist I was swatting at a bee. The entire match was considered the worst show of sportsmanship the game had ever seen. And of course, as I became unravelled, I fell further and further behind, finally losing in straight sets.

Phil didn't know what to say afterwards. He wasn't often left speechless, but he certainly was that day. And even someone as unselfconscious as I was couldn't help but be humiliated by the day's events.

I was suddenly famous all over again, only this time for all the wrong reasons, for being the biggest asshole in sports. Let me tell you, it's not how you want to be remembered. And yet the infamous are still popular guests at a Hollywood or London party, and I was still very much in demand, only now I was a bit of a dangerous curiosity. Another thing was the chicks. They were still really into me, though now it was a slightly more sinister kind of girl I was attracting, more often than not the kind that really digs criminality. And the skank factor climbed considerably. Once again my game suffered, and I began to lose earlier and earlier to an increasingly inferior class of player. Phil was at what he called his "wit's end." Truth be told, I think he was really just kind of fed up with me. More and more I went out on tour with assistant coaches while Phil stayed back in Toronto. He was still officially my coach, but I was seeing less and less of him. Before too long it would be never again.

February 18

I lost my first round of qualifying. What a shitty day. Cold and miserable and I couldn't get my racquet on a single ball. The guy playing me must have thought he'd caught the world's luckiest break in meeting Olie Wood so early in the tournament. Boy, won't the Tennis Canada guys be pleased. And now I've got to kill a week in fucking Lisbon (I'm sorry, but that's such a goddamned funny name!) before I'm due to head out to Mallorca, Spain for a Challenger. What the hell am I going to do in Portugal all that time?

(6:45 PM)

Okay, so there are lots of wine bars here, only they don't only serve wine. This is pretty sweet, I've got to say. Still cold, but it's got nothing on Ottawa this time of year. This isn't a bad way to live to be sure. Only problem is, I'm way ahead of "schedule" on my per diem. At the rate I'm going I'll be broke in like a week or so. Not sure what I'm going to do then.

February 20

Man, I've got such shitty luck. So I'm enjoying a little cocktail when I hear this voice behind me.

"Mr. Wood?"

I'm not used to being recognized these days, so it took me by surprise, especially since he seemed to speak English.

"May I sit?" He was what polite people would call swarthy. I call him dark, oily and really Mediterranean-looking, complete with long, overly-moussed hair and those Eurotrash sunglasses you still occasionally see around.

"Do you know who I am?" he asked me nicely. I was starting to get a nice buzz on so it took me a minute to get any kind of answer together. "Raphael Farnel is my name. You are familiar, yes?" My mood grew a little darker, especially when I noticed the four guys behind him.

"I've heard the name."

"Good, then you have something for me. Something from Mr. Goodie and Tennis Canada."

"Yeah, well, about that—"

"He would be very disappointed to hear the book didn't reach its intended . . . target audience."

"He would, and I'd hate for Goodie to be disappointed in me, but I have some good news and some bad news."

"Do you now."

"See, the thing is, on the upside, I have your book back in my room."

"Excellent."

"Less good is . . . well that's all I have."

"Meaning?"

"Meaning the contents went up my ass, and haven't really come back out yet."

"How . . . interesting."

"Isn't it. See, Goodie should've realized that a book isn't all that great a hiding place, especially when drug-sniffing dogs are waiting at the other end. Now if he'd told me what I'd be carrying, I might have been able to—"

"Please shut up," he said. "You have to tell me now what we are to do about this problem. Mr. Goodie has my money, you see, but I don't have my book."

"And you know, I'm sick about that, because I'm a big fan of your brand of literature, I really am. But you see, it's not really my problem. I didn't even know what I was carrying. I still don't know actually, and that's after tripping on it big-time. And I do mean *big*-time."

"This doesn't interest me. What does is how we recover what's mine."

"Listen, bud, there's been far too much action in and around my ass these last few weeks, and I'm not about to let you or anyone else go spelunking around in there trying to scrounge up whatever's left of your stuff. I'm sorry."

"As am I."

And that's the last thing I remember. Next thing I know is, I'm waking up in a tacky living room amidst so much bright, pastel-coloured furniture and glass-top tables that I was briefly blinded when I came to.

"Hey, this is just like my place."

"You are very amusing, *tennis player*," I heard Farnel say behind me, with a noted and rather nasty edge to the last two words. "My how I hate your kind. So arrogant. So full of yourselves. Always dressed in your token tennis whites. You are given the simplest of errands," he said, "and you destroy the very simplicity of that errand. Yet even so, most of the fools Mr. Goodie sends me are able to at least complete their assignment, like the stupidest of monkeys. And you fall short of even that."

"Hey dude, I told you, I had no choice. I was gonna get shaken down at the airport, and I did and worse. A *lot* worse."

"The idiots in Lisbon International would have done *nothing*. They are mine to do with as I wish. You understand this? All you had to do was get the book through customs on the Canadian side and deliver it to me, and yet you fail even this simple task. I should kill you, if only to spare the world your feeble brain."

"Think that bothers me? You're not the first person to suggest that, you know." Hah. Score one for the stupid monkey.

"I care not, but you will need to be dealt with," he said. "Dealt with" is never a good thing by the way. It never happens that you're going to be "dealt with" in a nice, pleasant, relaxing way, like with a foot massage from a nice buxom lady. "How would you suggest I deal with you?" he asked. I was glad to have an opportunity to contribute.

"How about letting me go about my business, since I didn't do anything to hurt you on purpose?"

"Naive little man. Arrogant tennis player. Maybe I should slit your throat?"

"Wouldn't be worth your time. Why would you want to stain your nice rugs here with the likes of me?" I was trying to appear calm, but felt I was failing miserably.

"This is a good point. Then again, I could kill you outside. Perhaps in my yard. It is beautiful out there this time of year."

"Yeah, that *could* work, I suppose. . . ."

"Perhaps we can work something out."

"I'm up for ideas at this point."

"Perhaps it would be best if you did not talk for some time. You are giving me a headache." I decided to comply, and after a time he said, "You deliver a package for me, and perhaps I don't kill you."

Again? What was I, a mule? A carrier pigeon? To hell with that! "Of course," I said. "No problem."

He handed me a piece of paper. "This address, do you know it?"

"Should I?"

"No, no, just nod. Please. I cannot bear to hear you talk any-more." I shook my head and he said, "All right. You will go to this address, and you will write on a piece of paper in your own handwriting, in English, 'The People's Republic of Portugal will not stand by any longer.' Do you understand this thing I say? Just nod." I nodded. "Next you will leave this on the front step of the building," he said, and handed me a small package wrapped in brown paper. "Can you understand this much, ten-nis player?"

I could and did. I mean is that all I have to do to get out of this? Drop off a package for some other fuck to pick up? That much I can definitely do, and with very little skin off my ass to boot.

And he let me go. Just like that. We parted with him saying, "Fuck this up and next time I remove your balls." Ha! Little does he know there's only one left! Score another one for the stupid monkey!

Later, I made my way to the address provided. It was a nice, old, ornate-looking building, but home to a great deal of activity. Seemed like a pretty busy place to leave any quantity of drugs, but then hey, I'm just the stupid monkey here, so what business is it of mine. If someone comes along and steals this stash, well that's too damned bad for Farnel. This is as far as ol' Olie Wood's involvement goes. End of the line for the monkey. I filled out the note like he'd asked, and left it next to the package under a rock. And that was that.

And that's that for Portugal. Good riddance, I say. I have a lot of travelling to do over the next few weeks and I don't have time for drug dealers. Especially European drug dealers with their sleazy yet (compared to their American counterparts I've had the opportunity to meet) not all that threatening demeanours.

I took the train to Mallorca where I'll hole up for a couple of days before my next tournament, this one a high profile Challenger. So here I sit, in another bad hotel room with funky sheets I really don't think I should sleep on. And considering some of the shit I've slept in/on/next to over the years, believe me that's saying something.

February 22

Andre Agassi won a big clay court event today in Madrid, not too far from here. We arrived on the tour around the same time. It's weird, what with him in his thirties and still winning against all odds and me . . . here. Not winning. Balancing the scales perfectly. We took similar career paths actually, both called "brash" (I still to this day haven't figured out exactly what that means), both with big flashy games and loads of talent just waiting to be fully formed. And both of us had mid-career dips, him out of the top 100 and starting to play Challengers, me out of the top 200 and lucky to even get into those. The difference was, he pulled out of his spiral while I just kept on spinning downward. He would eventually go on to win eight Grand Slams and regain number one on a couple of occasions. I would go on to stay in a D-grade hotel in Mallorca with sheets that smelled vaguely of body odour and headcheese. He's a multimillionaire and world famous legend of the game, even as he still actively plays. I'm neither of those things. So I hate him, and the bile in my stomach does a little dance every time I hear his name or see that pompous ass duck-walk across a court, and worse so when I hear of him lifting yet another trophy or becoming the eighth man in the history of the game to win his eight hundredth match. Fuck you, Agassi. Seriously. I find that hatred towards those more successful helps me feel better about myself. It's just my thing.

So I'm motivated to get out and practice and train. Only, going up against a ball machine bores me to tears, so I just do a little cross-training. I run for fifteen minutes until my breathing becomes short and then I try the weights in the club gym, but the Spanish women watching and laughing as I struggle with the thirty-pounders is a bit intimidating, so I power walk my way to a cute little bar a couple of blocks from the club. On the television there I see that some terrorist group has blown up the Portuguese Finance Minister on the parliament steps. Fucking monsters in the world, really. Can't imagine the mind of someone who'd do something like that. They suspect an English connection to the bombing. Can't make out the Spanish reporter too well, but something about a threat letter from the terrorist cell. The world just makes me shake my head sometimes.

Anyhow, I've had too much to drink and I've got to play tomorrow. Should sleep. Not feeling too good, but some sleep should perk me right up.

February 23

So sick I thought I might die. My stomach was making noises I've never heard before, and when there was no longer any junk left to throw up, I started throwing up stuff that's never supposed to come out of the human body. Last night I attended this reception party the tournament sponsor was throwing, and they were serving this fish-type shit on crackers, and I know well enough never to pass up free food, so I partook of it as often as I could. Now normally I never get sick. My body just doesn't seem to have the patience for such minor inconveniences. But I've got to say, I started feeling pretty queasy just as I was setting foot on the court today. I don't think I was looking my best, judging from the gasps emitted by the handful of people in attendance. But the funny thing? I was so distracted by this overwhelming need to throw up that I wasn't thinking about the thousand and one things that usually go through my head. Even when I actually did throw up on court I kept ploughing on, and before I knew it I was shaking hands with my opponent, with an actual, honest to God, non-default-related win under my belt. Way I see it, I still have all the natural talent I once had and I have it in spades, but now there's all this other shit going on in my world that keeps it at bay.

In fact I won both my matches. I have no real memory of either of them, what with the delirium and all, but I'm into the main draw! I'll earn actual money for whatever else happens from here. I'll earn actual ranking points! As long as I can keep most of digestive organs on the inside I might finally have a chance to see some serious results. In fact I'm already feeling better. Maybe I'll be well enough tomorrow to start taking advantage of this winning streak. I play Lincoln Holmes and he's never come up against me when I'm on a streak. I can be one dangerous son of a bitch when I'm on a streak.

February 24

Fine. Whatever. So he beat me again. I think the answer for me is to stay sick all the time. I'm going to look into that for my next event in Germany.

February 25

Dear Portuguese People,
As you can see by the enclosed photos, I have your skunk. I don't plan to harm him, and in fact, as you can see, he's recently enjoyed a little

excursion to Spain. It's probably the first time he's travelled, so that's nice, huh? I wanted to say I don't judge you for having a skunk for a lawn ornament. I mean it's tacky and all, and in fact it's the kind of thing my mother might have found funny and believe me that's no compliment, but anyway, I don't blame you. You are Portuguese and don't know any better.

February 26

On the train, Germany bound. Stuttgart, to be precise. Don't think I've ever been. Some Slavic-looking honey was eyeing me across the aisle, licking her lips at me. I was getting really turned on, and starting to imagine having a little of that anonymous train-sex you hear about, until I realize she was giving me the international signal for "You've got mustard on your upper lip, asshole."

I miss Miranda. I'd love to be able to bring her along on my road trips, but we could never afford it. Besides, she needs to work. What she does is demanding, and it requires her full attention, not to mention a full schedule. Those dudes need my girlfriend's bare ass pushed in their face and they need it nightly. When I'm alone I whack off way too much. Then my hand starts to cramp and that hurts my tennis. I suppose I could just abstain, as they say, but no, I actually really can't. I've heard that if you let it build up too much your testicles can and will explode, and that would suck. I think you need to keep the juices flowing continually, four times a day and sometimes five, to make sure there's no build-up because really, that kind of thing could fuck a man up for life. Especially if you have just the one, that's a lot of pressure to put on one lonely ball.

I sometimes think I should try a lot harder to be faithful to Miranda. The problem is, wherever I happen to be, she's not there while lots of other ladies are. Besides, with each passing year it gets harder to score chicks and it makes me realize that one day, maybe even pretty soon, the well will run dry. Then where will I be? I'll be an officially washed-up waste of skin. So I really feel I ought to be active while I can. Of course Miranda might well get fed up with my bullshit and leave me—in fact she probably should—but that's a chance I'm going to have to take for now. Sometimes I think that maybe she should find someone a little more grounded. God knows she deserves better than me.

Oh listen to me, poor little mopey boy. I think going several days without talking to another human being starts to fry your brain a little and you start talking like a sap. I've got to keep busy and active to make sure I don't start getting depressed or something like that.

I've got this new strategy I've been rolling around in my head a while, and I'm going to battle-test it in Stuttgart: make them think I'm crazy. I've never tried it before—at least not on purpose—and I think if I rush the net a lot with an insane look in my eyes, making as much noise as I can get away with—kind of like animal noises combined with whacked out head twitches like I might go off at any minute—then maybe I can frighten my opponents into committing a lot of "unforced" errors. I have to confess I'm running out of options pretty quickly. Unless I contract a serious disease in the next two days and get into my nutty "so sick I'm brilliant" phase again, I may be well and truly fucked in this game.

February 28

So, what I would have to call "interesting" results stemming from the implementation of my crazy-man strategy. I played some Japanese guy who moved really quickly and had a great ground game, but who also seemed rather easily startled. He played with a methodical, textbook style that fit right into my plan. He came in expecting to play a certain game a certain way. Olie Wood made sure that wasn't going to happen.

Net rushing on clay is rarer than on, say, grass because the ball moves so much slower. It's harder to get to the net because your opponent has more time to construct his point and fire off a passing shot, making you look like some dawdling asshole up there at the net with your dick in your hand. It's a major reason why the big serve and volley players almost never do well on clay, even the greats. But today I figured I was going to do what feels right, and if this Asian ass-hat on the other side of the net passes me, well I'm not going to give him much to shoot at. So I start rushing the net. Every point, not just on my own serve, but on his as well. He blows almost every shot past me and rarely breaks into any kind of facial expression, except for what Phil would have called "grim determination"—which is boring by the way. Meanwhile I'm showing him every wild and ridiculous face there is and then some, and finally get my racquet on an attempted backhand passing shot and drill a smash right at him. That throws him a little, especially when I point at him afterwards and nod my head as if to say, "That's right, dude, you might lose a limb out here today. I don't give a shit if I win or not. You've heard the stories. You know what ol' Olie Wood's all about. And since it's so unlikely I could win here today, I might as well burn off some of my homicidal tendencies and at least hurt someone." That's quite a look, hey.

So he takes the first set 6–1, but I clearly throw him a bit in the process, especially when I start waving my arms around at the net. I receive a warning from the umpire for "unsportsmanlike conduct," but at least it's elicited some sort of response from my opponent. Then on set point I buzz him a little, breezing a shot by his temple that, had it connected, would have resulted in some major bruising. And now he's genuinely rattled.

Next set I break his serve straight away and start to really apply the pressure. I'm actually having fun too, which seems to de-stress me a little, and so I begin to play okay, even without the bullshit head games. He starts playing tentatively and he makes a few mistakes, enough to hand me the second set 6–4. Third set I'm feeling tired (I'm not used to going three sets with a real touring professional, even when playing well, and my saggy ass starts to drag a bit more) but I keep up the pressure, including a guttural scream when approaching for another smash that actually makes the guy cover his head and crouch down as though his life might be in danger. I receive another warning, but he starts to crack up after that, spraying a lot of shots wide as he takes his eye off the ball and places it on me, just in case I'm going to do something really crazy. I take the third set 6–3, and with it the match.

I say "interesting" results not just because I won or because I scared another human being into thinking I might be a little nuts, but because it actually seemed to make me play better. I'd forgotten I actually know how to play *tennis*; how to go up against genuinely professional guys who do this every day. Guys with coaches and entourages who actually train and work out on a regular basis. I'm starting to wonder what I might be capable of if I begin to apply myself a little more consistently. For the first time in years I'm starting to wonder if I actually have some gas left in the tank, and if I do, whether I can get myself into a position to play a Grand Slam again. The mind reels.

March 1

And then it gets reeled back in. Just as I think I've got the goods back, I run into someone playing in the zone—Lincoln Holmes, who informs me after kicking my ass in straight sets that, after one last Challenger in Düsseldorf next week, he's now only going to play ATP-level matches. After winning two Challengers and reaching the semi-finals of two ATP events already this year, he feels like he's ready to make the fulltime leap to the majors. He even thinks he can get his ranking high enough to earn a direct entry into the US Open, or at the very least, impress the US Tennis Association into handing him a wildcard. I hate him for this and wonder if he were brutally murdered in, say, the locker room, would I automatically be dubbed the prime suspect in whatever investigation followed?

Am filled with self-doubt and violent thoughts. The world is filled with misery and horror and everything sucks worse than I ever imagined.

Did sit-ups until my whole body burned in an effort to prove to myself it's not all over, it's really not.

Then I broke into Holmes' room in the hotel and sprayed shaving cream all over his sheets and stole his wallet. Felt instantly better.

March 2

Jesus. Had a hell of a dream just now. I was living in the world of the "Peanuts" gang—you know, Charlie Brown and those dudes—and I discovered something: they all live next to a nuclear reactor. It all makes sense; it's why all the boys are losing their hair. And not just Charlie Brown, but Linus and Pigpen and all those other dudes, except maybe Schroeder who's probably using plugs or wearing a wig. They all look like they're on day fifteen of a major nuclear meltdown. Charles Schultz was one sick sick-ass motherfucker.

March 4

Kind of lost the last few days. I met some German kids from a local college and we partied hard for a while. They were impressed with the fact I'm a tennis pro. Well, actually they didn't believe me at first.

"No way, man. You're too fat," one of the little assholes said in his fruity-sounding broken English. I told him not to be deceived, and that more than one opponent had been duped by my deceptively unhealthy-looking exterior. Although, to be honest, I can't remember the last time someone was duped to the point of actually losing to me, but this little shithead didn't know that.

They made me prove it by firing a serve into the window of a nearby house. Now, nine hundred ninety-nine times out of a thousand I couldn't do that to save my life, but that night something came back to me and clicked and in it went—smash! I heard a lot of screaming inside the house, and I ran so fast my heart felt like it was going to explode right out of my chest. Maybe I am a little out of shape.

Anyway, they thought I was the shit after that, and so we went to this place that was kind of like a frat house but not really—more industrial and German—and we got violently drunk. And the only thing I remember after that was making out with some really fat chick at a bar I really don't remember the name of.

I thought this journal would give me some idea of what happened the last three days, but the only thing I wrote in it was some crazy shit about Charlie Brown and nuclear meltdowns and that doesn't help at all.

Still, it really does make you think.

March 5

When I was a kid I used to occasionally have what I called "pure moments." They were pretty rare, especially when I was still living with my mother, but every now and then they'd appear from seemingly out of nowhere.

Once when I was really young and still in school—this must have been the first or second grade—back when I still felt obliged to go, we went on a field trip to some shitty zoo. I don't remember where it was, just some town we had to drive an hour or so in a bus to get to, somewhere outside the city. It was all part of this short-lived plan to "broaden the experience of the urban, lower-income youth." The whole trip out there I was sullen and mouthy, like I usually was back then, but once we arrived stuff just clicked in like this really amazing way. The sun was blazing, which I always enjoyed, and while the animals were generally in bad shape, clearly not the cream of the zoo crop, I loved each and every one of them that day. I was fascinated by their sounds and smells, and by their exotic feel. The goofy penguins, and a clearly very old, very bored polar bear, were like a whole new world for me. And the black swan was like something out of science fiction or a fairy tale.

We had lunch at a hamburger place just outside the zoo, and the food tasted perfect as it cooked a little more in the sun. The mood was light and the kids were nice to each other, even to me. It felt like every part of that simple, otherwise forgettable day was pitch-perfect. There was absolutely nothing wrong about it. Until I got home, that is, to find my mother taking it from behind courtesy of the fat guy who was kind of like our landlord at the time.

"You back already?" she winced without stopping as I walked through the door. "Thought they'd keep you there until at least five. Go into your room now while Mommy works, okay?"

I did, and tried to replace the image of my mother's sad and sagging breasts with the eyes of the deer we were allowed to feed at the zoo, their noses nuzzling up against my hand as they sucked the feed I'd bought from a machine a nickel at a time. It worked pretty well. No matter what my life was really like when you pulled off the lid and looked inside, I'd had a pure day free from the outside world and it carried me a while.

Well today, in the Düsseldorf Challenger, I had myself one of those pure moments. In athletics you'll often hear the expression "in the zone." I don't know about other sports, but what it means in tennis is that you can do no wrong. Everything you do with your racquet just works. If you scratched between your ass cheeks with it, you'd uncover some lost drop shot in there. Put simply, you're blessed for whatever period of time the pure moment lasts.

Today I won my opening-round match and I did it in the oddest of ways: by playing good tennis. I can't remember the last time I could say that. My serves were clean, my returns quick. I covered the net well and my backhand was so fluid it was like my racquet was a physical extension of my arm. Like those few moments in Stuttgart, I felt like I belonged in this game, playing against good players and, for a change, beating them. Ran into Lincoln Holmes in the locker room afterwards and he congratulated me.

"You had a really good day today, Olie. I'd hate to run into you when you're in the zone like that, you might actually give me a tough match," he added with a wink and a laugh to let me know it was all in good fun, ribbing the old guy.

"Heard you lost your wallet in Stuttgart," I replied. That seemed to darken his cheery mood a little.

"Yeah. I had four hundred euros in there and a picture of my mother. I'd love to get hold of the fucker who broke into my room."

"Yeah, no kidding. Anyway, good luck in your match, Lincoln. Maybe we'll meet in the quarterfinals, and then we can see who the better man is when we're both playing to our abilities."

"Don't remember the last time you made a quarterfinal in an event like this, Olie. That would be something to see." He forced a smile again, and walked out onto the court to warm up for his match. I felt like I'd held my own just then. When shit works on the tennis court, shit starts working off the court too. The thought made me horny and I went out trolling for German skirt, but finding that none would talk to me I returned to my hotel and whacked off to European MTV, and it was pretty good. After all, it was a pure moment kind of day.

March 6

Beat a name player from Russia today. A long three-setter that left me as damp as a bar rag and my legs like jelly, but I'm officially kicking ass. I wish there was some television coverage of these events. I'd love for Miranda and Gary to see me winning again. Wonder what ol' Phil would think if he knew?

Phil and I officially parted ways one month before things really went south. I'd been playing solid tennis for a couple of years, and keeping myself amongst the top-ranked guys, but never quite breaking through to the top. I couldn't beat the Samprases or the Agassis of the day, and losing like that really played games with my head. For years I'd been told I was going to be the best, and when I fell a little short of that I proved unable to keep things together, and my life became quite craptastic.

My last year with Phil I set a new record for fines. Some fuck-munch from NBC doing commentary for my US Open quarter-final noted that, "Wood has a singular accomplishment this year—he has received fines on *four* continents! He may never win a Slam, but he'll certainly go down in the record books as the 'fine-est' player in the game!" And so on.

Phil wore a new look all the time now, one that said, "I had such faith and belief in you and you're pissing it all away." I did what I could to ignore that look. It pissed me off. We fought a lot.

"You have no idea of the gift you have, Olie. You have no right to waste it like this."

"You're just jealous."

"Maybe. Or maybe I can't stand the fact this talent had to go to a spoiled punk like you instead of someone who would've appreciated it and worked to develop it."

"Fuck you."

That was how our arguments tended to end, with that clever parry of mine.

Finally one day the other shoe dropped. I was playing the Paris Masters, and I was ranked number eight in the world. All I had to do was win a couple of matches and hold my ranking and I'd qualify to play the season-ending Masters Cup, in which the best eight players in the world square off in round robin play to determine the "best of the best." I just had to hold my own and play to my seed, the quarterfinals.

The Masters was a big deal to Phil. He believed it showed the sum total results of any given year of work, and of course it was a huge payday, even just for showing up. Naturally I screwed the pooch in the second round after I got caught up arguing with the umpire over a bad call. I lost the match and ended the year ranked number nine in the world. A hell of a showing for anyone, and it should have been enough. Of the thousands of people who play this game professionally I was one of the top ten, and it should have been enough. But it was not enough. And Phil blew a gasket.

"You don't deserve to be playing this sport!" he hissed at me afterward.

"I lost, man. Chill. It happens."

"You didn't just 'lose.' You tanked. You couldn't focus because you had to argue that one point into the ground. You had to scream at the umpire until he gave you a warning and docked you a point, and then you couldn't concentrate on the match! You pissed it away and now, no Masters Cup."

"Big fuckin' deal. This way I get a longer off-season, so lay off. I've played the Masters twice already, so the mystery is gone anyways."

" 'Anyway,' " he corrected me.

"What?"

"We tried to knock the street out of you, but still you can't so much as speak properly. You're still just a stupid street kid with a huge chip in his shoulder. Nothing's changed with Olie Wood."

"Now you're making fun of the way I talk? Fuck you, old man. Fuck you and your fine talk, and your fancy shmancy club, and your fucking history of the game and all that other crap. I'm so sick of you."

"You're sick of *me*? That's a good one. I try to give you a life, I try to give you your dreams, and look what you do with it. Nothing."

"*My* dreams? *Your* dreams, dude!" That froze him. "I'm so tired of trying to fulfill this fantasy you have of getting a second chance," I told him. "I wanna live my own life, and you're just here sucking the air outta the room. I'm sick of it. I'm sick of you."

He just stared at me. "I can't do this anymore," he said quietly.

"Fine, who needs ya."

"You do," he said. "Far more than you realize. But then you will soon enough, I suppose." He began to pack his things. "I wish you luck, Olie. I really do. I hope you pull your shit together and find a way to realize your potential. Best of luck." He offered me his hand, but I never broke eye contact and didn't move to take it. He waited a while, and finally lowered his arm and turned and walked from the room. I never spoke to him again.

I still saw him occasionally. He coached a young kid from Quebec a while, but that never amounted to anything and the kid never broke the top 200. Then he worked with this tall gangly girl from Nova Scotia, but she was never more than a third stringer. Finally he gave up coaching and returned to some administrative role at Toomey.

He died just before Christmas this year. I've tried not to think about it. I've tried not to feel sick to my stomach for not trying to patch things up with him while he was still alive. Cancer, it was. Pancreas. One of the worst kinds, they say, but I think it all happened pretty quickly. At least there's that anyway.

I find myself thinking about him a lot these days. I block it out as best I can since he passed away, but he keeps coming back to me. I think it might be one of the reasons I started keeping this journal. See, Phil died alone. He never had any kids, just the ones he coached, and his wife left him right around the time he retired from that part of the game.

He died alone. And no one will ever know what he meant to people like me. He will be forgotten except by those very few people he worked with. I figure whatever happens, even after I fade from any kind of public memory, at least I can leave behind some thoughts and some history so that someone, somewhere, might remember.

Jesus I get down easy. I should be celebrating a good win. It'll make for a not half-bad payday, and in turn push me a little closer to my goal of qualifying for a Grand Slam. This is a good day. I guess it's just that I think about Phil more on the good days than on the bad ones. We had a lot more good days together than bad, which is why it's such a kick in the ass that we broke up the way we did.

Tomorrow I will quietly dedicate my quarterfinal match to Phil. I will win one in his memory. In his honour. It's the least I can do for someone who did so much for me, and in the end received so little in return.

March 7

Okay, I'm not reading anything into my crushing defeat at the hands of the hateful Lincoln Holmes. He just had a good day, and I just happened to have a bad one. It's not like some kind of omen or, like, Phil looking down on me and sending me bad karma for being such an asshole to him or something. I refuse to believe that.

But just in case, let me make it official: Phil, dude, I'm really sorry for anything that happened between us. It was all my fault. So no hard feelings, okay?

Hopefully that will nix any curse he may have put on me. And no offence to Phil, but I think it's best I don't dedicate anything to him ever again.

March 10

Milan. Beautiful city. Plenty to do here too, only I've run through my per diem and the money I stole from Lincoln and I still have a week to go before I get out of here. Not sure what I'll do for food and such. At least the hotel is paid for. Maybe I can steal a little food from the hotel restaurant or charge it to the room. That would certainly make Goodie shit his pants. Might be worth it just for the fun of knowing that.

Killed the last couple of days kicking back, taking the train through Italy and trying unsuccessfully to pick up Italian chicks. I am seriously out of my league in this part of the world.

Looking forward to getting back home. I called Miranda collect yesterday and she sounded so far away it made me sad. She was upset because some customer had pawed her pretty aggressively. The rules are pretty clear on that sort of thing, and she was seriously pissed that the bouncer didn't step in before he did. Can't say I blame her. Of course they threw the guy out, but the damage was done. Geez, some people have hard jobs. I can safely say that I've never once been groped in the execution of my vocation. At least not that I can recollect.

Tomorrow I play an ATP tournament on indoor carpet. I used to love playing on carpet; the ball moved like lightning and it suited my attacking style of game. Now I just wish the damned ball would slow down a little and give me a chance to get to it.

This is my last chance to truly make a mark on this little mini tour. God knows if and when I might actually be able to come back here and play again. This could very well be my last time playing professional tennis in Europe. That feels kind of morbid.

Anyhow, I'm supposed to check in with Goodie the day after I get back and I'm kind of dreading it, both because I haven't really racked up any notable results to warrant their bankrolling me, and because he might be pissed off I lost his drugs somewhere up my rectum.

March 11

Sucked like a five-dollar whore this afternoon. Played like the old woman I sometimes feel like. Today was all about the agility, and I was utterly helpless as my Italian opponent whisked me about like a rag doll, the knees being my downfall. I've noticed lately that they're starting to creak and hurt like hell. I had arthroscopic surgery on both knees back when things started going wrong, and every now and then I still feel a possibly career-ending bout of pain in one or the other, but usually it clears up after some rest. Today though they were as bad as they've ever been.

I also received my first fine in a while today, but there was nothing I could do. See, I have an enormous bladder. A drinker's bladder. I'm kind of known for it in certain circles actually. I can go an entire day without having to piss, which Miranda insists is bad for me, but it's come in really handy during play, believe me. I only ever take a piss break when I need one strategically. (The ATP changed the rules during my time on the tour to allow for a certain number of bathroom breaks during a match. I never need one myself, but that doesn't stop me from taking one if I'm playing badly and want to throw my opponent's rhythm off.)

So today before my match I had a couple of beers on the hotel tab, just to loosen myself up. It seemed to work as I opened well with a good hold of serve. But things fell apart shortly after that.

I should mention here that there are few worse things in this game than playing someone on their home turf. Certain fans can get a little crazy, especially in some European countries, or worse, South America, where I was once beaned with a full bag of frozen peas by an overly enthusiastic fan. Worse still is playing the Davis Cup, which is team tennis played between countries. You think soccer fans can get ugly? Go see a Davis Cup match somewhere, like in Chile or Australia. Those people would just as soon kill you as look at you if you're from the opposing country. We get up for it in Canada too, in our own mostly polite but still competitive way. (And yes, I'm still on the Canadian Davis Cup team, officially at least, even ranked as low as I am nowadays. I'm still pulling hard for the old red and white, which is part of the reason I qualified for this recent round of funding.)

So here I am playing an Italian in Italy, and these people can get worked up over a tiddlywinks tournament, let alone a tennis match. So needless to say they were at full boil today. Which just pissed me off frankly.

I should also mention that I don't freak out quite like I did when I was a kid. I didn't know any better then. But now I know I can't afford the fines, and frankly it just isn't worth it. Now I just internalize my pain and suffering until it becomes a giant mass of resentment in my stomach that eventually develops into a bleeding ulcer that makes it difficult to eat or even breathe until I finally end up unbelievably sick and in the care of the Canadian healthcare system when I inevitably check myself in for an operation of some sort. It's much better this way. And even though, during rain delays at some events, they still run that TV footage of my freaking out at the Australian Open, I know that's not me anymore. When I do get pissed off and need to make a point I get a little more creative now.

So I'm starting to both suck and blow, and this de la Penti guy I'm playing is starting to embarrass me. He's playing games with me, bringing me into the net, then lobbing a shot back over my head, but softly enough so that if I run I can just get to it, at which point he places a drop shot just over the net to bring me scurrying back again. He's jerking me around like some kind of monkey and the Italian fans are loving it. Add to this my sudden need to urinate as a result of all the water I drank this morning, not to mention the three to five pre-match beers, and suddenly I find myself with a gusher all but ready to blow.

Now the bathroom break rule doesn't allow for mid-game visits. You have to wait until the game ends to hit the can, so while this de la Penti prick jerks me around, keeping the game going just for the fun of it, I start to feel that build-up behind my dick that says, "Hi, this is the world's largest bladder, and I'm now in need of release. And when I decide it's time to let loose, there is no debate." It's a very chatty bladder as well.

So I drop trow and take a piss against one of the decorative faux bushes they keep in the four corners of the court.

The Italian fans didn't find that amusing. No, they seemed to think I was personally insulting them by taking nature's call in front of them. Maybe I was a little. But then you just don't piss on Olie Wood unless you expect to get a little bit back, you know?

I was fined and threatened with disqualification from the match, but in the end they didn't bother considering how far behind I already was. It took just a few more games before de la Penti tore me a new asshole and I was done.

Italian TV was covering the event, and the episode actually ran on the nightly news, so high up in the line-up that it followed only the update on the Portuguese Finance Minister's horrible death and the utter lack of leads in the case. Who knew the sight of my schlong could elicit such a huge reaction? I should be flattered.

Ultimately, the fine I received amounted to about the same as my first-round prize money. I was planning on getting some peanuts at the airport when I leave this place, but those kinds of expenses will just have to wait till I get home.

I'm done with Europe. My ticket home is open so I can bug out of here first thing tomorrow morning. Might as well, I'm out of money and can't exactly do much while I'm here. And I can't charge much more to the hotel or Goodie will start to get suspicious. So home it is. Back to Canada. It's mid March so Ottawa should be a balmy twenty below zero, but fuck it. I'll get to see Gary and Miranda again and, in turn, get off courtesy of something other than my own hand. Yep, it'll be nice to see a friendly face or two—actually just the two. I don't know any more friendly faces than that.

March 13

Home. Or at least, Miranda's home. Got the once-over at the airport in Milan, but at least I wasn't carrying any drug-filled textbooks to incriminate me this time. Even without actual contraband on my person I seem to set off security alarms all over the world. I wonder if I should get a haircut or shave more often? It's just so hard to remember the latter and I can never be bothered with the former. I might ask Miranda to give me a cut, but she says she likes my hair long and I sure as hell ain't paying a "stylist" to do it. And besides, that's what the headband's for. No, for now I'll just have to put up with the token harassment from border guards and security personnel.

My next big project will be to raise some money for plane fare.
My next couple of tournaments are Challengers in Florida and
Arizona and a couple of tiny Futures in small-town California.
There's no way I can hoof it all the way to Hollywood, Florida,
for my next event in two weeks. I probably wouldn't even be able
to make it in time. I've got to get creative.

Miranda was pleased to see me home. Only problem is, she's
really starting to go on about the marriage thing again and that's
just not cool right now.

Gary says he might fly down to Florida with me if I'm able to
scrounge together the money for my ticket. That would make for a
better trip than usual. He's really happy these days because he's
started ministering at an "alternative church" (which basically
means a lot of crazies and drug addicts hanging out in a elemen-
tary school gymnasium somewhere), which reminds him of why he
was called to the Lord in the first place. He's also started handing
out weed as a kind of communion. I warned him that might get
him into trouble, but he believes it's what God wants him to do and
it's hard to argue with God. Or Gary, for that matter. Neither one
presenting all that logical an argument much of the time.

As for me, I'm feeling somewhat fucked. I have but one pair of
sneakers, one half of which now has a hole in the sole. I felt it during my match in Milan, but to be honest I was more focused on
the pain in my knees than the pain in my foot. So now I have no
idea what to do. Miranda's broke this month after paying rent and
I'm less than broke, and for what they charge for tennis shoes
these days I might as well mortgage my soul.

Tomorrow I meet up with Wesley Goodie at Tennis Canada. He
didn't sound all that happy on the phone, but then I get the
impression that, generally speaking, Goodie's not all that happy a
guy. I'm supposed to give him a report on the tour, and I have no
idea what I'm supposed to say. "Won a few, lost a few more"? In
fact I can't remember how I did in some of those events. My
mind still shuts down from time to time. Still, it should be recorded in this journal, so I'll just check.

Well, that's just lovely.

March 14

Problem solved with the sneakers. For seven dollars at Wal-Mart I was able to purchase a pair of canvas shoes with a sneakery feel to them with some loonies stolen from Miranda's dresser—last night's lap dance gratuities no doubt. Granted they look a little stupid, but they'll allow me to move around better than the giant hole with a little sneaker wrapped around it that I was sporting before.

On a less positive note, I met up with Wesley today and he was-n't in the best of moods.

"What's shakin', Wes?" I asked, strolling confidently into his office.

"Don't ever call me Wes," he said. "Now sit down."

"Europe was quite something."

"I'm glad you enjoyed yourself. Quite the record you've amassed." He paused to read from a file. "Five wins—which I find hard to believe by the way—and five losses, including two first-round defeats, as well as one missed tournament in Northern Greece." Greece? Oh, right. *Greece*! Shit, I somehow forgot an entire tournament. "Six hundred dollars in extra room charges," he continued, "one suspicion of drug smuggling at the Lisbon Airport, one fine for 'public urination'—nice touch there—and finally, one entirely plausible suspicion of breaking-and-entering another player's room."

"That's a lie! Whoever said that is, like, besmirching my good name."

"Yes. Right. So." He paused again. "And if that were not enough, on top of all this, a message from Raphael Farnel stating quite clearly how you managed to screw up the extremely simple assignment you were given."

"Hey man, I was going to get busted."

"Are you aware that monetary assistance from this organization has helped send scores of players all over the world, and not one of them has ever failed the simple task of delivering a *book*?"

"Yeah, well, I'm intimately familiar with what was *in* the book, and I was in for a lot of shit if I got caught."

"You're an idiot, Olie."

"Oh yeah? Well you're fat."

"So are you, Olie."

"This isn't fat, it's muscle. I'm a professional athlete—"

"Look, Farnel tells me you made good on what was owed him, and that's fine. Nevertheless, my reputation, and the reputation of Tennis Canada, is shot. Kaput. You just made the entire organization look ridiculous, not to mention inept, to one of its primary benefactors, which is something neither he nor we will soon forget."

"I'm told I'm a hard person to forget actually."

"And as for your 'accomplishments,' the program will be re-evaluated in light of the investment we've made, and the lack of return on said investment."

"Hey look, man, that was a hell of a month for me. Did you say *five wins*? I don't remember five wins, but if there were, well then I'm happy. Do you have any idea when the last time I had five wins in a *month* was? I think it might still have been the twentieth century. So I'm damned happy. Hell, I'm ecstatic. Now I'm sorry about the fine—it came out of my prize earnings— and as for the extra room charges, well, just consider it player development."

"You're thirty-one. How much actual development do you think you have left in there?"

"Maybe so, but I consider it a great success."

"I consider it a great joke."

"Well, good for you, dude."

We both fell silent a moment.

"Yes, good for me," he eventually continued. "In any case, there won't be any more supplemental funding coming from Tennis Canada on behalf of Olie Wood."

"Hey, like you say, I'm thirty-one. What do I care? This is my, like, swan song. I appreciate the little financial contribution to the cause."

"You are such a huge mistake, Olie."

"Yeah, well, I may be. But at least I'm something, *Wes*."

After I left his office, I found a doughnut with only a little bit missing on top of one of the garbage cans right outside Tennis Canada, and then I was able to take a cab ride to within a block of Miranda's place before dashing on it. Mistake or not, my life is pretty good.

March 15

I just found out, by mail, that the ATP is going to start drug testing soon. Officially it's for performance enhancing drugs, but I wonder what else they can detect. This could be challenging.

March 17

I was able to reach an old friend of mine today in Detroit. His name is Ahmed Khazaini and he runs a discount electronics store kind of like an independent Radio Shack, only not quite so classy. He played pro tennis briefly out of Iraq, but while he was out and about on tour one time he defected to the US for good. He was never very successful and didn't last too long, but he was one of the (very) few players who seemed to like me back in my prime.

"You are the shit, bro! The shit!" he was fond of telling me. "You are so cool, I want to befriend you very much!" And while I know that sounds, like, super gay, he was really just a pal of mine, especially because of the chicks I was continuously able to score back in the day. He hung around hoping to scoop up some leftovers, and I'm proud to say, every now and then, he did manage to pick up some of the less appealing babes that happened my way. I felt like I was doing someone a really big favour, not to mention everything I was doing for international relations.

Ever since he left the tour, Ahmed's been busy running his business, and whenever I talk to him he has big plans to expand, but they never quite seem to come together.

"You come in and join the business, bro!" he often says to me. "We'll be like business partners, and you can be the famous one who does the ads!" He still seems to think it's twelve years ago, and somehow doesn't realize I haven't been famous since we were both much, much thinner than we are now.

Yeah, about that. While people may occasionally suggest that I'm a little meatier than I was, say, back in my prime, Ahmed is like two of me. You can look at me and see that underneath it all I'm still a professional athlete. Ahmed, though, just seemed to exhale and let it all fall out once he left the sport. He seems happy being a fat dude, but when someone breathes heavy after crossing a room you've got to be at least a little concerned.

Anyhow, I'm going to hit him up for travel sponsorship for my next few events in the Southern US. I'm sure there's something we can work out that will help us both, and besides, it'll be nice to see him again.

March 18

Terrible fight with Miranda tonight. When I told her I had to leave earlier than expected so that I could drive to Detroit with Gary to see Ahmed, she freaked out and ended up busting my lip with her shoe, one of those classy, red, six-inch heels I like so much.

"You're never here, asshole. It's like having a phantom for a boyfriend!" she said, and I told her that actually sounded pretty cool and would make a really neat nickname for me—the Phantom—but she took that the wrong way and belted me with her shoe. She felt really bad for bloodying me up, but still said, "I'm not sure how much more I can take of you, Olie. You've got to be home more. You've got to be here with me. I can't do this long distance shit anymore. I need you here to help me move heavy stuff, you know? You've got to, like, commit more, baby. You've got to start thinking about our future. We're never going to be able to get married and have babies if you're not around to do your part."

She was absolutely right, which is one reason I made sure to get out of there pronto and on my way to Detroit, even if it was a little earlier than I'd intended (the middle of the night while she was sleeping to be precise).

So now here I am heading down south with Gary to get me some sponsorship dough. Been a long time since I had any of that. It'll feel pretty cool to be amongst the "sponsored" again. It'll make me feel like I did in the old days when people really wanted a piece of me, and didn't necessarily have to assault me with their footwear to prove it.

March 19

"No way, bro. Not gonna happen," Ahmed told me before I even got to the part about what he'd be getting out of the deal.

"I thought I was your bro, bro."

"You are the bro-est bro I have, bro, but who has the money to just give away like that? Business ain't *that* good, you know."

He had a point; the store was a major-league shit hole. "But I'm not asking for a gift. This is a serious *sponsorship* opportunity. This is a chance to have your store name seen by all the people watching the matches on TV."

"Since when did they start showing Challengers on TV, bro? Lot's changed since I played the game, I see." He laughed heartily at this.

"Well, okay, what about all the crowds in attendance?"

"*Crowds?*" he said.

"Okay, fine. Never mind."

"How much you need, bro?" he asked me.

"Maybe a thousand. Enough for a place ticket to Florida, bus fare after that, and hotels."

"Hotels. On my dime." He sighed deeply. "You still getting the pussy, bro?" he said slyly.

"I get my share, sure."

Gary, standing silently next to me throughout this exchange, rolled his eyes at that. You could literally hear them rolling back in his head in absolute mockery of me. I thanked him.

"Maybe when you fix me up we'll talk about money—"

"I'm not a pimp, Ahmed," I warned him, feeling a little like one already.

"I'm just kidding you, bro. Never mind. Okay here's what we do. I *pay* you some money—I can swing, maybe, five hundred—and you hand out flyers for the mail-order part of the business when you're travelling around down there. And then you wear a billboard when you play. So you're, like, working for me, instead of this sponsorship bullshit, okay?"

I breathed a sigh of relief. "Anything you need from me, bro."

I gladly took his money and his flyers and an awkwardly stiff placard he expected me to wear while playing, and Gary and I brainstormed to figure out if that would be enough cash.

"I've got enough to feed us both," he told me. "That's probably all I can swing other than my own plane ticket. I could just give you my money and you could go without me."

"No, I want you there. We can do this. I've just gotta be creative."

And I was. I remembered how they pay for certain things in the States that we don't in Canada. Things I have plenty of, like blood. And semen. So I travelled to three blood banks around Detroit and gave the limit at each one. I then found one fertility clinic that was willing to pay for spunk, but one look at me and apparently they already had enough. No matter, I was so tired after offering up all that blood that I probably couldn't have found the energy to work one off anyway. As it was, I was prepared to lie down on the sidewalk and have a nap outside the fertility clinic, but Gary thought that a bad idea and dragged me off to his truck to sleep for the night.

"Who do you pray to?" he asked as I began to doze off in the front seat.

"What makes you think I pray at all, Gary."

"Well, when we're travelling together, I sometimes hear you talking to yourself. Especially when you're falling asleep."

"News to me."

"Yeah, you do. And I often wonder who it is you're talking to."

"Well not God, if that's what you're thinking."

He shook his head. "Well that makes me sad. But also frustrated. Then sad again, then a little angry, then sympathetic, then sad again—"

"So sadness would be the one overriding emotion here then."

"Well if you're not praying, who are you talking to?"

"You know what? I have no idea." And I didn't either. Phil? My mother? 1920s tennis great and well documented pervert, Bill Tilden? Damned if I knew.

"Let me know if you figure it out."

"You'll be the first to know," I told him.

March 21

Very bad scene at the airport today when I got into my first fight with Gary since we were kids. He doesn't fly much—he's more of a road trip guy—so I gave him the benefit of the doubt when I realized he was carrying.

"I don't know how you got it across the border or where you were stashing it," I told him, trying to make him ditch his weed in the bathroom, "but trust me, they search these days. You'll get caught."

He shrugged. "If I get caught, I get caught."

"Yeah, you say that now, but just you watch. Trust me, I had a little run-in recently, and no way I'd want to go through *that* again." The mere thought of having to shove that big wad of pot up my ass made me itch uncomfortably in apprehension.

"I won't get rid of it."

"You've gotta."

"I won't."

"Then I'll take it from you and flush it myself."

"I won't let you."

"What, are you going to hit me?"

"If I have to."

"Yeah, right. Fuck you," I said with a laugh.

"I'm deadly serious, Olie. I will."

"Fine. But I want to sit in a totally different part of the plane than you. I don't want to be dragged into this shit when you get caught."

"No problem." And with that he got into line way up ahead of me, and I refused to make eye contact with him even though he kept shooting glances back my way. Finally it was his turn to pass through the security check—they gave him a really quick pat down but otherwise let him through without questioning. Then when my turn came they pulled me out of the line.

"Can you step over here, sir?" said the large back lady.

"What did I do?"

"Just a routine inspection, sir. Can you please remove your belt, shoes and headband?"

"This is nuts! I haven't *done* anything! For maybe the first time in my life I'm doing this absolutely straight and clean and *now* you stop me? This is fucked!" I said, but to no avail.

After a brief struggle, they forced me into a nearby room and shoved me into a chair and suddenly I was in Lisbon again, only this time, as I was in the States, the accents were different. Hispanic mostly. And some Iranian.

"Ms. Henderson here says you carry sometimes," a little guy with a bad moustache said to me. Why do these guys always sport moustaches? Weird.

"She's got it totally wrong," I told him. "This time I'm not carrying. *Not*."

"So usually you carry then." It wasn't a question.

"Yes. I mean no. I mean—what was the question?"

"You do drugs, huh? You carry?"

"No. I never have. Never."

"Your file says you were stopped in Portugal on suspicion."

"It was a mistake. Their mistake," I added quickly.

"So no drugs."

"Nope, no drugs."

"We'll need to do perform a cavity search then."

And so the public obsession with my rectum continued as yet again I was probed, poked and violated in search of the drugs I didn't have. Typical.

Of course I missed my flight while Gary continued on his merry way. When they finally let me through it was with a cursory apology, not to mention four and a half hours later than I'd been scheduled to leave originally. I landed in Miami in the middle of the night and couldn't find Gary anywhere. I was alone again, while my pal was off wandering the streets in this strange city.

I used to be greeted by a limo and driver. Sometimes there were even groupies. Groupies! Oh *God* I loved groupies, more than, like, anything else. More than the money or the fame or the trophies. Nothing felt as good as some young hussy willing to do pretty much anything for you or to you just because of who she thought you were. There is no—NO—greater rush in the world than the tactile attentions of a good young groupie. Now I arrive to stale Florida air and a whole lot of nothing.

Back in the groupie days I was still actually winning of course. In fact I came within a hair's breath of winning a Grand Slam at one point.

The Australian Open, of course, was the site of so much of my misery over the years. Something about that country just isn't right. The animals look like something out of science fiction, and the people are way too tanned and *way* too chiseled for my liking. And you've never heard people supposedly speaking English sound so much like they're speaking a foreign tongue. And the tournament gave me fits. When I started out there, they'd just switched from grass to a surface called "ace rebound," which in those early years sometimes bubbled a little and pitched in one direction or another. It was unpredictable and way too hot, especially in January, and it brought me a lot of misfortune. And for all that, I still came so close to winning there.

The year after the horrible flare ups and the spitting and the assorted and seemingly arbitrary acts of violence, I returned to what is commonly referred to as "a chorus of boos." The Australian fans had completely turned against me, but I played well enough to win my first few matches regardless. To make matters worse, it seemed like every round I was matched up against another member of the host country. Now in a draw of 128 players, coming from every corner of the globe, what are the odds that I'd meet such a long list of Aussies one after the other? Well I did, and with each win I only made their fans hate me that much more.

And yet I was somehow (and somewhat uncharacteristically) able to block them out, as I seemed to find my old form. It was the first time I'd played a big event without a real coach in my corner, and it almost seemed to liberate me. I played a little more loosely and a little more aggressively and it definitely paid off, because before I knew it I was in the semi-finals dispatching yet another top-ranked Australian in straight sets. I was suddenly in the final, playing on arguably the biggest stage in the sport.

Center court, at the final of a Grand Slam tournament, is the holy grail of the game. It's like the tennis equivalent of a cathedral, only a really exclusive one. It's always sold out, with row after row of people seated so high up you have to squint to see their faces up there at the top, and there are more television cameras than you can count. The air feels a little thicker and your breath comes a little shorter. It's like no other place in the world. The Grand Slams also post this wall of past champions you can't help but glance at from time to time, knowing you're three to five sets away from joining the likes of Borg, McEnroe (neither of whom ever won the Australian Open, so you'd also know you had one up on them), Sampras, and that little shithead Agassi who's won this thing like a gazillion times already. You can also see the big ass trophy they have standing by for the winner. Those things are huge, like giant mortar shells. (Little known fact: the winner doesn't actually get to take home the huge, wonderfully obnoxious trophy you see them hoisting on TV after the win; they get a little wee facsimile to stick on their shelf. That always felt like a lie to me. But then what I wouldn't give to just once be lied to like that.) All these distractions, all these big beautiful distractions, and you still have to play the fucking match.

I won't say who I played, but let's just say you know him. He's one of the famous of our ilk, and over the years his lawyers have been on my case over a few issues, not the least of which was (after his wife gave me a handjob) our having what the police called "an altercation" resulting in a restraining order being slapped on me (*Me!*). Anyhow, best I not tempt fate and anymore lawsuits here. It doesn't matter anyway; we played a tight five-setter, and I actually got the better of him in the fifth. I somehow managed to find another gear at exactly the right time, and I broke him twice to take a four-nil lead. I was coasting toward my

first Grand Slam title. I was going to become famous all over
again. It was all going to turn around for me.

I held serve to go up five-nothing and I could taste it. I was four
points away from that big obnoxious trophy (or at least the mini
version of it). I was one game from history.

He started tentatively, netting his first serve before lobbing me
a puffball of a second serve. I took it on the rise and nailed the
corner of his court. Love–15. Three points away.

Next, he fired off a nice kick serve that I was just able to catch
a piece of, and I was so in the zone that it was a sufficient enough
piece to guide the ball down the alley of the ad court, utterly un-
returnable. Love–30. Two away. This was a done deal. He was
clearly rattled and it looked like he was about to fold up his tent
and go home.

He served, placing it nicely, low to the corner of the box. I dug
it out however, hitting a nice defensive forehand. He took a swat
and slightly miss-hit the ball, hoping for a solid forehand with
pace but instead just sending over a floater. It was a perfect setup
for me to make my mark on this match. I hauled back and took
it out of the air with a smash. The ball connected with the sweet
spot of the racquet, and I could feel the perfection of the shot
reverberating up my arm.

At that moment a kookaburra flew across the court, intercepting
the ball and exploding in a mass of feathers. It actually disintegrat-
ed from the power of the shot. The crowd went silent. I'd actually
been winning them over a little over the course of the match, but
now I was getting "evil bird killer" vibes from some corners. I was
freaked. It was like some kind of horrible omen. No one said anything. Time seemed to stand still. Finally the umpire called over the
microphone: "We will take a break while the ballboys clear the . .
. uh, feathers from the court." The tension broken, some people
laughed uneasily, while others squirmed in discomfort. The camera guys, however, were ecstatic. They snapped everything, from
my reaction to the crowd's unease. They already had the story; it
didn't really matter to them who won anymore. This was the front
page of the sports section, if not the whole paper!

I tried to regroup. We were told to replay the point, and I knew I was close to shutting this thing down. I just needed one more point and I could clear out, and to hell with the bird. But I was thrown. Bad karma comes from stuff like that, you know? Curses have been known to stem from such things. Voodoo shit. But still, I had to buckle down. Just one more point and I'd be through to the Promised Land.

I took one more glance at the trophy on its stand and gritted my teeth in anticipation of the serve. He served it up—it was hit right to me—and I nailed the fucker. A perfect cross-court winner. I'd done it. I'd finally done it. I dropped to my knees the way Bjorn Borg used to and raised my fists in the air. I admit I started to cry a little. I struggled to my feet and started to lap the court, passing by my chair to grab a Canadian flag I kept in my bag just in case this moment occurred, and I let it fly behind me as I made my lap of triumph, tears streaming from my eyes. Occasionally I let out a little whoop of joy to punctuate the victory. I realized I'd forgotten the traditional handshake with my opponent, so I ran back to the net to meet him. It was then I realized people were acting somewhat strangely. They weren't cheering me; they were actually laughing at me, which hardly seemed appropriate. The cameras were rolling and there was plenty of commotion, but something seemed wrong.

"What are you doing, you *idiot*?" my opponent hissed when I went to shake his hand.

"Sorry I forgot the handshake, dude. Let's just do it and get the hell out of here."

"Love-forty," announced the umpire over the mike. Then the crowd laughed even harder, like a huge pocket of air had suddenly been released from their midst.

Fuck. With all the confusion around the bird I'd miscalculated the score. I looked around, and the cameras were all trained on me. Now there'd be a contest for the leading sports story the next day. I looked to my player's box for some kind of moral support, but of course I had no one there to offer any.

"Get back there and let me serve," whispered my opponent, by now no longer angry but instead clearly embarrassed for me.

I tried to put on a brave face, shrugging to the crowd with a sheepish smile as I sauntered back to my place on the baseline, but I tripped on the Canadian flag tied around my shoulders and hanging down to my feet. I landed on my face and knocked out my two front teeth. Blood poured from my face, and the umpire climbed down to check on me.

"You want a medical timeout, mate?" he asked, genuinely concerned as he gingerly untied my flag and removed it from me.

But I couldn't let this horror show drag out any longer. I was just a point away from bringing an end to this, and even if my glory was wiped clean away I'd still get the win. "Leth do thith," I lisped through the gap in my teeth. And I prepared once again to receive serve.

My opponent went to my backhand, and even though the serve wasn't all that hard, I was so distracted by the way my mouth kept filling up with blood that I whiffed it. 15–40.

His next serve was an ace. Nothing I could do. Then he hit a nice spin serve to my forehand which I shanked, taking us all too quickly to deuce. Finally, fuelled by a fresh surge of confidence, he finished me off with a pair of aces.

But no problem. I still had a 5–1 lead and the chance to serve for the match and the championship. Only thing is, the laughter from the crowd was really throwing my serve off. I hit a personal record four double-faults that game, and he tore me a new one with the one serve I did manage to get over the net. This continued for a while until he pulled back even at 5–5. It all happened so fast. Just as I started to dig in again and focus, I began to picture the headlines that would appear if I actually lost this thing: "Biggest Collapse in Sports History"; "One Dead Bird + One Serious Choker = A Bad Day at the Office for Wood"; and of course the inevitable "Olie Wood . . . Not!" I started to hyperventilate as I pictured them all, and tried to call for a bathroom break, but you can't take a break mid-game and it was my serve. I don't think I hit a ball anywhere even close to the service box that game. He finished me off on his serve and suddenly I was back shaking his hand again, only this time for real.

"Sorry, man," was all he could say. "Tough one." He'd beaten me 7–5.

It was so unbelievably horrible that the crowd finally stopped laughing at me, and seemed to start pitying me. I was happy to accept it. During the trophy presentation ceremony, when they presented me with my sad-assed little runner-up plate, the tournament director announced to the crowd, "He always entertains us—he always puts on a good show, and never more so than today—your runner up, Olie Wood!" I wanted to bite off his ear and puke it down his throat.

Something I've never admitted before, I tried to kill myself that night. I tried to overdose on pills, but I just ended up getting really stoned. I'd already built up quite the iron constitution by that point.

The press was unusually cruel the next few days. I'd correctly guessed the headlines of course, but hadn't even scratched the surface of the corresponding articles. I was being called a "cautionary tale" and "the poster boy for humiliation in sports." I tried to hide out, even missing a few tournaments. In fact it became difficult to even *conceive* of playing tennis again. When I finally did, though, at a clay court event in Monte Carlo, I couldn't help but hear the titters and giggles from the crowd, and I couldn't really concentrate on my game. I lost early, and they fined me when I refused to do the mandatory post-match press conference. I just couldn't face those same questions over and over, like, "Was it the most humiliating experience you've ever had to endure, Olie?" and "Do you feel like a loser, Olie?" I'm serious, they asked those exact questions.

Worse still, my knees really started to hurt. So bad in fact that I had to pull out of the next couple of tournaments. Finally I saw a doctor, and he told me I needed arthroscopic surgery on both of them. It seemed I'd ground down most of the cartilage, and without surgery might never be able to play again. I went in for surgery in April, and was off the tour for the remainder of the year.

I never really got it back after that. The knees seemed to take years to fully heal. I was in pain all the time now, but at least I was able to move. Nevertheless, for a player with a serve and volley style of game who relied on his speed, my goose was fucked, or cooked, or however that saying goes.

I started losing early and often, and even when people stopped laughing at me as the memory of my humiliation faded (buoyed whenever the networks played it as part of their yearly highlight packages, which they still fucking well do all the time of course), no one took me seriously anymore. I was able to compete at the Slams and major tournaments for a few more years, but as my ranking slipped I was forced to play qualifying matches for the big events before I found myself being relegated to Challengers, and then when things got real dire, Futures and Satellite events, the bottom of the tennis barrel.

Blink, and before you know it here I am, trying to flag down a cab at four in the morning so that I can go get rested up in my third-tier hotel to play in my third-tier tournament in hopes of pulling something meaningful out of my third-tier life. Man, looking back sucks. I had no idea how good I had it when I couldn't remember anything anymore.

March 22

Dear Portugeezers (What the hell do you people call yourselves any-way?),

As you can see from the photo your skunk is enjoying the Florida sun. He caused me quite a lot of trouble getting through the airport. Thankfully the x-ray scan showed he was hollow, or else they might have busted him wide open. And that would have been sad since we've grown quite close. But not in a creepy way. Don't worry, I'm not fucking your skunk or anything weird like that. I'm not that desperate.

Anyhow, it took some doing, but we finally found my friend Gary. He was sitting on a beach near our hotel smoking a bud with a bunch of chicks. I tried to bag a couple, but even stoner-chicks don't seem all that into me these days.

So here's the skunk doing his thing by the ocean. It must be nice for him; it's probably the first time he's been this close to an ocean, coming from Portugal and all.

March 23

So I play my event in two days. Enough time to soak up some rays and chill with Gary. Only Gary's decided he's going to walk up and down the beach preaching his version of the Word. Now, in my limited experience, Catholics aren't too big on the public preaching thing. You don't typically see some dude in a black dress and white collar standing on his soapbox and preaching to the masses—unless of course he's insane and/or the End is Nigh. It just seems, well, absurd. But Gary has never been your typical priest. And since forming his new congregation, he's been all about the pot-infused public proclamation.

Of course he gets the usual "Fuck off, man" and "Keep it in the church, dude" and of course the odd visit from those strangely comical beach police who order him to "cease and desist," but Gary's been having a ball.

"It's a fucking riot," he told me at one point. We were sitting on the sand and he was busy rolling himself a joint of course.

"You shouldn't do that out in the open, man. I mean this isn't Canada, dude. I'm fairly sure American police take a pretty dim view of toking up on a public beach. They won't look the other way like back home."

He ignored me, and continued to roll his joint in silence.

"I'm serious. We could get busted, Gar."

But naturally not only did the police not bust him, but one by one the straggling spring-breakers gravitated to the smell of weed, and before we knew it a large group had surrounded us, passing a bud around while Gary pontificated on the connection between nature and the Lord. And they all really dug it of course.

Eventually I excused myself, retreating to a dark bar where I felt a little more at ease. Now *this* was Florida as I imagined and hoped it would be this time of year. Let Gary have his throngs of

kids and his sunshine and his marijuana. There are other pleasures
in life.

Speaking of which, I've had the worst luck with chicks lately. And to make matters worse, when I actually started to score
with this drunk girl at the bar who'd probably have let me do
whatever to her, I suffered a pang of guilt. I've never had a pang
of guilt before, at least none that I can remember. This journal's
gotten way too long for me to check, so we'll just assume there
haven't been any pangs before. We'll consider me pang-free till
this point. So what the hell does this all mean then? Miranda
and I aren't exclusive, or at least I'm not, so what the fuck? I
mean here I am, alone in my room on a warm Florida night
jerking off because I feel *guilty*, like some fag. Meanwhile Gary
sits on his beach, illuminated by a bonfire, surrounded by chicks
that, if it weren't for his stupid Catholic vows, he'd have his
pick of. What I wouldn't give to have a little of that holy mojo
right now.

March 26

I've come to hate Florida. Gary's making me feel guilty about
my plan to abandon Ahmed's portable billboard for the tournament. I tried to explain that it just wouldn't work—that most
sponsors provide a shirt or a sewed-on patch or some such
thing—and he reminded me that, according to the deal we'd
made, Ahmed wasn't technically my sponsor but my *employer*. But
how was I actually supposed to play with a big cardboard sign
hanging around my neck?

"So you took Ahmed's money without any intention of hon-
ouring the deal? That blows, Olie."

"He can afford it. He was just helping me out. He didn't really
expect me to wear the stupid thing."

"I don't think he would've sent it along if he hadn't intended
for you to wear it. For you to do anything but wear it would be
to steal from him. And that's a sin."

"Yeah, well, I'm not alone in that, so spare me the
Commandments, pusher-man."

But he was right. Man, this new guilty conscience thing is really starting to piss me off. And so before my match, because I figured I owed it to Ahmed and his business, as a compromise I wore the sign around the streets of Miami so that people would have something to throw empty coffee cups and insults at as they drove past. Meanwhile I look like the world's biggest jerkoff for hauling around this stupid cheap-ass sign that reads "Ahmed's Radio Stack" (which is sure to get him sued for copyright violation eventually). I even wore it to my event, though I was told I had to take it off before the match, which came as something of a relief. At least I'd fulfilled my obligation and worn the stupid thing. Not that it mattered; I went on to lose in the first round to some Norwegian player I'd never heard of. A Norwegian. Christ. No one loses to Norwegians at anything except maybe cross-country skiing and that fruity tobogganing thing. It was a humiliating loss. I was only glad it wasn't televised, so that Ahmed didn't have to see me wasting his money and my time on some stupid trip that's netted us absolutely nothing of value.

Tomorrow I start this grind all over again, travelling west. (I think Arizona is west of here, though I should probably check a map to make sure.) This is getting increasingly difficult for me to do. Even when I do scratch up a bit of money, this "arrive, lose and move on" routine is really starting to suck the life out of me. My mind keeps wandering back to this idea that I might have to come up with something to do when all this is over. It's not just the income thing (hell, it's not like I'm making any doing what I'm doing; I'm almost through Ahmed's sponsorship dough and I'll have to start dipping into my blood money soon), it's that I simply won't have anything to actually *do* anymore. And while I'm among the laziest people in the world, and would happily sit on the sofa eating Cheetos and watching TV all day long, eventually I'm going to have to figure out what the hell the next stage of my life is going to look like.

Meanwhile, I'll make all these nasty thoughts about my future go away by dipping into the blood funds to score a little cocaine. I hear Florida is a great place to score blow. Hey, as long as it puts off all thoughts of tomorrow, I'll continue to blow my mind today!

March 27

So I'm back on the bus for what should prove to be an excruciatingly hot, sticky and long trip to Arizona. And I'm going alone. Gary's decided to stay in the Miami area a while to tend to his new flock. I can't blame him, really. Blind adoration from a gaggle of scantily clad young women isn't the worst thing in the world, I'm thinking. But I'll miss him. I was looking forward to spending some time on the road with my old buddy, but I understand where he's at. I'll think of him as I continue with this trip.

And what a shitty trip it's been, so far. I'm so hot I feel like I'm stretched on a rack on the surface of the sun, being cured like a piece of meat. Being hot is one thing, but being hot on a *bus* is another. At least it's a quiet group. A lot of older people, mostly dozing. But one thing they all seem to have in common is that old-person smell. I know it well from my time working with the elderly, but it's not a smell you ever get used to entirely. It gets in your nose like some kind of pre-death rot and you can't get it out. Anyone with a grandparent they don't see very often will know exactly what I'm talking about. This sort of sour, musty, rotten vegetable aroma. In fact this lady sitting beside me here pretty much epitomizes it. And worse, she's sleeping and her dentures have come loose in her mouth, and there's a whole other smell coming out of that orifice. Even with the window cracked there's no getting away from it. God I don't ever want to get that old. What would I do knowing that I smell like that, and that I'm physically falling to pieces with each and every passing day? (Actually, a I write this, I'm conscious of the fact that I've been told I don't smell so hot myself on occasion, and that I too am "falling apart," but I think in my case it's more of a metaphor. At least I'm pretty sure it's a metaphor. What's a metaphor again?)

I'm supposed to play another tournament in three days in a town called San Pedro. Now this is really quite typical of the Futures tour. San Pedro isn't on any map I've found so far, though

I know it's located near the border. Let's just say it's a small event, but one I was able to gain entry to, so ready or not here I come. So many of these events are located in places you'd never find yourself visiting in normal life. In fact I often wonder who actually lives in some of these ghost towns. Take San Pedro. It borders a desert and has a population of, like, five hundred. Yet someone in his or her infinite genius decided to stage a professional tennis tournament there. Why there? Because I think they're fucking with us, seeing just how far we'll go to play this stupid game. How small a town we'll visit; how poor a set of conditions we'll tolerate. And we keep doing it because we might actually scrounge together a few ATP points in hopes of earning ourselves a place in the real events in the real cities with the real modern facilities and equipment. It's one sad hamster wheel we're on, but we spin away, regardless of the outcome.

Math was never one of my strongest skills, I admit. Before I went to Toomey, I was told by one math teacher I scored the first zero she'd ever seen not counting the kids who, like, died halfway through the school year yet were still on the books, or those who never actually did any of the work at all. I actually did the work, yet somehow scored an actual zero. I believe, looking back, that I was just too smart for her class, though I do admit that math is not my strong suit. Yet even with my shitty math skills I realize what an uphill climb I have ahead of me, trying to qualify for a Grand Slam this year. The French Open is in a few weeks and out of the question. Wimbledon is in July and it would take some kind of miracle to get me there. My only hope is the US Open around Labour Day, and even that is beginning to look unlikely.

Looking over the computer rankings, I discovered two things. The good news is I'm about to crack the top 300 for the first time in three years. The bad news is I need to be ranked at least 180 places higher in order to have any chance of playing in the qualifying rounds. And that's all I want, really. I don't expect any more than that. Because playing in the qualifiers at a major would mean real money and real pro courts. The best this world has to offer. To get even a tiny taste of that again is a dream worth hanging onto. But moving up that amount of rankings in such a short span of time is starting to look nearly impossible. I must ask Gary next time I see him to run the numbers for me, statistically speaking. At what point in the year does it become outright impossible? Can't think about it now. Got to focus on this next event here.

(9:45 PM)

Ah Jesus, gross. The lady next to me is dead. We had to pull the bus over, which of course means the trip will now be even longer while they clean her out and ship her off to, well, wherever it is they ship dead people off to. And the real kicker is, they're making me sit in the same seat I was in (the bus is full), right next to the dead lady's aura. I am *so* creeped out right now. No wonder she smelled so bad. I wonder how long she's been gone. What a way to go. On a fucking bus to nowhere. Christ, I've really got to start thinking about my life and what it's all supposed to mean before I end up just like her. Talk about your messages from above. "Get your life on track, asshole." Must start taking that to heart. Must start using my time to reflect more keenly on my place in the world. Meanwhile, I've got to ride with the ghost of the denture lady all the way to Arizona. On the upside, I think it'll smell considerably better.

March 29

Most of the players are staying in the only hotel in San Pedro. Things are pretty cramped here, and it's all we can do to stay sane and not kill each other. We practice on the same ramshackle courts we'll be playing on once the tournament begins. Meanwhile the guys are hanging out, just trying to make the days go by a little quicker.

So I recently made a resolution to endear myself to my fellow players. When I was at the top of the game, most of the other players hated me because I was somewhat arrogant and seemed to consider myself too good for them. They hate me now because (I hear) they find me completely rude and utterly un-likable, not to mention totally pathetic and embarrassing. I always wanted to know what that professional sportsmen's camaraderie felt like and now, before I'm finished, I'm determined to spend some quality time amongst my contemporaries.

With that in mind then, I decided to invite myself along when the gang headed out for pizza tonight.

Once you achieve the highest echelons of the game, there aren't a whole of lot of friendships to be had amongst the players, but those still working their way up the ladder tend to be more cordial with one another. They share hotel rooms and split travel expenses, and generally find the trench warfare conditions they're forced to endure bringing them closer together. And sometimes, to blow off steam, they head out on the town together. My strategy was to hang around the courts where we train, eavesdropping on their conversations in the hopes of discovering what these kids did for fun.

"Hey, pizza tonight next town over. You in?" I heard one guy ask a couple of the younger up-and-comers.

"Absolutely," I said with a smile, striding over as though the invitation had been intended exclusively for me. "I'm all over it."

The guy making the plans—Jensen was his name—looked a little thrown. "Uh, yeah—Olie, right? Well, yeah, I suppose that would be okay. I guess you could come too."

I could feel the love, but made plans to drive out to some pizza place outside Phoenix anyway. This was exactly what I'd been looking for. Michael Zahn was there, and as he was one of the few players who owned a car, he was the one in charge. I was surprised he didn't seem either upset or startled when he found out I was coming along for the ride.

"Hey, Wood. Nice to see you, buddy," he said as I came out to meet the gang in front of the hotel. He actually seemed sincere. Maybe I was breaking down their collective resistance after all. I was really feeling like one of the guys.

Zahn drove, and the six of us carried on like old pals. It was quite the trip. Jensen said this pizza place was a little out of the way, and that very few people knew about it despite the fact it served arguably the best pizza in Arizona, so our trip took us off in a pretty remote direction. In fact, before I knew it, the pavement gave way to sand.

"We're in the desert," Zahn explained. "This place is really remote, but it's part of what makes it cool. Part of its charm, kind of like you, Olie. Don't worry, it's just a little farther."

Finally the car rolled to a stop and we all piled out. It didn't look like much to me. In fact, to be precise, it looked just like desert. "I don't get it," I said.

"It's right over that way," Zahn told me. So I started walking. Then I heard the car start up again, and when I turned around it was pulling away in a hurry.

I stood there a while, in the dark, wondering how these fuckers could leave me alone to die in the remotest part of the Arizona desert. So I started walking, hopefully in the direction we'd come from, but then I must've started going in circles or something, because it all looked the same to me.

I've been out here now for hours and I'm starting to get a little concerned. I really think I might be lost. Still, I have faith the guys will eventually see the error of their ways and come back for me.

March 30

Okay, I can't be certain, but I might be fucked. In the last day I've seen a sidewinder snake, some rocks, a few vultures, the carcass of something that looked vaguely human, and nothing else. When we drove out here it seemed to take no more than an hour and a half. Now, again, my math skills aren't the best, but I calculate that should take like maybe six hours to retrace on foot. Now obviously I've been out here a lot longer than that, and I have no idea where the hell I'm at. I could very well die out here. Not the way I wanted to go, I've got to say. I'd almost rather check out on a bus like that old lady.

I tossed my shirt a while back, and now that I'm starting to burn my nips I'm wishing I'd hung onto it, or at least tied it around my head. Now, to help keep the sun off, I've tied my pants around my head like a giant turban, but it isn't helping much. All I feel is heat.

Walking around without my shirt reminds me of just how horribly out of shape I've become of late. I tend to avoid myself in the mirror when I'm naked these days. The spare tire and bulging man-boobs are just too depressing a sight to behold. Now every time I glance down I can't help but see them. My God, getting old sucks. When I see these kids today so young, so quick and with so much of their future still ahead of them, it almost makes me want to cry out loud. But I don't of course, because I'm a man, and I'm proud.

On a positive note, maybe this little desert adventure will sweat off a few pounds, and I'll bounce back all trim and fit like I was when I was twenty-one. Yeah, right. Who am I kidding—I'm old. Just take a gander at this gut of mine.

Jesus I'm thirsty. I've taken to sopping up my head sweat with my pants and then sucking on them to retrieve the moisture, but I'm starting to perspire less and less. That really can't be a good sign considering how much I normally sweat, like even when I stagger from the couch to the fridge.

I'm also starting to get quite hungry. Man, I know it's dumb, but I really wish there'd been a pizza place out here after all. Maybe I should open one.

March 31

My pen is starting to go dry and I'm not sure if I can keep toting this journal around. I've got to get lighter somehow, and since my man-books aren't going anywhere the literature might have to go.

(7 o'clock. Maybe 8. Fuck if I know.)

It's so cold out here. Did I say it was hot before? Well it's not, it's cold. And I mean really cold, after that fucking sun goes down. It wasn't nearly this cold last night, so what gives. Who knows. I've never hung out in a desert before. You learn something new every day, I suppose.

April 1

April Fools Day? Ha! Fooled me, guys! Come on back now, y'hear?

Found a cactus. Broke it open and sucked out some nasty juice. Cut my hands on the spines. Fucking spines. Spines? Spines. Ever say a word a few times and have it start to sound weird? *Spines.* Ha. Funny.

April ?

Cactus water crappy. But can't leave my cactus. Need my cactus. Found some grass, just a little bit, tasted bad but had to eat it. It told me to, and you never say no to talking grass.

April 8

Well, I've always known I live what could be called a strange life, but sometimes I amaze even myself. God knows how many days I was actually out there, but I really did start to see things, and I'm not even sure where to begin.

I survived by sucking the moisture from a cactus, but in the process I scraped up my face and scratched my cornea on a needle. As a result I'm now wearing a patch over my right eye, possibly a permanent addition, which would mean my peripheral vision, not to mention my depth perception, is now officially fucked for this lifetime. But I survived. In a deluded state I staggered around until I came across some grass, which I proceeded to eat in order to stay alive. Then there was more grass and less sand. Then I saw an animal approaching, and I figured I was either going to die, or else I'd somehow be able to kill it with my bare hands and consume it. I readied myself to pounce, and then I realized it was a cat. In the desert. Of course I had to be hallucinating, but then the cat came over and gave me the evil eye.

Naturally it was Blanche Dowling.

I picked her up and stared at her in utter disbelief. She looked deep into my eyes, and then gave me a swat across the bridge of my nose, drawing blood. That was when I knew she was for real all right.

"How in the hell did you get here?" I croaked, my voice rusty after several days of silence. She said nothing. She just squinted at me with that token pissed-off look on her face. I put her down and she started trotting off in the direction she'd come from, opposite the beach volleyball court I was now inexplicably standing alongside. We walked a while until the grass got thicker, and then suddenly we were moving across pavement. I looked around and we were standing in the parking lot of an outlet mall. I was saved.

The volleyball players, upset this sunburned man dressed in little more than his underwear, but with his pants wrapped loosely around his head, had come staggering out of the desert and into their game, aimed some choice words at my back, but I couldn't be bothered to respond.

I'd somehow made my way to the very town in which I'd set Blanche Dowling free. She'd survived, and when she sensed me close, chewing the grass alongside a beach volleyball court to be precise, she came back to me. I've heard about animals walking across entire countries, sometimes for years, and their radar or whatever eventually enabling them to find their masters. Seems like that's what Blanche Dowling did, even if it was technically the other way around.

Cat in hand, I made my way to a hospital (and I normally avoid American hospitals like the plague) where they checked me over, and in addition to the cactus lacerations and the scratched cornea, I'm now suffering from severe sunburn, heatstroke, dehydration and a severely debilitating bout of the runs resulting from all the grass I've eaten. Otherwise I'll be fine after some rest, which I'm now getting in a cheap, rundown motel in Phoenix, having run out on my completely unreasonable hospital tab.

The kicker is, turns out there was a US Open scout at the San Pedro tournament I missed, checking out potential talent for possible wildcard consideration. I could kill. Those guys not only cost me an event and whatever money and points might've been had as a result of playing in it, but a possible ticket to the big show, which I understand Michael Zahn may now get after winning the event. Life is so cruel and unfair it boggles the mind.

But no hard feelings. These guys needed something to keep them amused, and though it didn't last too long, it was fun being part of the group. I might've done the same thing if I was their age, and I probably did when I was young. No point looking back though; got to keep my one good eye on the future. Onwards and upwards. Next event's in Macon and I'm raring to go. That is, once I get this IV needle out of my arm.

April 10

Dear Portugeusians,

I had no one to speak to today so I figured I'd send along another photo of your skunk, this time hanging out by the pool at a local motel here in Phoenix, Arizona. As you can see he's still being well cared for, and he's already seen a little more of the world than you probably have yourself, so that's good. I'm sure you're happy for him, since he's probably having a much better life than you could give him. You're welcome. Anyhow, I'll send you more pictures as he travels the world, or at least the parts of it I'll be visiting. See, I don't know how much more I'll be able to see this year since I'm desperately low on cash because this fucking sport is so hard to make a living at. Sorry, that's not really relevant to your skunk is it?

Oh, I don't know if he had a name before, but he's now called Sparky. Sparky the skunk. I think it's got a nice ring to it.

April 12

Good day today. Got the feeling back in my extremities! I was able to get out and move around a little, and even mowed some old lady's lawn for ten bucks, so I'm feeling flush and ready.

Still, I'm not sure I have enough cash left for the bus to Macon. I'm wary of hitchhiking, but I may have no other choice. And now that I have Blanche Dowling back, it's going to be all the more difficult to get around.

She's settled in like nothing happened. She's her old ornery self, paying me as little mind as possible while still managing to keep me in her sights. It's like being married to a little hairy person with a bad temper.

Speaking of which, talked to Miranda today. She's worried about me and said, "If anything really bad happened to you, I probably wouldn't even get a call. You have no next of kin. If we were married everything would be a lot easier. . . ."

She's really on about this. Not sure how I'm going to keep dodging that bullet. Of course the larger question here is why she'd want to marry me in the first place. I know I'm not exactly a catch, and the more I see of myself the more I think a woman would have to be a little twisted to want to have sex with me. Unless she was in love with me. And how that might have happened is completely beyond me.

We started off so casually. We were simply servicing each other. She was such a fine piece and I was, well, I was conveniently located at the time, it seems. Even the way we started living together was so gradual we hardly noticed: I needed a place to crash, and she was looking for some company and hated sleeping alone at night. We were just kind of hanging around each other, and after a while we started developing feelings for each other. It's only recently though that she's started talking about making things permanent, and it's the first time I've gotten a little antsy. My parents, needless to say, never got married. I never knew any of my family, so I never really got to spend time around married couples on any sort of regular basis. The only married people I really knew were Gary's parents, and since they couldn't have found anyone else to marry them, they don't really count. It's just such a weird, foreign concept to me. Like, what if I needed to have sex with someone else? I would think that's frowned upon in marriage. What's *that* all about. And what about if I want to, say, go to another city for a while, just to chill out a little? Am I supposed to like take her or ask her permission, or what? I just don't understand the whole process. Besides, would I be expected to wear a tuxedo and *go into a church*? I'm not sure I could do either. Anyhow, I pretended the connection was bad and got off the phone, but I'm going to have to see her soon enough after the Macon event. She's really adamant about this, and she's saved up enough for a pretty swanky wedding, so there's no getting out of it unless I simply walk away from her, and I'm not sure I want to do that. I really like the bitch. I might even—well, never mind. Can't even think about that right now. Got to clear the head. Supposed to be getting well again now.

You know, as I look at my reflection, I don't mind the eye patch. Kind of got a pirate thing going on, and it's actually kind of hot. I could be, like, the pirate tennis pro. It could be my gig. My shtick. That would get me on TV at the US Open for sure.

April 13

So I bit the bullet and hitched a ride with a big friendly woman driving an old pickup.

"Well, hey honey, park that ass o' yers right here," she said. "How come yer bag's movin'?"

"That's my cat," I told her. I hadn't had time to get another cage for Blanche Dowling yet. The woman, whose name was Thelina, didn't seem to think that odd at all. She had a number of tattoos, and caught me staring at what appeared to be a shaved poodle splayed across her chest.

"Lahk that one, do ya?" she asked.

"It's rather unusual."

"Ah lahk ma body art that makes ya think, ya know?"

"Sure," I said. I didn't though.

"Got any?"

"What, tattoos?" I did actually, but lied and said no. Most women, when you first meet them, don't really like to look at your dong, I've found.

Thelina was actually quite fun. She laughed a lot and seemed to really enjoy life. She didn't even bat an eye when I told her I was a professional athlete, as most do these days, which was nice.

"What'd ya play?" she asked. When I told her she just shrugged. "Never follered it much m'self. D'only sports ah foller is baseball and car racin'. So are ya famous or what."

"I used to be."

"Yeah, lahf's like that. Ah used to be a beauty queen, y'know." Looking at her, I had a pretty hard time believing that, but didn't say so. "Ah was Miss Georgia once upon a time. Men lahked me an awful lot. Ya think lahf's always gonna be that sweet, that y'always gonna be ridin' that high, and then one day it all turns to sheet." She laughed. "But ya get on and make due, dontcha? Y'accept that lahf's a bitch and ya get fat and ya get married to an asshole and he beats on ya so ya leave him and hafta start all over agin. But ya keep on getting up offa yer ass and ya keep dustin' yerself off and gittin' on yer way. Ah just farted, excuse me."

She was right of course. If we're famous or at least successful in whatever we're into, eventually we've got to realize we can't make it last forever. Eventually we've all got to get old or fat or ugly, or just plain tired, and call it a day. I took a look at my bag, at the two racquets I carry, sticking up out of the opening and wondered, Could I just hang it up and walk away? Could I just give it up once and for all and accept that it's not going to come back? Maybe. Not yet, of course—I've still got something to prove before I let them drag me away—but one day, if I'm not careful, a time will come when that decision is made for me.

"You try to hang onto it, Thelina?"

"Nah. Who's got the taam."

"Yeah, I guess."

"Y'all tahk funny. Where ya from anyways?"

"Canada. Toronto."

"Well, sheet. Ain't that sum'n? Ah got me a sister up in Halifax and they all tahk funny too. Ya know her? Pearlabell Winter? Livin' in Halifax?"

"I'll be sure to say hello."

She laughed. "You're a sweetie, sugar. Some woman better snap y'all up real quick. Charmer lahk yerself ain't gonna be 'vailable for long, this ah know."

"Yeah, someone has. Someone already has," I told her.

April 14

Thelina drove me all the way into Macon, bless her heart. We talked about a lot of things, particularly what it's like around these parts and what I should expect while I'm here. I played events in

Atlanta back in the day, but Macon's nothing like Atlanta. They seem to sense I'm different; the locals have shot me a few challenging looks already. I really hope I don't have to fight while I'm here. As I think I mentioned, the eye patch really screws with my peripheral vision and depth perception, and I wouldn't be able to defend myself too well.

I'm here ahead of schedule, so I'm taking the opportunity to practice a little. Today I tried to work on my spin. As I get older (read: slower and weaker) I tend to have to rely on spin to stay with some of the stronger players. Playing with a lot of spin is a way of neutralizing all these power hitters. It's a way a weaker player can remain in the match, and the only reason I don't lose every one of them 6–0, 6–0. Once upon a time I was a real ball-striker—I could trade blows with the best of them—but with each passing year I've had to take something off the ball and manoeuvre it around the court a little more. And the way you do that is through spin of course.

People play tennis differently. There are as many ways to play the game as there are people who play it. You can be aggressive and charge the net or you can stay back on the baseline; you can play defence and be a counter-puncher or you can dictate the play with hard punishing groundstrokes; you can chip and charge and use the drop shot and other assorted tricks or you can just plain out-slug your opponent; and you can hit the ball flat or with spin. When you hit it flat, the ball just flies hard, fast and deep. When you hit it with spin, you sacrifice some power for control. Topspin is when you bring the racquet over the ball, which keeps it from flying too long, enabling you to hit with pace as well as control. Backspin is a trickier shot, in that you hit *under* the ball, almost bringing it back towards you when it contacts your opponent's court. Backspin is nasty. It can really fuck up your opponent. You're hitting it forward, but in the process you're also making it rotate backwards, creating an unpredictable bounce. I've come to depend on backspin to stay in matches of course.

Some people hit with a lot of topspin—they're all about careful control and balance. Some people just hit out with flat shots and don't worry about control—it's all about power and domination. Then there are those of us that need to skirt convention a little and make shit up as we go—it's ugly sometimes and not exactly honest, but we've got to survive too, you know? My worry is, as I get older, I'm finding it harder to win even with backspin.

Anyhow, I'll do whatever I have to, to survive. A desperate man doesn't care what it looks like, just so long as it gets the job done. Two days until my next event and I'm going to keep practicing my backspin until I have it down.

April 19

So here's what qualifies as a shitty day. Three days ago I'm playing the Macon Futures and something starts to feel—odd. I'm playing okay—I'm losing of course but not badly, a few bounces here or there and I could've taken the first set—and I'm still in it well into the second. Then I feel more than hear a slight "pop." Suddenly my knees go all rubbery and my left one won't bend properly. I try to stick it out but I can hardly move.

Still, I had that one little record that had remained intact, and I wasn't about to let it go. In all my many years of playing this game I've never retired from a match due to fatigue, or injury, or heat-stroke, or cramps, or impending terrorist attack. No matter what's happened, I've stuck it out to the end, even if it meant playing to a humiliating loss in the process. My medical advisors, back when I had medical advisors, told me I was stupid to push through injuries, but I figured they were just covering their own asses so I ignored them. So here I was feeling a disturbingly familiar pain, but since I owed it to myself to preserve the one thing I'd remained true to all these years, I played through it. Even when I could hardly stand on my left leg and my opponent was blowing shots by me with ease, I still stood firm. I lost the second set in a blow-out but at least I went down fighting.

Problem was, even with the match over, the pain was still dancing around my knee joint. I tried to ignore it as long as I could, but that became impossible after I found myself crawling to the crapper in my hotel room. A thing like that's hard to overlook.

Desperate, I tried to work my way northward. I have a paralyzing fear of the American medical system, and I was very scared of having to visit another hospital there, especially after having skipped out on one bill already. I had no money as it was, and a US medical bill could very well have landed me in some kind of debtor's prison. They have those, if I'm not mistaken.

I looked so bad I couldn't even hitch a ride. I tried walking, but couldn't very well do that, and in the end couldn't even make it out of Macon. And so I paid a visit to a free public clinic, which basically meant a thirty-six-hour wait to get examined. The doctor who finally saw me grimaced when she looked at the x-ray.

You never, ever want to see a doctor grimace. It's never good.

"I understand you've had arthroscopic surgery," she said, and I found myself mildly turned on by the way she said it. I've always had a thing for chicks in white medical jackets, and despite the pain I was experiencing, this time in Macon proved no exception. "Looks like you've been pretty hard on your knees. This looks bad, Mr. Wood."

"Call me Olie," I said.

"Mr. Wood, you're going to need another surgery on your left knee. And I'm going to have to advise you give up this sport. Pretty soon you won't have any cartilage left, and if you keep this up you could find yourself unable to walk."

I didn't know what to say. So I asked her what she was doing later.

"And your tests have shown even worse news," she continued on unabated. "You have an advanced form of kidney disease. Actually, both your kidneys are diseased to such a degree I can't believe you're still walking around. I can't even begin to imagine the kind of abuse you've put yourself through to get to this point. You could very well be dead in a matter of two years."

My God, I thought. This is horrible. I just can't believe the knee has gotten this bad again! I told her I needed to think about it, and she gave me a cortisone shot to dull the pain.

When she stepped out of the office to write me up a prescription for painkillers, I stole some drugs from her cabinet.

Turned out they were mostly for constipation and asthma, but I was still able to pawn them off on some blind junkie outside, which earned me enough money for a bus to Lexington, Kentucky. From there I borrowed a minivan I was able to hotwire (I still retain some of the more useful skills from my childhood), which I drove as far as Lansing, Michigan before being tailed by two police cars. I abandoned the van near a public library, and together with Blanche Dowling, hid out in the Canadian Literature section where no one seemed to be and where no one thought to look for me. I remained there until closing, and then slipped into a bathroom stall when they locked up, spending the night curled up around a remarkably clean toilet with an automatic flush. It was the most time I'd ever spent around such a large collection of books, and when I slipped out the next morning I actually felt a little smarter because of it.

A combination of public buses and inspired limping got me out of Lansing, at which point I managed to hitch a ride to Detroit. The seven hours they kept me at the border giving my ass the usual going-over was nothing in comparison to the discomfort that followed, when Miranda drove down to meet me in Windsor.

"I am so fucking sick of having to take time off work, and having to spend my own money, to come get your sorry ass out of trouble," she told me in greeting. "And did you get another goddamned cat? And what the hell happened to your eye? Jesus, what's *wrong* with you?" She seemed even more agitated than usual.

She couldn't quite believe my story about how Blanche Dowling had come back to me, and she insisted it was a different cat until she looked more closely.

"Yeah that's the same lovely kitty," she told me derisively.

Miranda was prickly the whole drive home. I thought she'd be glad to see me, but instead seemed to almost wish me dead. Finally, just as we were coming into Ottawa, she jammed the rental car to the curb and turned to me with a hard look.

"Now looking at you sitting here, I can't believe I'm actually going to say this, but I have to know, and I have to know right now. Olie, are you going to marry me or not."

Well after all I'd just been through, I couldn't think of what to say. The first thing that came out of my mouth was, "How long do I have to decide?" And, well, that just didn't go over very well at all.

"Lazy-assed, ungrateful motherfucker!" she screamed, kicking me out of the car. It could've been far worse though; at least she kicked me out in the city. I walked the rest of the way home and, once there, sweet-talked her through the locked door.

"Come on, baby," I purred.

"You don't deserve me, Olie."

"I really don't, you're right, but come on. Let's have a proper reunion. I'll let you wear my eye patch."

Finally she took the chain off the door. "You know, if you weren't so fucking ugly, I'd have nothing to do with you," she told me, which is probably true unfortunately.

Things are better now though. No commitments for a week. It'll be nice to just kick back and do nothing for a bit. Besides, I need to rest and give my knee a break. I've got an event in Saskatoon next week and I need to make sure everything is still working like it should. Just nice and easy and then I'll be as good as new.

April 20

Sweet sleep. Nothing but sleep. I've missed sleeping in till three in the afternoon.

April 21

It's always so hard watching tournaments on TV, especially the ones I've won before. I lose track of time when I travel, and I was surprised to come across the Nasdaq Masters Series while flipping around the channels. I won the thing when I was like nineteen, and now here I am watching it in Miranda's fuzzy green bathrobe, sipping a cup of herbal tea.

This Andy Roddick guy is doing well. He's typical of these new young guns starting to dominate the tour: strong, with a big forehand, a heavy stroke off the ground, and a monster serve that seems to come at you from out of a tree. I hate them so much it hurts me. When I watch the top pros I can't help but wonder what the hell I think I'm doing here. I have nothing close to what some of these guys can offer, and the idea of coming up against them in some ATP event actually scares the hell out of me. I've never been frightened of an opponent before, and now a whole generation of them has me worrying. Back in the day I could stay up all night snorting cocaine off Carmen Electra's breasts, and then roll out of bed a half hour before a match and still hold my own against any of the top players in the world. Now I could spend a week in a hyperbaric chamber, eating nothing but dry pasta and tomato juice, and I'd still have my ass handed to me. Even if I somehow manage to make it into a Grand Slam before I have to call it a day, the first of these guys I face will make me piss my pants in anxiety. That's not the way a grown man should have to live.

They seem so young, these guys. So healthy and in such terrific shape. You can see the tendons in their necks pull tight when they serve, and the muscles in their forearms ripple when they slap a forehand. When the hell did this happen? Was I ever like that? I remember being young and full of energy, sure, but I don't ever remember looking like that. I don't remember striking a forehand with that kind of power and depth. Was I simply one of the best in a very mediocre time? These guys make me look like a chump. Even the lower-ranked pros make me feel old and fat and tired. Though I'm not really fat of course; I'm just retaining a little water. It happens in spring. Once I get back in the gym it won't be a problem.

Finally I got so depressed that I had to turn off the match and plug in some porn. That always has the opposite effect on me, cheering me up instantly. Oddly enough, it was one of the films Miranda made back when she was considering a career in cinema. It didn't really take though, frankly because the Canadian adult movie industry just doesn't pay what these girls deserve.

Still, she made some nice art during her brief tenure in front of the camera. The one I watched today, *Saving Ryan's Privates*, was downright lovely. If nothing else, it took my mind of the top pros with their big paycheques and their huge televised audiences and their enormous shiny trophies.

I have my share of trophies, only it's been a long time since I won any, and the last few I did win were getting awfully small in stature. I keep them on a shelf in the bedroom. There aren't as many as I remember—in fact the sheer number of trophies seems to shrink every time I take the time to look—but that shelf represents the sum total of my existence on earth, and I can't afford to dwell on its lack of size. I should count them though, and keep a running total, just to make sure they aren't actually disappearing, like someone's breaking in and stealing them and pretending they're me, Olie Wood, Professional Athlete. I'll have to remember to look the last day I'm here. It'll give me something to do.

April 22

I'm officially bored. This happens every time I'm on a bit of a layoff. I sit at home, I watch TV, I jack off a few times, then Miranda comes home and we fight a little, we make up, and then we have sex. I know it sounds fun, but it actually gets to be a bit of a grind after a while.

Gary calls what I have "wanderlust." It means I can't stay in one place too long. It's one of the reasons I find it hard to imagine being married and tied down. I'm starting to feel the pull of the road already, more so with Miranda constantly ragging on about settling down.

Wonder how Gary's doing. Haven't heard from him in a while. Hope he's happy there on his beach, or wherever the hell he is now.

April 23

I asked Miranda if she'd take care of Blanche Dowling while I travel to Saskatoon, and she blew a fuse.

"You're going to leave again, and stick me with that animal? You're crazier than you look."

"Honey, it's just so hard to travel with the cat and her carrier. I mean it's hard enough getting rides with*out* her."

"I'm this close to dumping you, Olie. You have no idea."

She's been so angry lately. I can't figure out what's going on. Then, sometimes, she just starts crying for no reason. And believe me, Miranda's no crier. She didn't cry when that customer slapped her. And she didn't cry when someone broke in and stole her TV and stereo. She didn't even cry during that scene in *Dumbo* when Dumbo visits his mother who's locked up, and she strokes his head with her trunk and rocks him to sleep in her makeshift trunk-bassinet. Jesus, that's a hard scene to watch, even now.

No, Miranda is one hard chick to set off, so something's up, something hormonal no doubt. Of course I have no idea what that actually means, but you hear enough people say it that it just seems to explain what women are all about.

Anyway, she's actually agreed to watch the cat a while, which is even more suspicious. Worse still, she then tried to cuddle Blanche Dowling. Of course the cat was so shocked to be touched by anyone, let alone Miranda, that she totally freaked out and started scratching her face and hands, kind of spoiling the moment from everybody. Even then Miranda didn't react the way she normally would have, which you'd think would involve kicking the shit out of the cat. Instead she just sat quietly, nursing her wounds.

Jeez, it could be something serious, like brain cancer. I don't know. I don't pretend to understand chicks, what with their crazy hormonal ways.

April 25

Here I am, on a train to Saskatchewan. Miranda paid for the ticket, God bless her, pooling all her available funds, and so here I sit in relative comfort on my way to yet another event in yet another town. The knee feels okay. I haven't tried playing on it, but it's had a chance to rest, so hopefully it'll hold up throughout the tournament. This'll be a good chance to put together some wins. A Futures event in Canada doesn't tend to attract too much high calibre talent from the rest of the world, so I figure I'll have a pretty good chance against the various Canadian juniors and American wannabees that even think to enter. And it'll be a nice chance to see this country of ours in early spring. Even though it actually looks more like the dead of winter with every passing station.

Fuck I hate Canada.

April 26

So I met this dude on the train who says he's an alien from a planet called Aries. Well of course he is. Funny thing is, he's probably the most interesting person I've met in ages. His name is Xarkon and he's quite entertaining.

I was starting to get bored. Plus the scenery whipping by was all the same white and grey, and it was really starting to depress me. Canada in April isn't a good thing, especially here in the hinterland, and so I'm sitting here wishing I had enough money to upgrade to a sleeping car when this bald guy plops down beside me. Barring all the moles and the spider web tattoo covering his skull he actually seems pretty normal, and he starts chatting me up immediately.

"You look like you could be from away," he says matter-of-factly.

"Yeah, I am actually. Ottawa."

"I was thinking more *away* away."

"Like what, Europe?"

"I'm getting a real extraterrestrial vibe off you."

Now you might think this was the first time someone had said that sort of thing to me, but you'd be wrong. "Sorry, dude," I tell him. "I'm from closer than that."

"Not me," he says. "I'm an out-worlder." That's right: an out-worlder. Now some might run for the hills at the sound of that, or at least the tiny train bathroom at the end of the car, but I was bored and willing to hear the guy out.

"Xarkon," I said, "tell me about your planet." And he did, sharing the details for the next two and a half hours. I've got to tell you, Aries sounds like one kick-ass place. It seems Aries is one of those free love societies. I've always dreamed about living in a free love society. I mean really, what could be better? No weird arguments about marriage; just good, solid, old-fashioned hard-core boning amongst friends. I so envy Xarkon his cool world. He offered to take me with him, but to be honest I don't know if I could handle the pressure.

Xarkon got off the train in Winnipeg, but promised to come see me play some time. I was sorry to see him go; he was such a great distraction. For the rest of the trip I tried something Miranda's always on about, this "creative visualization" thing, which is kind of like imagining good things that should be happening for you down the road. Miranda says it really works for her when the club is slow and she wants more dudes to come in.

Anyhow, to kill some more time, I started imagining myself winning matches for a change. I imagined myself ending a match on a confident forehand winner. I imagined holding up the trophy at the end of the tournament. I could see it all so clearly, me with a big shit-eating grin on my face, and the runner-up sporting that dignified loser look when all he really wants to do is cry, beat the shit out of me, and run and hide, in that order. It's a sweet sight all right. I figure, if this stuff works, I'll keep seeing those moments as clearly as I can until they actually arrive. Hell, for good measure, I also started imagining a few hot naked chicks running through the scene, those surgically enhanced Hollywood chicks I used to hang with when I was big. There are six of them, and they start jumping all over me and rubbing their hard little bodies against mine, trying to burn away my clothes with their grinding pulsating body heat and it all becomes too much for the audience to bear and they have to look away and—shit, that was pretty good. Wow. Yessir, creative visualization is definitely the way to go.

April 28

Flat. That's the only word that comes to mind as you ride the shuttle bus through the outskirts of Saskatoon. I'm reminded of my theory that Futures organizers seem to seek out the shittiest places on earth to hold their events in, just to break us down and weed out the ones who can't take it. Well I've seen and played the worst, believe me. This may be a soul-sucking place to play tennis in, but Olie Wood is up for anything anywhere anytime.

I have a day to practice, but I haven't picked up a racquet since my knee went out. I'm a little nervous, I admit, but I've got to push on through. If I don't get back on the horse I may lose my nerve, and I don't have the luxury of time to dick around. I've got to plunge right back in no matter what pain and/or humiliation may await me.

April 29

Life is unfair and God hates me. There is simply no other explanation for what's just transpired.

So I'm looking at the draw and can't help but smile a little. The average age of the players in the tournament is nineteen. Now, sure there are nineteen-year-old prodigies who have these amazing innate skills (I was one myself), but usually these kids are still finding their feet, especially in a smaller Canadian city like Saskatoon where most of the kids are born and raised. Now I may not be able to beat the top ATP players anymore, but I know I can handle Canadian kids in my own backyard. Well, okay, not exactly my *backyard*, since I live on the other side of the country, but my "figurative" backyard. Like it's not really, technically my backyard, but, like, the backyard of my country, so I know it pretty well. Even though I've never been to Saskatoon before, and for very good reason it turns out.

I drew this junior from Quebec; he must have been sixteen and all of ninety-five pounds. I laughed a little when I saw the kid, but then he looked at me and laughed a little too. More than a little, actually. So of course I had to teach this punk a lesson. And I did. I taught him how to glide effortlessly around a court, striking the ball at will, while a much older, fatter version of himself skittered around like a sick blind rat in a maze.

He was beating me senseless and never seemed to run out of energy. My knee was holding up, sure, but what good was it doing me? None. None good. None whatsoever.

Then I got angry. No theatrics like in the good old days, but my temper certainly got the better of me. A few of the officials who know me and my history seemed to tense up, but I wasn't going to do anything to anyone but myself. I was just so frustrated at my lack of speed and at how ridiculously weak I'd become in recent times. So I started hitting myself. Over the head. And I continued to hit myself over the head until I got a warning from the umpire about violence on the court. I argued that since I was the only one getting hit it shouldn't matter, but she didn't buy that and docked me a point. That only made me angrier, so I started smashing my racquet methodically against the ground. Finally I caught myself though, as I realized I only carry two racquets with me and I'd just kicked the shit out of half of them. I was docked another point for the outburst, and that was enough for me to collect myself. I changed over to my other, shittier racquet and tried to regroup. But things didn't get any better. Playing bad is one thing, but being run around the court by a teenager is the worst thing in the world. It makes you feel stupid and helpless and I got angry all over again. Things only got worse when I broke a string. I went to replace the racquet, but then I remembered how I'd broken the other one like ten minutes earlier, and I was screwed. I boldly tried to play on, but every ball I managed to hit fell to the earth like a stone. Then I got super pissed off and beat the shit out of that racquet too. Now I had no racquets. This was seemingly unprecedented, and at first the umpire didn't know what to do.

"I'll have to default you," she said. "I think."

"But I've never defaulted before."

"Be that as it may, if you can't play on I'll have to give the match to your opponent."

I stood there, helpless, in the middle of the court, not sure what to do. The entire crowd of four people was staring at me in disbelief. It was a horrible moment. Then my sixteen-year-old opponent did something no hardened pro would ever do. He reached into his bag, pulled out a racquet, and offered it to me.

"I'd hate to see it end like this," he said. "Besides, my sponsor gives me loads of them."

I fought off the desire to strike the kid, and instead embraced with gratitude such a grand gesture. I gratefully accepted the racquet and played on with new determination and life, and a funny thing happened—I continued to play horribly and lost my temper again, this time kicking the shit out of the racquet I'd been given, simply out of habit. Now even my opponent had no sympathy for me, and I ended up defaulting for not being able to continue. I offered to play on without a racquet, but that suggestion just seemed to piss the umpire off, and she waved me off the court. It was humiliating, and for something to actually humiliate me, you know it takes some doing.

I was sitting in the shitty little locker room afterwards when the kid came in to shower.

"That was one of the more pathetic things I've ever seen," he said as he stripped down, revealing an underdeveloped but oddly fit body that made me suck my gut in instinctively.

"We've all got our own style," I said airily.

"You call that a style, huh. Shit, they must've done things different back in the 70s."

"Fuck you, punk. I wasn't playing in the 70s. I was goddamned *born* in the 70s. Or at least close to it."

"Then you look like shit for your age. Might want to look into a little moisturizer or something. Your skin looks like a walnut shell."

I tried to recall which one the walnut was so as to determine just how deep a cut that was. Meanwhile he shed the rest of his clothes and jumped in the shower, as unashamed of his nakedness as I'd become sensitive of mine.

I stood in front of the mirror and checked my skin. To be honest, it's far from the worst looking thing about me. Sure I've got a few wrinkles. Probably a few more than I should have at my age, but don't they say wrinkles add to a man's character? Or is it gray hair that's supposed to do that—because shit, I've got that too. I never noticed before. When I let my hair grow long and it got a little unruly I stopped noticing the colour, but as I stood checking myself over I realized I had at least fifty of the little buggers. The young punk got out of the shower and saw me checking myself over.

"Staring at it won't make it any prettier, you know."

"I played Wimbledon, asshole."

"Sorry?"

"I played Wimbledon when you were sucking on your mommy's tit. The US Open too. Reached the final of the Australian Open."

"Oh I know, dude," he laughed. "That one's a classic. I must have seen that meltdown, like, twenty times on TV. That was pretty nasty. So what's your point?" he asked.

"I wasn't always like this, you know. I used to be one of the best in the game."

"So?"

"So cut me a little slack. Shit, I never talked to a veteran like that. No, I showed those guys a little respect," I said, though even as I said it I wasn't entirely sure that was correct.

" 'Veteran?' " he said. "I like that. Makes you sound noble or something. Most of the guys prefer 'has-been.' A little more accurate, I'm thinking."

"Suck my balls."

"Yeah, about that. Is it true you've only got one? Man, you're really a wreck, aren't you. Why are you still even *doing* this. I mean isn't it long past time you hung it up?"

"What's your name?" I asked him.

"Dylan. Why?"

"Well, Dylan, some day you're going to be standing right where I am. That's assuming you ever actually achieve something in the game first."

"Oh I will."

"We'll see. And don't be discouraged by the fact that I was the only Canadian player to be ranked in the top ten. Ever. In the history of the game. Don't be turned off by the fact that other than a few doubles players, you can count on one hand the number of

Canadian players who ever made any impression at all on the circuit. And never let yourself get down over the likelihood you'll be doomed to playing bullshit penny-ante tournaments like this one for most if not all of your career, and if you're lucky, at the end of it all, wind up looking a little something like me. Face it, bud, you may have beaten a creaky, beaten-down old nag today, but I've played against the best and rest assured, you ain't got what it takes. Sorry to be the one to break it you."

That threw him a little. "Whatever, old guy. Whatever." He made a sharp turn away from me, his dick swinging threateningly, but I saw the hint of fear I'd placed there. On his face, not his dick. I didn't place anything there. But I knew that look, that "How the hell am I ever going to make a go of this?" look that most young players get when they first try to make the leap from obscurity. I never had that look. In the early days it all came to me so easily. But this kid had the look and I smiled a little, knowing I could still ruin someone's career given the opportunity.

I felt a little better in spite of my loss until I realized I had only the one racquet left and it needed new strings, which I couldn't really afford. So I noticed one of the guys getting ready for the next match had an armful of racquets, and when he was pulling his shirt over his head I stole one and ran like hell. And it's a hell of a nice racquet as well. Looks almost custom-made. Maybe it'll help me with my next match in Victoria.

April 30

I got a call late last night in my room, which freaked me out because no one calls me, even Miranda now that she's so pissed at me. I assumed someone was busting me for stealing the racquet, but instead it was one of the ATP officials informing me that I was to report for my "random" drug test.

"But this is just a Futures event," I whined, sounding like a little kid without the slightest hint of embarrassment.

"Yet you've played ATP events this year," the guy said. "Though looking at your record here, I'm not entirely clear how that happened. . . . In any case," he said, "I've been asked to

administer your test, so I'll need you to do that first thing tomorrow morning."

Well this wasn't good. I haven't used anything of late, and that's
comforting, but I can't begin to imagine what's still lurking in my
system. I've done some things that tend to linger, let's say. Could
be a problem. If nothing else, any test I take will no doubt detect
a fairly high alcohol content from all the post-match partying I
took part in with all my friends, here alone in my room. Don't
know if that's against the rules, but it sure won't make me look
too good. And I already don't look all that good these days.

So this morning I rolled out of bed as early as I can remember—I must have been up and about by, like, 9:30—and tried to
corner some of the other players.

"Hey, buddy, can I borrow your urine?" I whispered at one. He
just gave me a look and scurried away. I tried this approach on
several others, but no takers. Finally I got a nibble from an
American named Jake Nielson.

"What'll you give me?" he asked me.

"Dunno. What do you need?"

"How 'bout a blowjob?"

"You're gay, dude?"

"Nah, but I been out here on this shitty tour a long time."

"Tell me about it," I said. "But sorry, man, can't do it. Not for a
glassful of piss."

Then I saw Dudley and thought I'd be okay. I don't tend to talk
to Dudley if I can help it. I actually try to avoid him whenever
possible. See, Dudley was an aspiring young player who once
worked as a ballboy at some of the bigger Canadian events. He
was a nice unassuming kid with a little talent, but he was a better
ballboy than he'd ever be a player. Anyway, I was playing a match
in Toronto one really hot summer day, the kind of day where you
sweat even *thinking* about playing, and as I believe I've mentioned,
I sweat an awful lot. I have no idea why. I've come to terms with
it over the years, but back then I was still struggling with it.
Anyway, I was playing the Canadian Open and I was on serve, and
when I went to hit the ball my racquet just flew right out of my

hand. It shot almost straight up and out of the court. I was worried it might hit a fan, but instead it flew into another court and hit a ballboy, which obviously wasn't as bad. Except for the ballboy of course. Dudley went from being your normal average kid to a total retard. He was physically fine, but he had absolutely scrambled eggs for brains after that. In those days of course I was quite the big deal, and no one even thought to hold me responsible—after all, I didn't *make* myself sweat like that—but I still felt bad. Dudley never did piece it together that I'd been the one that brained him, and in fact seemed to love me above all other players. Whenever possible he would follow me around like a little lost puppy, but I tried to keep my distance.

Since his accident he lives off his disability and the settlement money he received from the ATP, travelling around the country with his mother as a volunteer ballboy. And every time he sees me it's always the same.

"Hooray for Oliewood!" he screamed. "Hooray for Oliewood!" he repeated as he scampered up to me, pawing me lightly.

"Heya there, Dudley. What's shakin'?"

"Nothing is shaking on me, Oliewood. Nothing shakes on Dudley."

"Hey, can I ask a favour of ya, pal?"

"Sure, Oliewood."

"I need to borrow your pee."

He frowned and shook his head spastically. "Ooh, dunno, Oliewood. Dunno, dunno, dunno."

"Nothing weird, I just need you to pee in a cup for me. Come on, it'll be fun."

He shook his head again.

"Dudley, I really need your help here. I'm serious. I need to give the tennis people some pee, and I don't have any in me."

"Really, Oliewood?"

"Yep, really."

He considered things carefully.

"So what do you say, Dudley. Can you help out your old pal Oliewood or what."

"Well," he said, "I'll need some help with my bag. . . ."

Turns out Dudley uses a catheter and bag. Can't be trusted to piss the old-fashioned way, I guess. This, of course, presented a pretty unpleasant situation for me as we gathered in a bathroom stall, trying to figure out how the hell the goddamned thing worked. I didn't trust the piss in the bag. I mean who knew how long that crap had been hanging around? No, I needed the fresh stuff. Dudley, of course, was of no help whatsoever, and at one point got pretty angry with me.

"Not my pee-pee!" he hissed.

"Listen, I'm not trying to check out your dick, dude. I'm just trying to figure this shit out."

We struggled a while, until we discovered the needle-like thing inserted in his cock, which he was afraid to remove by himself. So I actually had to extract it myself while he groaned and shuddered in discomfort.

Finally I was able to remove the thing, and with it came a wave of thick brown piss snaking through the air and landing on my thigh.

"Nice."

"Oh jeez," said Dudley, embarrassed for me.

"Just get it in here," I said, trying to get my Styrofoam coffee cup in place.

Eventually I had enough, and after painstakingly putting Dudley back together (Ever tried to insert a catheter up someone's cock? Not easy.) and drying myself off, I hoofed it over to the office where the two ATP folks were holed up. I hid the cup in my jacket pocket, hoping I wouldn't upset the contents too much. "What would you like me to do?" I asked.

"First off, we'll need a urine sample. Then we'll need to ask you some questions."

"Piss then questions. Gotcha."

They led me into a nice clean bathroom where I transferred the contents of the Styrofoam cup to the plastic one they provided, spilling a little more on myself in the process. All worth it, I figured, when the bald guy named Bates turned his nose up at the stench afterwards. Between the shot from Dudley's catheter to this latest spill, I guess I was giving off a bit of an aroma. But then they weren't here to grade me on my aroma.

"Have you used any illegal drugs at any time in the past year?" asked the other one, Morris.

"Drugs are illegal, sir. Of course not," I replied with the most innocent smile I could muster.

"Any use of performance-enhancing substances in the past year?"

"Absolutely not. I run on pure talent and hard work."

Both guys stared at me a while, unsure of how to respond. "That's very funny," said Bates finally. "But seriously, any perform-ance-enhancing drugs?"

"No. None." In actual fact I did try a steroid-type thing a few years ago, back when I was trying to get strong enough to com-pete with these powerful young bucks that kept spilling out onto the tour. But instead of making me stronger, it only made my temper shorter and my already impressive breasts bigger. At the same time, though, it gave me a wicked sort of high, so I kept using it until my supply ran out. Bitch tits were a small price to pay for that kind of quality buzz. But I've done nothing like that in years, and thus the "No. None."

"Okay, Mr. Wood. You are aware of course that if anything in your urine sample shows us a picture that differs from your answers here today, it could result in a suspension from the tour."

"Sure. You bet."

"We should have your results in a few days. Hopefully all will be well."

"I can't help but wonder why the ATP cares about me at all."

"We share your wonder, Mr. Wood," said Bates. "But everyone gets it eventually. It's just your turn."

"Well, it's nice to feel like part of the tour again, even if it's just because I get to piss in the same cup as the top guys."

"Well, not the same cup. . . ."

"Well, I know not the *same* cup, but the same *kind* of cup."

"Actually, oddly enough they tend to use a nicer cup for the top forty players," Morris informed me.

"Can I go?" I asked.

"Sure thing. Good luck in your next event. I believe you're in Victoria?"

"Yeah, Satellite event."

"Hope you win a match or two."

"Hope to do better than that."

"That's also very funny, Mr. Wood."

God, I hate ATP guys.

May 3

Hit balls against a back wall of a school for a couple of hours today. I'm in Victoria, getting ready for my next event, sharing a room with three other guys. Boy, you really don't want to share a room with that many men. The smell is just indescribable, even without our actually doing anything.

I can't usually get other guys to share a room with me, but some of the younger guys are desperate to find a way to afford their rooms and the more they can pack in, the better, even if I'm one of the packees. They just ignore me, I do the same, and together we save a little money in the process.

I never had to experience this sort of thing when I was their age. Four, even six to a room, over an entire year in which your tennis income is maybe a thousand bucks all told. Meals split amongst the group, which often amount to little more than a pack of noodles. It's like student-living without the school. Odd to get to know it now, in my thirties. Gives me an entirely new perspective on things. Though honestly, perspective is overrated. I'd just as soon go back to the nice hotels, the big money, and the cameras trying to capture my every move. But I know those days are gone. I have to make the best of sharing a room with three guys, one of whom leaves his soiled, skid-marked underwear lying in the middle of the floor. It takes a lot for me to feel like the clean one, but I do.

It was nice to find a wall to hit the ball against today. When I was a kid, before Phil discovered me, I spent a lot of hours doing exactly that. It's where I learned all about timing and the basic construction of strokes. It's where I still feel I can hit out and hit loose, and few things feel better to a tennis player. When you play against the wall, you can hit the ball as hard as you want and any frustrations you might have just fly off toward the wall and stay there. When I was a kid, I sometimes pictured my mother tied against the wall as I let her have it over and over again, forehand, backhand, smash. A shrink would likely tell me I had issues. I'd likely tell that shrink to fuck himself.

When you step out onto a court you could be moving badly, or your rhythm could be off, or you could just be facing down an opponent far better than you. None of that matters with the wall. Hitting a ball against a wall might be the purest feeling in the world.

I was really grooving and stroking some solid forehands until I hit a shot wide and broke a school window. I ran like hell, and suddenly had flashbacks to when I was a kid. Tennis and breaking things and running like hell. That was my childhood to a T.

May 4

Awkward moment while I was warming up for the Satellite event today. I was hitting serves into an empty court and feeling pretty limber when I felt someone come up behind me mid-service. I whirled on the guy, because you never interrupt a man while he's serving. I didn't recognize him, but he seemed to know me.

"Nice serve, Olie Wood."

"Thanks," I said. "But I really need some room to groove here." I turned and made ready to serve again, but he grabbed my arm.

"Leggo my Eggo," I told him.

"That's my racquet."

"No way, dude, I bought it mail-order." I've always been quick and natural with a lie. I don't even need to think about it really; it just comes out. It's like a talent I have.

"Seriously, man, that's my racquet," he said, and now I recognized him. And yes, it was his racquet.

"No, it's not your racquet," I told him.

"Look, stop messing around. My fucking name is etched into the frame."

"No it isn't."

"It is. See, right there. Prakesh."

"I don't see anything."

"Right *there*!"

"Well that's my name too."

"No, it isn't. Your name is Olie. Olie Wood."

"No it isn't."

"Look, I know it is."

"Wood is my married name. My maiden name is Prakesh."

"That's ridiculous."

"You're ridiculous."

"What does that even mean?"

"What do *you* even mean?"

This went on for a while, until Prakesh got frustrated and punched me in the nose, taking back his precious racquet in the process.

No matter, I snuck into the clubhouse and stole another, making sure it had no one's name on it. I mean jeez, etching your name into your racquet? Isn't that a bit extreme? I mean doesn't anyone trust anyone anymore? What kind of a world *is* this?

In any case, new racquet or not, I lost my opening round match, though I played pretty well. I really feel like I'm on the cusp of a breakthrough. I really think I could've won this one had my opponent not been better than me, and that's encouraging.

Then some good news as I heard back from the ATP guys who informed me I was clean. No sign of any banned substances, though they did tell me I had a serious liver infection. Ha! Little do they know it's not even my piss! I haven't got any problems with my liver, other than the ones I already know about.

Though I suppose I ought to let Dudley know. He's here in Victoria, so it shouldn't be hard to track him down.

May 5

Could've sworn there was something I was supposed to do today, but I'm drawing a blank here. Ah well, I've got nowhere to be, so I'm going to chillax here in my smelly motel. The guys have it for the week, so I can just hang.

May 6

Still can't remember what it was I was supposed to do. But now there's a Gilligan's Island marathon on late night TV, so I gotta go.

May 7

Sadly I must leave the west coast behind as I head for Oregon. I leave knowing there was something I forgot to do, but I checked and sure enough I remembered to pack my newly stolen racquet. I said goodbye to the guys I bunked with and threw a salute to good ol' Dudley as my bus pulled away. Sometimes I do still feel that sense of connection to the people in the tennis community. Sometimes we really do look out for one another and that feels pretty damned special.

I need to win some matches in Port Widdly, Oregon or else I'm sunk. I have no money. When I get off this bus I will do so with exactly seven cents—Canadian. Once I would have found it exciting to travel around with no idea where I might be bunking down or where my next meal might be coming from, but at my age I'd kill for a little predictability. As it is, I have no idea what will happen when I step off this bus.

May 8

So I was mugged getting off the bus. Haven't been mugged in a while; forgot what that feels like. Funny thing is, they picked the absolute worst time to rob me.

"But I've only got seven cents," I told them. "Canadian."

"The fuck you do," one of them said, pushing me to the ground outside the station.

And this group of guys was big and scary. Well, okay, when I say group I mean two, and when I say guys I mean girls, and when I say big I technically mean small—kids, actually. But they had a mean, desperate look about them, believe me. And they could certainly kick, which they demonstrated for me quite willingly.

"Gimme your money!" the one with the ponytail told me.

"I'm a professional athlete!" I informed her, trying to get to my feet. Unfortunately the other one had a pretty nice leg sweep and I ended up back on my ass immediately.

"I'm so sure," she said with a sneer. "Professional ass-leech maybe!" Okay, that was a pretty good one, I had to admit. Made me laugh even as I sat there.

"What happened to your eye? Got hungry?" the leg-sweeper asked me.

"Lost it in a knife fight with a bunch of bikers," I told her. "Big ones. But I took a few of 'em down first, believe me."

"The only thing you could take down is a cream pie," Ponytail informed me as she kicked out again, this time planting a dirty white sneaker on my forehead. She tried to kick me again but I grabbed her ankle and twisted it around, hard. She fell to the ground and I bit her on the shin; she let out a very satisfying scream. Leg-sweep then tried to leap on me, but I straight-armed her, and she tumbled off the other way. The first one cocked her leg and fired off a kick at my knee, and it exploded in pain. I was able to punch her in the stomach anyway. Leg-sweep jumped on my back as I tried—again—to struggle to my feet. The pain in my knee was excruciating.

"Just give us your money!" she screamed into my ear, pounding away on my back and head. Then she dug her long black finger-nails into the soft flesh of my throat. I growled out an obscenity or two as, balancing myself on my one good leg, I grabbed her by the wrist and flung her over my head, kung fu style.

Meanwhile, Ponytail had gone for my bag and my tennis rac-quet, the only thing of value I had left. I leapt at her, batting her out of the way with an elbow. She crouched as if to spring, but I pulled out my racquet and executed a perfect backhand, laying her out cold across the sidewalk alongside her comatose partner.

I was feeling pretty proud. Not everyone can say they've been able to fight off two highly motivated attackers. For good measure, I rooted around in their pockets and found maybe twelve dollars. I don't think I've ever felt quite as cool as I did at that moment.

May 10

So I lost my opening-round match, but at least it went three sets. I feel like I'm getting closer, and I only cheated on maybe a half dozen line calls. The one good thing about Futures tournaments is making your own line calls—it's nice. But even without the cheating I held my own; a few points here or there and it could easily have gone the other way. I'm a little screwed money-wise now, but I'm feeling pretty good anyway.

The French Open is in a couple of weeks, the clay court Grand Slam. Clay has always been my worst surface, but I can hold my own against anyone but some of the Spaniards and South Americans who seem to thrive in the mud. A couple of times I reached the quarterfinals in the French. A quarterfinalist got around $113,000 back then. More now, I presume. I can hardly comprehend that kind of money though. What the hell did I do with it all? I know there was the coach and entourage I hired after Phil and I parted ways, and they sucked a ton of money out of me. A lot went to drugs and booze, and then a few lady friends helped themselves along the way. I also bought a lot of shit I didn't need, like big noisy cars and big noisy clothes. I was the one with the bling. But bling doesn't last when you aren't bringing it in. God, I could live off the loot from a French Open quarterfinal for, like, two or three years now. I can't even imagine it though.

More than the money, I miss the audience. You never realize how much you like playing for an audience until you start playing to crowds of three people, one of whom is asleep, or possibly dead. A Grand Slam audience is like this big ol' wall of people, tens of thousands of them, and you can hear their collective breath as you hit a shot that lands just inside the line, or reach for a long ball and get just a piece of it with your racquet. Every single thing you do on a court is magnified by ten thousand in a place like that. I miss the audience more than all the rest of it put together.

On the other hand, when you lose at a Futures, there's no one there to be disappointed in you. So it cuts both ways.

The kick in the ass wasn't the loss though, it's what happened after. Back in the clubhouse I was told to call Miles Aveldson immediately. Miles is this ATP official who handles a lot of the North American Futures and Challenger events. I hadn't talked to him in years.

"Olie Wood," he said when I got him on the line. "It's been a while."

"How you been, Miles?"

"A lot better than you, boy. Jesus Christ in heaven, have you looked at your win-loss record lately? Almost makes me want to weep."

"I had no idea you were so emotional, Miles."

"We have a few problems here," he told me.

"Look, man, I passed that drug test. And anything else you heard is just a rumour. An *unfounded* rumour."

"It's not your test—though I can't help but be sceptical about those results—it's your match record."

"Yeah, I'm in a little bit of a slump. But I won a couple in Europe."

"Listen, Olie. I like you. Even with all our history, you're a character and God knows our sport needs more characters. But to be completely frank, I don't see how we can continue to offer you places in event draws."

"And that means . . ."

"That means we're not going to let you play any more tournaments for the foreseeable future. There are other players who deserve those draws who might actually have the potential to do something with their game."

"You can't prevent me from playing, Miles."

"No, but I can advise tournaments to refuse you. Your ranking doesn't warrant a fraction of the events you've played in. Half the time tournament directors are letting you in for nostalgia's sake."

"I'm not sure who that would be or why they'd care, but it doesn't matter. Event directors get to decide who plays, not you."

"But I can advise them that the ATP is recommending they go another way. It will have some consequences."

"This is because of what went on between us, isn't it?"

"Olie, if it was, do you think I'd have waited this long? It's your horrendous ranking."

"You're just jealous of me, dude. Always have been."

"That's enough, Olie."

"How's your wife by the way?"

"That's *enough*, Olie! Enjoy your retirement."

Then he hung up. How rude. Not good. This could really have some negative effects on my season if I'm not careful.

May 11

Hopped a train this morning. I've never done that before. Felt like some kind of hobo or something. It's a freight car travelling up through British Columbia before heading east. No idea how far east, but the further the better.

May 12

Dear Portugs,

Once, a few months ago, I was experiencing some hard times. And people in hard times sometimes need to steal to stay alive. So please don't judge me, and please try to understand.

What I was after was beer, which they sell in corner stores here. Long story short, the old Asian woman running the store caught me trying to walk out with a case and pulled a shotgun on me screaming, "You no beer here! You no beer here!" and I dropped the case and ran. But feeling like I'd invested so much in the exercise already, and not wanting to leave empty-handed, I grabbed some crap as I ran, not realizing until later that most of it would be useless to me, except of course the beef jerky. I love beef jerky. Other than that, though, all I was able to grab was a cheap point-of-purchase Polaroid camera, a couple of books of stamps, and an "America—Love it or Leave it!" key chain. Now, since I don't actually own any keys, I tossed the chain, and since I don't know anyone I'd ever send a letter to (besides the occasional one to yourselves, that is), the stamps were pretty much useless to me, and after taking a few token pictures of my girlfriend's tits, even that got old pretty quickly. When I do steal, I tend to do it blindly, and as a result end up with a lot of garbage. So I want to thank you for helping me put to use both of the things I haven't thrown away from my big Oregon crime spree. And accordingly, please note the picture of Sparky hanging out in beautiful downtown Port Widdly! You'll notice he's enjoying the one public bench they have here, waiting for the one public bus on the one paved street that makes up "Downtown." You see, when it comes to these sorts of towns, I've experienced more than my share. I've played every butt-crack in North America, and plenty in your part of the world too and really, they all look alike. You start to feel like the weight of all these lost days will eventually come crashing down on your head, killing you instantly. That's the life I chose for myself though. So don't feel sorry for me.

Anyway, Sparky's well cared for, and I'm sure he thinks of you a great deal. Oddly enough, though I haven't actually met you, I do too.

May 13

Border issues. The train was forced to stop for inspection, and so I hid out in a car full of some of the most hardcore porn I've ever seen. And trust me, I've seen my share. Actually, the car was full of ant traps, crate after crate of them, but when you hide in a giant crate of ant traps and muck around a little, you oftentimes find porn. Don't ask me why. Anyway, it was magazines mostly, but we're talking crack whores taking on entire barnyards of animals type stuff here. Not pretty, but then there's an audience for everything, they say. They do say that, don't they?

Anyway, I crouched down low as the car door slid open. I could hear muffled voices and footsteps as one of the crates was pried open.

"Ant traps. Why's it always ant traps?"

"Check another one," another voice said.

"Ant traps. A whole lot of fucking ant traps—wait."

"What is it?"

"Uh, nothing. Let's move on. You go ahead, I'm just going to replace these lids."

Before too long we were on our way again, and I slept a long time. I didn't dream; usually I don't. On those occasions I do dream, I tend to remember them pretty vividly, but usually my mind doesn't shut down enough. When I was a little kid, I learned to sleep really lightly, just in case. To this day it doesn't take much to rouse me. For example, the sound of someone taking a crap in my train car.

"What the fuck?" I shouted at the ratty-looking dude continued to defecate in the corner.

"Wasn't sure you were alive," he said, "sleepin' s'long and all."

"Christ, do you have to do that in here? It's gonna stink like hell."

"Can't help it. Gotta go when nature calls. And ain't no toilets on this car. Ain't like it's the goddam dinin' car."

"Where'd you come from?" I asked.

"Slipped in after the border guys checked out. You were sleepin' like a baby in your crate of skin mags there."

"Well I might puke, so you're warned."

"Ah suck it up. Worse things in the world than a little shit. 'Cides, you ain't gonna be on this here train forever."

"No, thank God."

"Where ya headed?" he asked, finally yanking up his pants.

"As far east as this thing'll take me."

"That so. I'm just lookin' for a nice place to settle down in is all. I'm a Canadian. Tried my luck in the States, but it ain't got a lot to offer the likes o' me."

"Yeah, well, same here."

He actually wasn't a bad guy. Called himself Elmo. It was better having someone to talk to. Helped take my mind off the awful stench now permeating the train car.

He asked what I did for a living and I told him.

"Professional athlete, eh? Can't imagine the sport the likes o' you might play for money. Professional tiddlywinks maybe," he ventured with a wheezy laugh.

"Tennis."

"Eh? Girl's game."

"I used to make millions a year at it."

"Where're your millions now, Professional Athlete?" he laughed.

"Hard times, dude."

"To be sure. They happen to us all from time to time. Yeah, to be sure." He seemed sad suddenly. "Used to be vice president of a bank back in Hamilton," he eventually went on. "Made me a mint at that racket."

"You're a long way from banks, old man."

"Sure as shit. Shot all my money up my nose and in my arms. You make your mint when you're young and you never learn no responsibility. You never learn no limits. Fucked me up good. Right some good, let me tell you."

"And now you're here taking a shit in a train car."

"That I am. It's the one activity that truly binds us together as a society. Lowest common denominator. Got a woman?" he asked.

"Yeah, I do. Good one actually."

"Well you should be gettin' a leg over her right now, not talkin' crap with the likes of me."

"I wish I was, believe me."

"So what're you here for?"

"My tennis. My career."

"Some career," he told me. "A guy like yourself's got no business leaving a woman to come out here ridin' the rails and playin' tennis. Gotta think, man!"

He was right of course. "Don't know what else I'd do," I mumbled.

"You got two hands, two legs and a dick, don'tcha? Well you combine that with a bit of brains and you're all set. That's all you need to make a good go of it."

"You mean like you."

"Ah, you laugh but I'm happy. I'm doin' my thing. But I'll tell you somethin' for nothin'. If I had me a bird back home, or even a home for that matter, I'd be there and a damn sight happier still. You dig?"

"Yeah, I dig." Actually I had no idea what he meant, but I liked the guy. Elmo was one of the better travelling partners I'd had in a long time. He smelled like crap but he had a lot to say, and a lot of what he said was actually kind of interesting. He told me all about his travels, some of which made mine look like a spring holiday. He told me about his downfall, and how he'd socked just enough money away to keep himself alive. He lived mostly hand-to-mouth, but still had a bit put away, enough to prop himself up now and then. I couldn't help but admire his unconditional acceptance of life. Made me think of all the things I ought to be thankful for.

Elmo seemed to like me too. "You're a good egg, Mr. Wood," he told me shortly before we pulled into the outskirts of Moose Jaw. "I like people who persevere. There ain't too many of us left, but those of us who are left, we shall inherit this good earth. I get off here," he told me as the train came to a clunking stop.

And that was the last I saw of ol' Elmo. I hopped trains until I got home to Ottawa, starved and sick. It's not the best way to travel, and I can't say I'd recommend it, but it did get me home. I don't think I can do this much longer though.

May 22

Home. Fed and rested and feeling much better. Looking forward to settling back in with my lady a while.

May 23

The day started out so well. It was the first truly nice, truly spring-like day of the year, and the sun was warm as I practiced my backspin on the local public court.

It's good to be home. I missed Miranda more than usual, probably because I didn't get laid the entire trip, and it's great just to see her, even though she really doesn't look very good. She's put on a lot of weight since I saw her last. My mistake of course was commenting on it this morning.

"Fuck you," she told me when I suggested she get out and walk a little more. "You don't know the first fucking thing, do you. I'm *pregnant*, asshole. I was just looking for the right time to tell you."

Well now, what do you say to that? Believe me, it's like nothing you've ever heard before. It certainly sent me reeling, let me tell you. Oh, and I learned something else you should never, ever say to a woman at a time like this: "Is it mine?"

Well I'd rather not go into too much detail of what transpired next, but I will say that the two fingers she dislocated were a small price to pay for my indiscretion. Right now I'm in the emergency room having them taped up after being reset with a horrible "snap." Miranda feels bad though, and she's crying a lot.

"I'm so sorry, baby. I don't want our child being born into a violent household. I feel so *bad*!" But then, just as passionately: "Dumb-ass! Don't make me yell in front of the baby!"

It's going to be a long however-many months.

May 24

I didn't sleep at all last night. It's weird seeing the sun come up, and while it's obviously beautiful, it's also a little unnerving when you realize you just went an entire cycle without sleep.

A baby. *My* baby. I have no idea what that means. Even writing the words down doesn't seem to make sense. It's like I'm writing random words on a page that have no relation to one another. I might as well be writing "hotel" and "flamingo." Or "snow" and "ball." Oh, well, right. Anyway, you get the point.

It's one thing to imagine what having a kid might be like, but it's another thing entirely to realize it's actually happening now. I'm not happy. Not happy at all. Oh sure, in an ideal world it would be nice to have a little daughter around who thinks the world of her old man, or a son I could teach tennis to while we bond over beers in the backyard, but knowing my life and my world, it would more than likely end up being a little crack whore of a daughter or a convicted sexual predator of a son. The risks are really high, especially if you consider where it is I come from and how close I sometimes find myself to being back there again. I mean what do we do when Miranda gets too old to take off her clothes for money? Or I'm too old to chase a little yellow ball around a glorified playground? We're just a couple more bad decisions from that shitty little apartment I spent my first few years in.

On top of that, I quite simply can't imagine being any kind of father. With the reality of the thing thrust in my face, it rears up even clearer: No one deserves to end up with Olie Wood as their Dad. This poor little kid—Jesus Christ.

But in the interests of stabilizing Miranda's ever-decreasing sanity, I've put on a brave front.

"It's good news, baby," I whispered as we went to bed that night.

"We're going to raise this baby right," she whispered back.

We discussed our options, and she said she'd be taking time off from dancing in a few weeks. She's going to ask Paulo, the guy who owns the club, if she can start tending bar after that. Might be nice actually to have my girlfriend doing a job that doesn't involve her showing her vagina to strangers.

"I think we ought to get married now that the baby's on the way," she told me. Christ, I hadn't even thought of that. Marriage is yet another thing on my growing list of things I definitely don't feel ready for.

"We so don't need to bother with that conventional horseshit," I tried.

"Sometimes I feel like a little conventionality might be nice."

"It's a racket."

"You know, it might be, but I don't really care. It's something I'd still like to do. I'd like this baby to have the same name as its parents."

"Oh. Right. We'd have to name it."

"Yeah we'd have to name it. What, did you think we were going to call it 'You'?"

"I actually hadn't thought about it."

I was thinking LaShawn if it's a boy."

"Lovely."

"Or Crystal if it's a girl."

"Even better."

"Crystal Wood-Escobar. Hmm. Crystal Escobar-Wood. Maybe just Crystal Wood. See, we really should get married and share the same name. It's so much easier."

"Sounds like a hooker."

"Excuse me?"

"Crystal Wood sounds like a hooker or a porn star. We're so fucking low class it's making my teeth hurt."

She just lay there in silence. I felt like shit, but didn't know what to say to make things better.

"I don't think we're low class," she said. "I think Crystal's a classy name. Sounds like a princess."

I sighed. "I'm sorry, baby. You're right. A princess is what we'll have. I'm just wound up about it all. It's just so much information to take in that it's going to take a little time is all. I'm sorry. Really."

"Okay," she said quietly. Now, in all the years I've known Miranda, she has pretty much never said anything quietly. It's unsettling, and I braced myself for the imminent attack.

But it never came. She simply went to sleep. I really don't deserve Miranda or this little baby.

I need to get away for a while, I've decided. There's a tournament in Mississauga, outside Toronto, next week. Even the Miles Aveldsons of the world can't keep me out of the smaller Canadian events. These ones are so tiny they make even Olie Wood seem like a big fish, and the Canadian pool of decent players is so ridiculously small that they practically can't refuse me. Still, as my career winds down, I hate to think of being relegated to playing only a few Canadian events. And there's no way I can get into the qualifying rounds of the US Open playing just this handful of tournaments up here. I have to find a way around Aveldson and his arbitrary rules. In the meantime, I need to smooth things over with Miranda before I can hoof it out of here.

May 26

So some clashes are occurring. Miranda keeps trying to get me excited about the impending birth, and I'm finding it increasingly difficult to fake enthusiasm. God love her for trying, but there's only so much I can do here.

"Would you like to go shopping for onesies?" she asked me this morning while I was trying to watch Springer.

"I have no idea what that is."

"Like little bags you put the baby in before they wear proper clothes? Like when they're really little?"

"Yeah . . . it, uh, feels maybe a little early to be thinking about that, doesn't it?"

"It's not too early anymore. From here on out it's never going to be too early again."

Everything she says now has that air of inevitability to it. Words like "every," "never" and "forever" keep popping up, words that really make it seem like a permanent kind of thing. Which I suppose a kid will be. Yikes.

"I love how my body feels so alive. I'll never forget this feeling. It's making me feel more like a woman all the time," she just said, though I'm not entirely certain she was actually talking to me. No, if anything, she's talking to her stomach again, which is exceedingly creepy if you ask me.

She's negotiated a new gig at the club. For the next year or so she'll be tending bar, though she'll still dress skimpy for a few more months. Some of the dancers there are fat *without* being pregnant, and they're taking everything off, so Miranda ought to be able to get away with a skirt and halter-top for at least a couple of months. She performed her final set last night; I went to watch and show support. She still moves pretty well, even with the baby in there. But there were no lap dances, I made sure of that. That'd be pushing it a little.

She seems really happy about her new gig. She certainly never minded her old job, but I think being a mother makes her feel like she shouldn't be batting men's faces around with her boobs. She's really quite traditional.

She keeps asking me if I love her. It's actually starting to get annoying. But I do, I really do. It's just I'd rather not have to keep telling her every fifteen minutes.

"I just want to make sure," she tells me. "You seem so, you know, distant. Every time I try to look you in the eye you seem so far away."

"That's because I only have one good eye. It makes it hard to focus."

"So then you do love me?"

"What do you think?"

And so back and forth we go. A man really doesn't need this crap. No, what a man needs is to be left alone with his thoughts. Better yet, a man needs his allowance from his girlfriend so he can go drinking at another strip club.

May 27

I haven't been able to practice. The weather is great and the days are getting warmer, but every time I step out on the court all I'm able to think about is my life careening to a sudden stop.

I don't enjoy this game anymore. I go through the motions now. I hit the ball and don't really care where it ends up. I'm so depressed I can hardly get out of bed in the morning.

Though I did have one nice moment today. As I was warming up on the court, an old guy came by, looking impatient.

"What's up, dude?" I asked.

"My partner seems to have stood me up," he told me. "Not for the first time either. Asshole."

Assuming he was talking about his friend and not me, I asked if he wanted to rally for a bit. He looked me up and down and smiled, "Why not?" We rallied for a while and I got a little winded. I hate what's happened to me.

Anyway, after a little while he said, "Want to make it interesting?"

"What you got in mind?"

"Twenty bucks?"

Now I didn't have twenty bucks. I didn't have twenty cents, but I figured this felt too much like old times to pass up, and if he beat me I could always just run away. So we had ourselves a little match.

You can look at it two ways: a professional tennis player went three close sets with a guy twenty years his senior, and it should have been a blow-out and the so-called professional is a joke; or, on the other hand, an out of shape, formerly talented tennis player pulled his act together long enough to push a pretty good club-level player to the limit.

We went back and forth a long time. It was a pretty intense match. The guy didn't like to lose a point, and his anger and intensity made each game sweaty and tight.

It went the distance, but I finally took him out. I was an exhausted wreck afterwards but I won, and that's what counts. I was so happy I did a victory lap that reminded me, a little unfortunately, of my horror show at the Australian Open all those years ago, but I kept it up.

The guy was pissed off losing to the likes of me, and pitched his racquet over the fence in frustration and disgust. He hemmed and hawed about having a sore back and the sun being in his eyes, but eventually coughed up the twenty. Hey, that's more than I would've done, believe me.

As I walked home I was filled with a funny feeling, however briefly. I know I just barely beat some old guy, but it didn't matter. Too often I forget what it feels like to win, and even a half-assed win like this one made me feel new again. It doesn't take much at this stage of my life, I suppose, but it doesn't matter. Today I was a winner, and twenty bucks richer for it as well. I was also reminded of why I started to play this game in the first place, that *feeling*. That unbelievable feeling you never get anywhere outside a competitive arena. Suddenly I wanted to get back out on a professional court in a professional match against some real professional opponents. All at once I felt ready again. But then I got home and saw Miranda all fat and happy and the feeling disappeared, and I'm back to feeling miserable again.

May 29

So I'm practicing again. I still have a few days to get in better shape. I'm up against the clock now, true, but I'm feeling determined. Miranda did her part to bring me down this morning though by saying, "Now here you go again, getting all revved up. I've seen this so many times before. Just don't get bored again and quit; I'm so sick of that. I hate to see you lose your spirit every time things get tough." But for once I didn't let someone else's opinion distract me. I'm determined to pull my shit together and make this work.

I tried some deep knee bends to warm up, but I heard an awful lot of popping and got scared and had to stop. So then I tried some sit-ups, but the handful I actually managed were really hard and hurt like hell, so I figured some light running might be more my speed. I was able to do that for a good fifteen minutes and felt a lot better. I spent the rest of the morning working on my serve, which I think was a real help. I was even able to land a few.

Funny thing is, when I practice, I see the one thing that never really goes away. My talent. It's in there somewhere, sometimes just barely peeking out, but it's in there regardless. I know I *can* hit a deep crosscourt forehand with power; I just can't seem to make my lousy body *do* it right now. But I feel it in my bones that the shot's there, waiting to come out. I know how to execute the shot; I just need the ol' Olie Wood to execute. See, that's one of the reasons I still do this. If I actually lost my fundamental abilities there'd be no reason to keep going. But to know it's just a matter of training and conditioning and focussing helps a lot. I know on some level I can get it back, and it all starts here as I hit twenty-five crosscourt forehands with some pepper and a few finally go in.

May 30

Starting to feel ready for Mississauga. The shots are coming and I get a little less winded when I'm running. I'm feeling pretty good and focusing on the tournament. Miranda, of course, keeps going on about this baby business, but I remain focused on what's important.

Speaking of which, when I was combing my hair this morning I nearly fell on my ass when I saw how much came out in the comb. I can't figure it out. Something's happening where I can still grow my hair long and thick in the back, while my hairline creeps steadily back across my forehead like a gradually receding tide. It's not a good look for me, I have to admit. Maybe I'll start wearing a hat. Or stop wearing the headband. Whatever the case, something's got to give.

June 2

Just off the bus and feeling fine. A day to warm up, with my first match to follow. I stepped on the scale last night, and while I won't divulge my weight (because it's no else's business, quite frankly), I will say I lost three pounds in the last couple of weeks. Good for me.

This motel ranks amongst the worst I've ever seen, and that's saying something considering some of the places I've holed up in. But it's all Miranda could afford to spot me after bus fare. I promised to pay her back with my winnings, and you'd better believe I'm coming back with some winnings.

One of the nastier by-products of the gradually improving weather is all the newly hatched insects. My room seems to be a nest of some sort, and the little critters are just now springing to life. It's not the flies and maggots I mind so much, and hell, even the cockroaches are okay—almost like old friends, really—it's these big, weird, beetle-like things that kind of freak me out. It's actually hard to go to sleep, what with all their scurrying about.

June 3

Mississauga Invitational Futures tomorrow. I'm checking out the draw and feeling pretty good about it. First round I've got a new kid I've never heard of, and after that it doesn't look too bad until the semi-finals. I could actually do some damage here.

I like playing new kids because they're usually so piss-nervous. If there's one thing I am, it's calm. Well, okay, maybe not calm so much as composed. I like the sound of that better anyway. I never get nervous, really. When I was younger I always knew what I had going on, and when it turned out I didn't have it going on quite like I thought I did, I'd already been around so long that nothing phased me. But most new kids are wrecks until they get a couple of matches under their belts.

So tonight I'm in a local bar called Smiley's and a chick comes up to me. I'm sucking back a couple of shots, steeling myself for tomorrow's match, when she starts to hit on me. That doesn't happen as much as it used to. I mean the chicks still dig me—like a lot, actually—though maybe they don't hit on me with quite the frequency they did before. But this hottie here is a combination of my two favourite things in women: sexy and drunk.

"My friends tol' me to come over here," she slurred.

"What excellent friends you have," I told her.

"They dared me to flirt wi' you. Said I wouldn't have the guts," she burped. Now I've had that effect on women before. Sometimes they get really nervous around a professional athlete. "They said I was'n drunk enough to talk to someone like you, but I tol' them I sure as shit *was*," she continued, and I liked where this was going frankly. This chick was totally into me. "So here I am, talking to you, 'cause I am the dare *queen*. No one ever fuckin' dares me and has me, like, not do that shit."

Now by "talking to me" she obviously meant something completely different. And I can honestly say that the fact she was so sloppy and drunk did give me pause, however briefly. I do have standards, see, but thankfully they weren't getting too much in the way presently.

"So what do we do now?" I asked.

"Let's go to my car," she told me.

And so off we went. Only my legs felt a little heavy. It's like they didn't want to go along. Shut up, legs, I said. I'm in charge here.

"Whasa matter, old guy?" she asked outside. "Afraid o' lil ol' me?" And with that she started laughing hysterically and fell to the pavement in a heap. This was going to be easy. I tend to do a lot better with chicks when they're falling down and/or passing out, believe me. But even watching her flop around in the parking lot, which I normally find totally hot, didn't feel all that attractive suddenly. I kept picturing Miranda at home with our baby swimming around inside her like some kind of fish, and my desire for sexual conquest went right out the window. I honestly can't remember a single time in my entire life that I've lost my desire for sex. Like, never. But here I was, actually feeling bad for this chick. I almost thought of helping her up, but even that didn't interest me. Something was making me go back to my scary room alone to drink seven mini bottles of Old Viking vodka, and that's exactly what I did. If nothing else, it'll help me get some good solid sleep for my match tomorrow.

June 4

Okay, so not my best day ever.

Where to begin? Shit. Some days you just know will stay with you forever. On the plus side, I did play a great match. Not too often can I say that anymore, but I did genuinely play well. I was serving well, I was moving the kid around a little, and my fore-hands were solid and effective. I took the first set in twenty-five minutes and rattled the kid something awful. I took the lead in the second, and then some bad shit went down. And I mean that literally.

Okay, I'm not proud of this, but it's not like it's the first time it's happened, and it's not like it doesn't happen to everybody. I need-ed to let one rip. I was in such bad shape from last night's booze that I was gassy, and it can be quite uncomfortable running around a court when you're gassy. So I figured I'd release one of those nice controlled silent farts. Only when I went to do it, I actually—well I believe the term is "shit myself." When some-thing like that happens, your brain kind of short-circuits. It's hon-estly not entirely sure how to compute what's just transpired. I mean I've shit myself before. Plenty of times. But doing it on the court? Not cool, it turns out.

There are no bathroom breaks in a Futures match. I might've been able to beg off at the end of a set, or even, if my opponent was really cool, on a switchover, but not in the middle of a game. I had to play through, and let me just say, it's not a good feeling. Especially if you have to, say, make a *lunge* for a backhand that's just out of reach. Now there's a feeling you'll remember the rest of your life.

I actually got a little used to it after a while, but it was still a crappy feeling by and large.

It wasn't the worst part of my day. No, that title had to go to what transpired next. I was two games away from scoring my first win in ages when I came into the net to retrieve a drop shot, and the load in my pants shifted in a really uncomfortable, distracting way. It caused me to lose my balance a little on the full run and I kind of, well, flew off the court. I crashed headlong into the net of the next court over, causing it to fly off its post. The cord that holds the net to the post whipped up and, well, things definitely deteriorated after that.

Okay, so if you've ever seen a televised tennis match, you've seen these really beautiful, well kept courts. The nets are removed in case of rain and kept in perfect shape. However, on the shittier— sometimes public—courts we play Futures on, things aren't always held to that high a standard. For example, the cord that attaches the net to the post is usually a wire wrapped in some kind of plastic casing. And after years of neglect several different things can happen: the nets can develop holes, cracks can develop on the courts, and the plastic casings on the wire cords can come off leaving bare, sharp and, as it turns out, pretty dangerous wires exposed.

At first I didn't notice anything out of the ordinary, though I was a little embarrassed as I got to my feet and slumped back to my own court. But the handful of people in attendance were looking at me strangely, and I winced at the notion they'd some- how realized I'd shit myself. My opponent was supposed to serve, but he wasn't moving at all. He just kept staring and then, even- tually, pointing.

"Shut up, just play," I yelled, waving him off. Only as I waved, a large spray of blood arced out from my left hand, painting the court.

Well I'd never seen anything quite like that before. I stared at my hand, trying to figure out what was wrong, but couldn't quite put my finger on it. Finally my opponent pointed out, "Your fingers are missing!" And sure enough, they were.

It was the first two fingers on my left hand, and they were nowhere to be found. Or to be more precise, they were actually to be found on the ground under the net of the court beside us. Seems the wire whipped up so fast that it sliced cleanly through my hand, taking with it two of my favourite fingers in passing.

My first reaction was pissed off (that qualifies as a reaction, right?). I was so close to winning this thing—finally—and now this motherfucking finger thing was going to derail me? Well not if I could help it.

"Play on!" I barked at my opponent, now looking a little green at the opposite end of the court. A crowd started to gather as tournament officials descended upon us. I didn't help the situation when I waved again, sending another stream of blood arcing across the court.

"You need to get to a doctor," my opponent said.

"Yeah you'd like that, wouldn't you? Well no dice. Serve, fucker!"

"Mr. Wood," said the tournament director, standing courtside. "You have to get to a hospital!"

"No way, you can't make me default. Now come on, punk, serve!"

"But there's, like, blood all over the court," he said weakly.

"That's my business! Serve!"

"Seriously, Mr. Wood," urged the tournament director, "I need you to get off the court and straight to a hospital. I'm not going to be liable for—"

"Back up, man," I said as he moved onto the court. "Hey, interference from tournament officials!" I pointed out. "I should get a default win! You can't come out here!" I scooted away as he tried to grab my shoulder. Soon a couple more tournament guys were trying to grab me, but they couldn't catch me, until finally my opponent barfed on the court. "I get the default! That dude's sick!" I yelled, but it was suddenly getting harder to speak. I couldn't project my voice at all, and my eyesight was also starting to get a little wonky. "Not feeling so good," I muttered, slipping in a pool of my own blood just as two guys tackled me. I'm not entirely sure what happened next, though I do recall an ambulance coming to get me.

July 21

Nearly two months. Hard to get back into the flow of trying to keep track of my life again. Where to start?

Well I'll start by saying: Hell of a way to spend the summer! I've basically been living the life of a househusband this past little while. Miranda even bought me a goddamned apron, which sucks mightily.

I'm only able to write this because I'm right-handed. In other words, they weren't able to save the fingers. They tried to reattach them but it didn't take, or so they say. So now I'm a deformed freak and life suddenly has a few more question marks. Meanwhile I watch Wimbledon on TV. I get to enjoy the sight of Lincoln Holmes playing through to the quarterfinals, and listen to the commentators speak about him as the Next Big Thing. I used to be the Next Big Thing. Now I'm the Big Deformed Has-Been.

It's getting used to the simple things that's proving the most difficult. Any time I reach out to grab something with my left hand, I drop it. It feels like my fingers are still there, but trust me, they aren't. I just thank God for three things: 1) I wipe my ass and brush my teeth with my right hand, though not necessarily in that order; 2) I jack off with my right hand; and 3) I play tennis with my right hand.

Now Miranda would chew my ass out if she heard me even mention tennis, but it's the most important of all (okay, maybe a close second to #2). I know what you're thinking: Is he nuts? Here he was barely getting by as it was, and now he's talking like he could actually *play* again? Well, yeah. See, the only thing I need my left hand for is tossing the ball in the air on my serve, and I've been practicing. Now I haven't actually *tried* to serve—hell, I haven't picked up a racquet in six weeks (speaking of which, those petty little assholes recorded my last match as a loss/default; I may sue)—but to be perfectly honest, I don't feel like my game has to suffer at all for this.

Oh sure, it looks terrible. They botched the stitching and the scar looks ugly. But I don't see why that would have any effect on the way I play tennis.

Miranda wants me to heal fully and then get a job. She suggested I be a bouncer at her club. She figures I might look scary with my missing fingers, like people would think I lost them in a knife fight or something. Not how I wanted to end up, bouncing in a titty bar. But then it is what everyone would have predicted for me growing up. I have to say, I really loved being able to prove people wrong back when I was on top of the world. There I'd be in the back of a Rolls, doing a line of coke, getting sucked off by some young starlet on my way to the ESPY Awards where I was up for Best Newcomer in Sport or some such shit, and all that would be going through my mind was, "If only they could see me now." Even when things started to go bad for me, part of what kept me going was knowing people would enjoy seeing me fall apart just a little too much. I've seen the looks I get from people who knew me growing up. More than anything else, I hate knowing how much they must be enjoying my demise. But then I know I still have it in me to wipe the smirks off their faces. Just one more big score and they'll be all like, "Wha?" That's all I want.

And the baby is getting closer and closer. And I feel more panicked than ever. Miranda loves the look of me cleaning up around the house and cooking for her. (I'm good with eggs. Oh, and pasta too. And toast. And I can make frozen juice with the best of them. I got mad skillz in the kitchen, let me tell you.) I think she has this dream of the perfect little family all settled down and happy and I've never wanted it less.

There's a small tournament in Muskoka next week, a tiny little thing that's considered a kind of warm-up for young Canadian players. It could be a possible comeback venue. I talked to the event director and he offered me a wildcard (he always found me amusing and thinks I'd add some character to the event if nothing else—probably nothing else), only I'll have to make up a reason to go or else Miranda might blow. Maybe I'll say I'm being head-hunted by a big Muskoka company. She might buy that.

July 22

She didn't buy that. She knows why I want to go to Muskoka and thinks I'm nuts. Only instead of freaking out and hurting me, she just sat there looking sad. I hate more than anything to see her sad. It's so much easier when she takes a shot at me or shouts. But I've got to go. I can't sit around like this forever. I mean I'm already starting to go nuts. It's bad enough when I can't be out there earning my own way, but a lot worse when I have to sit and watch people like Lincoln Holmes have his Grand Slam break-through at the holiest shrine in the sport. Fuck that. Now Muskoka might be a long way from Wimbledon (I looked it up on a map, and it is), but I've got to get back into this thing some-where, and it's as good a place as any. I feel bad for Miranda, but it's what I have to do. If I can just get myself back on track it'll all be worth it, and then Miranda will appreciate how hard I'm try-ing to keep this thing together. I was getting so close when I had my finger accident, and I'm still close. She's just got to let me go and try.

July 25

Man, this Muskoka sucks. Boringtown is more like it. This country seriously blows, and if my girlfriend wasn't here I'd so take off for somewhere cooler. Even the shitty little towns seem that much shittier and littler here than in, say, the States or Europe. Though Canadian buses seem a little cleaner. So I sup-pose that's something.

I notice I've lost a little weight during my layoff. I caught a glimpse of my reflection when I walked out of the bus station, and I was looking pretty slim, I must say. I tend to collect my fat upfront, on my gut and in my face, and though my face still looks kind of puffy, the gut is definitely a little smaller. I won't go so far as to say I'm in the best shape of my life, but I can say I'm probably in the best shape of my year. Except for the fingers and the eye of course, but they don't matter so much to the way I look. I'm glad men can put on a few pounds and still look, like, distinguished. It would suck to be a chick; once they balloon up it's all over for them. Once a chick gets to be a chub, who wants to have anything to do with them? I mean really? But guys can pull off the look, especially if they're otherwise stylin', like say a professional athlete such as myself.

Speaking of fat chicks, I've screwed more than a few and I'll say this for them, they're a grateful bunch. They'll often do lots of funky shit just because they can't believe how fortunate they are that you're actually taking the time to stick your dick in them. You'd be surprised by how, uh, "enthusiastic" they can be, given the opportunity to perform.

I mention this at all because I realize this is the longest I've gone without screwing more than one person at a time since, like, forever. I guess I really am tied down, and it's a little freaky. If I marry Miranda, is this how it's going to be forever? Just her? Is that even normal? Like who actually does something like that? You know, that being monotonous crap? *Please*. One chick only? Come on. But then I haven't really felt like it, to be honest. Maybe it's because she's pregnant and I feel bad for her being, like, pregnant. I don't know. Maybe I'll scope out the babes of Muskoka and that'll get the ol' juices flowing. There's got to be some half decent tail around here somewhere. Lot of rich folks anyway, and rich folks tend to be better looking, in my opinion. But then maybe I'll give Miranda a call and have phone sex with her instead. I tend to enjoy that more anyhow.

July 26

Good practice today. Still having trouble with my ball toss though. It's hard to get a good grip on the ball with just three digits, two of which are, like, the loser fingers. A big part of the serve depends on the toss. Different people toss differently; I tend to toss the ball a little higher than most, and then take it out of the air early on the drop. It's one of the reasons I always had a good, solid serve. I was able to come high over the ball and get some good power on it. Now, though, the ball kind of veers to the left every time I toss it, and it's hard to get any control. That could be a problem. Still, I'm moving okay, and my strokes aren't all that bad. Two days and I meet my reckoning. I have no idea what that means, but it sounds threatening.

July 28

So it all comes down to this. I played my first tournament since the great bloodletting and it wasn't pretty. Not because the injury hurt my performance or anything, but because I genuinely sucked in all other areas of my game. (I'm so embarrassed by the score that I'm not even going to mention it, except to say that more than one goose egg appeared on the scoreboard alongside my name.)

I took a look at a calendar today and realized my time is up. It's impossible for me to get my ranking high enough to be considered for the qualifying rounds of the US Open, the last Grand Slam of the year. So I'm well and truly fucked. I'm surprisingly calm considering, but it still sucks to know my one dream that's kept me going all these months is over. Kaput. I couldn't be more miserable.

So now what? Do I keep trying to gain entry into these bullshit backwater events, where the competition keeps getting younger and younger, with no idea where this is all supposed to lead me in the end? And what end is there after all this is over? I mean I always knew the US Open was a bit of a pipedream, but I didn't have any other kind of dream to move me along from dink town to dink town. All I know is, I'm in Muskoka and I want to go home. In two weeks I play a Futures in Duck's Blind, Iowa and after that, well, fuck if I know what's after that.

July 29

Miranda loaded me up with enough money to catch the bus back home, and I travelled throughout the night to get back to her. She's started dropping hints again about me getting another job, or as she put it, "a real job." That hurts, but it's hard to argue when I need her money just to get home, forgoing the pleasure of riding the rails while someone takes a crap in your train car.

I actually flipped through the want ads in the paper today to see what might be out there. Not sure what I could do. I have no education to speak of, no job experience at all, and let's be honest, no real skills. I do have a couple of ideas though, and a good idea can change the world.

July 30

Miranda is really showing. She's one big ol' cow now, and I told her so. But I meant it in the nicest possible way. She's over four months, which means I'll be a father some time in maybe February or March. January? Yeah, Miranda says January. Jeez she's smart. I really do love my big ol' cow.

I've been practicing holding things in my gimp left hand, and I'm getting a lot better lately. Sometimes I forget I'm missing the fingers; it actually feels like they're still there. Other than occasionally dropping things though, which to be honest I sometimes did before, life isn't all that different. As I think I mentioned before, most of the important things in life I do with my right hand anyway, so really it's not like it's holding me back all that much. Though I do look pretty freaky, I must say. With each passing month I seem to lose some new part of myself, like some kind of modern-day leper. Naked, I'm quite a sight. But once you get past what I look like, I'm still the same ol' Olie inside.

I hope the kid isn't freaked out by my missing fingers. I've seen kids scream and hide behind their parents when they see me coming down the street. I assume it's because of the missing digits and eye patch; otherwise I've got me some bigger problems to deal with.

The kid. Shit, I'm just now really coming to terms with it. I know I'm a horrible person for thinking I don't want this baby, but I can't help it. My life feels like it's slipping away anyway, and all this does is speed the process up. I wish I had someone to talk to about all this, but I can't reach Gary and, well, Miranda probably wouldn't be the best sounding board, I'm thinking. Still, I suppose I do owe it to her to at least share what I'm feeling, even though the last time I brought it up I caught some serious hell and a punch in the stomach.

(3:05 AM)

So now for the big news. Who should show up at our door in the middle of the night but Gary. God it was good to see him again. It's been months and he looks just great. I finally understand the concept of a "sight for sore eyes."

"Dude," I said to him.

"Dude," he said back.

"You're back."

"That I am."

"What, the sun and hot chicks get boring?"

"Actually, yes. Quite."

"Get the fuck out of here."

"No, seriously. Everything just seems the same down there. Every day the weather is pretty much the same, and even the people all kind of look the same. It's depressing."

"Yeah, all toned bodies and tiny swimsuits. I'm already jealous, dude, don't make it worse."

"I also felt a kind of calling back here."

"Your church?"

"You, actually."

"No shit."

"I shit you not. Also I ran out of product. And money. But mostly the first thing."

"Well I'm touched, man, and I missed you, but I'm not having any kind of crisis." I thought better of it. "Well, no more than like five or six crises, but none you can help me with."

As if on cue, Miranda came shuffling into the living room.

"Gary," she said sleepily. "Nice to see you. Did Olie tell you the good news?" Oh shit, I thought, I suck, and I'm in trouble for not making it the first thing to come out of my mouth. But Gary didn't skip a beat in coming to my rescue.

"Of course he did. And with pride too, I might add. Congratulations, Miranda," he said, getting up to give her a hug.

"I feel in my heart this child is blessed." Well of course that made Miranda start to cry, and back she went to bed with a smile on her face.

"How'd you know?" I said.

"Because I'm not an idiot, and I can see she's clearly pregnant." I didn't mention that I hadn't noticed myself until she told me. "I can't believe you didn't think to mention it."

"I was getting to it," I lied. "I just figured you wouldn't want to be hit with that kind of news straight off."

He looked sceptical. "I get the feeling you aren't as sold on this as you should be."

"Ah, you know, it's just, well . . ."

"You don't feel ready."

"Yeah. I guess."

"Well you'd better *get* ready. Because it's coming, and that baby's going to need you."

"You know, I just can't really think about it right now, okay?"

"I can't believe you'd be able to think about anything else."

"I have a tournament in a couple of weeks."

"*Ah.*"

"What the hell's that supposed to mean?"

"The tennis can't always be number one, you know."

"It can for the next two weeks. And for a few more weeks after that."

"How's it been going anyhow?"

"Not bad," I lied again. I couldn't tell if he believed me.

"How's your ranking? Are you in position to qualify for the Open?"

"Well . . . it all depends on how you look at—"

"There's something different about you," he cut in.

"Well I think I may have lost a little weight. . . ."

"Are you . . . are you missing some *fingers* since the last time I saw you?"

"Oh, that. Yeah, you know how it goes."

"Oh, yeah, sure. . . . Actually no, I don't. I don't know how it goes. Enlighten me."

"You know, you're playing tennis, you lose a couple of fingers—shit happens."

He nodded as though he understood. Meanwhile, Blanche Dowling came meandering into the room and stared at Gary a while. Finally she coughed up a hairball, and turned around and left.

Gary and I continued to shoot the shit a while. Eventually, though, the sun came up and he had to go home.

I couldn't get back to sleep. I kept thinking about what he'd said. This kid is going to need me. *Need* me. Who the fuck does he think he is anyway? Is this what the next eighteen years of my life are going to be like? Being *needed* by some helpless infant? I never had the chance to be helpless. No, I had to get self-sufficient fast. I can feel my soul being sucked out already, and the child isn't even born yet.

August 1

Gary is always a great help. He drove me all the way to the Gene Toomey Tennis Centre today so I could look for work. It wasn't the most humiliating experience of my life, but it was definitely up there.

The new Director is a guy named Marcel Montclair. He was a student there the same time I was, and like most of the guys who watched me become successful while they wallowed in mediocrity he hated me a great deal. It probably didn't help that the first time we met I told him I hated French people. I'm not proud of it, but come on, you know you've felt the same way at one time or another. Anyway, he never seemed to let that go. And when we'd play, he'd never win, and it started to drive him a little nuts eventually. He actually became a little obsessed about it. He did turn pro for a short time, but never managed to crack the top 900, and eventually started teaching fulltime, winding up here at Toomey. Now he's in charge and, like most of my peers, seems to really enjoy watching the downward spiral Olie Wood's currently on.

"Wow. Olie Wood. Someone I never thought we'd see here again," he said as we sat down in his office. "Still on the tour aren't you?"

"I am. As a matter of fact, I have an event in Iowa next week."

"Ah yes, Iowa. Home of all the great tennis events."

"An event's an event, Marcel."

"I suppose," he said. "Oh I heard about your accident. That looks nasty," he said, indicating the stumps where my fingers used to be.

"It's okay. I survived."

"So I see," he said, and we sat there together silently for a time. Finally he said, "So why don't we cut the chase, Olie. I have a great deal to do here as you can see."

"Well, yeah, of course. Of course you do. Me too as a matter of fact. No, I just stopped by to see the old alma mater," I said. "And, well, to see if there's any way I can, you know, help out around here or something like that. You know, to kinda 'give back' and all that crap."

He just stared at me for what felt like a really long time. "You know, I kind of hoped that was why you'd come," he said after a while, and I started to feel a little more hopeful until he added, "so I can tell you to go fuck yourself." I felt a little less hopeful now. "I can't believe that, you of all people, would come back here to ask a favour of me. Of *me*!"

"I'm not looking for favours, Marcel. I'm looking to share all the shit I've learned with some of the kids here. I'm thinking of, like, a higher calling. This isn't about me."

"Oh but it is, Olie. It was always about you, wasn't it? Everything revolved around the one and only Olie Wood, the little orphan saviour of tennis. The one who was going to go all the way to number one, and win all the Grand Slams, and teach the world a thing or two about Canadian greatness!" At that point he started to rant in French, and he kind of lost me.

"Calm down, dude," I told him. "I know you don't like me, but it's been a long time. Can't we get past whatever shit might have existed between us when we were young?"

"You'd like that, wouldn't you? Everything to suit the great Olie Wood. Perhaps you'd like my job too? After all, you're entitled to it of course. Whatever the great Olie Wood wants, the great Olie

Wood gets. Do you want my shirt? Here, surely you want my shirt," he said, quickly removing both his Toomey blazer and shirt before tossing the latter in my face. I started to get a little freaked out when he began removing his shoes and pants, and decided to get the hell out of there before things went any further. Let it never be said that I haven't left a mark, however.

On the drive home I felt totally depressed.

"There's nothing else I can do, Gar."

"You're a man of considerable talents, Olie. You just haven't come to grips with all of them yet."

"Well that's helpful. If I'm not on the tour, what exactly is it I'm supposed to do for a living?"

"Toomey's not the only teaching centre."

"Yeah, well, I've been around long enough to know most of the people running the other ones as well."

"Well that's good."

"No, that's definitely *not* good. I've burned a lot of bridges in my time."

"Ah."

"Yeah."

"Well," he said, "God will show the way."

"Well that would be just super of him," I said.

August 3

Back to playing househusband. I'm as miserable as I've ever been in my life. I make Miranda her breakfast and see her off in the morning while she runs errands, then I clean the house and watch shitty daytime TV until she returns later on. Some days I get out to the neighbourhood courts and practice a little, or try to go for a run, but that usually doesn't work so well. Then Miranda comes home, we have dinner, and she heads out to work while I watch more TV until I fall asleep on the sofa, wallowing in self-pity and my own filth. I imagine once this kid comes I'll be the babysitter too, since Miranda's the one who goes out and works to pay the bills. This genuinely sucks. I never thought I'd say it, but I'm actually counting down the days until I can leave for Iowa. Problem is, after Iowa, I don't have any more wildcards or invitations to play qualifying tournaments, not that Miranda is willing to tolerate much more anyhow. As much as I'm looking forward to getting out of here, part of me feels like I'm walking towards the gallows. This is the end, my friends. Retirement is a fate worse than death, I'm finding.

August 5

I've left the family home, maybe for good this time. Had a horrible fight with Miranda, the kind you just don't come back from. We fight from time to time—we're both fiery people—but this one was worse. I swear it wasn't my fault though. She just pushed me too far this time.

I was packing my things for Iowa (I actually rented a car for the occasion) when she blurted out, "I don't think I can afford to pay for any more of your trips, Olie." Well, fair enough. She shouldn't have to and I don't blame her for saying so, but her tone is what got to me. It was one of those, "You're a pathetic asshole and you have to stop playing games and get on with being a grownup" kind of tones. Or maybe I was just reading into it. In any case I got defensive.

"So don't. I don't need you."

"What's that supposed to mean?"

"It means you're not in charge here."

"I never claimed to be. I just think this should be where you call it a day, baby. Don't you agree?"

Well that made me mad. I mean who the hell is she to make the call? "Maybe I don't," I said. "Maybe I have enough belief in myself and my abilities to actually still make a go of it."

"Baby, you're starting to look desperate," she said, putting a hand on my arm. I shook it off.

"Don't call me 'baby.' And look who's talking. Desperate is someone who deliberately gets pregnant so they can trap a man into marriage and a family he doesn't want."

That might have been pushing it a little too far, now that I look back on it.

"Fuck you, Olie. Is that really was you really think?"

"Maybe. Maybe I do."

"Wow. Congratulations. For someone as wrong as you are, as often as you are, you have just outdone yourself."

"Well there you go."

"What exactly are you saying?" she asked.

"Maybe I'm saying I don't want this baby," I answered.

She grabbed me by the throat. "Don't you think it's a little late to be coming to that particular conclusion? Or have you not noticed the shape of me."

"How can I help but notice? You're the size of a fucking back-hoe."

"That's what happens when a women gets pregnant, asshole."

"Who are you calling an asshole?"

"I'm calling *you* an asshole, asshole!"

"Christ, I'm so sick of taking this shit from you. I'm sick of all of this."

"What, like the rent-free place to live? The spending money? The sex on demand even when you smell like crap?"

"No, like the nagging, and the insults, and the mocking of the way I choose to live my life and the constant questioning of my career, how's that."

"What *career*? I haven't noticed one creeping around here any-where, have you?"

"I gotta get outta here. I gotta get away from all this. From this baby, from you—"

"Abandoning us, huh? I guess the apple doesn't fall far from the tree after all."

Part of me wanted to hit her. I've never hit a girl before (except in self-defence), but I can't help but admit that I want-ed to now. But instead of hitting her I tossed the rest of my shit in a bag, grabbed Blanche Dowling, and left. She didn't try to stop me.

I walked around, dragging my bag behind me for like an hour, until I finally ended up at Gary's place. He took me in without a word.

So now I'm here at Gary's, and in a few days I leave for my last scheduled tournament. And while I do feel a big baby-shaped weight off my shoulders, I can't help but feel something else weighing them down all the same, something I can't quite put my finger on. Guilt maybe.

August 7

Man I hate border guards. Every goddamned time they see me they end up sticking a hand up my ass. It's like they can't wait to see me bent over with my clothes off. It's not like I'd be so stupid as to bring anything over the border. I'm not an idiot.

Really, I'm not.

So I'm back to travelling with Blanche Dowling, and it's like nothing has changed. We're right back where we started. Somehow that's not as comforting as I thought it would be.

I've never known a creature so fixed in her ways. You'd think that over time she might mellow, or becoming a little more affectionate, or, you know, die—*anything*. But she still snarls seemingly at random, and she still growls when you go near her, and she still scratches the shit out of you whenever possible. Not very nice traits in a travelling companion.

And to make matters worse, she now has a way of making me feel like I might be going crazy. When it's just me I keep my thoughts to myself, but when I travel with her I start talking to her like she's a person. And that's not good. Because, like, she's not a person.

"Looking forward to the trip?" I asked her as we eased into the line-up at the border. She had nothing to say, so I just kept on going. "Yep, I have high hopes for this little tourney. Could be the big turnaround for me," I said, and I swear she almost smiled. Yeah, I still hate her.

Anyhow, there's no law about my bringing a cat across the border—I've done it plenty of times—but they still hassle me about it.

"Mr. Wood, is your cat up-to-date on all its shots, vaccinations and other relevant medications?" the big woman with the moustache asked me once I'd been brought inside. Again with the moustache? What gives with these guys?

"You bet," I replied.

"And I assume you have the paperwork to verify this?"

"You betcha, baby. Ma'am," I quickly added.

"I'm going to have to ask you to remove your clothing and place all your belongings on this table," she told me. "Bernie here will be conducting a search," she added, referring to the little weasel of a guy standing next to me. At least he didn't look too thrilled about it.

Bernie snapped on a pair of rubber gloves and started to pat me down. "I ain't dirty, man," I told him.

"Just a precaution, sir. Please remain quiet while I finish the search."

"Why you guys always single me out, huh? I don't have a record."

"Maybe something about your appearance screams out, 'Search me, I could be trouble,'" he told me.

Hey, at least he was honest with me. And to his credit he didn't probe too deep, and they eventually let me go with a minimum of further harassment. I've been through this so many times that it almost felt mailed in. They tried to give Blanche Dowling the once-over too, but she hissed and spit and tore a long enough strip out of Bernie's forearm that they decided the animal was clean. They wondered aloud if she might be rabid, but I told them, "No, she's just a bitch." They seemed to agree and let us through.

"I suppose you have your uses," I told her as we drove off, leaving the border behind. In answer, she began to lick her ass. At least we're still communicating, after all this time.

August 10

Almost no memory of the drive down, but here I am in Duck's Blind. It looks like it sounds: rural, small, and more than a little creepy. But, like a lot of small towns, they have a tennis club, and pretty much every tennis club holds some kind of tournament.

And so here I am, ready to kick some serious Iowa ass. Tomorrow I play my first match, and for a change my opponent is actually kind of interesting. Local guy named Mirth Minter, the club pro and occasional tour player. More interesting still, he's actually a year older than me. I almost never play guys older than me. Mirth doesn't play too much anymore, but I do remember him from back when I was on top. He was what they call a journeyman, someone who makes a decent living by occasionally putting together a string of wins, but who never really makes a big impact on the game. Even at that, I think he was ranked as high as #42 in the world at one time. He won a small tournament in India once, and that was about it in terms of major accomplishments. We played a few times back in the day, and I took every match. He always offered a good game, but he never had the will to seal the deal and finish it off with a win. He faded from the top 100 after a few years and started playing Satellite events, finally ending up in a shit hole like Duck's Blind teaching hick kids and fat old women how to hit a proper backhand. In a nutshell, he's basically me in a year or two. Encouraging, really. Something to look forward to.

I actually kind of like the guy. He's unpretentious and seems to relate to some of the crap I go through on a day-to-day basis. We went for a drink tonight to catch up.

"It's not bad, you know," he said, referring to his latest gig. "It sure beats traipsing around from town to town, never knowing where your next dollar's going to come from. I mean I still try to get out and play some events in the area, but that's about all I can handle anymore. It's become more of a way to stay in shape than anything else."

"But don't you ever miss it?"

"What, the sharing of shitty motel rooms with a bunch of kids half your age? The busting your ass for a couple hundred dollars and a ranking point or two—if you're lucky? Not a lot, no."

"No, the glory of it, man," I said, gesturing with my beer. "Don't you miss the big matches, the ones that mark you for life?"

"Well that's the difference between you and me, Olie. I never really had too many of those to miss."

He had a point. It was easier for someone like Mirth to walk away. It had obviously been a dream at one time, but never having flown too close to the sun he never had the chance to get his wings burned off. (I think I read that on a Styx album once.)

"I'm having a hard time walking away," I told him.

"Are you waiting for something in particular?"

"I want to play another Slam. Just one."

He laughed. "You and I would be lucky to get tickets to *watch* a Slam right now, my friend. We have to come to terms with the fact that things do eventually come to an end. Everything. Even this."

"Yeah, so people keep telling me."

Despite my feelings for Mirth, the conversation made me sad. And what's worse is knowing that he's right. So now I'm willing myself to beat him tomorrow. Nothing against him personally, but if I'm going to go out, I want to go out on a high note. I'm entitled.

August 11

I'm not saying I hate Mirth Minter, but he didn't need that win. I did, and he took it away from me like the greedy bastard he is.

It was actually a good match, a hell of a lot better than up in Muskoka at any rate. I actually played pretty well. Even my gimp hand wasn't too bad a distraction, and my ball toss seemed okay. We must have been a sight, though, couple of old guys battling away out there. I noticed a few spectators, and several of the other players who'd stopped by to laugh, staying to watch. Even I could see this was an entertaining match. We both clearly wanted to win. The harder he hit the ball, the harder I hit it back; the more balls he kept in play, the more balls I kept alive. It was truly what they call a war of attrition. If by attrition they mean hitting the shit out of the ball and wanting the other guy to die.

We went the distance, deep into the third set and further. Neither of us was willing to give an inch. More and more people were lining up to watch us. I haven't had an audience like that in years (not counting the great bloody hand incident of a couple of

months ago, but this was more about the actual tennis than waiting to see if Olie Wood actually died on court). In the end
though, it was the unthinkable that killed me: I got tired. After
nearly three hours of brutal, high quality tennis, I ran out of gas.
I was suddenly an old man just trying to keep up (never mind that
my opponent was an even older man; I guess teaching kids and
old ladies keeps you in some kind of shape). The one thing that
never happened to me finally brought me down.

Mirth was really gracious afterward, but then it's easy to be gracious when you win.

"Match of a lifetime, Olie," he said. "Thanks for that. I needed
that more than you'll ever know."

I muttered something in response, I don't remember what
exactly, but it didn't matter; Mirth wouldn't have heard me, he was
on such a high. I know that feeling well. Even as an old man I can
still remember what it feels like to win a match like that.

And now, I suppose, I'm done. So what's next? I can't very well
stay here in Duck's Blind. The only job in tennis here is occupied
by the jerk that just kicked my ass. And I can't go home to
Miranda because that's simply not my home anymore.

Instead of making myself think (which made my head hurt), I
used the last of the money Miranda gave me to score some down-
ers at a bar, and then went back to my room to crash.

                                              August 12
A brief reprieve. Got a call at the Duck's Blind clubhouse from
Martin Haslan of Tennis Canada, asking me to play a Davis Cup
tie next week, filling in for both Sebastien Laliberté and Steve
Turrell, our top two guys who are both out with injuries (man,
the younger guys are pussies these days; they should take a look
at me and what I play through). The Canadian tennis talent pool
is extremely shallow, and they're a little desperate trying to field a
team for the next tie against the US in Rhode Island.

Anyhow Haslan, like Mirth Minter, is an older guy who always
seemed to like me, and I'm grateful to him for thinking of me.
There's no money in Davis Cup ties but they'll fly me out there,

and even arrange a rental car to get me back home. They'll also put me up in a nice hotel, which is something I haven't experienced in a really long time. It's totally worth it of course.

Davis Cup is a funny thing. It's the only time outside of doubles that tennis becomes a kind of team sport. It's essentially a group competition where you represent your country against other, preferably shittier countries. Normally tennis is all about you, and fuck everyone else. Davis Cup is odd because it's about the so-called "bigger and better" things, like country, national glory, international relations and crap like that.

I used to hate playing Davis Cup, because it totally went against what I felt the game was all about, but Phil forced me to play those couple of years I was at the top. Canada had gone so long (read: forever) without producing a top player that Tennis Canada was desperate to have me represent them, and I got the team into the World Group both years I played. See, the best sixteen teams play best-of-five series, called "ties" for some fucked up reason no one can explain anymore. To get into that group, you've got to beat out one of the lousier top–16 teams from the previous year. Teams have to win regional qualifiers and whatnot just to be considered in the running for the World Group, and Canada typically couldn't get past the lower levels of regional qualifying. Not only did Olie Wood single-handedly propel the team all the way to the World Group, but twice we got all the way to the semifinals where we lost to the Germans. Have I ever mentioned that I hate the Germans? No? Well I do. Them and the French. And the Dutch too, though I can't really say why. Their accents just piss me off, I guess.

Eventually though I grew tired of it and quit the team, and that was pretty much the end of any Canadian Davis Cup success. Now the team is playing a regional qualifier for a spot in the World Group against the Americans, who had a shitastic year this year and have to scramble to even stay in the group they used to dominate. The Canadian team won't pose any real challenge, but it might be fun to play my part in our country's inevitable demise.

And yeah, I do see some irony in these guys giving me the chance to extend my career by another week long after I turned my back on them, but fuck it.

No word yet from Miranda. Not that I expected one. To hell with her. It's not like I miss her or anything; I've got Blanche Dowling to keep me company, and we're bonding like crazy. For instance, when she tried to scratch my one good eye out, I felt like her heart really wasn't in it. It was like she was just going through the motions. Just playing a part. Deep down I think she really didn't want to blind me. That's progress.

                                                              August 15

Dear Portuguese dudes,

You'll notice Sparky is now in a place called Newport. This is the location of the Tennis Hall of Fame and also a tournament called the Miller Light Hall of Fame Championships. I personally love the events sponsored by beer companies; the combination seems somewhat poetic, and a win almost preordained.

All the greats are in the Hall of Fame, anyone and everyone who ever meant anything to the sport of tennis. I won't ever be in there myself, but I'm cool with that. I don't want people being able to come here and look at my shit. All those displays dedicated to the best players in the game, it's way too invasive. Still, you can't help but come here and get a little caught up in the amazing history of this game. Or maybe you could, I don't know. You could be some cold-ass motherfuckers for all I know. The Portuguesians I met seemed overly emotional if anything, but I suppose there are always exceptions. I can't tell if having a skunk lawn ornament means you're fun-loving and emotional, or just tacky and pathetic. Let's assume the former and just say, if you came here, you'd enjoy yourself. Just look at how much Sparky is.

Oh, and sorry about the chunks missing from Sparky's ear. My cat has been attacking and eating little parts of him lately. I will do my best to put a stop to this before he starts to look as messed up as I do.

August 16

So this is what they call getting thrown into the deep end. No sooner do I arrive than they start putting me through my paces, even though I might not even play. I'm scheduled to play what they call reverse singles should the situation warrant it. After two singles matches, usually going with the best players you've got, you play one doubles match. If no one has won three points by then, you play two more singles matches. I'm scheduled for the last match if it ever gets that far, which it won't. We'd be extremely lucky to get even one point off the Americans, but that doesn't mean the coach, some guy with a French name I'm not even going to try to pronounce, isn't working me like a dog.

"Crab walk! Crab walk!" he screamed like some kind of drill sergeant as he forced me to do sidesteps back and forth across the court. I started to remember the downside of having a coach.

"You are so out of shape, Mr. Wood," he said. "I have no idea how we are going to get you ready. Do you have any idea why Martin Haslan would have recommended you?"

"Fond memories maybe?"

"Yes, well, my own memories of you are not so fond. I remember some embarrassing moments from you on court back in the day. I confess I wasn't even aware you still played."

"Futures mostly. Some ATP events."

"I see."

"So, what, more crabwalking?"

"Absolutely. More crabwalking please."

He drilled me for hours. Finally, though, I got to practice with the rest of the team, and we're a pretty motley crew, I must say. Even with Sebastien Laliberté and Steve Turrell the Canadian team wouldn't be worth shit, and without them we're several degrees worse.

One neat thing about being able to play here, though, is the chance to play on grass again. I haven't played on grass in a long time. Newport is the only grass court tournament played in North America, and one of the few remaining in the world. Grass isn't quite like anything else in this sport. You can play on hard

court, clay, indoors—all have their advantages and disadvan-
tages—but regardless of the play of a grass court (I don't usually
play all that well on grass; the bounce is too low for someone who
has the kind of trouble I do bending over), what's so cool about
it is its connection to history.

Now I'm not some kind of fag or anything, don't get me
wrong. I don't get all romantic and crap over this kind of stuff. It's
just that, well, when you play on grass, you can't help but feel like
you're connected to something bigger somehow. This is what they
played on a hundred years ago. This is what they've played
Wimbledon on for even longer, and there's no tournament that
means as much as Wimbledon to anyone who has played this
game professionally. I used to have a handful of grass stolen from
center court at Wimbledon from the year I reached the semi-
finals, but I've since sold it on eBay. Still, I can remember playing
there as well as I can remember anything in my life. That's why
I'm glad I may get the chance to play on grass one last time. We've
just got to get our act together and actually win a couple of
matches so I get the chance.

August 17

Okay, so not the best start. We dropped our two matches today,
meaning a loss in the doubles tomorrow and we're outta here.
There's a chance I might get to play anyway in what we call a
"dead rubber," essentially a match that doesn't mean anything to
anyone, but remains good practice for whatever American player
didn't get enough of a workout in over the course of the tie. On
the upside, doubles is the one thing Canada seems to do well in.
We've had plenty of great doubles players over the years. Only
thing is, no one cares about doubles. Outside Davis Cup of
course; here it could keep us alive.

August 18

We won the doubles match in a close one. We're still in this
thing. Tomorrow come the reverse singles matches, and if by some
miracle we win the first match, I get to play in something that

will actually matter. It hurt me a little when I overheard this kid named Pelletier, who has the first match tomorrow, talking to the coach tonight:

"So what if I do win. All that'll do is just buy us a little time. Wood'll have to play anchor, and we all know how that'll turn out."

"Don't think about Wood. Sure, if it comes down to him, we're screwed, but at least if we force the Americans into a sudden death match we'll have done more than anyone thought possible of us."

"If only we had someone—*any*one—half-decent to step in. God, he looks like shit. And his hand creeps me out too."

" 'If only' is right, but we don't. Losing Laliberté and Turrell at the last minute put us in a bad spot, and he was the best we could come up with at the last minute. That says a lot about Canadian tennis right there."

And then they both laughed heartily for an oddly long time.

That's not what you want to hear the night before you potentially play a critically important tennis match. And yeah, it hurts to hear it, but what can I do? Oh, I mean, I can slip Neet into their shampoo after tomorrow and let the hilarity ensure (and don't think I won't either), but that doesn't really help my mood or my game in the meantime. I guess all I can do is go out there and show them a thing or two. Show them the old guy still has a little gas left in the tank.

August 19

A day to remember, that's for sure. Pelletier got lucky when his American opponent, leading in the fifth set, pulled up lame and had to withdraw, giving us a default and tying the series at two apiece. That brought me up—against Lincoln Holmes of course. Holmes has been the big story on tour this year: huge break-throughs every week, shooting up the world rankings, considered a serious threat at the upcoming US Open, and a member of the US Davis Cup team in his first year on the ATP tour. And I get to play him in the deciding match.

But see, I always believed I could beat this guy. We've played a few times in the Futures and I know his game and, more importantly, his weaknesses. I was determined to exploit them.

I worked his backhand, which I know is his weakest shot, and I hit balls with plenty of backspin, making sure they bounced low, forcing him to bend and stretch a lot. I was mostly hoping to knock him on his ass a few times, just because. But he's a young guy in really good shape, and everything I threw at him he managed to return. In the end I put up a good fight, but he took me out in straight sets.

There were actually a few Canadian journalists on hand to see this. I should have known. Any time we play the Americans in any sport the national press is going to get all horny and throw a few cameras at it, purely out of reflex. So, just to make my painful loss that much worse, I had reporters sticking microphones in my face and asking me, "Do you feel like you let a huge opportunity for Canada slip away?" and "Do you think the team would have been better served by having a younger, more active player in the anchor position?" Like the Canadian press cares about tennis all of a sudden. All I could say was, "I was filler. It wasn't even supposed to get down to me. No one thought I'd even get the chance to play." And, "There was no one else." I also caused a bit of a stir by swearing on camera, telling them to "Fuck off and leave me alone." That should make the Tennis Canada folks really happy. I probably burned the last bridge I had right there.

So that was it. My last match, and a loss of course. Now what? I've got nothing else scheduled and no money and nowhere to go. It all ends like this. Wow. What a downer.

When I started this journal I guess I intended to write about my last year on tour, but I never thought it would end quite like this. But there you go. I guess I've got nothing else to write about. I guess this is the end of my story.

So I guess that's it. Thanks for reading, whoever you are. If you're interested in a cat, check me out in Newport. I may have to bunker down here a while. Maybe I'll get a job as a tour guide at the Hall of Fame; that way my various failures can be rubbed into my open sores every day. Or maybe I'll go back on the road and see where it leads me. We'll see. At least I seem to be taking it all well, so that's something.

(2:38 AM)

Okay, maybe not taking it as well as I thought. I called Gary (collect) sobbing to come and get me.

"Please please *please* come down here man," I blubbered. "I'm all alone and my career is over and no one here likes me and Miranda's gone and I lost today and the whole country is going to be laughing at me and hating me more than they already do and I just want to go home except I don't have a home anymore and everything sucks and please please *please* come get me!" And with that I slipped into full-blown hysterics, with the heaving and the total-body sobbing and the kind of howling you only do when you're a little kid and you feel like an absolute injustice has occurred. That was me on a street corner in the phone booth I'd decided to sleep in after having been kicked out of the hotel because I had no money to pay.

All Gary said was, "Okay, Olie, no worries." And then he hung up. I'm not even sure what that means exactly, but he's coming. I think.

August 20

So no Gary yet. I spent part of the day begging for change, but all I got was sixty-one cents and a lecture from a cop concerning the illegality of panhandling. It was enough for a doughnut, so at least I've eaten today. Hope Gary gets here soon though. I need someone to talk to, and even with letting Blanche Dowling out to walk around, she still has very little to say to me.

August 21

Still no Gary. I took refuge in a local church where I was able to get myself a bowl of soup and some milk for Blanche Dowling. Sometimes these religious dudes can be okay. I walked around the town a while but it started to rain, and even though she was protected by her cage, Blanche Dowling started to freak out and I had to beat it back to the church. I keep checking over at the Hall of Fame for Gary but there's still no sign of him.

So I think I'm now officially a vagrant. And I'm so tired and drained I don't even have the energy to, like, go steal some stuff to sell or anything. Being a vagrant kind of sucks, I have to say.

                                                                    August 22

Thank God Gary's shown up. He drove straight here but, for once, got held up at the border. Despite the robes and collar they actually searched him this time, but not all that penetratingly the way they always do with me, and therefore didn't find anything. (Fortunately Gary tends to keep his stash jammed up his ass when he travels in the States, and few if any are willing to search a priest's ass. And, I should add, this it yet another reason why I've never partaken of Gary's merchandise.)

Gary's sold a lot of his weed to some college kids here in Newport, and we've been able to get a room here at the Holiday Inn. Blanche Dowling seems a lot happier now, hanging from the curtains by her claws.

"So now that I'm here," Gary said, "what now?"

"I was hoping you'd have some ideas."

He thought deeply a moment.

"Nothing?" I said.

"I was focused on getting down here."

"I see."

"Yeah."

"Yeah."

We sat there quietly another moment.

"Sorry to hear about you and Miranda," he said at length.

"Yeah. Sucks."

"And the baby?"

"Still inside her, I'm guessing."

"So you're leaving the baby behind too?"

"I dunno, Gar. I haven't thought that far ahead."

"Yeah."

"Yeah."

This conversation was getting us nowhere.

Then, suddenly, Gary said, "Tell me Olie, what would make you happy?"

"Happy? Fuck if I know. I don't know happy. Not familiar with happy. No, I just need to get through the day."

"But seriously."

"I really don't know, Gar."

"Well when I was down in Florida, I was struck by how happy some of those kids were. Not a care in the world, or so it seemed to me. And I haven't seen *you* like that since . . . well, since I don't know when. Maybe when you were first playing professionally."

"Yeah. I was happy then."

"Why?"

"Huh?"

"Why were you happy then. What exactly made you happy?"

"The money. The chicks. The fame. Take your pick."

"I'm not sure I believe that."

"Trust me, dude. I like that sort of shit."

"No, seriously. I think it was something more than that. I think you were happy because you were doing exactly what you were put here to do."

"It was never that mystical, Gary. It was just something I was good at, and had the chance to make some decent scratch doing."

"It was also the first time you felt like you were realizing your potential. I remember. Phil seemed to be able to bring that out in you."

"Yeah," I sighed. "Phil. Well we see where that got him, don't you."

"And you were happy," he continued.

"And I was happy. True."

Gary paused. "Is there a computer here?" he asked after a while.

"Here?"

"Well obviously not in our *room*. I can see that."

"Well I'm sure there's something down in the lobby or at the front desk. Why?"

"Let's go see."

We went down to the lobby and found a complimentary guest computer.

"What are you doing?" I asked as he logged on.

"What's your world ranking?"

I had no idea. Maybe 450?

"Tell me something honestly, Olie. What would it mean for you to play in the US Open?"

"I think you know, dude. Even qualifying would be huge, not to mention enough money to keep me going a good long while. Why?"

"But what would you do with that kind of opportunity. That's what I'm wondering."

"Well, to be honest, I wouldn't stand a chance. I can barely keep up with the players on the Futures circuit, let alone bona fide ATP guys."

"But winning, that's not really the point is it. What would it *feel* like?"

"To play on those courts again? Well, it would feel . . . it would feel amazing. Yeah, just to have one more moment like that would be absolutely amazing. But why?" I said. "What's your point?"

He smiled, but just barely. "I want to show you what I've been working on this last little while," he said, pivoting the screen so that I could see it more clearly.

"What. What is it. Oh my God, Gary, what did you do."

After all these years it's easy to forget some of Gary's more latent talents. One of the best hackers in Canada as a kid, he always had a way of seeing around barriers, slipping through loopholes, and getting himself into places no one had any right to be. Lord knows how long he'd been at it, but the end result was right there in front of me.

"Holy shit."

"You ain't kiddin'. The key was to raise your ranking just high enough to make you eligible for the qualifying rounds, but not so high that anyone would notice the sudden surge."

"Come on, they'd know in a second."

"Not if you came in around, say, one hundred and twenty, they wouldn't."

It had been, he said, surprisingly easy, taking him all of a few days to work around the ridiculously feeble ATP firewall. Once in, of course, he'd had to go back a ways, manufacturing a history of fictitious results to show a steady climb up the rankings over the course of the year, so if anyone thought to really look into it, they'd have to look a really long way. To be honest, though, it felt kind of good. Especially as I hadn't had to actually earn any of it. Olie Wood, it seemed, was ranked #121 in the world.

Later that night I contacted the ATP and requested an entry into the qualifying rounds of the US Open. Time will tell if we get caught and if I am—worst-case scenario—banned from ever playing again. Which is more or less where I'm at now anyways, so fuck it.

August 24

So we've been hanging out at the hotel the last couple of days, shooting the shit, waiting to hear back from the ATP. Which we did. Today. I am to make my way to New York, where I will play first-round qualifying at the US Open in three days.

I have been reborn, all thanks to my old pal Gary.

August 27

So I'm in New York. It wasn't a long drive from Rhode Island, but now we're tapped out again. All Gary has left of his stash is what he's going to need personally over the next week or so, and so he has nothing left to sell. I thought that maybe we could sleep in the truck, but that's probably not such a good idea when I'm supposed to be preparing for such an important match.

I actually have a friend in Manhattan; I still have a few out here. We went to check him out and damn if he didn't offer up a place to stay.

See, people who play professional tennis early in life can spin off into any number of careers if and when the game doesn't click for them. They can open an electronics store, become a local club pro or, as in the case of my old friend George the Jew, become a very successful pimp of sorts.

Before he was known as Snow White, George Goldstein was a half decent player on the Challenger circuit with a killer serve and shitty knees. He never went anywhere as a pro, but after leaving the game and falling on hard times he eventually moved back into his parents' enormous Manhattan apartment and started up the successful phone sex business 1–800–HARDASS—perhaps you've heard of it, I don't know. Anyway, George was the owner, operator and talent, selling himself as a rich blonde Jewish kid in his early twenties desperate to be trained in the ways of aggressive homosexuality. Actually, that described him pretty well for the most part, though he didn't need any lessons from anyone and definitely liked the ladies, only the ladies don't often call phone sex lines, he all too quickly found out. Over time he grew his business and branched out into the escort world to "manage" an ever-increasing number of surgically enhanced girls whose augmentations he paid for out of his own pocket. I got to know two or three of these beauties myself in my earlier visits to New York. I'm an old friend of George's, so it seemed only appropriate that I do a few laps around the talent pool myself.

Today he owns and operates a very exclusive and expensive brothel on the Upper East Side where he greeted Gary and me warmly.

"Wood-man! My nigga!" he said, greeting me with an overly complicated handshake that seemed to mean he was glad to see me. At some point George "Snow White" Goldstein must have decided he was pure black, even though he's so incredibly pale he makes me look positively African by comparison. "And the preacher man? I surrender!" he went on with hands in the air when he noticed Gary standing there behind me, done out in his full regalia. "We ain't had a priest 'round here in, oh, some time. Since I stopped taking calls on the phone lines. And the Wood-man, we ain't seen yo white ass 'round here since I don't know when. What'll it be then, the usual?"

"Believe it or not, no. I actually just need a place to stay."

"And what, I suppose you'd like to park yo ass in my establish-ment free of charge, is that it? What an interestin' development this is. My, my."

"I hate to ask, but I'm desperate. I'm playing the US Open and I need a place to crash for a couple of nights. I won't be around long; just until I play and lose my match."

"Yo, back yo ass up. US Open? You? The Wood-man? Fuck dat shit, you ain't been in d' Slams in years."

"I'm in this year. Swear to God."

"Well, if dat don't beat all shit. And the preacher man? He stayin' too?"

"If he can. This is a really big deal for me, and I couldn't have gotten this far without him."

"God on yo shoulder, huh? Well, yeah, this could be a'ight. I'll tell you what, if we got rooms free you can crash here as a special guest of Snow White hisself. But if d' rooms fill up with payin' clientele, well then you gotta move yo ass on out, you dig?"

"Yeah, George, I dig."

So Gary and I are sharing a room with a lot of Goldstein gold—curtains, paint, bedspread—and it's making me a little nauseous, but it's cool because it's all part of the process. I'm in the US Open and it doesn't matter where I stay, just so long as I have a half decent roof over my head. Even if I've got to listen to some weird shit though the walls, like the rabbi who's in there now screaming, "Pinch my nipples, Nazi! Pinch them!" I've heard worse. Hell, I've *said* worse. I'll survive.

August 28

Flushing Meadows, New York. The US Open, final Grand Slam event of the year. Main draw of 128 men and 128 women, pre-ceded by three rounds of qualifying of 128 more. Best of all, $7,946,000 in prize money is up for grabs. I can pull a few grand out of here even if I lose in first-round qualifying, and an unbe-lievable $14,000 if I make it into the main draw. Which I admit isn't going to happen. But that's okay; just to be here, playing among the best in the game, is more than I ever could've hoped for. I owe Gary everything.

I practiced on the outer courts today, and I forgot what it feels like to hit a ball on a court of this quality. It changes the way the ball feels; it changes the way you play the game. I almost felt overwhelmed as all the old memories came rushing back to me.

I suddenly remembered when I was about nineteen and warming up for this very same tournament, and Phil told me something important:

"Remember how this feels, kid. The feel of your shoes on the asphalt as you run, the clear blinding contrast of the white-painted lines in the sun, the ballboys in their crisp matching uniforms buzzing by—you won't get this feeling anywhere else. This is the purest place on earth, between these lines." I thought he was full of shit and told him so, but as I look back now I realize how right he was. This is the grail for me. This is the place I was always meant to be. Even just warming up here is something special, and it took a few years in exile to fully appreciate what it means.

Be that as it may, tomorrow may be my last match and you know what? That's okay. It was supposed to finish here. Not in Duck's Blind, not in Newport, but right here. And if that Brazilian turd I have to play tomorrow wipes my ass across the beautiful clean asphalt between these white painted lines, I'm okay with that too. And the four grand I'll walk away with will be enough for me to live on a long time.

This is a good place for me, in more ways than one.

August 29

Well, interesting day. Let me first say, it's easy to forget how well world-class players can play this game. The intensity and talent is miles above what you find on the Futures circuit. It takes you by surprise at first: "Oh, right, *that's* how fast some people can serve the ball; *that's* how fast some people can move toward a drop volley."

My opponent today was a Brazilian named Andre Fernandez. Now, most of the South American guys are clay-court specialists;

they prefer slow, methodical rallies to anything fast and short. That was the only thing I had to count on going into the match, but even with that in mind I was no match for this guy. He's young, fit, fast, and has been practicing a lot more than, say, I have.

He blew me off the court in the first set. I was lucky to have taken a game off him, and even that, I think, was a direct result of pity on his part. That and the fact I was an easy mark, and therefore a good opportunity to experiment with some trickier shots.

I'd also forgotten what it feels like to play in front of people. At most of the events I play, the "crowds" are nothing more than a handful of bored, morbidly curious halfwits with little better to do. Here, even the qualifying matches attract crowds. Now I suppose by most pros' standards they're tiny, but trust me, I can't remember the last time I had a few hundred people watch me play. Admittedly they probably weren't here to watch me play *specifically*, but nonetheless there were a couple of hundred asses planted in a couple of hundred seats while I banged a tennis ball around. It freaked me out a little, to say the least.

And meanwhile the end of my US Open experience was rapidly approaching as Fernandez wore me down with deep groundstrokes, pushing me from side to side like a dog chasing a stick. It was all too much; I was completely overwhelmed. Within twenty minutes of starting the second set my tournament was pretty much over. Over before it even began.

That's not to say I didn't play well. Something kind of interesting happened, actually. I've heard it said on many occasions that when you play against the best, they bring out the best in you. Actually, Phil always used to say that, but I never quite understood what it meant since at the time I kind of *was* the best.

But now I was suddenly getting it. I always knew I had talent, but over the years I'd let it slip away. I lost the will and then the ability to keep up, and with each loss those things receded further and further behind me. But here I was playing a really good opponent who, sure, was kicking my ass, but who was also forcing me to play purely on instinct, with no time to think or do much more than react. And as it turns out, my reactions are pretty damned good, even after all these years. I mean, yeah, he's better than me and he was playing much better than me, but I didn't feel humiliated. And that alone was kind of a novel experience for me.

I was just about ready to call it a day with him leading 4–1 when something interesting happened—he started to limp. Not a lot, mind you, but enough for me to notice. Now let's be honest, he still would've beaten me had he been missing both feet and walking around on his hands, swinging his racquet from his ass—just so long as he actually finished the match.

I saw the look in his eye that said, "Let's finish this quick because I'm starting to hurt a little." I assumed he'd landed a little funny on his leg or twisted the wrong way on a return because it sure as hell wasn't anything I was doing to cause him to pull up injured. But nonetheless, there it was, my opening. And I took it.

Again, even injured, he was still clearly going to beat me—it was just a matter of time, he was just that much better—so I decided to do the one thing I'm still good at: I dug in for a war of attrition. Instead of going for winners, I simply tried to keep the ball in play; kept making him move on what was looking increasingly like a pulled hamstring. I actually smiled as I realized it, because a pulled hamstring hurts like hell. I was starting to enjoy this. I won a couple of games, but he still took it to 5–4, and was preparing to serve out the match. All he had to do was stay on serve, but I kept making him move until, suddenly, without warning, he stopped cold in the middle of the court. His hamstring had pulled tight and he couldn't seem to walk.

I waited. The umpire (and how nice it was to play with an umpire again!) waited. "Do you need to call the trainer?" he asked at length. Fernandez thought about it.

"I can't walk," he finally said.

"What are you going to do?" asked the umpire.

"It's very bad," Fernandez said.

"I understand, but I need a decision, Mr. Fernandez."

And just like that it was over. He hobbled to the net and offered me his hand. At first I wasn't sure what to do with it. I'm not used to being on this end of "the handshake" anymore. Then he said, "Even if I pull this out I'll have to default in the second round. I had this injury last year and, well, I know what it'll mean for the rest of my season if I go on."

Without a word I shook his hand, and with what I imagined was a pretty stunned look on my face, made my way back to my chair.

I hadn't actually thought about what I'd do if I won. That wasn't part of the plan. I'd beaten a better player. All right, sure, he'd pretty much beaten himself, but I was there to accept the win on his behalf. And so it's Olie Wood going on to the second round and not Andre Fernandez, which was what was *supposed* to happen.

Back at the bordello, Gary and George were a little speechless.

"My nigga," said George after I'd explained what happened.

"Holy God," added Gary with what was obviously the only possible explanation.

That pissed me off a little. "Maybe it's because I was actually good enough to beat the guy," I said. Then I thought about it and changed my mind. "No, you're right. Godlike intervention's more likely."

I spent the rest of the evening replaying over and over the moment of that handshake in my head. Okay, masturbating and replaying over and over the moment of that handshake in my head. It was a huge moment, believe me. Still, I'm realistic. I'm now living on borrowed time. Tomorrow I'm to play Günter Smoltz of Austria, and he's six-foot-six and a net-rusher to boot, making him pretty much impossible to pass. I'm in some serious trouble here, and I know it. All the same, I'm still in this thing, and every day I'm in is another day of living the dream the Olie Wood way.

August 30

Today was hot. Like really hot. But you know, I always loved the heat. Made me horny, if anything. Some people have trouble staying active in the heat, but my body chemistry or some such shit is designed differently, it seems. You just don't survive several days in the Arizona desert if you don't have some kind of special capacity for dealing with the heat, and that's me.

For the second time in as many days I got off to a bad start, dropping the first set 6–love. Playing this guy was like playing against a wall: no matter how well you hit the ball, the wall will always eventually win. I couldn't pass him and I couldn't lob over him. All I could do was wait for him to make mistakes, and he wasn't making many.

But he did seem to be bothered by the heat. I could tell he was relieved to be winning so easily, as he was dragging his ass a little and hunching over occasionally between points. I redoubled my efforts to stall and take as long with my serves as possible, just to keep him out there a few extra minutes. It started working as I finally won a game midway through the second set.

Then he started having a few problems with his serve, and this big guy, having to carry all that weight around, started to sag a little and somehow I broke him. Suddenly I was actually in this set. I pushed harder than I can ever remember pushing before, and battled him to a tiebreaker. He asked the umpire about calling the match due to heat, but the US Open doesn't have a heat policy unlike some other events. So he had to play on, and by asking that question confirmed for me that he was indeed hurting now. Meanwhile I was soaking up the sun. I may be a bit of a sloth out there, but I do love the sun.

He couldn't get his act together in the tiebreak. I wasn't winning any points—this guy was still miles ahead of me in terms of quality of play—but he was starting to make a lot of mistakes and it was getting easier to place the ball just out of reach. He double-faulted away the tiebreak and we were suddenly in the third set.

His body language at the changeover said it all. It said, and I quote, "I can't believe I'm still out here against this loser. I don't know how much more of this shit I can take."

I was starting to feel a little peppy out there. I was enjoying the conditions, and since he'd done all the work tiring himself out, I had energy to spare. The sweat pouring off the guy really wasn't pretty, and that comes from someone who, as you know, has a little bit of a perspiration problem himself. I played to my only advantage, doing everything I could to move him around the court. I wasn't going for winners at all; I was just keeping him moving. Then, suddenly, at 4–2 for him in the third set, he keeled over and fell flat on his face. A collective gasp went up from the few people in attendance, and I did everything I could to avoid punching the air in victory.

The umpire and trainer came scrambling out onto the court to tend to him. It looked as though he'd passed out from heatstroke. Weather like this is hard on tennis players, especially the big ones.

But the guy really wasn't moving. The umpire looked ashen, and suddenly started waving his arms to the tournament officials nearby. Before I knew it an ambulance had pulled out onto the court, and Günter Smoltz was the recipient of some aggressive CPR courtesy of the paramedics. But it was no use. Günter Smoltz was dead.

I was concerned of course, and jogged up to the umpire to offer my condolences.

"Wow, I really didn't want to win it this way," I said quietly, and when he didn't respond right away, added, "I mean I did win this thing, right?"

The guy just looked at me. "Yes, Mr. Wood, you won—by default. Congratulations on your glorious achievement."

So it was true! I'd won another one! I'm into the third round of qualifying at the US Open! This is *unbelievable*! Playing to my strengths and actually winning as a result!

Oh, yeah, and too bad for Smoltz by the way. Shitty thing to have happen, that's for sure. I feel for him and his family and, well, let's all have a moment of silence as we all remember Günter's sunny demeanour and colourful character.

(Go, Olie!)

August 31

Well now this is weird. I never really expected to be playing with something on the line. A win today and I'm into the main draw of the US Open with its gruelling five-set matches. A loss and it's like I was never really here to begin with.

There's been a lot of fallout from Smoltz's death yesterday. Everyone's pretty down and there was even some talk of cancelling the entire event. Thank God they didn't; I haven't enjoyed this much success in ages. No way are the pulling the plug on me now.

New Yorkers are a pretty bloodthirsty bunch, and as a result of Smoltz's timely demise people who've never attended a tennis match are suddenly curious to check it out. Don't get me wrong, the US Open is an extremely popular event. Tens of thousands of people will be swarming all over this place over the next two weeks, but the qualifying event is usually pretty small potatoes. And yet here today we have a nearly full house, no doubt eager to get a look at the guy who was on the same court as "the guy who died." It all adds to the pressure of playing, but there was a time when I loved an audience. I just needed to channel that old confidence again.

I came onto the court with a big smile, determined to win over the audience, but something about me seemed to piss these people off.

"You suck!" yelled one.

"You're fat!" shouted another.

"Killer!" screamed a third.

"You're fat!" chimed in a fourth.

"Hey, someone already said that!" I shot back.

These people seemed to actually blame me for what happened. All I did was benefit from a better resistance to the sun, for God's sake. I became determined to win the match, if for no other reason than to show these assholes up. Nothing motivates ol' Olie Wood like revenge and spite, I can tell you that.

As we were taking to the court, my opponent, an American named Danny Carroll ranked just outside the top 100, grabbed me by the arm, pulled me toward him and whispered in my ear, "Günter was a personal friend of mine. This one's for him, you fucking old man."

"I'm sure your boyfriend would be touched," I whispered back. "Now take your hand off me, or this is what'll happen to it," I added, holding up my deformed hand for him to examine more closely. He seemed either horrified or stupefied. At any rate, he drew back.

"I have no idea how you got here. There's no way you're ranked high enough to be in the draw. You've been sucking at the Futures level. Something smells fishy here."

"Just your wife, dude," I said, backing away with a smile on my face, a smile that disappeared entirely as soon as I remembered that Danny Carroll's wife was in fact dying of brain cancer. So I felt a little bad, though it did at least shut him up for now.

Things started off badly, what with my dropping the first set, but then that seemed to be my pattern this week, so I wasn't all that worried just yet. Danny was a good solid player, but one without any particular flair or big shots; he had a decent return game and didn't make many mistakes you could exploit. He was also pretty healthy, so I didn't think waiting for him to die from the heat was going to work this time. So again, I used the tools at my disposal.

"Günter looked like hell yesterday," I mentioned during a changeover. "I mean when he went down face first like that . . . damn that had to hurt. But then they say he'd already kicked the bucket by that point, so maybe not so much," I added with a smirk.

"Asshole," he said, making one of those clichéd hand-cutting-the-throat motions. As we took to the court he bumped me hard, earning himself a warning from the umpire.

"You know who'll really miss Günter?" I said on the next changeover. "Your wife. Yup, she surely will. But then I hear she'll be seeing him again soon enough anyway." Now I know, I know, what a horrible thing to say, and yes, I actually felt kind of bad for saying it, but it did achieve the desired result. He looked me square in the eye, wound up, and belted a ball straight at my head. Danny was docked a point for unsportsmanlike conduct when I just managed to duck out of the way.

"You know what Günter's last words were?" I said as we switched sides. "Danny Carroll's wife could suck-start a tank."

"Olie, you're so fucking immature," he said as he pushed past me, earning himself another docked point. He barely noticed though, so full of loathing was he now. My strategy wasn't really working however. Except for the couple of points he was penalized, I was barely winning any. The angrier Carroll got, the better he seemed to play. And so I wasn't long for this tournament when finally, out of desperation, I stuck my tongue out at him. Now that's immature too, sure, but I was frustrated, and I never imagined the reaction it would get. He upped and hurled his racquet at me, missing by a mile but still drawing the ire of the umpire and the hoots of the crowd, the latter suddenly seeing me as the reasonable one of the match. And I can honestly say that this was the first time in my career—hell, in my *life*—that I've ever been considered the reasonable one. Felt kind of cool.

"Game, Wood," said the umpire, and Carroll suddenly seemed to realize what was going on. He went nuts.

"You're penalizing *me*? Instead of *this* asshole?" he screamed as the crowd started getting into it.

"Play on," replied the umpire.

"This fucker is saying unbelievable things about my wife and Günter Smoltz," Carroll tried to explain.

"He's lying, sir," I managed. "I'm not saying anything of the kind."

"Play on," repeated the umpire, ignoring us both.

I winked at Carroll while the umpire was looking his way and the guy snapped, lunging at me and throwing a punch.

"Game, set and match, Wood," said the exasperated umpire, leaving the chair without another word. A security guy had to pull Carroll off me as I feigned innocence. He just kept trying to get at me, but to no avail.

So Danny Carroll is suspended from the tour for a month while Olie Wood is moving through to the main draw of the US Open. I won't say the ends justify the means because, well, honestly, I'm not exactly sure what that even means. Or ends. Anyway, you use the tools you have at your disposal to win, and I did exactly that. Do I feel bad? Sure, a little. But then this is who I am.

There was no celebration at George's last night due to the period of mourning being respected for ol' whatsisname, but tonight we partied it up good. The weird thing was how much Blanche Dowling seemed to be enjoying herself. She had the run of the place, and the girls really seemed to like having her around. She was suddenly like a totally different cat, hopping up on people's laps and even purring from time to time. I wasn't actually aware she had that mechanism. What do cats purr with exactly? Doesn't matter; whatever they use, turns out Blanche Dowling has one and it works.

September 1

Day off today while the main draw gets underway. I've drawn an Australian named Arthur Munney, ranked #56 in the world. He's miles above me of course, and the highest ranked player I've gone up against all year. He's considered a bit of a pin-up too, so the television cameras should be there; they always cover the pretty boys. I've never met him but I already hate him, what with his stupid ponytail and dimpled chin.

I wonder if Miranda will watch the match on TV. One of George's girls offered me a blowjob last night, and though I thanked her for thinking of me, I wasn't really interested. Chicks aren't my main focus right now. Though I generally do enjoy blowjobs. Mostly, though, I wish Miranda was here in my player's box. At the big events like this one, each player is given a section where their friends, coach, and family can sit and cheer them on. I'll probably have Gary and, if he's free, possibly George. That seems sad somehow.

Fuck it. I have lots going for me. I'm into the main draw of the US fucking Open, and my payday will be a big one regardless of where I go from here. Even if I lose now, it will be losing on one of the biggest stages in professional sports, so to all you assholes who said I'd never get back here, FUCK YOU. Sure I had to pull a few strings to get here, but here I am and where are you?

I sat in the stands and watched a couple of the first-round matches today, and I must say, it scared me a little bit. These guys are like really, *really* good. All of them. There isn't a player in this draw who doesn't deserve to be here. Well, maybe one.

I feel like so much of the game has passed me by. I mean these guys don't need tricks to win; they win on talent and fitness and fortitude. Part of me is saying, "Who am I kidding, I'm totally out of my league here." But then another part of me is saying, "Who gives a shit? I'm thirty-one and on my way out, and I don't have to prove anything to anyone." I'm definitely liking that second guy more.

September 2

Scared shitless for the first time in a long time today. When I was a kid and playing events like this regularly, I was too young and too stupid to know any better. But now I understand what's at stake when I step out there, and it's downright terrifying.

Or take the locker rooms. You forget shit like that. People being paid to clean up your crap. Stars of the game everywhere you look: Roger Federer taking a long noisy piss; Marat Safin picking at a zit; Andy Roddick relentlessly readjusting his underwear (boxer-briefs; I know people will ask). Just regular people at their most genuine and vulnerable. It's weird, seeing them like that.

I'm having flashbacks of being the poor kid without the proper gear. All these years later and I'm still playing in my crappy Keds with my stolen racquet while my opponent, Arthur Munney, has a bag full of top-quality gear and tennis shoes that cost more than everything I own put together.

I had one nice surprise when I walked out onto the court this afternoon though: a full player's box. George had been nice enough to give a bunch of the girls the day off to come cheer me on. Admittedly my box looked a little different than most players' boxes at an event like this, but beggars can't be choosers.

One cool thing about the middling popularity of this sport is, while ESPN does cover it, except for the biggest names and matches they almost always show it on tape delay, which means I was actually able to watch the match later on in the day. It was interesting to note how many times the cameras panned to my box. It was also interesting to hear the commentators John McEnroe and Mary Carrillo weighing in on me prior to the match.

JM: "I remember this guy from way back when *I* played. What on earth is he even *doing* here? I mean just look at the guy. Look at his hair!"

MC: "He's not the healthiest looking guy in the draw, that's for sure. But remember, he did have to fight through three rounds of qualifying to get here."

JM: "Yeah, one injury retirement, one default, and one death. Quite the track record for ol' Olie Wood, that's for sure."

MC: "I barely remember him actually being on the tour. Wasn't he a top player at one time?"

JM: "He was a blip for a while. Had a couple of good years followed by a whole lot of bad ones. Kind of an embarrassing record actually. He's totally out of his league here."

And though he was being an asshole, McEnroe was right: I was out of my league here. You could see it in our warm-up. Munney hit the ball with a confidence and power you just couldn't manufacture. He was the real deal. I hit the ball with discomfort and desperation. And I was out of tricks here. This was going to come down to how much gas I had left in the tank, which wasn't a hell of a lot, let me tell you.

I found the crowd difficult to adjust to. Every time you look up you're staring at thousands of people, an actual *wall* of people, and they're all staring at you. I suddenly felt fat and wished I'd cut my hair. Or maybe changed my headband for a clean fresh one. It made it far more difficult to concentrate on the job at hand, and before too long Munney, far more used to this than I was, took the first set. I was getting used to that anyhow.

Then fortune stepped in.

I was spraying a lot of balls—wide, long, everywhere. I was having a hard time contending with the pace of the ball, and I couldn't control it even when I managed to get my racquet on it. Anyway, one of my errant shots took Munney square in the nose. I seem to have a unique talent for nailing my opponents.

He went down hard, clutching his face. It seemed to really hurt, and when he stood up it was, well, flat, for lack of a better word. Suddenly it was wider than it was long, and that's saying something. I never knew that could actually happen in real life, but trust me, it can. I've now seen it firsthand.

JM: "Ooh, that looks bad."

MC: "I've got to think it looks worse than it feels."

JC: "Yeah, but when you're one of People Magazine's Twenty Most Beautiful People, I would almost think that's worse."

I didn't know he was on that particular list. I suddenly felt a little less bad.

Munney looked seriously rattled. And while it seemed to me a wildly out of proportion response to the actual severity of the injury, he got himself an injury timeout while the trainer scrambled out to check on him. His nose didn't seem to be broken so we played on, but he kept playing with it and couldn't seem to concentrate. Suddenly I'd taken four straight games and the second set.

"Dude," I said as we were sitting side by side between changeovers. "What's wrong with you?"

"It won't go back, mate."

"Huh?"

"My nose, it won't go back. My whole face looks different now. Looks *wrong*."

"Hey, yeah, I'm sorry. It was actually an accident."

"No worries, mate. I know you couldn't have done that on purpose if you tried. Still, just *look* at it."

He couldn't take his mind off it. Funny enough, neither could I. I was so distracted by how awful he looked that I wasn't really thinking about my game, and the less I thought about it the better it became. I started hitting some really solid groundstrokes, and before I knew it I had the third set in hand.

Munney took a timeout after the set and was gone a ridiculously long time. They couldn't seem to get him to come back out of the locker room. When he finally did emerge, he looked terrible. My guess is he'd spent the entire time in the mirror playing with his nose, readjusting it, whatever. I decided to end this match while I was still in it.

"Jesus, it looks awful," I winced. "It must really hurt."

He covered his face with his hand. "It's sore, but it's okay. But it does look really bad, doesn't it? What the hell am I supposed to do?" He was genuinely upset about it.

Now we all know Anna Kournikova. Pretty blonde thing. Never all that much of a player (never won a title in her so-called "career"), but known far and wide for the way she looked and for what she wore. For someone like that, tennis is no more than a means to an end. They aren't the best in the sport, but they know how to parlay their exposure into something far more lucrative and long-term, like modelling or acting. Not many tennis players make the transition, but Kournikova definitely paved the way. I say this because Arthur Munney was clearly looking to follow in the footsteps of Kournikova, and I'd just ruined his big ticket out of here.

"I don't know, Arthur," I said. "I don't know what you should do. You look almost as bad as I do."

That did it. "Umpire, I have to default," he said at once.

"Are you serious?" asked the umpire. "It doesn't seem that bad."

"I'm deadly serious. I have to get this examined immediately." He quickly shook my hand, then the umpire's hand, and then he was out of there, bags in hand. No one in the crowd seemed to know how to react. Neither did the television commentators.

JM: "I can't believe what I'm seeing here. This guy is *defaulting*! The injury is not that bad! You *can't* be serious."

MC: "He's definitely beating it out of here in a hurry. There's got to be something else wrong, though I'm not sure what that would be. The trainer seemed to give him the go-ahead, though. Maybe he knows something we don't."

JM: "And unbelievably, Olie Wood's strange journey continues for another day. This guy's somehow through to the second round."

MC: "I don't think anyone would have looked at the draw and predicted this. It's true what they say: In sports sometimes *anything* can happen."

And that's true by the way.

September 3

Day off today. George took Gary and me on a tour of some of his favourite places in and around the city, including Times Square, the Empire State Building, and the police station where he sometimes goes to bail out one or more of his ladies. I realize now, that even though my life at times seems odd, there are far more bizarre paths I could have taken.

I've decided to leave Blanche Dowling behind when I leave New York. She's become kind of the official house cat here at the cathouse, and I've never seen her so happy. I can't get my head around it. She still takes swats at me if I go near her, and she still seems to hate Gary, so it's not like she's mellowed any. She's still a bitch, just a more discriminating bitch than I gave her credit for initially.

Tomorrow I play a Swede named Gustov Bjornson. Judging from my press conference after last night's match I'm basically on a death watch, with people just waiting for me to lose humiliatingly. And when I say "people" I mean the two or three journalists who actually bothered to attend my press conference.

The "PC" is a funny little thing, and a mandatory part of all Grand Slam tourneys. After each and every match both players are required to face the press, and if you don't you can be fined pretty severely. So even if there's no one around who actually gives a shit about you or what you did or didn't do out there on the court, you're still required to plonk your ass down in the press room and wait to see if anyone cares enough to show up. Being something of a curiosity, I attracted a few reporters interested to see if I was for real. They asked a couple of questions along the lines of, "Being saved by another man's vanity, how's that make you feel?" which I didn't bother answering. I mean what the hell do you say to something like that? Other than the fact I just keep on winning, or at least getting through my matches, as a result of my opponents' various vulnerabilities.

After the press conference, Gary and I went out for a drink at a bar close to Flushing Meadows. I noticed Bjornson, my next opponent, nursing a bottle of water over at the bar, and told Gary I wanted a quick moment alone with the guy. Gary obliged, and to no surprise, disappeared into the bathroom to roll a joint or five.

"Bjornson, my man," I said, slapping him on the back as I took a seat alongside.

"Do I know you?" he asked in heavily accented English.

"Olie Wood, dude. You know, from your match tomorrow?"

"Ah, yeah. How are you doing? Why are you here?"

"No reason. Just thought I'd say hi. And to tell you I'm sorry about the whole April thing."

"What April thing?" he said suspiciously.

"Well, you know, how she's leaving you for Colin Farrell."

See, a couple of things you need to know about Gustov Bjornson are: 1) he's a very insecure person because he's basically ugly; 2) he dates supermodel April Meadows and quite rightly worships the water she walks upon; and 3) he's not Colin Farrell.

Bjornson is that breed of athlete prevalent in almost every sport. He's big as hell, he's got a face that looks like it's been smashed to smithereens and then rebuilt several times over, and he does things like grow his wispy blond hair long in an effort to hide his horrible looks but just ends up drawing more attention to them. He's also a really talented player with a huge forehand that he hits with more power than you'd get out of most automobiles. He's got hands the size of hams, and together with his huge arms, uses them to pummel the living crap out of his opponents. I would never be able to compete with that kind of power, but again, it helps to know a thing or two about your opponent before you ever set foot on the court to face him.

When you look like Bjornson, you're going to feel a little funny about your relationships, especially when they happen to be with tiny, stick-thin supermodels that most of the world has seen at least partially naked at some point. Funny thing is, I wasn't making anything up this time. I actually heard from another player that she's humping the Irish actor who's something of a personal hero of mine.

"You lie," Bjornson said.

"Yeah, maybe," I said, gazing cursorily around the bar. "Where's she at anyway? I thought she'd be here with you. You know, night before the big match and all."

He stared down at the floor. "Not feeling well. Had to get out by myself a while."

"I know what you mean, man. It's hard dating a whore."

"Sorry?"

"Hey, I'm just saying watch out. Word is getting around that yours isn't the only pole she's smoking. It's even in the papers. Go look if you don't believe me."

I got up to rejoin Gary at the table he'd moved to, and watched Bjornson out of the corner of my eye. Finally he came storming over to growl in my face, "You know nothing. April's a good woman. She's not a whore."

"She's an American model, dude. Wake up. Look at yourself— and I say this as someone who's pretty challenged in the beauty department himself—you're a fucking gargoyle. No offence, but what would someone like April Meadows want with someone like you?"

Now I should probably point out that my logic here was pretty flawed. Beautiful women date big ugly guys all the time. Why, you ask? Well it's simple, really. There are two reasons: money and fame. But even when someone is wealthy, like Bjornson, and well known in his sport, like Bjornson, and athletic, like Bjornson, he can't get away from whatever insecurities have dogged him his whole life.

"Have a drink with us," I suggested when he started to die inside.

"No, no, I shouldn't," he said, wiping away tears with the back of an arm. "I want to be alone. We'll meet again tomorrow, Olie Wood. I thank you for your candour." And with that he was gone.

Gary hoisted his glass. "To you, Olie. And to your continued success, however undeserved."

"To me," I said, and we clinked our glasses.

"Great things are happening for you, my friend. I can feel it."

I tipped back my glass and thought for the first time in a long time that he might actually be right.

                                                    September 4

I took to the court today trying to think of what I was going to need to beat someone like Bjornson. That is, until I saw him slouch his way onto the court, late and looking like shit warmed over.

"You okay?" I asked as we began to warm up.

"I confronted April last night. She confessed to everything."

"Sorry to hear it, dude."

"She's left me. She says it has nothing to do with me, and I believe her."

"Sorry again."

"You were right, Olie," he sniffled. "It's this Colin Farrell character. They've been fucking for weeks. *God*, what a jerk."

"Sorry all over the place, bud. But please don't cry out here. That's just not cool."

The warm-up completed, we started the match with me on serve. Bjornson took a wild swing at the ball, but missed by about two feet. Then he crumpled to the ground and started to cry wildly. The umpire jumped down and scurried over, asking if he was hurt. Bjornson didn't answer. The officials tried to get him to his feet, but he was all loose-legged and floppy and unable to stand up straight. Finally they had to drag him from the court, by his ankles no less. As they escorted him from the stadium, the umpire breathed into his microphone and with a bit of reluctance said, "Game, set and match, Mr. Wood." He gave me a look that said, "I don't know what you did, but I'm watching you." I shrugged and offered my bows to a crowd too stunned by what it had just witnessed to notice.

The press conference afterward featured a few more reporters than I'd ordinarily attract.

"A pretty weird way to work your way through the draw, huh?" asked one.

"As long as I get through," I told the guy.

"You haven't seen a lot of court time, Olie. Doesn't that worry you, not being ready for when you finally have to play an entire match?"

"Maybe I'll be the first guy to get through to the final without actually playing a match," I said, which to my surprise earned a chuckle from the crowd. Not all of them were so friendly however. I got into a fight with a reporter from *Sports Illustrated* after she accused me of cheating, more or less suggesting I was a washed-up hack with no business being here at the US Open. I admit to calling her a bitch, yes, but nothing more than that. Regardless, it definitely got people talking about me again. They even ran a piece on me on ESPN tonight:

"A lot of people are asking, 'Who *is* this Olie Wood guy,' and to be honest, we had to go back a ways to find out ourselves. Rarely has someone disappeared so entirely from a sport that we hardly remember him, but Olie Wood was once a promising, highly touted young player in the game. Most who do remember him will do so from the oft-repeated footage from a now infamous appearance at the Australian Open," announced the voiceover, and of course they showed the clip of me and the kookaburra, the victory lap, and the ensuing meltdown. "Mr. Wood's path through this year's US Open has been one of the stranger ones we've witnessed, resulting in a vicious verbal exchange between Wood and Louise Colbert from *Sports Illustrated* earlier this afternoon. However, whether a result of his unorthodox look and style, his combative yet entertaining manner, or his improbable run through the draw, Olie Wood is fast becoming the talk of this year's US Open."

So there.

I play none other than Lincoln Holmes tomorrow, which doesn't bode well for me. In fact, I may be bode right out of this tournament by this time tomorrow if I don't figure out a way to get under his skin, and Lincoln's never shown a lot of emotional weaknesses, at least not to me. My work is definitely cut out for me.

September 5

Today was my toughest match to date. The damnable Lincoln Holmes has been on fire all year, and he's beaten me badly each and every time we've played. And now he's being tapped to go deep into the second week of the tournament, while Olie Wood is been tapped to need directions to the bus station home. I've had to sit back and watch while this son of a bitch lives out the life I was supposed to have. Well fuck him. Fuck you, Lincoln Holmes.

In the locker room prior to the match he tried to ignore me as I began to implement my strategy.

"I'm cookin' with gas, dude. I've played you the way I have these last nine matches just to lull you into a false sense of security and confidence, and I can see it's worked. You won't believe what you see out there today—"

He stopped me, but just barely. "Olie, I've been watching your matches with a kind of morbid curiosity, and I know you too well—you're a scam artist, and always have been as long as I've known you. I'm not going to let you trick me into flipping out, I don't care if I get hurt, and I'm better in the heat than you are. *Way* better. So it's going to come down to tennis, and we both know you're totally out of your league when it comes to that."

"Yeah? Well fuck you," I said, smiling at my cleverness. He just sighed.

"You've tricked your way in here somehow, and you're pretending to be a tennis player, but you're not," he went on. "Not anymore. I don't know who you think you're fooling, but remember, I've been down there with you. We crossed paths as I was coming up and you were heading down. *Way* down. I know what you are, Olie, so don't fuck around. I tired of your bullshit long ago. This here is my coming out party, and I'm not about to let someone like you spoil it for me."

"Coming out. Now is that, like, a gay thing?" I asked.

He just threw his hands up in surrender. "I give up, Olie. You're obviously running dangerously low on brain cells, and I'm not going to tax what few you have left. Let's go and get this over with."

Without another word I grabbed my gear and stood up. He started to walk out, but at the last second stopped and turned back.

"You know what's so upsetting about you, Olie?"

"Well I've heard a long list, Lincoln. I'm not exactly sure which one you're thinking of—"

"When I was young I watched you play Wimbledon," he broke in. "You were this rough-hewn kid without a lot of style, but you had a real gift. It was obvious to anyone who watched, this gift, and you were beautiful to see. I was a fan of yours, Olie. And I always imagined how great you'd be to meet. What makes me sick is how disappointing it was when I actually got the chance. How you'd fucked it all up and let it all slip away. That's the saddest thing," he said, and with that turned and walked away.

I followed numbly. I mean what do you say to something like that? "Fuck you, Holmes?" Hardly fitting. Not again.

He was right about one thing though: I was a disappointment. I was. But not today. I was into the third round of the US Open, and no matter what this jerk said, I'd gotten here my way, on my own steam. So yeah, fuck you, Holmes.

I'll say this for his little pep talk though. I've rarely, if ever, played as focused as I did today, even back when I was on top. I was thrown by what he'd said, but it didn't matter. If anything it was going to help my game.

I hit a backhand crosscourt totally on instinct that made the crowd go wild, and even Holmes had to nod in respect. That evening's broadcast only reinforced what I already knew.

JM: "You've got to take your hat off to Olie for a shot like that."

MC: "I have no idea where that came from, John. He's got some shots, I'll say that. Who is this guy?"

I played one of the best sets of my life, running around like a hot sweaty madman. I worked Lincoln to a draw, and in the tiebreak started playing more aggressively, taking the game to him, which I know he doesn't like. But knowing something, and being able to do something about it, are entirely different matters, it seems. I've always known Lincoln Holmes likes to play long rallies, and hates it when his opponents attack the net with any kind of regularity. But in the past I couldn't ever quite make this knowledge work for me. Today, though, something was clicking, and I was able to work through his defences and take a few balls on volleys.

I won the opening set in the tiebreaker. It was the first time I'd taken the opening set in the entire tournament.

JM: "This is totally bizarre. This guy comes out of nowhere, and takes a set off one of the top young players in the world. This should be a totally one-sided match, and yet this out-of-shape *Canadian* is putting the spurs to Lincoln Holmes before our very eyes."

I took the second set quickly. Clearly Holmes didn't know how to deal with me on these terms. But then things started to shift. I ran out of gas early in the third set, and he cleaned my clock as he started to find his rhythm again. He kicked the shit out of me in the fourth too, and I was starting to look and feel a little desperate. The worse I felt the more confident he got.

JM: "Well, we're seeing things return to normal now. Holmes got over his nerves and seems to be pulling out of this potential disaster."

MC: "Good thing he turned this around when he did. It could have been the most embarrassing loss of his young career. Getting beaten by someone like Olie Wood will kind of stick to you for a while."

He broke me to open the fifth set, and I was pretty much done. I started getting frustrated and really swinging out on my forehands, sending a lot of them sailing long. But it still felt pretty good to be knocking the shit out of these balls. Even if I was on my way out, at least I was going down swinging.

Then, on a breakpoint down, I let fly a forehand—and killed a bird flying across the court. Obliterated, really. Talk about your deja vu. I'd been to this party before, and couldn't believe I was back.

For a moment everything went completely silent. Though, this being New York, a few people let out a whoop after a while, and then someone shouted, "It ain't the bird's fault you guys are playing this bad!" which got a nervous laugh from the crowd. But they had no idea what this meant to me. Only the true tennis aficionado would remember my involvement in the incident in Australia. Even though it's still shown on TV quite often, no one really remembers the player involved, kind of like that "agony of defeat" ski guy on ABC's Wide World of Sports.

But I remembered. And what's worse, I know I only saw it for a second, and that later on the sports shows called it a pigeon, but I'm pretty sure it was a kookaburra. Now I know this is New York and that they don't actually, technically exist here, but I'm pretty sure that's what I saw. How that could be, I have no idea, but that's what I saw.

And I experienced a kind of epiphany at that moment. Life is fucked. Shit happens—weird, incomprehensible shit—and that bird, before it bought it, or perhaps *by* buying it, was trying to tell me something important. Maybe you're walking around with all sorts of nasty things swirling around you, waiting to see how you spin them. Maybe you have the power to turn your shitty luck around and start doing something good with your life, if only you put the proper spin on things. You've been walking around under such a dark cloud for so many years, waiting for some kind of sign that your life doesn't suck, and, well, here you go. Here's your sign. You take one step forward by taking just a little back. All it takes, it seems, is a little backspin.

I smiled a little as we replayed the point and I hit my first ace of the match. I was still tired, but not really feeling it much anymore. I pulled out the game, and got myself on the board in the fifth set.

JM: "Most people don't remember much about this guy's history on the tour, but believe it or not, that exact same thing happened to him years ago at the Australian Open. It happened right around the time his game really went to the birds."

MC: "That's funny, John. I actually didn't realize that was him. I've seen that footage. *Every*one's seen that footage. He's got to be the unluckiest person on the planet."

But she was wrong.

Holmes started to panic a little as I picked up my level of play even further. I broke him to even the set at 2–2, and held serve again. The idea of my playing this well this deep into a match of this magnitude seemed to rattle him, and I managed to break him again. I stopped caring whether I won or not and just started concentrating on playing well, and goddamn it if I wasn't playing better than him.

I beat Lincoln Holmes 6–4 in the fifth. My first five-set win in eight years. And most importantly, I actually beat him. I beat a better player by playing better tennis. I had no tricks to pull, and yet I still somehow managed to pull out the victory. Holmes was gracious in defeat, certainly more than I've ever been with him. He just shook my hand and said, "That's what I'm talkin' about. That's what I saw at Wimbledon that day." Maybe he's not such an asshole after all. Or maybe I'm just feeling mushy in my post-victory glow, I don't know.

And while I am experiencing excruciating pain right now, with every muscle in my body screaming out in agony, I've never been more proud of myself. My bird-butchery was of course the top story on the news tonight, but attached to that was a nice little piece on Olie Wood and his incredible journey getting this far in "Olie's Open." They opened with the line, "Who is this guy?"

JM: "I guess there's still room for miracles in this world."

MC: "I never thought I'd see the day. A truly entertaining match, and I guess the big question is, how far can this guy actually go in this tournament?"

September 6

Thank God, another day off today. Because I'm so wrecked I could hardly walk when I finally got up this afternoon. A little of George the Jew's blow and a few drinks and I was right as rain, but Jesus, my body can't take another match like that again.

Hung out with Gary today, just checking out the city. A couple of people actually recognized me, which was nice for a change.

"Bird killer!" said one.

"Monster!" shouted another.

"Who *is* this guy?" said a third with a wink, quoting the line that had become almost synonymous with me over the previous twenty-four hours.

"Seems like people are getting to know Olie Wood all over again," said Gary, stating the obvious.

"Yeah, weird shit," I agreed.

"God works in mysterious ways," he sighed, and I frowned. "There's obviously something bigger at work here, Olie. I trust you recognize that."

"Well if it's your boss, you tell him thanks," I said. "This has definitely been a week to remember."

"I'm just glad to see you happy again. I don't see you happy enough anymore."

"Hey, just give me something to be happy about and I'm all over it, pal."

He asked me what I was going to go when all this was over.

"Well I dunno," I said. I admit I've sort of allowed myself to forget this was going to end, more likely sooner than later. "I'll start thinking about the next big project, I guess. Who knows, this week might even move my ranking up high enough to get me into more big tournaments. Maybe this is a second chance I'm getting."

"Or maybe a final chance to make good on all your early promise."

"Jesus, bring me down a little why don't you," I said, more than a little irritated, even though I wasn't entirely sure what he'd meant.

"Well wasn't that was this was always supposed to be?" he said.

"God, you're starting to sound just like Miranda. Why are you guys so keen to see me quit?"

"I'm not. That's not what I want at all. I just happen to think you have other things to offer after all this is over, that's all."

"Well I'll decide when this is all supposed to end, Gary, not you and *certainly* not your God. And while we're on the subject, it's me that got me into this position, not God. Was it God that fucked up Arthur Munney's nose? No, that was me. Was it God that made Danny Carroll go nuts? No, again that was me. *I* got me here, no one else. *I* outplayed Lincoln Holmes yesterday."

He paused a moment. "So what got you into the tournament in the first place?" he asked, and I stopped dead on the sidewalk.

"Well that would have been you, Gar."

"Okay," he nodded suggestively.

"Oh, God told you to hack an international sporting organization's computer system, did he. Well isn't he just the little radical."

Actually, at the press conference following yesterday's match, I was asked about a possible higher power at work here. Not surprising, really, as Americans seem to love that kind of thing. "Just the higher power of my own talent," I answered, trying to play the room but receiving no laughs. I never get any laughs. No one gets my sense of humour. It's way too sophisticated for most people.

"You've got to agree this is one of the most bizarre stories we've seen in the game for a long time," the reporter continued.

"I just think it's taken a long time to get back to where I belong in the sport. It's not bizarre," I said, "it's just things righting themselves eventually."

"But you're well past your prime, and you've benefited from an awful lot of good luck, don't you think?"

"Hey, you make your own luck, dude. I know what I've done. It's not some higher power at work here, it's me working my ass off," I said, ending the press conference right there.

September 7

My next opponent, a Russian named Ivan Dubenko, is one of the more popular players on the tour. He's what they call amiable, and nothing ever seems to get to him. Part of that may be because he doesn't speak a word of English except, for some reason, "I am afraid the Indians are quite indigestible." I speak English and I'm not even sure what that means. He was going to be tough, this guy.

Weird moment as I was heading over to the facilities this afternoon. A large tattooed woman came bouncing up to me, throwing her arms around me in a big bear hug. "Ah saw it on the teevee, and says to mahself, that there's the same boy I drove into Macon. How in the hell are ya?"

"Thelina! My God, what are you doing here?"

"Ahm watchin' the teevee and seen this story on ya and I says to mahself, Self, get yer ass up there to New Yawk City an' see yer boy play his tennis. So ah drove ma car all the way up here and here ah am. Y'all're doin' some great stuff out there. Beat that negra boy real good."

I asked Thelina if she'd like to sit in my box, and once I'd convinced her that this wasn't some sort of lame come-on, and that the seats were actually pretty amazing, she was thrilled. Then, and I swear to God this is true, what do I see through the crowd but another familiar tattoo bobbing its way toward me.

"Earthling!" the man announced. It was that weird dude from the train to Saskatoon.

"Xarkon," I replied. "What brings you to New York?"

"I've been monitoring your progress from Aries, and thought I'd use up a few vacation days to observe you in your indigenous environment."

"Got any pointers for me?"

"Just win, baby. Just win."

I pointed him, too, in the direction of my player's box, then shook his hand and went to prepare for my match.

It ended up being a real up and down affair. Dubenko's the better player, but my win against Lincoln Holmes has given me new reservoirs of confidence. It also helped that Dubenko seemed to be suffering from leg cramps stemming from that ridiculously humid New York heat we'd experienced earlier on in the week. I surprised myself by playing him pretty even, early on. The crowd actually seemed to be rooting for me, and my motley crew of a player's box was cheering for all they were worth.

I rather enjoyed watching the match later that night, and listening to the commentary.

JM: "I've gotta say, this Canadian guy has some talent. It may be wrapped in a pretty unappealing package, but it's in there somewhere under all that fat. If you squint just the right way, you can almost see the player who had a successful run on the tour once upon a time."

MC: "Yes, to go from playing Futures—and not doing all that well—to going toe to toe with a quality player like Ivan Dubenko is really quite remarkable. I don't know what's more entertaining, seeing him actually start to play well, or waiting to see what bizarre incident befalls him next."

I didn't disappoint. When some heckler kept calling me out on each lost point, I eventually hit him a solid forehand, catching him square on the forehead with a resounding "thud." This not only shut him up, but got a huge roar from the crowd. I was docked a point, but it was totally worth it, as he was completely silent after that.

Dubenko and I split the first four sets. I was counterpunching for the most part, and occasionally blunting the power of his shots with backspin, forcing him to race to the net bent low to retrieve the ball (always a fun tactic against these bigger guys), a ploy which won me my share of points. But in the meantime I was getting bone tired, and wasn't even sure whether I'd be able to finish the match. It was an evening match, so I didn't have the better part of the sun and heat to work with—it would have made Dubenko's cramping even worse while I reenergized under the sun's rays. As it was, I had to contend with a fairly nice New York evening, much to my chagrin.

At 4–4 in the fifth, he was serving at deuce and I hit a solid return up the line. He hit it back harder crosscourt; I hit it with no pace whatsoever down the middle of the court; he ripped a return right at me; I caught it on my shoetops and fluffed it just over the net; he dove to retrieve it and popped it back over; I dove to the net, hearing a crack in my knee as I did, and popped it back again. There we were, both at the net, knocking the ball back and forth, faster and faster as the rally picked up steam until finally, mercifully, he flubbed it, and the ball bounced off the net on his side. It was the best rally of the night and I'd somehow come out of it on top. He double-faulted on the next serve and I'd broken him, and made ready to serve for the match.

The next couple of minutes went by in a blur as I took him out with four straight points. I was serving like a man possessed. Even with no strength left in my arm I was able to backspin my serves, forcing him to stretch and lunge every which way in an effort to retrieve the oddly bouncing ball. A purely defensive tactic, mind you, but one that worked well against a guy who liked to go out there and bash the absolute shit out of the ball.

I'd won. I was into the quarterfinals of the US Open. The folks in my box went nuts.

Dubenko was gracious in defeat. I was touched when he pulled me close and whispered, "I am afraid the Indians are quite indigestible."

"Thanks, man," I told him. "That means a lot."

The press conference afterwards was an absolute nuthouse. It was standing room only, and reporters were throwing questions at me so fast I barely had time to answer.

"How have you been able to do this? Is this truly the comeback of a lifetime?"

"How did you do it? He seemed to be outplaying you from the first point, but somehow you stayed with him."

"Since killing that bird you seem to have turned your game around. Are you a superstitious person?"

"Do you think that heckler might sue?"

And finally: "Who *is* this guy!" Which got a huge laugh.

As I left the grounds, I actually had people approach me for autographs. I hadn't signed an autograph since I was about twenty. It was quite a rush.

People seemed to recognize me everywhere I went. It always seems like not that many people watch or care about tennis, but when something odd happens they start tuning in by the millions. I was that something odd, it seems.

I'm now back at the brothel, and as soon as the girl and her date in the next room call it a night, I'll sleep the best sleep I've slept in a very long time.

(1:00 AM)

Well as if things couldn't get any more emotional, but who should show up tonight but Miranda. She almost seemed shy when I came down to meet her at the front door.

"How'd you find me here?" I asked, unsure how to react.

"I followed you from Flushing Meadows. I didn't want to get in the way of all the people wishing you well and asking for autographs. And then . . . well, I just needed to work up the nerve."

"Since when do you need nerve to talk to me?"

"Since you became this big celebrity."

We stood there awkwardly a while. In the meantime, an old black dude cruised quietly by.

"Damn, girl," I said to break the silence developing between us. "You're so *fat*!"

"Yeah, the baby and all."

"Right," I said, remembering. "Right."

"So, congratulations on, well, everything. You know I was, like, wrong and all."

Well now that came as quite a shock. I'd never once heard Miranda say she was wrong about anything before.

"Thanks," I said.

"So you miss me or what."

"All the time," I told her.

"And the baby?"

"Not so much."

"Yeah. Right. Okay. Well I brought your mail," she said, shoving a stack of envelopes at me. "And this shirt you left at the house."

"You came all this way to give me a shirt and some junk mail?"

"No. Well, yeah—and this," she said, pushing a bigger envelope at me. Inside was a kind of x-ray type thing. "I had an ultrasound. You know, just to make sure the baby is healthy—and he is, just in case you're wondering—and, well, I thought you'd like a copy."

It was a picture of Miranda's stomach (not that you could tell it was her, really, but I'll have to take her word for it), and inside it was this "shape." It was the outline of a baby. Of *my* baby. I couldn't stop staring. It was so bizarre. I hadn't expected it to look like that, or to feel whatever it was I was suddenly feeling inside.

"This is so wild," I whispered.

"I know," she said, smiling.

"Fuck me. Fuck me!" cried one of the girls from a nearby room.

"That's your kid. *Our* kid," I continued on seamlessly.

"Yeah, I know. It's a boy. You want to feel?"

It turned out she didn't mean quite what I thought, and she slid my hand down to where this thing was kicking the absolute crap out of her stomach.

"How could I raise him?" I asked.

"How couldn't you?" she shot back. "And why can't we do this together?"

"You know I'm not equipped for this, Miranda."

"Who is, Olie. Everyone has to learn on the job."

"But I never learned what it meant to *have* a father, let alone be one."

"I could help you," she said, "if you want me to."

When I asked her why she'd want me to be a part of this thing, especially after everything I'd put her through, she told me that, despite all of my various shortcomings and some of her better instincts, she still loved me. "And when I saw you play that Holmes guy on TV, I saw a passion in your eyes I hadn't seen in a really long time, if ever. It was the first time I got a sense of the person you were before we met. It was the first time I think I really understood you." She breathed deeply as though she'd been practicing that.

"I don't like it when you yell at me and hit me," I told her.

"I'll stop. I don't like it when you disengage from me."

"I can try to stop."

"So now what?" she asked.

And so I took my girl to bed in our whorehouse guestroom, and it was a night I can honestly say will stay with me the rest of my life.

September 8

Andre Agassi has won the US Open twice and been ranked number one in the world for more than one hundred weeks. He's one of the oldest players on the tour—older than me even—but still manages to keep himself ranked amongst the best in the world. I've never liked him. I respect him for his skills, yes, but I've never liked him. And he was my quarterfinal opponent today.

Now beating Ivan Dubenko or a still-green Lincoln Holmes is one thing, but taking on someone like Andre Agassi is an entirely different matter altogether. I was terrified going in and couldn't even speak to him in the locker room beforehand. I was in no position to trash-talk this time.

What I did have going for me was my growing entourage, what with Miranda and our unborn son joining the other assorted freaks and geeks already on display in my player's box. Xarkon and Thelina seemed to be really hitting it off, while the prostitutes were growing increasingly familiar with both Gary and the game. And to top it all off, who showed up but my old buddy Dudley.

"Dud, dude!" I said when I saw him sitting there, squeezed in tight between two sexy Asian transvestites (those are still girls, right?). "How'd you get here, man?"

"Oh, saved my pennies, Olie Wood. Yeah, saved 'em up and came down to see you."

"You don't look so good, Dudley."

"Yeah, Dudley's sick as a dog, they say. Scary plane ride today."

So there they were, my cheering section, screaming full blast as I came trotting out onto the court for my match. The media were out in force, waiting to see how far I could take this thing, and the crowd was treating it like some kind of carnival. It was all pretty intimidating, though Agassi didn't seem all that phased by it. I was, however, and prior to the match I sat rubbing my sore knee and staring out at the crowd of thousands, completely over-whelmed by it all. Did I have anything left in the tank? Could I possibly keep up with this guy? Only time would tell.

And not much time at all, it turned out. My first serve he blast-ed crosscourt, nowhere near me. My second serve he answered much the same way. In about a minute and a half he broke me to start the match, and it wouldn't get much better after that.

Agassi played me like the chump I was. Suddenly it felt like I was back on the Futures tour again, badly outmanned and with no hope of even keeping up. The energy quickly drained from the crowd, and the atmosphere we'd arrived to was conspicuously absent barring the odd shout of encouragement from my box. None of it helped. He bageled me in the first set 6–0, and I was humiliated. I've often wondered if my ability to be embarrassed had faded over time, but it hadn't evidently.

In the second set I was going to try everything I had, but I just couldn't get to the ball to try it. I was a step too slow on every point. I was lucky to pull a game out, so my humiliation wasn't complete. Though even my box was quiet by now.

As the third set opened I felt totally drained, and my arms and legs felt like they were filled with lead. He broke me again to open the set, and I was sunk. As the match was being shown live I never got to hear the commentary, but I could easily imagine it.

JM: "This is more like it. This is the Olie Wood we all expected to see from the outset."

MC: "Absolutely. The thrashing of his life and well deserved, I might add."

Then a funny thing happened. He hit me. It was nothing real-ly, just a miss-hit that took me solidly in the chest. It didn't hurt, but it pissed me off. He apologized immediately, as was protocol, but the look on his face told a different story. I lost that game too, and as we changed sides he bumped into me accidentally-on-pur-pose, grinning a little in passing. I knew what he was trying to do. I'd done it a thousand times myself. But it made me angry, his doing it to me, and I started hitting out a little. Everything hurt, but I pushed through the pain to break his serve and win a service game of my own after that. I was on the board now, if nothing else. My only goal at this point was to go down fighting. No more bagels. No more embarrassments. No shame in losing when you're trying your damnedest. I mean, what was I even doing here in the first place, right? This was all gravy. But I wasn't going to go down like a loser. No way. And with that in mind I stepped up my game even further.

I never seem to learn that I play my best when I "hit out," or, in other words, when I simply wallop the ball whenever it comes into my court. I've always been a player who thrives on instinct and guts, and when I try to over-think things it just screws me up. Hell, that's the story of my life—when I try to think, everything goes to shit. So, once I started smashing that fucker and not giving a shit about losing, my shots started landing and suddenly I wasn't the only one out there scurrying after the ball.

I played him to a third-set tiebreaker, at which point my second wind started to kick in. I began to hit some glorious shots, like the one I hit in desperation backwards and between my legs that somehow made it over the net, surprising him and winning me the point. It was close, but in the end I took the third set 9–7 in the tiebreak.

But when I walked back to my chair on the changeover I felt— no, more like heard—that telltale pop in my knee. I sat down immediately so as not to reveal my injury, but the pain started crawling up my leg and I knew I was fucked.

When the umpire called time, I remained in my chair.

"Is there a problem, Mr. Wood?" he asked.

"I just need a minute," I told him.

"You don't have a minute."

"Okay," I said, but still didn't move.

"Are you able to return to the court?" he asked.

"You bet. No problem."

"Well then please do so, Mr. Wood."

I had no choice. It was either get up now or default. I slowly rose to my feet, and as I started hobbling out onto the court gasps could be heard throughout the capacity crowd. I grimaced at Miranda. She gave me a look that said, "What? What is it?" But all I could do was shrug in answer. This was not the way I wanted to go out.

I took my place and prepared to serve, but as I shifted my weight onto my knee I buckled and fell hard to the ground. The crowd gasped again.

The trainer came running out onto the court. I was permitted an injury timeout as he worked my leg over as best he could.

"This is bad," he said. "You're going to need surgery again by the looks of it. This match is over, I'm afraid."

"No way," I protested. "I didn't come this far to default. It takes a lot more than this to make Olie Wood pull out of a match."

"I'm familiar with your resilience, Olie, but I'm serious. This is bad."

"Can't you give me a painkiller?"

"I can give you a shot."

"I may need a big one. My tolerance for that sort of thing has gotten pretty high."

"Well this here is pretty potent stuff—"

"No, seriously, dude. It's *really high*."

"Okay." He froze my leg and gave me a shot; it was lame but better than nothing. At least I was able to stand up, but there was no way I was going to be running down balls any time soon.

I went to serve, and in desperation used an odd sort of underhand. Agassi was caught off guard, and as a result completely whiffed on the ball. I smiled for the first time all day. I noticed he'd twisted a little funny when he lunged, and now he, too, was limping visibly.

"What's up, dude?" I said. "Problem?" He just glared at me and paced a while. Eventually, when I served again, he didn't even move. Now *he* called the trainer over.

After a while he returned to his place on the baseline, but looked extremely uncomfortable doing so. I was able to win the game just by getting my serves in. Agassi looked scared all of a sudden.

The next two games went much the same way, with each of us winning with dinky little serves the other simply wasn't able to get to. On the next changeover we had ourselves a chat.

"It's your hip again, isn't it," I said.

He nodded reluctantly. "It's your knee again, isn't it."

I smiled half-heartedly.

"Well this should be interesting," he said with a wince, and we went on to play one of the strangest sets in the history of tennis after that. Or one of the slowest at least. Two of the oldest guys in the game hobbling around hitting lobs and dropshots, trying whatever unconventional bullshit they could come up with to stay alive in the frame. It was a kind of elderly version of your classic war of attrition. I won that fourth set 6–4 by the way.

The fifth set was even worse. Twice I had to crawl to the ball when my knee gave out, and Agassi, all he did was throw up in the middle of the court from the pain in his hip. Neither of us was willing to give this one up, and I knew that if it was going to come down to pure pigheadedness, I had as good a chance as any.

At one point both of us were literally down on our knees, smacking pitty-pat volleys back and forth. I actually began to feel some admiration for the guy. No dilettante would *ever* have risked serious, even permanent, injury by continuing to play on a hip like his. I needed this, and I was never going to give up, and yet he stayed with me, pushing me to the absolute limit of what I was capable of. I'm sure he felt the same way about me.

When I got to match point on serve, and wheeled my racquet back ready to attack, the pain went screaming up my spine in spurts. I gasped, and stood there a long moment before pushing through the pain, letting out a scream, and a serve, much more powerful than intended, or what you'd think was even possible at this point. I heard a sickening crunch. I wasn't even able to see Agassi net the return through the tears in my eyes, but I knew I'd won from the reaction of the crowd. I'd never heard a noise that loud, that genuine, and it suddenly occurred to me how quiet they'd been throughout. I'd never been a fan-favourite back when I was on top, and we all know what people have generally thought of me since, so this was something entirely new to me now.

A thoughtful ballgirl helped me to the net to shake Agassi's hand. He embraced me at center court, which admittedly caught me off guard, but I was more than a little moved when he looked me square in the eye and said, "One for the ages, Olie. You're a hell of a player, my friend."

They carried me out on a stretcher while Agassi, to his credit, was able to leave under his own power. Out of the corner of my eye I saw the jubilant crowd offering us both a standing ovation. I'll never forget that moment as long as I live.

(10:00 PM)

Typical of my life that on one of the most emotional days in memory it would just keep pouring on. I'm catching up on my rest in bed at a medical facility at Flushing Meadows when a nurse comes in and says, "Mr. Wood, your mother's here to see you."

"Nah, that's just my girlfriend. She doesn't look so good at night sometimes."

"No, sir, the woman says she's your mother."

It took a while to process this. Thelina? No. Gary's mother? Hardly. No, it was obviously a stalker, which was kind of intriguing, so I let the nurse show her in. And lo and behold it *was* my mother. She wasn't dead after all.

"Hey there, Oliver," she said with a deep, cracked voice just this side of masculine. I wondered where Miranda had gone while I was sleeping. "You played good out there," she went on while I scrambled for something to say.

She was thin. Like really thin. And she looked pale, almost ashen, beneath what appeared to be a jet-black wig. Yet, oddly enough, she didn't look nearly as bad as the picture I'd held in my mind all these years. No, more than anything else she looked old. She couldn't have been more than, what, fifty? Fifty-five tops? And yet she could've easily passed for seventy. She had deep dark circles under her eyes and her hands shook a little.

"It's good to see you, honey," she told me.

"Wow, a little notoriety and all the skeletons start coming out of the closet," I said in a voice far softer than I'd intended. She laughed and it sounded like ripped metal.

"It's not every day you see your baby on the news. How could I not come show my support?"

"I was on the news plenty when I was younger. Don't remember seeing you then."

"You know how it is. I never sat still long enough to really get a bead on what you were doing."

"That maternal instinct just comes so natural to you, doesn't it?"

She laughed again. "You're so much my boy. You've sure got your mother in you," she said, coming closer.

"That's a pretty shitty thing to say," I said, pulling back. She circled the bed, studying my IV bag.

"Does it hurt?"

"It's better than it was."

"I'm glad. I saw you earlier with a nice looking lady. That your wife?"

"Something like that, yeah."

"Bun in the oven, huh?"

"Wow. Observant. So that's where I get it from."

"A grandmother," she said, smiling. "Somehow I don't seem the type."

"You're not."

Her face sagged. "Are you angry with me, Oliver?"

"That's one way of putting it, sure."

"A lot of water under the bridge with you and me."

"You left me. You abandoned me."

"I was in no condition to be a mother. It was the best thing for you."

"I thought you were dead."

"I was once or twice," she said, scratching her arm all too tellingly.

"Why are you here?" I asked.

"Can't a mother come watch her son do something special?"

"A mother can, yeah. But that still doesn't explain what you're doing here."

Her eyes wrinkled up at the corners. "Yeah, well, you got me there. Touché (she pronounced it "toosh"). I just wanted to, you know, see you enjoying all your success."

"Meaning?"

"Nothing, honey. Just wanted to be here for you in your big moment of glory."

"So then I guess they mentioned how much I'm earning at this event on the news."

She sighed. "I don't remember exactly. At any rate, it's not important. What is important is that I'm here, and we're all getting reacquainted as a family."

"That's what's important to you, huh? Family?"

"Honey, that's all that matters to me."

"Okay, 'Mom.' I'll tell you what, you meet me here tomorrow for lunch. I have a meeting with some tournament officials at eleven, and afterwards you can meet Miranda and feel the baby."

"Sounds lovely," she smiled.

"But let's be clear. You aren't getting any money. Not one penny, no matter what sob story you come up with. I'll say it again, just so there's no misunderstanding: whatever money I take out of this event stays with me and *my* family. So don't even ask," I said, and with that the smile drained from her face. She looked even paler than when she'd come in. "So if that's something you can handle, and you still want to see me, you come have lunch on me tomorrow. I'm willing to give you at least that much."

They say I have no business even trying to play the semi-final in two days. They say I'll have no chance of being able to get well in that time.

They're wrong.

September 9

Started the day off with a slow walk. I'm not pushing it, and have no intention of playing on the knee before I have to. After a while it was loose enough that I was at least able to walk, which was something to build on. I'm wearing a knee brace that offers me a little flexibility, and I continue to take mild painkillers and anti-inflammatories to help keep the swelling down.

I'm officially a celebrity again. Everyone seems to know who I am. I'm front-page news in one of the New York papers (though admittedly on my knees, hobbling around the court), and I got a call from Regis Philben's show earlier. For today at least I'm the biggest name in sports, and for once it's not because I did something stupid or embarrassing. How novel.

Anyway, I had a meeting with the US Tennis Association and ATP folks this morning. I wasn't sure why they wanted to see me, but I assumed it had something to do with publicity requirements or something.

It was two guys, Owen Lieberman from the USTA and Tony Tucker from the ATP.

"Have a seat, Olie," said Tucker, and I did. "How are you feeling?"

"I'll be ready for the semis."

"We have a problem, Mr. Wood," said Lieberman.

"No, seriously. I'll be ready."

"We've been reviewing your records. There's no way you're ranked inside the top two hundred."

I paused, not sure of what to say and not wanting to walk into a trap.

"Did you hear what I said?" Lieberman asked.

"Yeah. . . ."

"So you see the problem then."

"No. . . ."

"Someone's been tampering with the computer system. We've traced it back a long way, and there's just no way you could have accumulated the points necessary to be invited to qualifying play."

"I'm not sure what you want me to—"

"Mr. Wood, someone has cheated the system, and clearly with the intent of benefiting you."

"I don't know anything about that."

"Regardless, I'll say it again: we have a problem here."

"What do you want me to do?" I said, feeling the panic beginning to rise. I mean here they were talking about taking away my wins, my newfound celebrity, and my money. My fucking *money*! These guys were talking about disqualifying me! "No way, man," I said. "No way this is happening."

"I'll tell you what we're going to do," Tucker said. "We're going to declare you a special wildcard. That's if someone asks. Otherwise, this will remain between the three of us and no one else."

I ran that over in my mind a few times.

"We need you," said Lieberman, seeing that I was clearly confused.

"You do?"

"At this moment you're the biggest name in the sport," Tucker explained. "Tennis remains a tough sell in this country at the best of times, and yet here you've somehow captured the public's imagination, and not just those who follows sports. We announce that Olie Wood is a big fraud and, well, quite frankly we're a big fraud."

"I see."

"Wesley Goodie at Tennis Canada started the investigation," Lieberman continued. "For whatever reason, he seems to have some real issues with you. Fortunately he knows nothing about our little deal here. Let's keep it that way. He can be a bit of a . . . stickler with the rules, especially when it comes to you."

"Oh can't he," I said.

"Just know that we can't tolerate this kind of thing in the future," Tucker went on. "We're not saying you had anything to do with it, but let's just say we've been alerted to a weakness in our system we'll be safeguarding from now on."

I met Miranda for lunch at a café in the complex. We waited for over an hour for my mother to arrive, but of course she didn't. No surprise.

"Are you sad?" Miranda asked.

"A little, maybe. No, not really. It's hard to be disappointed by someone who never earned a big enough spot in your heart in the first place."

"Wow. That's pretty fucking profound."

"You're right. And you're pretty fucking fat as well."

We both laughed.

"I want you to know something," she said. "I'm never going to leave you, and neither of us is ever going to leave this kid. We're better than that. We're better than *her*."

And she was right. We were.

September 10

I woke up this morning and felt sick to my stomach. My legs were like rubber as I stood there in the shower quietly contemplating the tile work. There was just too much going on for me to process. After the business at the hospital I half wondered if my mother would show up at the court today, if for no other reason than to prove I was wrong in my assumptions about her. To be honest, part of me was rooting for her. But even without all the family drama of the last couple of days, I had enough on my plate to feel entirely overwhelmed by it all. Once upon a time this kind of day wouldn't have been out of the ordinary at all. I've played in several Grand Slam semi-finals, and though the thrill never wears off, the terror certainly does. And now after all these years it's back with a vengeance.

Today I played Roger Federer of Switzerland, the number-one ranked player in the world. The guy who took all his potential and harnessed it, turning himself into arguably the greatest to ever play the game.

People say he could be the perfect tennis player, free of any real flaws. Thing is, people used to say the exact same thing about Olie Wood at one time. Well sometimes people are wrong. But they're not when it comes to Federer. He's the guy I was supposed to have been, and probably could have been, though perhaps in another lifetime. Needless to say, I've never played the guy before.

I was able to move around all right in the warm-up. My knee was bugging me, no question, but not so much that I couldn't play. It was game on.

The thing that surprised me most about that match was how well I stayed with him. At times our rallies seemed to go on endlessly, and the knee loosened up as the match wore on. Yet it didn't matter how well I stayed with him; he always found a way to win the point in the end. He clipped me 6–2 in the first set, and redoubling my efforts I managed one more game in the second. I broke him early to open the third, and held serve to lead 2–0, imagining another great come from behind victory when my knee completely gave out. I went down hard as though someone had pulled my legs out from under me. But I was an old hand at this by now, and I started to get up to the appreciative roar of the crowd.

But I couldn't get up. The knee had no strength left in it at all. The umpire climbed down from his chair. "Mr. Wood . . ."

"I'm okay. I can play. Ask Andre Agassi."

He sighed and returned to his chair. I limped to my position on the baseline with the crowd going nuts, and Federer let fly a serve I simply couldn't get to, though God knows I tried. He served again, and I could barely hold my racquet up. I collapsed on the spot, writhing in pain, exhausted.

The crowd started shouting, half of them encouraging me to get up, the other half pleading with me to stay down. Miranda was definitely part of the latter. I could see her there in my player's box with tears in her eyes. I tried to reassure her with a smile, but only managed to grimace a little. Then I tried to get up to extend my hand to Federer. Classy guy that he is, he jumped over the net and came to me.

"No shame," he said. "A good match. I'm honoured to be here with you."

It was over. I received my second standing ovation of the tournament as Federer walked me back to my chair. The roar of the crowd was all you could hear.

Later, Miranda and Gary and I got ourselves a hotel room. It was expensive, but I'd earned $260,000 for my efforts so I wasn't too worried. Not bad for two weeks work.

In the post-match press conference, a journalist asked how I was going to build on this success and what tournament I was planning on playing next. I told him there wouldn't be another tournament for me. I'd already gotten more out of this game that I could've possibly hoped for. I was going home with my wife and son and really, who could ask for more?

September 11

As we packed up our things at George's place last night, I said goodbye to Blanche Dowling.

"See you around, cat," I told her, feeling a little stupid but saying it just the same. I turned to leave and felt something push against my leg. I looked down and saw the flat of her head pressing up against me. Not rubbing as cats usually do, and not biting as Blanche Dowling typically does, but just resting there. "Take care of yourself," I said, pulling my leg away, but she just took a step forward and planted the flat of her head against me again. This was odd. I looked at Gary, and he shrugged. Then I picked her up. She was my cat after all.

Oh and Roger Federer won the US Open today. Good for him; he's good for the game.

September 12

Reporters keep asking me if I'm upset about how it all ended. I don't think they really understand what I've been through in the past year to even get to this point. If they did know, they might ask me instead, "Is this a genuine miracle?" and I'd have to say, "I think so."

We're all heading back to Ottawa in a couple of days. We're going to enjoy New York a little first, and then we can actually fly home. I love to fly, and Miranda's never been on a plane before, so it's long past time she experienced that as well.

I suppose we'll get married at some point, though there's no rush. We don't *need* to get married—I'm not going anywhere, regardless of whether we make it official—but if that's what Miranda wants, well then there you go. We'll still love our kid just the same. I'm really starting to look forward to meeting the little guy. I want to see what something that sprung from my genes might look like, given all the appropriate opportunities to fulfill its potential. I've got my fingers crossed, but something tells me it'll all come out like it should. I've never been an optimist before. Feels a little weird.

I'm going to teach at Toomey when I get home. I got the call after the semi-final. I guess with me in the news so much this week they saw an opportunity to increase their exposure. I'm a shitty teacher, but what do they know? I'm officially retired now, it might be a fun thing to do and, who knows, maybe I'll remember one or two useful pointers from everything Phil taught me all those years ago. I think he might enjoy the idea of me teaching. I think he'd approve somehow. And do I hold a grudge after the way Toomey and Tennis Canada treated me a few months back? Hell, yeah. But I figure this might be the first time in my life I'm in a position to be the bigger man and not lord it over them. Well, okay, I'll still lord it over them. Hell, that's half the reason I'm taking the job.

More than anything I'm relieved I was able to find one last highlight in this game. After all, for a while there I was really beginning to think my life was finished; I was terrified of fading to black against this terrible backdrop of failure. That's been my story these last few years, and it means a great deal to me that I was able to change the script in time, before it was too late, before it was over. Now I leave on my terms. Who knew such a thing was even possible.

Miranda is curled up on the bed with Blanche Dowling. She's watching the Weather Channel and loving it; I think she's feeling like she's in some kind of palace here, though in actual fact it's just the Ramada. Still, it's a damned sight better than anything we've known in recent memory.

Gary is starting a journal of his own, telling me he's inspired by the commitment I've shown. He's struggling a bit and keeps asking my opinion of everything he writes, but he'll get it. I told him it starts to come easier after a while.

My son swims in liquid inside Miranda's stomach. How bizarre is that. And how bizarre is it that this is my family I'm staring at.

My *family*. As messed up as it might seem to someone else, I'm happy as hell with that.

September 13

Today I imagined a conversation Phil and I might have had were he still around.

"I do okay?" I'd ask.

"You did okay," he'd say.

"Just okay?"

"You did me proud, my son."

"Well that's more than enough to take out of this couple of weeks, huh?"

"Sure. But the title would have been even better."

And everything would be okay again. Everything would be back to the way it was supposed to be. I don't know where Phil is, but for the first time I think he knows all about me. I really think he knows, and likes what he sees.

September 14

Dear Portugalians,

This is a photo of Sparky the skunk at the US Open. I don't know if you follow tennis, but this is a big deal for us. Sparky has seen a lot over the last few months, but nothing quite so eventful as these last two weeks.

You know, sometimes we can pull off something incredible, even when the whole world thinks it's beyond us. I was glad to have ol' Sparky along to witness this important time in my life. I finally feel proud of myself. You know, I had no idea what it was I've been searching for all these years. I thought it might have been money, or glory, or fame, but I've learned these last two weeks that it's actually none of these things. I've had all those things at one time or another and they never really made me happy. No, the thing that makes life liveable is being able to take a little pride in yourself. Not so much in your accomplishments—you don't even need to win—but in the fact you fought the good fight to get where you are. Because it's what you endure that defines who you are. I know that now. And I think when my kid is born I'll be able to tell him about this chapter of my life with a smile on my face and with some pride in my heart. And that's a pretty damned good thing, it turns out.

I was going to leave Sparky here in honour of this memorable occasion, but I think I'll take him home with me to Ottawa if it's all the same to you. If you ever come to the city to visit, take a look around and you might see him on a lawn or in a window somewhere. If you do, feel free to give the little guy a buzz. If nothing else, I'm sure Sparky will have plenty to tell you about his various adventures. Just look for the home of a little Canadian family with a lot of laughter seeing them through. See you there.